'The Keneallys have produced a strong murder mystery of admirable depth.'

Sunday Times

'The evocation of place and time is splendid.'

Mail on Sunday

'Meg and Tom Keneally, daughter and father, are on a roll with their crime series set during the early days of Australia's colonial settlement.'

Sydney Morning Herald

'There's a crime at the centre of the story, but it is the detail of early Australian life, the atmosphere and great writing that make the book special.'

Choice

'Introduces a totally different kind of detective, while at the same time exploring with perception and wit the forces that shaped a nation…the father and daughter duo have hit on a real winner.'

Crime Review

'The Keneallys have hit their straps with this Monsarrat outing… The third instalment of Monsarrat's dangerous tour of the convict settlements of Australia can be anticipated with relish.'

…ustralian

About the Authors

Tom Keneally won the 1982 Booker Prize with *Schindler's Ark*, later made into the Academy Award-winning film *Schindler's List*. His novels *The Chant of Jimmie Blacksmith*, *Gossip from the Forest* and *Confederates* were shortlisted for the Booker Prize.

His daughter Meg Keneally has been a journalist and radio producer, and has spent more than ten years working in corporate affairs for listed financial services companies. Both live in Australia.

Also by Meg and Tom Keneally

The Soldier's Curse
The Unmourned

THE POWER GAME

THE MONSARRAT SERIES

MEG AND TOM KENEALLY

POINT
BLANK

A Point Blank Book

First published in Great Britain by Point Blank,
an imprint of Oneworld Publications, 2020

ISBN 978-1-78607-687-8 (paperback)
ISBN 978-1-78607-688-5 (eBook)

Printed and bound in Great Britain by Clays Ltd, Elcograf S.p.A.

This is a work of fiction. While, as in all fiction, the literary perceptions
and insights are based on experience, all names, characters, places,
and incidents either are products of the author's imagination or are
used fictitiously.

Oneworld Publications
10 Bloomsbury Street
London WC1B 3SR
United Kingdom

For Jane, daughter and sister

Prologue

Maria Island, off the east coast of Van Diemen's Land
January 1826

Bart Harefield loved laughing at them. The ones who thought they had power. The ones who alighted from his boat without a nod or a glance. They were the ones who felt the carefully woven skein of half-truths tighten around them, choking their air of respect and reputation.

They did not know why it happened. They put it down to happenstance, a misunderstood word here or an odd look there. Then they stepped again onto the boat without any idea the agent of their downfall was piloting them over the pitted grey water. The officer sent away for a reputed affair with the daughter of an overseer. The reverend replaced thanks to rumours of his over-enthusiasm for a soprano in the convict women's choir.

Harefield was particularly proud of his latest triumph: the commissary dismissed when the amount of rice and flour in the stores did not match the inventory. No one thought to look under the floorboards of the bosun's hut for the missing supplies. And all it had taken was a whisper, which Harefield delivered to the Hatter along with a threat to withdraw supplies of contraband rum, a low mutter in the vicinity of a person known for gossip, a quick glance to check they weren't being overheard.

None of them, from the commandant down, realised how completely they belonged to Harefield. He was the only person on Maria Island who could guide the little cutter through the sea's worst moods, through scudding clouds and squalls, so that people and goods were able to continue passing between Maria and the larger island of Van Diemen's Land it hung off.

With Harefield, things got done. Goods delivered, information traded, rumours started. Even better when the rumours were true, and profitable. Harefield kept quiet about the convicts he ferried over from the island to work on the commandant's house in Orford, when the King would be expecting them to be working on roads and reservoirs. He would continue to keep the secret until it suited him to do otherwise.

On days like yesterday, though – when the wind stood the waves up in serried ranks and dared a sailor to try to smash through them – even a brave sailor like Harefield knew to stay in port, temporarily silencing the murmurings with which he crossed the water.

Harefield could read the sea. He had grown up on it. A boy with straggly hair and missing teeth grown to a wiry, pinched man whose childhood beatings had pushed him to master an element that was indifferent to force. He was no fool. And he would not be thanked for the loss of the small government cutter if he put to sea recklessly. The loss of a bosun was less of a problem. Flesh and muscle were easier to come by here than good timber and flax.

Those times he was stuck idle on the mainland because of maritime conditions could get dull – unless you had some reading. Harefield's favourite cargo was letters. Most were mundane. They started and ended with ridiculous obsequiousness: 'I have the honour to inform you' and 'your most obedient servant'. How any man could style himself thus, and remain standing upright from lack of hilarity, Harefield had no idea.

He forced himself to read them, though. Occasionally his persistence was rewarded. In recent times there had been one letter in particular. He'd been so entranced as he read it that he tipped his tallow candle over the page a little too far, sending a fat wax droplet onto it. It irritated him because he liked things clean. But it didn't really matter. The intended recipient knew the letter had been read because Harefield himself had answered it.

On a piece of old parchment, he had scrawled: 'I was very interested to hear of your plans. I believe those in authority would be even more so. I imagine they will also be fascinated to hear about a certain relationship that many would consider inappropriate. You may, if you wish, buy my silence, but I'm not certain you can afford it.'

～⌒⌒～

Today the wind was a little less wild and abeam than it had been the night before, and Harefield decided to set out on the five miles of water between Triabunna and Maria Island.

The wind had brought with it a blinding rain, which saw him nearly tipped into the ocean as he was trying to tie up to the dock on his arrival. That simpleton was standing there and made no move towards him, did not reach a hand down to help Harefield up the slippery ladder. 'Too much to hope you've come to help,' Harefield snapped, as if the fool was even capable of it. 'I thought I'd come down and see the storm,' stuttered Walter, almost backing into the ocean.

'Well, I hope it devours you and leaves the rest of us alone. At least then you'll be of some use,' said Harefield, carrying a sack of letters up towards the commissary.

3

He delivered them only after having secreted the most interesting-looking. Then he went back to the dock, telling himself it was too much to hope for that the halfwit had unloaded the rest of the goods from the boat.

Perhaps the man had a small amount of sense, as he was no longer on the dock. Harefield decided that one of the bottles of rum, which was to go to the Hatter and from there to those who were thirsty among the convicts, should instead accompany him to his hut.

The rum was rather too pleasant, and Harefield woke as the sun was beginning to sink, sitting upright and panting from the remnants of an already forgotten nightmare. He pulled on his coat and went back to the dock, to check that the boat had not been dashed against it.

Lieutenant Holloway intercepted him. Harefield had nothing on this one, not yet – a man who wore propriety like a corset, stiff with judgemental efficiency. Might be worthwhile making something up, though. Especially given the pursed lips and lifted chin with which Holloway communicated his distaste for the ragged boatman sodden with sea water.

Holloway was leaving the outbuilding the commandant used as an office. 'Harefield, you are going to the light, yes?' he asked.

As well as keeping the penal station supplied, Bart Harefield was responsible for a small light on an outcrop near the island's chief inlet, Darlington Bay. Whales liked to frequent these waters, and as a result so did whalers. It wouldn't do to have one sail directly into one of the island's striated cliffs; nor, since some were Yankee whalers, to bring the taint of Yankee republicanism too close to the convict station.

'It would be a difficult trip now, lieutenant,' said Harefield. 'Not the weather for it.'

'Of course it's not the bloody weather for it! That's why we need it lit. If I do not see a glimmer from the headland within

4

an hour, I may decide to visit your hut, see what I find there. I know that the commandant is myopic when it comes to some of your activities, but I assure you I am not.'

Holloway didn't see the glare Harefield gave him from under the sodden felt brim of his hat. He turned, went to his hut to get rags and oil, and started the long trudge to the painted cliffs.

The light was housed in a square box of glass lenses designed to magnify passing shipping. This apparatus sat high, on top of a rickety latticework structure so it could be seen from as great a distance as possible. It required a long ladder to ascend, and a steady head to lean out and insert your hand through the base to coax the lamp into lighting.

The clouds were allowing only a glimmer of sun to seep through to the surface of the grey sea, and even that small ration had dwindled as the afternoon had worn on.

Halfway up the ladder Harefield heard a voice calling his name. He looked down, unable to resist a grin when desperation stared back at him from a familiar face. Desperate people were lucrative. This one, though, would have to wait.

He hauled himself up the ladder bit by bit. But the wind must've been stronger than he thought, for the ladder wobbled. He cursed, gripped onto the light's frame. It didn't help. The ladder shifted again and again.

When he looked down, he saw that the wind wasn't responsible. The expression on the face looking up at him was grim now, perhaps a little frightened, but resolved. And the brows were drawn together in concentration as the hands around the ladder pulled again.

Finally it lost contact with the light's frame and came plummeting down, with Harefield on it. The impact of hitting the ground knocked the breath out of him, and a snap accompanied by a jolt of pain told him that something had broken. But no one would be allowed to pull him down like that, not with impunity. He staggered to his feet, realising as he put weight on

5

his right ankle that it had made the noise, but determined to give an answer for the insult.

He knew he must be careful in this low light if there was to be a scuffle. The cliff edge was very near and did not announce itself. His attacker, he saw now, was holding an axe. It was down, though, at the end of a slack arm that was having trouble lifting it. There was no delaying – Harefield knew that hesitation was death.

He lunged, knocking his attacker to the ground, falling heavy on the arm with the axe in it, sending the weapon flying. Grinning as a pleasant prospect suddenly occurred to him. Before he could take things further, though, he heard movement behind him. He turned his head and saw the flash of a bright line of metal, the edge of the rusted axe as it was hoisted – not as well as he would have done it, but well enough to be effective – and arced down towards him. He feared the edge was aimed for his throat and ducked, only to receive a blow on his shoulder. He felt such huge and deep pain that he tried to appease the person with the axe, wanted to utter an assurance that whatever grudge there was, he would attend to it. 'Leave my head,' he tried to say. He was shaken out of speech by two other great blows, and had an impulse to shout, 'That's not a square way to behave.'

But before he could even gurgle out the words, a final blow split his shoulder. By the time he hit the vicious rocks below the cliff top, he was well and truly dead.

Later, a convict sent by Holloway spotted Harefield's body, which looked to be the victim of a fall. Only when a party had worked their way around to the cliff's base was it found that the bosun's right arm hung by a filament of flesh, that there were deep axe wounds in his shoulders, and that he had already been dead for several hours.

Chapter 1

Of things that couldn't be trusted, the ocean sat at the top of Hannah Mulrooney's list. And on her third visit for the day to the bucket in her cabin, into which she had emptied her stomach countless times on this journey, she confirmed its place there. The sea had not the decency to announce its intentions, all blue innocence followed by grey temper, slapping the hull of the ship, making its displeasure known, eloquent in its threat.

There was no fire to boil a kettle on, not on this flimsy collection of planks they insisted on calling a ship, to which Mr Monsarrat had casually agreed to trust both their lives. Even if there had been, it would have been more efficient to pour the tea directly into the bucket.

Hannah had thought she was done with ocean voyages. Certainly she expected to make the occasional journey down the river from Parramatta to Sydney and back again. But the river was more predictable than the ocean, and she had made her peace with it. This heaving mass of peaks didn't seem to care, though. It simply did its very best to impede the progress of the brig *Cyprus* as it slowly picked its way through the wave-littered expanse which separated Van Diemen's Land from the rest of God's green earth and its creatures.

I was born on one island, she thought. Crammed into the hull of a ship on another, exiled to a third. I truly should not be asked to deal with a fourth.

To the north, somewhere in the vastness they had left, her son rode or sang or swore or prayed or slept, but did not write – had suddenly stopped answering the letters she poured into the silence. Helen, the convict servant, sat by the fire in Parramatta, hopefully with her daughter, Eliza, still playing nearby and not reclaimed by the orphan school.

Mr Monsarrat needed *her*, however – he had said so, repeatedly, even when he was not in fear of receiving a scolding. And Hannah was grateful for the extra day he had managed to negotiate in Sydney, when he'd called on Harcourt's Auctioneers, depositing with them some jewels, in fire-damaged settings but with their value still intact. The jewels, which she hoped to never see again, would be sold off at the earliest opportunity, their proceeds to await her return and to be used to set her son up in colonial respectability. The thought of giving him the news for a moment quelled the low hum of fear which rose and fell with the waves. When she found him.

If, she thought, the sea doesn't decide that I have traversed it too many times, that it is time to claim me.

There was a knock on the door of her small cabin. She shared it with the maidservant of one of the officers aboard, a surly girl who was hardly there anyway. Hannah, in contrast, rarely left.

'Come in, eejit of a man.'

Hugh Llewelyn Monsarrat opened the door slowly, cautiously. He was well over a foot taller than her, and her employer

8

besides, but they both knew she would not have displayed such timidity had she been at his door.

'I've lost count, my friend, of the number of times I have told you you'd be better off on deck. Fixing your eyes on the horizon can help with the sickness, you know. And fresh air, well, it's a commodity we've both been deprived of in the past. I for one intend to avail myself of as much of it as possible.'

'You can tell me all you like,' she said. 'But if I allow you to tempt me up onto the deck, to breathe great lungfuls of fresh sea air, what happens if I'm taken by a wave and find myself breathing in great lungfuls of sea water instead? Will your fine words save me?'

Monsarrat shrugged. 'In any case, it's as well you've not taken my advice,' he said. 'Your temper would probably pollute the atmosphere. Better it bounces off the walls in here, harming no one.'

She narrowed her eyes, stood and reached for the waist of her skirt, where a cleaning cloth habitually rested. Her weapon, though, was absent, very possibly being applied to a Parramatta skillet at this moment.

'I am joking with you, of course,' said Monsarrat. 'Trying to, anyway . . .'

'Well, I'm glad to see you deprive yourself of that fresh air for such a noble purpose,' she said. 'Perhaps you should take yourself back up onto the deck for more of it.'

Monsarrat smiled. 'Hobart Town is near: we are entering Sullivans Cove. I thought you might wish to see your salvation come into view.'

◦⁀◦

A remarkable woman, Hannah Mulrooney, Monsarrat thought as they made their way up the ladder towards the deck. Highly intelligent, perceptive, kind, practical. But a God-awful temper on her when she was in any way constrained, whether by an injured ankle, or a rough sea.

And one was now putting pressure on the other. He knew she tried not to think of her healing sprain, was working on the principle that if she completely ignored it, the ligaments would mend themselves out of sheer humiliation. She was applying the same principle to the frayed edges of her mind, still jangled from her near-immolation in Parramatta at the hands of a murderous woman. But both tasks were harder to do on a pitching sea, and more than once Monsarrat caught her as she stumbled.

He had not been entirely joking about the wisdom of her remaining confined below, and he would be as delighted as she to see her once again restored to the more trustworthy land. He could not help feeling grateful that she had subjected herself to the ocean, though – facing a terror, which she hid in irritability, to accompany him. They both knew he needed her if he was to have any hope of accomplishing his task.

It was a task whose nature had not been made entirely clear to Monsarrat. Yes, there had been a murder in the remote penal settlement of Maria Island. Monsarrat had heard little of the place. It was either mentioned as an afterthought, a colony too small to think much of, or it was whispered of – an ocean fortress which held a mysterious prisoner who'd been given immunity from death.

But the person whose murder Monsarrat was being sent to investigate, the circumstances of his dispatch, and why the crime was sufficiently sensitive to warrant help from Sydney, had not yet been revealed.

It was unusual for a commandant to send for help over such a distance. And the only assistance Ralph Eveleigh, Monsarrat's superior on the governor's staff in Parramatta, had given him was snuggled in a blue velvet box in his trunk. Monsarrat would have preferred a detailed brief, but would have to make do with the gift of an ornate magnifying glass, a spare one Eveleigh had been given and passed to Monsarrat.

They were still a little too far out to see Hobart Town clearly but Monsarrat could make out the British flag on one of the hills of their island destination on their port side. He saw Mrs Mulrooney glance at it, then frown and look away. It was a design she had seen flying over her own dead.

Used to the encompassing glare and unapologetic heat of Parramatta, Monsarrat could not help feeling that he had been taken back across the oceans to Plymouth. This place had the same low sky, and even on the summer's morning a piercing wind scudded up the river and found its way inside his coat.

While it was an outpost, Hobart Town was a well-developed one. Slabs of pinch-windowed, honey-stoned buildings, warehouses of the chief merchants, found themselves reflected in the harbour, or those sections of it which weren't obscured by the hulls of boats. Small craft swarmed between the larger brigs, with their cargoes of wool or flour or fish. Men called between boat and dock, ropes were thrown, and the occasional splash announced that someone had been less than cautious in the throwing. Empty carts lined up near the dock to swallow cargo, full ones to disgorge it. Some of those who should probably have been handing crates ashore were disappearing around corners with women who had artfully pulled down one shoulder of their dresses. And behind the town sat the megalith of a mountain, like a divine presence, almost too big for the landscape.

The boat, when it docked, was still being rocked from side to side by wavelets fed by the river wind, worsening Mrs Mulrooney's temper as she was hauled ashore by a young sailor and then tripped on a protruding nail, which she no doubt felt had been put there specifically for the purpose.

Monsarrat, engaged in helping the muttering woman to her feet, failed to notice immediately the man who had approached them. He wore a brown jacket, with the seam attaching one of the sleeves to the shoulder slowly unravelling. It was impossible to tell whether his neckerchief was clean – Monsarrat always told himself such things shouldn't matter, but could never resist checking – as it was black and tucked in to a grey shirt, which might once have been white. The man did not introduce himself, or smile, or raise the broad-brimmed hat on top of his head. He simply stopped a few feet from them, standing with his arms crossed, staring. Monsarrat felt oddly offended. The man was probably a former convict. Surely, in a world which viewed them as animals, their only hope was failing to behave as such. 'Good morning, sir,' Monsarrat said, in a more clipped manner than he'd intended. 'Can I help you?'

'Doubt it,' the man said. 'I'm here to help you, though. At least, help you into Marley's office. After that, you're on your own.'

'And Marley is who?'

The man snorted. 'You've obviously not been to Van Diemen's Land before,' he said. 'Richard Marley. Comptroller of convicts here. Wants to see you – that is, if you're the governor's man from Sydney?'

'Yes,' Monsarrat said wearily, bending to pick up Mrs Mulroony's shawl from where it had fallen as she tripped. 'Yes, I'm the governor's man from Sydney.'

And he really should have found out Marley's name, he chided himself. He had been told only that he was to report to the Van Diemen's Land comptroller of convicts for further instructions. That somebody would meet him. There had been no time to ask more, the fastidious Ralph Eveleigh being in a tearing rush to bundle them onto a boat. But placing one's reliance on such vague directions, even when they came from one of the least vague men in the world, was probably unwise.

'Come on, then,' said the man. 'And bring your missus, if she is up to it.'

Mrs Mulrooney opened her mouth, but Monsarrat caught her eyes and shook his head. No point making corrections until they knew whether such scruples would serve them.

He had expected a small carriage or horses to be waiting, but none seemed to be. Instead, the man led them on foot around to the eastern shore of the cove, to a dun-coloured slab of a building on which no creativity had been lavished, with small black windows which would surely struggle to admit any of the light frugally dispensed through the low clouds.

The man stood aside when they reached the door. 'Second floor. He's expecting you.'

Or at least expecting *someone*. Monsarrat found it hard to believe that, as a ticket-of-leave convict, he himself fitted satisfactorily into that expectation. He knocked on the door of the first office at the top of the stairs, Mrs Mulrooney dragging herself up behind him.

The man inside, who had been reading a document which appeared to be some sort of list, looked up. He took off his pince-nez glasses, massaged the bridge of his nose, stared and waited.

'Mr Marley?'

The man nodded.

'Hugh Monsarrat, sir. I believe I am expected.'

The man said nothing, raised his eyebrows.

'From the governor's office in Parramatta, sir,' said Monsarrat. 'You sent for me.'

'Ah,' he said. 'Yes, come in. Your servant may wait downstairs.' Again, Mrs Mulrooney opened her mouth to object, but Monsarrat turned and raised his eyebrows at her, an apology and entreaty. You are not a servant to me, he thought, but you'd better pretend to be one right now.

As her footfalls, made heavy by irritation as well as her injury, receded down the stairs, Monsarrat took the seat Marley gestured towards.

'Apologies for not meeting you off the boat,' he said. 'Quite a task, this. Comptroller of the uncontrollable.'

Monsarrat was amazed at this confession, as to an equal. 'Yes, I imagine it would be. I have known commandants of small penal settlements who find the same.'

'And this is no small penal settlement, Mr Monsarrat. I am what stands between the convicts and the civilised.'

'Surely, sir, some of them are civilised. Some of those who have finished their time.'

Inwardly, a more cautious Monsarrat said, 'Don't argue with him, you idiot.'

'They're amongst the worst. Redeemed? Delirious, most of them. They see things through the same false medium as ever – a medium they cannot understand, any more than they understand us. Under such circumstances, outrage is to be expected from time to time.'

He doesn't know I am one of the damned, thought Monsarrat. He can't, not if he is speaking like this. For the present Monsarrat decided to hold off on enlightening Marley that the man was conversing with someone who had viewed the world through that same false medium. 'I'm sure, though,' Monsarrat said, 'that a man with as many calls on his time as you have has not invited me from New South Wales merely to discuss the obdurate nature of convicts.'

'No, indeed. Although the obdurate nature of one convict in particular may become relevant,' Marley said. 'I have asked you here, in point of fact, in relation to the murder of a man who might have run foul of that very delirium of which I spoke. Fellow nearly had his arm severed at the shoulder by an axe before being thrown over a cliff. He was found in the shallows, rolling back and forth between some rocks.'

Monsarrat had shared a small penal settlement with several people capable of wielding an axe. But to share a small island with someone who had actually picked one up to do such

14

damage so brutally – that was a different matter. How did I let myself be put in this situation, he wondered, of being brought in to identify the culprit? It seemed to him pure chance that people in power had decided he was a superior detector. Thank God Hannah was with him!

'I stand ready to assist,' he said. 'I must ask, though, would somebody familiar with Van Diemen's Land and Maria Island not be better equipped to deal with the matter?'

'Perhaps, but because this death occurred in a place so far removed from civilisation, it can hardly lay claim to being part of this outpost. Even I received word of it a full week after the event. When the murder takes place on a small island, and the victim is the only free man there with the skill to steer a small boat through high seas, getting word to Hobart Town can take some time.'

Maria Island, Marley told Monsarrat, had around three hundred convicts. But it had one prisoner who figured above all others.

'His name is Thomas Power,' Marley said. 'And I suspect it was he who killed the bosun.'

'Thomas Power?' said Monsarrat. 'Surely not the revolutionary?'

Marley thumped the desk, a move so sudden that Monsarrat started backwards.

'Is there anyone who has not heard of the man? That he should achieve such fame off the back of his crimes against the Crown of Great Britain is simply ... *appalling*. Were his name to fade into obscurity, he would probably count that as a far worse punishment than incarceration. But no, the Whiggish newspapers in England – as well as troublemakers in other countries – continue to write about him. They place inhuman pressure on Lieutenant Governor Arthur to be kind to him. Yet these scribblers on the other side of the seas are safely insulated from the reality of the truth by leagues of ocean.'

Monsarrat could not help feeling a shiver of excitement at the prospect of meeting Power, a man he had read about in the *London Chronicle*, as well as reprinted passages from the London papers in the *Sydney Chronicle*, which he tried to peruse after Ralph Eveleigh was finished with it.

Power was an Irish nobleman, who had lent his strategic skill and charisma to the cause of freedom in Colombia and Venezuela with Bolívar himself, and then returned to Ireland with the military skills he had learned. He had taken a seat in the House of Commons, waking up some members who had been asleep for decades with his fiery speeches, and had become the leader of a failed attempt to wrest his country from the grasp of Britain.

He was lucky to have survived, but the authorities feared making a martyr of him. Best not to turn him into St Thomas by pulling him apart with horses (quartering, as they called it) and hanging and eviscerating him.

They tried to tilt his halo by offering him a bargain: they would give him a ticket of leave, freedom of movement and being his own man in a country district of the colony, in exchange for his promise not to escape. Other politicals had accepted those terms, happy to exchange untarnished heroism for food and comfort and nights at the inn. Power said he would prefer to keep open the option of escape if by some chance it was ever offered to him. So he was tucked away on a remote fragment of rock, in the hope that he would diminish in the world's memory.

Marley growled, 'You might remember, Monsarrat, that Power gained a special notoriety after he refused to take his freedom: two of his accomplices, transported with him, were offered a ticket of leave each, in exchange for a promise not to escape. The same offer was made to Power, who said he could not, in all conscience, make a promise he did not intend to keep. Men in London and Dublin who would cheerfully have attended his hanging decided he was clearly some sort of a man of honour.'

Power had been on Maria for well over a year now, but resolutely refused to abandon the Irish rebel stance he had adopted when he and his followers had attacked a fortified police barracks in Cork and were rounded up.

'The fellow's a showman – he did it to burnish his image,' Marley said. 'The best way to punish him is to remove his access to adoration, to erase him from the public memory. That's why, Mr Monsarrat, we did not simply leave this matter to the local constabulary. We need somebody discreet. Somebody who can be relied on to avoid Power's blandishments.'

'I can assure you, Mr Marley, I am reasonably resistant to blandishments.'

'I am glad to hear it. Until we know what we're dealing with, any intrigue surrounding the name Thomas Power must be avoided at all costs.

'You will also need to make sure others there are not in his thrall. There were rumours that Power had the run of the island, that he was dining nightly with the commandant of the place – stable enough fellow called Brewster. Not as stable as I would have hoped, though, for he was indeed entertaining Power. Such is the diabolical nature of the man, you see. He is able to charm almost anyone.'

'But not you, sir,' Monsarrat could not resist saying.

Marley sat straight in his chair, raising his chin defiantly. 'Certainly not,' he said. 'Power is now confined to his cottage and is not allowed beyond the small yard outside. More space than many prisoners are given, and more than he deserves. He is no longer able to treat the island as his private kingdom.' Marley lowered his sturdy and opinionated voice. 'And this is another reason we asked for someone from Sydney. Not a local

17

gossiping constable. It would be a wonderful convenience to the lieutenant governor if it were discovered that Power were responsible for this crime.

'We could find someone to prove he did it if we wanted, but the world and even elements of the Commons, let alone Ireland, would not accept it unless the evidence were overwhelming. For that reason it is important I offer you no inducement of any kind and no promise of preferment if you find he is indeed the one. Now, I believe he had some motivation, but we will need more than that. Essentially, if this darling of the radicals *were* found a common murderer, it would be a wonderful thing for certain powerful men in London, let alone for His Excellency and myself.'

Monsarrat left the office with every display of politeness. And yet he felt annoyed. Try to find Power guilty, please powerful men in England? The powerful men in England could be damned! They were the sort of men who would consider him dregs. As for pleasing Marley . . .

On the other hand, what if Power were the killer?

I must clear my head, thought Monsarrat, of all I know. As impossible as it is, I must be delivered to Maria Island as a clean slate, a blank page. A man of good will.

Chapter 2

'Bounced around in a cart for the better part of the day, and then another boat? Another island dangling off an island dangling off an island?'

Monsarrat had been dreading Mrs Mulrooney's reaction to the next stage of their journey.

'I know, I know – it's not your favourite mode of transport. I promise, though, it will be a short trip. Your agreement to undertake it is yet another testament to your fortitude.'

Mrs Mulrooney glared at him for a moment, then sighed and sat down on the bench in the scullery where he had found her, attempting to teach appropriate tea-making procedure to the Orient's cook.

'I don't blame you for it, Mr Monsarrat, and I'm sorry for my temper – no, I am, although do not expect to hear me say it again. Padraig has not answered any of my letters for some time. And I worry, you know, about Helen and little Eliza.'

Monsarrat could sympathise. He, too, found his thoughts were returning to Parramatta. In his case, though, they by-passed his comfortable cottage and landed in the third-class penitentiary of the Parramatta Female Factory, where a convict called Grace O'Leary awaited her imminent freedom.

'Your forbearance is remarkable,' he said. 'Don't frown at me, dear friend – I mean it. If it's any consolation, I imagine it will be several weeks before we return. Time enough to enjoy the feeling of solid ground beneath your feet.'

'As long as they've tea there,' she said, 'I will be right enough. Flour, butter and sugar would also go a long way towards improving my mood.'

'Well, while I can't promise Maria Island will provide you with everything on your list, it does seem to have an intriguing man caged up there, so I'm sure it will provide us both with an interesting experience.'

~⁊≈⁊~

In the end, Mrs Mulrooney resolutely refused to take to the sea again that day. Not, she told Monsarrat, without some time for a woman to come to terms with the situation. She had, after all, been carted over rutted roads on the journey south from Hobart Town, and could not be expected to deal with a turbulent ocean so soon.

It was as well, then, thought Monsarrat, that the cutter which would ferry them to Maria Island had not yet arrived in the little inlet with the small village of Triabunna on one of its shores, so he was able to settle her at the inn there.

The boat materialised a short time later as Monsarrat watched from the porch of the inn, its sail slacking and snapping according to the whims of the wind, its nose dipping and rising enough to tell Monsarrat that they were not in for a peaceful crossing. As its skipper brought the boat into the dock, the reason for the delay was evident. A man in the black coat and white bib of a magistrate sat on its rear bench, gripping on, looking from side to side as though he expected attack from under the water. He was avoiding looking behind him, though – the boat's gunwales were closest to the water thanks to the man's girth, which would have been impressive in London and was even more so here, where corpulence was rare.

His dumpling face was stippled with evidence of a childhood bout of the pox, and overlaid with small red lines which told of more recent bouts with rum. His eyes, though, even darting in panic, rested on the shore, the water, the sky for long enough to give Monsarrat the impression a certain corner of the man's brain retained the ability of calm assessment, cordoned off from the anxiety which was consuming the rest of him.

He seemed to relax as the boat was tied up to the dock, but walked stiffly ashore, his eyes fixed on the door of the pub.

Monsarrat was tempted to let him walk past, to be another man among the inn's many who were here for trade or whaling or any number of other purposes. But the opportunity to talk to someone who had recently been on Maria Island was too great. He stood suddenly to get the man's attention, and bowed. 'Forgive me, sir, but you have come from Maria Island?'

'Yes, well, it would be difficult to imagine where else I could have come from,' the man said, not slowing as he made his way in towards the warmth behind the inn's doors.

'I am sorry to bother you, sir,' Monsarrat said. 'But I am bound there myself, you see.'

The man stopped. 'I do apologise for my discourtesy,' he said. 'Sea journeys always put me in a bad frame of mind.'

'Yes, I happen to know someone of the same temperament,' said Monsarrat. 'Please don't trouble about it.'

The man held out his hand. 'Henry Ellison,' he said. 'I have the honour to occupy the position of visiting magistrate to Maria Island, and a great many other places in Van Diemen's Land.'

'Ah. So you will have been exercised, I'm sure, by recent events,' said Monsarrat. 'Forgive me, I don't speak out of prurience. I've been sent from Sydney to investigate the slaying of the bosun on Maria Island.'

'Oh! Marley told me they were sending someone from the governor's office.' Ellison was silent for a moment, and then said, 'May I suggest that you join me? I find myself in need of port, and would be most amenable to continuing our conversation once I have one in front of me.'

❧

'I must say, it's odd,' said Ellison.

'Odd?'

'That Marley felt the need to send for assistance from Sydney. Not that I begrudge your presence, sir.'

'Indeed. But my understanding, having spoken to Mr Marley, is that the case is somewhat delicate.'

'Ah, yes. Thomas Power. They will do anything to avoid publicity being attached to that name, unless they are able to proffer unassailable proof of his complicity in a crime worse even than the high treason he was sent here for.'

'Like murder.'

'Yes . . . like murder.'

'Were you on the island when it occurred?' said Monsarrat.

'No,' said Ellison. 'I only visit every month or so. Deal with anything a little bit thornier than a fistfight or the theft of rations. Not this thorny, though.'

'You're acquainted with Power?'

'Oh yes. He used to have more freedom than he does now, you know. Used to enjoy company, conversation. Quite a charming fellow, actually. And whether you believe his revolutionary leanings are right or wrong, the man certainly has the courage of his convictions.'

Monsarrat was surprised. True, magistrates could be a diverse group – back in Parramatta their number had once included the humane Samuel Cruden, the corrupt Socrates McAllister, and the zealous and unyielding Reverend Horace Bulmer. But to hear a legal officer do what Marley proclaimed some gentlemen did, and gloss over the treason which had sent Power over here – that was extraordinary.

'You admire the man?' Monsarrat asked.

Ellison straightened, squared his shoulders like a schoolboy who had suddenly remembered he was supposed to be paying attention.

'Oh, I don't admire the attempt of an uprising he was involved with in Ireland. Though there is some suggestion that he was among the voices calling for moderation. And in any case, the man has honour. I suppose you know he was offered a ticket of leave in exchange for a promise not to escape, and he refused?'

'But surely that means he is intending to escape?' said Monsarrat.

'Oh, not a bit of it,' said Ellison, rather quickly. 'He simply says that he does not recognise the right of the state to constrain his liberty for doing what he did, so he intends to refuse any kind of bargain which might legitimise his sentence. No, I think he is quite content on Maria Island. Well, perhaps content is too strong a word, but he is well aware of conditions at places like Macquarie Harbour, knows he has a comparatively comfortable imprisonment. I'd be amazed if he tried to escape, particularly when you look at the question of where he would go. America, yes. Or to South America perhaps, where he has a name in places like Colombia and Venezuela. But we're a long way from anywhere here, Mr Monsarrat.'

Another man was approaching them, dressed in sturdy canvas, a neckerchief and a broad brimmed hat tied underneath his chin with some rough cord.

'Ah, Jones,' said Ellison. 'Thank you for making the journey as comfortable as possible under the circumstances.'

'My pleasure, sir,' said Jones, in an accent of rounded consonants which sounded like they might have come from Cornwall. 'I am hoping for better weather tomorrow.'

He turned to Monsarrat. 'Jeremiah Jones, sir. I assume you're the man from Sydney? The one I am to convey to Maria Island?'

'Yes. How long will the trip take, do you think? I'm not concerned about heavy weather, but my housekeeper deplores it.'

'I'll tell you a secret, sir,' said Jones. 'All of us do. We just get used to it. But no one relishes sailing into a wave which is taller than the commandant's house, and there are a few of them out there today. Might take some hours to cross in these conditions, and they'll feel like days to your housekeeper. Best, I think, to leave the sea to exhaust itself. And there is usually a cup of tea awaiting me in the kitchens here. If you'll excuse me, I'll avail myself of it.'

Ellison seemed delighted to have a companion to drink port with, even though he was the only one doing any drinking. After his third glass, he said, 'Do you think, Mr Monsarrat, that a good revolutionary needs charm? I used to believe that the most defining characteristics of the revolutionary, or of anyone who manages to convince a large number of people of something, were intelligence and conviction. Now, though, I wonder if it is not a magnetic capacity to attract volunteers.'

'Well, I imagine intelligence and conviction are necessary,' said Monsarrat. 'But that magnetic capacity you mention might help a fellow bring people along with him.'

'Quite right, too. I've not much of it myself . . . No, no, please don't object, it's the truth. Might be why my wife, God rest her, did not feel compelled to come when I made these trips.' He laughed at his self-disparagement. 'But Power – he is one of those people, you know, who seems to be able to say precisely the right thing at the right moment. If he wasn't a revolutionary he could have been prime minister, especially with his high birth.'

'Yes, I've heard he's some sort of nobleman.'

Ellison nodded. 'A baronet. Has a wife and seven children waiting for him in a castle in southern Ireland. Was a Member of Parliament, too, at the time he led his attack in Cork. Tried to plead the Irish case there but, well, you can imagine the good it did him.'

'I understand there was some sort of friendship between him and the commandant.'

'Well,' said Ellison, 'I'm not sure Brewster has what you might call friends. But it suited him, for a time, to entertain the man. And Power couldn't have refused if he'd wanted to. Brewster doesn't allow refusals to pass without retribution.'

Ellison picked up his port, drained the rest of it in one gulp, and stood, wobbling slightly on the way up.

'I fear, Mr Monsarrat, that I'm going to have an even more uncomfortable journey back to Hobart than usual, given the state my head will be in tomorrow. I do apologise if I've rambled, but it's been a pleasure to pass the evening with you. Those of us who spend our lives surrounded by convicts appreciate some intelligent conversation.'

Ellison turned, and then turned back so quickly he almost fell. 'Oh, I imagine they'll accommodate you in the cottage they keep for my use,' he said. 'Mind the floorboards in front of the hearth. They're a little rotten. And take care not to anger the geese.'

'The geese?'

'Yes, you'll see.'

And he tottered towards the stairs, leaving Monsarrat wondering how he was to conceal his own past crimes, investigate those of someone else, avoid falling under Power's enchantment, and placate both the geese and Mrs Mulrooney.

❦

'They've tea, don't trouble yourself about that,' said Jones, deftly avoiding even the smallest of watery ridges in deference to one of his passenger's naked alarm. 'The stores are well run. The last

25

storekeeper was told to leave – thought to be dishonest. Not sure who he was going to trade stolen goods with. The wombats don't have anything anyone wants.'

Jones looked at Hannah Mulrooney, gave what was clearly intended to be a comforting smile, which brought her no comfort at all – anyone who felt the need to smile like that knew something quite alarming was in prospect.

This was correct, as it turned out. The arms of the bay had been providing them with a measure of protection. But the sea's height was increasing as they inched further out, and when the bow poked out from behind the protection of a crumbling grey arm of land, bristling with blackened tree stumps, the full force of the ocean hit them.

Hannah knew she looked terrified, and realised her white hands were clenching the bench. Now this is not the way you behave, she told herself. You can't have the man thinking you're a silly weak woman. You might need him to think well of you before this is out.

He did seem to believe she needed some distraction. 'Missus, would you do me a service?' he said to Hannah. 'There's an oilcloth under the bench there. It has a new dress for the commandant's wife, and a new shirt for her brother. I'd as soon not see them soak – would you mind holding them on our way over?'

As she clutched the parcel, she determined to visit her place of greatest comfort. 'Have they a well-appointed kitchen, there?' she asked.

'I daresay the commandant and his wife do. The rest of us, we cook our own food. Not that they are uncharitable. When I arrived a few weeks ago, I was invited to dine with the Brewsters. The doctor is there once a week, and Magistrate Ellison whenever he's over. I suppose it's the isolation, you see. You wouldn't believe how it affects people, for good or ill, when they're cut off from the rest of civilisation.'

'Oh, I think I would,' said Hannah. 'You see a lot of odd behaviour then, on Maria Island?'

Jones looked out to sea for a moment. 'People are different when they think they're not watched. Or when they think those doing the watching don't matter.' He turned to her and smiled. 'Now, you're not to worry about the voyage,' he said, as the cutter's nose pierced a wave, which broke over the boat, dousing them efficiently enough that Hannah thought Monsarrat would have to remove his jacket and wring it out once they landed. 'We're nearly there, look.' Jones nodded ahead through the air which still shimmered slightly with suspended droplets of water.

The dark shape of a considerable island with notable peaks and coastal cliffs crouched on the horizon, sway-backed and brooding, its arms stretched out in front of it, its middle providing shelter for a small crescent of white sand, almost perfect but for the grey, wooden tongue of the pier which protruded out from it. It looked too credibly a place where murder might occur.

'That's Darlington,' said Jones.

Hannah squinted, saw a utilitarian, rectangular two-storey building, a few smaller outbuildings, and some cottages slightly further up the hill, which rose at the back of the bay.

'Darlington? Behind those trees the other side of that building, you mean?' Monsarrat asked.

'No, nothing behind the trees, except more trees,' said Jones. 'That's all of it. Unless you count the commandant's house, and Ellison's cottage. They're over there.'

He pointed to a hill which rose on the southern side of the bay, from which two buildings had unimpeded views of the entire settlement.

'The island itself is fifteen miles long. There's room to build more,' said Jones in tones of amusement.

Now they were close to the dock, Hannah felt her reason returning, and with it a question.

'Were a soul to wish to get a letter out, how would they do it?'

'I can take one for you, missus,' said Jones. 'Put it on the coach to Hobart with the others. And if I miss the coach, Magistrate Ellison will mind the mail until the next one arrives. He likes to see it anyway – look at the convict letters for any criminal or rebellious sentiments.'

'Only the convicts' letters?' asked Monsarrat.

'Oh yes, he wouldn't dream of opening anything else.'

'In that case, would you be kind enough to take a letter for me?' asked Monsarrat, looking almost embarrassed when Mrs Mulrooney smiled at him. If he was writing to Grace O'Leary, he knew she'd be willing to swim back to Triabunna with the letter in her teeth. Grace was a far better prospect than that vapid Stark woman of Parramatta he had once been enamoured of, a woman Monsarrat had considered marrying until it became apparent that her hunger for social advancement would never be satisfied by a former convict.

Jones managed to avoid another drenching and gain the small bay, tying the boat to a ladder which led up to the dock.

While the wind had been a bother on the crossing, the day was clear, the low clouds of Van Diemen's Land having lifted, so Hannah and Monsarrat had no trouble seeing the three people who were walking down past the buildings towards their landing place.

One was wearing a red coat, almost a copy of the ones Hannah had seen each day in Port Macquarie, but with black facings instead of buff ones. Probably the commandant, judging by the fact that he was striding ahead. His coat was missing a button, something Port Macquarie's commandant would never have countenanced. He was a small man, thinning dark hair and thick eyebrows, and almost swamped by the expansive red fabric, but walking with his shoulders back so that his rounded belly was thrust forward, a smile on his face as he made his way down the dock.

Just behind him was a woman about the same height, plainly dressed in faded muslin, and she was an exceptional sight for such a remote place, her face almost perfectly symmetrical, grey intelligent eyes rolling curiously over the visitors, honey curls escaping undisciplined from her bonnet. It seemed miraculous to find such a creature here, an unadorned beauty in a place of squalls and rough men.

Hannah had almost resolved to tell Monsarrat off later for staring, but she took pity on him. This woman was a vision of possibility. Apart from her height, she looked very much as Grace O'Leary would had she enough food and a respite from the brutality of Parramatta's Female Factory.

Trailing behind both of them, looking around him, was a taller, broader man, younger than everyone else. His long dark hair was not tied back, and his cravat was loose. He did not wear a coat and his waistcoat was buttoned unevenly. At one point he became so engrossed in the path a pelican was making across the water that he nearly walked off the side of the wharf, and had to be pulled back and gently admonished by the woman.

The officer held out his hand before he reached the small group, propelling it into Monsarrat's grasp. 'I have to say, I am relieved Marley is taking this seriously,' the man said with an economical smile. 'Calls for more than the usual amount of tact, you know. Certainly more than the average constable out here possesses. And a man of Governor Darling's staff – when I heard, I was gratified. I knew things would be brought to a satisfactory conclusion. We named the town after him, you know. Darlington. Do you think that helped?'

Monsarrat had to remind himself that the governor's name was no longer Thomas Brisbane, but Ralph Darling, a man Monsarrat had yet to meet: Darling had stopped in Van Diemen's Land on his way to take office, and had only reached Sydney as Monsarrat left. In fact Monsarrat could be considered 'a man of Governor Darling's', but when should he admit that he was a ticket-of-leave man, if at all?

'I am certain he was most flattered,' said Monsarrat, 'However, I doubt he could be swayed in either direction by such honour.'

'Of course, of course. A man above reproach, I'm sure. As must you be, naturally.'

For the third time, Monsarrat cursed Eveleigh for omitting any mention of his convict past, prejudicial as it might have been in the minds of people like Marley. Now he was faced with two equally unpalatable choices: conceal a crucial piece of information about himself, or risk losing the trust of the ranking man on this small outcrop, a trust he would need to bring any investigation to a satisfactory conclusion.

He chose the former. Eveleigh must have had his reasons, mustn't he?

While still treating Monsarrat's arm as though it were a pump handle, the man said, 'I, by the way, am James Brewster. Captain. And commandant here, obviously.'

He looked expectantly over Monsarrat's shoulder.

'Ah,' said Monsarrat. 'This is Mrs Mulrooney, a member of my household staff.' He hoped the man did not see him wince – Monsarrat knew immediately there would be a payment extracted for such a description.

'How sensible to travel with a servant, especially to a place as remote as this, although I assure you, your needs would have been well looked after regardless. Thankfully there is a small room to accommodate her in the visiting magistrate's cottage. He is not visiting at the moment, you see, I feel sure he'd not begrudge his lodgings. A ticket-of-leave woman, I take it?'

Mrs Mulrooney, who had never subscribed to the convention of being seen and not heard, stepped forward. 'Yes, sir, ticketed twenty years now and in honest labour since then.'

The commandant nodded absently, seemed to remember there were others waiting to be introduced. He turned to gesture the woman forward, sweeping his arm in an arc which made her flinch, though she was some feet away. 'My wife, Elizabeth,' he said.

Elizabeth stepped forward and smiled at Monsarrat, who feared he was beaming back in a most unclerical manner. She also sent a brief, welcoming nod in the direction of Mrs Mulrooney, earning her a frown from her husband. Perhaps, Monsarrat thought, Brewster saw pleasantries as a commodity, and not to be wasted on the servants. Monsarrat could see a tension in Elizabeth's face that had not been visible from a distance, a discontent dragging at the corners of her mouth.

The fellow behind Brewster seemed intent on a cloud being herded across the sky by the same winds which had made the sea passage less than comfortable. Brewster turned towards him, 'Walter, try to concentrate. We have guests.'

The man stepped forward, smiling broadly.

'My wife's brother, Walter Gendron.' And then, and Monsarrat could have sworn there was mockery in his tone, Brewster said, 'Also our new assistant storekeeper.'

'New?' asked Monsarrat, shaking the young man's hand.

'Assisting my wife, for the moment. A harmless fancy of hers, I suppose. We had some ... administrative trouble with the old one,' said Brewster, still with that edge of bitterness so hard to read. Could be hard man to live with, thought Monsarrat.

Mrs Mulrooney smiled at Walter, who beamed back.

'You are the gentleman I'll see about tea, then,' she said.

'Yes. Tea,' Walter smiled. 'We have plenty of it, I assure you. And I do love the stuff, although I wish the summers here weren't too hot for the drinking of it.'

'Walter, there will be plenty of time for discussion of tea later,' said Brewster. 'For now could you please follow Jones

31

up the hill and make sure all is in readiness in the visiting magistrate's cottage?'

'I shouldn't leave the store, though, you told me,' Walter said.

'It will be all right, just this once, Walter,' Elizabeth Brewster said, in a high, clear voice. Walter smiled, nodded, and loped off.

'A very hard worker, my brother,' Elizabeth said. 'Needs, perhaps, a little direction at times, but a man with a soul of his own; you'll find none better.'

'Depends on what you're looking for,' said Brewster. 'Now, Monsarrat. You have heard of our special guest?'

'Yes. Mr Marley acquainted me with the sensitivities.'

'Not long ago, I wouldn't have believed it of him. Killing on the field of battle, yes, I always knew he would do that in a heartbeat. But something more singularly violent – I would have thought it was beneath him. Now, though . . . well, you will see for yourself, of course.

Chapter 3

All penal settlements had them – a commandant, a commissary, and some sort of official building bespeaking British authority rising from the earth. In Port Macquarie, it had been a church. Here, it was a hospital, though it was currently just a rectangle of foot-imprinted mud framed by a low wall of clay bricks. Convicts were moving aimlessly around. Some were engaged in the painfully slow process of adding brick to brick, others appeared to be shambling about in penal limbo. Monsarrat found it a dispiriting place and wondered if it would have the same impact on sturdy Mrs Mulrooney, who had yearned for land but not necessarily Maria Island.

He and Captain Brewster were being watched by a tall fellow – what Mrs Mulrooney would call a long streak of a man – in a red coat like Brewster's, although this one had a full complement of buttons. Its owner's blond hair was closely cropped and the fellow's manner was less precise than his dress, alternating between barking commands and glaring.

'Holloway!' Brewster called as they approached. 'I had hoped to see more progress.'

Holloway bowed, hinging himself at the hips in a gesture which seemed rusty from lack of use. 'Yes, sir. However, a craftsman is only as good as his tools.' He pointed at the collection of felons.

At this Brewster began stalking through the mud, yelling at those not obviously occupied. Most of them obeyed without any obvious sense of urgency. They began to pick up bricks and carry them from one side of the site to the other, or ambled down towards a pile of timbers next to the commissary to haul some up. One thing he could be sure of, Monsarrat knew with the convict side of his soul: Brewster was not a man happy within his skin.

One man gave the commandant a jaunty, gap-toothed smile. A small, whippety fellow who had perhaps just left his twenties behind. He was perched on the incomplete section of the wall.

'Milliner!' Holloway screamed. He had clearly decided to demonstrate his disciplinary skills to his commanding officer. 'Get off that wall and start hauling some wood up here!'

'I would, Lieutenant Holloway,' Milliner said. 'But I've been told not to. Dr Chester's orders, sir. Have to wait for the wound on my foot to stop suppurating.'

'What damn wound? First I've heard of it.'

'Oh . . . well, I can show you, if you like,' said Milliner, reaching down to unwrap a dirty cloth bandage and remove a shoe that was more hole than leather.

'Never mind, never mind,' said Brewster, clearly not anxious to see, or smell, a dirty foot with a rotting sore. 'We're on our way to Chester anyway, and I assure you we will check with him.'

'Of course, sir,' said Milliner, smiling and settling back onto the wall.

Brewster leaned conspiratorially towards Monsarrat. 'Of course, we have to rely mostly on convicts for labour,' he said.

'The overseers, the baker, the tanner. Most of the positions here are held by convicts. Harefield was an exception. You wouldn't give one of these men a boat.'

He turned to his subordinate. 'Holloway!' he barked. 'We have a representative of the governor here, you know. Important to look efficient, even if you can't make the actuality match the perception. Holloway will, naturally, give you any help you need, as will I.'

'Naturally,' said Holloway, a clipped word he choked out in the least natural way possible.

Brewster clapped his hands, as though the sharpness of the gesture could make the convicts move faster, took Monsarrat's elbow and guided him to a crouching, earth-coloured tent on the perimeter of the building site. Monsarrat still felt the vertigo of being invoked as a man from a larger world whom Milliner should try to impress.

'I shall now,' Brewster said, 'introduce you to the first person to examine Harefield after his death. And it may interest you to know that you have just met the last person to see him alive – apart from his killer, of course.'

'Ah. I shall want to interview Holloway then.'

'Time enough for that. First, though . . .'

Brewster pulled back the tent flap and gestured Monsarrat inside. His eyes slowly adjusted to the dim light, and took in the folding desk at the end of the room at which sat a man in his shirtsleeves, holding a paper up to a gap in the tent through which a weak beam of sunlight permeated. Monsarrat's shoes squelched on the muddy ground beneath, covered by sodden straw that was beginning to sink into the mire together with the legs of two unoccupied cots in the middle of the room. The desk and its wooden chair were saved from a similar fate by a piece of canvas stained by wet, brown blotches.

'Mr Monsarrat, this is Dr Chester,' Brewster said. 'Tries to keep them alive, and writes long reports when he fails.'

Chester stood, grasped Monsarrat's hand, held it slightly longer than Holloway had.

'I would offer you a seat, but, well . . .' he said, looking around the room.

'Quite all right,' said Monsarrat. 'I have been doing a lot of sitting on the journey here. Perhaps, though, we could walk?'

Chester needed no second invitation, immediately unfolded himself from behind his desk and made for the tent flap.

'Chester is not the only one with reports to write,' said Brewster. 'I shall return to mine, if you've no objection. I'm sure the doctor will make sure no harm comes to you.'

'Why would any harm come to me?' asked Monsarrat.

'Why does harm come to anyone?' asked Brewster. 'But it came to Harefield.' He dropped his voice. 'For the sake of everyone's composure, I have asserted that Harefield was clearly targeted by a murderer aggrieved with him, not the entire human population of this island. But how can we be sure? If Power is guilty of this . . .' He left the confidence unfinished. 'Later, I shall take you to see Thomas Power,' he said, then nodded to both of them, turned and made his way back down the hill towards his office.

'He says that sort of thing, from time to time,' said Chester. 'I wouldn't trouble about it. Simply his manner – he seems to like drama and warnings.'

'You know him quite well, then?' said Monsarrat.

'We all know each other well here. Whether we wish to or not. The inevitable consequence of our confinement. I don't want to sound ungrateful – the commandant and his wife have shown me nothing but consideration since I arrived here. It's simply . . . well, there are few enough here who have not committed a crime.'

Interesting, Monsarrat thought. He was forming the impression that Chester would not have chosen Brewster's company were the alternatives more plentiful. He also suspected Chester wanted him to know that.

They were walking down the hill with the white dot of Power's cottage almost lost in the distance against the background of the convict and military barracks, and the looming massif of the island's mountainous spine.

Chester nodded towards the cottage. 'The United States Congress, the government of France, they are worrying about Thomas Power, about his welfare,' he said. 'You would not believe such a man could be contained in such a tiny cottage on such a tiny island at the limit of the earth. Like a goblin in a fairy story.'

'Do you think he's the one who killed Harefield?'

'Sometimes I do. But then I ask myself, by day's light, if I'm really convinced. You can ask him yourself.'

A line of convicts was now dribbling out of the barracks, prodded along by an overseer swearing at them. Some had that same shamble as the men at the hospital site, the gait of men who were dead but hadn't yet realised it.

'The convicts, are they generally a healthy lot?' he asked. 'There were no patients in your tent. And the worst injury at the hospital site was a man with a suppurating sore on his foot.'

Chester laughed. 'Milliner? I believe that was self-inflicted. He created the wound somehow, and used it to get out of going up with the work gang to the reservoir. All his profits are in Darlington.'

'Profits?'

'For a group who are forbidden alcohol, the convicts manage to get drunk on a regular basis. I suspect Milliner had some sort of, shall we say, import arrangement with Harefield. He was transported for fencing stolen goods. Loves making a deal.'

'And what of his infection?'

'I believe it's neither deliberate nor serious. I presume he told you he was resting on my orders.'

'He did.'

'Milliner is rarely to be believed, except on the price of rum. The commandant turns a blind eye, but you can always tell what you will pay in Hobart by halving his price.'

'Yes, these things do tend to go . . . unnoticed in penal settlements, where there is so much requiring noticing,' said Monsarrat. 'And I must say, in my experience sly grog and violence seem to co-exist. Particularly when there's competition. Were Milliner and Harefield competitors, do you think?'

'Associates, more probably,' said Chester. 'The rum didn't swim here by itself.'

'Perhaps Harefield wanted a greater share in the profits? A disagreement, something like that?'

Chester was still. 'No,' he said after a minute. 'No, Milliner's not the type.'

'Everyone's the type, given sufficient provocation,' said Monsarrat. 'At least, many have suggested that.'

'Oh, yes, well, perhaps when it comes to killing. But as to *how* he was killed. Milliner's too lazy for that type of exertion.'

'Exertion?'

'One of the axe blows went through the deltoid and managed in one clean stroke, practised or otherwise, to sever the humerus. When they found him, that arm was hanging by a little gristle of biceps and skin. The other two blows cut the trapezoid and shattered the clavicle of both collarbones. Great passion or great strength in those blows. That's at least three swings. Forceful ones. Hard to get Milliner to pick up a trowel, let alone an axe.'

'And you are certain it was an axe?' asked Monsarrat.

'Yes, it was found on the headland. Bloodied, of course.'

'I imagine there would be quite a few of his bones broken by the fall, given he was found at the bottom of a cliff,' said Monsarrat.

'Above all,' said Chester, 'his skull was fractured, frontal and parietal bones both in fragments. It might have been the intention of the murderer to fracture the skull with the axe, and the wounds to the clavicle on both sides might have been near misses. But the killer certainly got him in the end.'

'Mind yourself around Power,' said Brewster as they approached a wooden gate set into a whitewashed wall. 'The man deals in half-truths, just enough veracity to take a person in, coated in the charm to make it go down easily. You wouldn't be the first to be fooled.'

'Oh?' said Monsarrat. 'Who has he deceived?'

'Not me, certainly!' Brewster barked, almost losing his footing. 'Damn creatures here can't stop digging holes.'

The gate, when they got there, did not look very sturdy, but the guard beside it did. The man stepped aside wordlessly as Brewster approached and extracted a ring of keys from his pocket.

'He has not yet tried to rush the gate,' Brewster said. 'But it's a possibility we need to be alive to.'

Indeed, no one hurled themselves at the gate. The only person beyond it did not seem inclined to hurl himself anywhere. He looked up, caught in the middle of pacing up and down the small, barren yard. He was dressed for a London spring, and a fashionable one at that, a well-cut coat in a fine fabric, a silk cravat of an extraordinary blue, and a waistcoat which looked to Monsarrat, who considered himself something of an authority on these matters, to be shot through with gold thread. He had a face which few women would describe as handsome but which an artist or draughtsman could not fault, so precise was the slope of the nose, the distance between the eyes. And his eyes were the most disconcertingly piercing shade of blue. Clearly, thought Monsarrat, the colour of the cravat was no coincidence. This was a man who wanted his eyes to be seen at best advantage, whether or not anyone was there to do the seeing.

'My dear Brewster,' he said, not moving towards them, perhaps fearing any attempt to do so would be misinterpreted. 'You have brought me a guest. How kind.'

'It's not kindness which motivates me,' Brewster said. 'Not anymore. This is Mr Monsarrat from the governor's office. He is here to investigate you.'

'Well, investigate away, dear fellow,' Power said. And then he did approach, took Monsarrat's hand, put his other over it. 'Just before you do, though, I have an important question to put to you.'

'Of course,' said Monsarrat, a little disconcerted by the man's two-handed grip, and even more uneasy when Power leaned in so that his face and Monsarrat's were inches apart.

'Tell me,' Power said. 'Do you have any books?'

⁓◦⁓

Brewster shut down the conversation about books before it could get started, leaving Monsarrat with the distinct impression that similar conversations in the past had gone on for rather a long time.

Power, at Brewster's urging, showed them into his small cottage, a set of three adjoining rooms so that to reach the kitchen one had to walk through the sitting room from the bedroom. Power had a small fire in the tiny sitting room, with one chair in front of it, angled so its occupant could ignore the papers spilling over the edges of the desk in the corner. He offered it to Monsarrat, who declined.

'Shall we all sit on the floor then?' said Power. He did not appear to be joking.

'I am happy to stand, thank you, Power,' said Brewster. 'As, I'm sure, is Mr Monsarrat.'

'Of course. As you wish, gentlemen. Now, I imagine your time has many calls on it, Mr Monsarrat. So I expect you want to get started. I suppose you're here to ask me about the bosun.'

40

'Yes, as a matter of fact,' said Monsarrat.

'You believe I killed him.'

'I believe nothing, at present.'

'Quite right. No point making assumptions.'

'Yes,' said Brewster. 'I did, and look where it got me.'

'My dear commandant,' said Power. 'I assure you, there was nothing—'

'No, nor will there be if I can help it. And it's not relevant, so let's not discuss it.'

'But my friend—' said Power.

'I am your jailer, not your friend, Mr Power.'

Brewster turned to Monsarrat. 'Mr Monsarrat, should you have no objection, perhaps I had best get on with my administrative duties. I think you're safe with Mr Power, but I would advise you again to apply the utmost scepticism to any word he utters.'

'Yes,' said Power, nodding solemnly. 'Especially words like hello or thank you. It is very easy to imbue them with a double meaning.'

Brewster glared at Power and stalked out of the cottage.

'I should not have done that, but I found it irresistible,' said Power. 'Still, it has angered him. Unwise to anger a small man with a large amount of authority.'

'There has been . . . a disagreement between you?'

'He doesn't want it discussed, so I'd best not. At any rate, he's right. It's not relevant to your quest. Would you care to take a turn around the grounds with me?'

The grounds to which Power was referring was the twenty-square-foot patch of walled dirt, to which, opening a door, he now led Monsarrat. They strolled side by side, Monsarrat rather astonished to be in the great patriot's company.

'The island was just bearable when I could walk where I pleased,' Power said. 'Do you know, a little to the south there are some extraordinary cliffs? You can still see the indentations made in them by creatures of incredible age. Little shells and

41

so forth. God knows how old they are, possibly millennia. And to the west are some more cliffs, ones with colours so artful it's impossible to believe they weren't put there by a brush. I am not a man made to be confined, Mr Monsarrat. And to be locked in this yard on this island is confinement within confinement, and almost intolerable.'

'I can imagine it must also be tedious,' said Monsarrat.

'Oh, indeed. I have my journals, and I write in them when I can – musings, and so on. But they get a little repetitive after a while, and what have I to write about beyond the contents of my own head? If I were to focus on the external, there would be a long list of entries saying things like, *I awoke, rose, washed, and paced around the yard 256 times*. Books, when I can get them, they're the ticket; the only things that keep me from losing my wits. Which brings me back to my first question – do you have any?'

'Is Catullus to your taste?'

'Anything is, by now. And, yes, especially Catullus – naughty boy that he was, eh? Had I his skill, I would do exactly as he did – send threats and dinner invitations and promissory notes in verse. If you can bear to part with it, Mr Monsarrat, I would be most grateful to give your volume a temporary home here.'

'I may be just about able to bear it, for a few nights, yes,' said Monsarrat, unable to resist smiling. 'And I have some *Blackstones Quarterly*s.'

'Oh, the Tory rubbish in those. I took you for a man of intellect, Mr Monsarrat. Tell me you're not polluting your spirit with such bile.'

'If I am, it's only for the pleasure of disagreeing with it. I find the *Edinburgh Review* more to my taste.'

'Ah! Yes, as would I in your circumstances. In any circumstances, really. I don't suppose you have some with you? I'll even take a *Blackstones*, if you're willing. Yes, these are the depths I have sunk to.'

He chuckled, an oddly satisfied sound from a man who had just completed his umpteenth circuit of the small yard.

'Tell me, Mr Power,' said Monsarrat. 'It's my understanding you're confined to this yard as a result of being too friendly with the commandant, for being too much at liberty here. If I may say so, though, the commandant appears to share the view that this is where you belong.'

'Yes, he does now. Wasn't always the case. Ultimately, though, the dinner invitations stopped. I imagine the Brewsters must be terribly bored now. The wombats, I hate to tell you, are not very good conversationalists.'

'Well, if I may, I'd like to call on you again, once I've found out a little more about the murder of Mr Harefield. In the meantime, I must ask one question.'

'Did I kill the bosun? No, sir.'

And it was hard to believe he had, though Monsarrat recalled Mr Marley's words. Indeed, while in conversation with roguish Power, it was hard for Monsarrat to remember he was on a search for the bosun's killer.

Monsarrat was ill-prepared, then, to feel a jab in the back from a forearm and to be rammed by Power's left arm. The political prisoner had him in a vice-like hold, leaving Monsarrat without breath.

'Do you feel I have dominance over you?' Power hissed in Monsarrat's ear.

The man is mad, thought Monsarrat. He managed to find the air to affirm this was the case. 'Yes. You have ... dominance.'

'Do you feel I could easily finish you?'

'I wouldn't be surprised if you could,' Monsarrat gasped.

'At the battle of Boyacá, seven thousand feet up in the Andes, Bolívar ordered my Irish in on the flank of the Spanish royalists. When my sword broke, I was forced to strangle a Spanish officer who was trying to kill me. Do you think I could strangle you?'

Pulsing with unfamiliar fear, Monsarrat murmured, 'I'm hopeful you won't try, Mr Power.'

He was released. He stood before a smiling Power and felt light as a feather.

'Why do you think I'll not do it?' asked Power.

'Well,' Monsarrat said. 'Unlike the Spaniard, I've got no ambition to kill you.'

'Forgive me,' said Power. 'I was just making a point. And you seem to have grasped it. Nor did I kill Harefield. Why would I, any more than I would have you, when I look forward to freedom and have a future to plan? But I bore Harefield no love, that I will tell you.'

'Oh? Any particular reason for that?'

'The man possessed a nasty vicious soul. This place is so isolated, and in those circumstances someone with knowledge of everyone else's affairs can do well if they use that knowledge immorally. Harefield understood the value of mean intelligence and set about collecting it and using it at every opportunity.'

'And who did he use it against?'

'Who didn't he? Anyone whom he felt wasn't being respectful enough, for a start. Who didn't appreciate his skills. He upset a fair few people. If you wish to find his killer, you will have to cast the net a lot wider than my small yard. I hope that whatever crimes I commit are directed at unjust rulers, not at bosuns.'

It took Hannah Mulrooney no time to find the stores. It was hardly possible, anyway, to get lost among the works of man here, few as they were.

That said, there were those who seemed intent on trying. Men walking with the assurance of those who were used to these paths would glance at her and suddenly quicken their pace. The works of nature looked to be another matter entirely. One presented itself as she picked her way down the hill. She took it for a log until it moved. The flat-faced dollop of brown fur meandered slowly across the grass, pulling tufts up noisily by the roots, methodically covering the patches of sustenance the hill had to offer. Beside it, a smaller version, about the size of a loaf of bread, tried to do likewise, but had not yet developed the ability to crop the grass to its roots.

She had seen these creatures before from time to time. Occasionally they would appear out of the trees in Port Macquarie before scuttling away, and every few months she would come across one by a roadside, although they seemed to prefer to keep to the woods. This one, though, seemed far too intent on its meal to be scared off.

She tried to call the creature's name to mind, and couldn't. Whatever they were, they showed no interest in moving. She made her way around them and continued down to the two-storey building near the dock.

She was surprised to see Mrs Brewster, as well as Walter, behind the counter. They were bent over a ledger, and Mrs Brewster was making marks in it while Walter looked on. She looked up and smiled as Hannah entered.

'The Sydney servant,' she said. 'I'm sorry, but we were never introduced. I am Elizabeth Brewster, although I suppose you could hear that perfectly well for yourself on the dock.'

'Hannah Mulrooney, ma'am,' said Hannah, remembering to show appropriate deference by bobbing a curtsey. She hid her surprise at Mrs Brewster's friendliness. Few in her position would have wasted the breath.

'And how can we assist you, Mrs Mulrooney?'

Hannah looked around the room, long and high-ceilinged, neatly arranged, with sacks of flour and kegs along the walls and shelves above them holding sugar and pitch and any number of substances in jars.

'I was hoping, ma'am, to be able to procure some tea. Perhaps some butter, flour and sugar, too. I am told my shortbread is rather fine so I thought to make some for yourself and your family.'

Walter looked up from the ledger. 'I myself am partial to shortbread,' he said.

'As are we all, of course,' said Mrs Brewster. 'And with such a lovely offer, how can I refuse? Walter, would you?' she said, as he moved along the shelves, running his fingers across each of the earthenware containers.

He nodded, set about getting the supplies ready.

'Where's the flour?' he called over his shoulder.

'Second barrel over,' Mrs Brewster called back. 'I think.' She turned and smiled at Hannah. 'We are new to this, Walter and I,' she said. 'The commissary needed to be replaced rather urgently.'

'Oh. Illness?'

'No . . . in any case, we are getting better at it day by day. Keeps us occupied here where occupation can be difficult to find. Tell me, Mrs Mulrooney, in addition to shortbread, has your employer any particular likes or dislikes with regard to food?'

'He is grateful for anything.'

Mrs Brewster frowned.

'As is anyone who appreciates the bounty of the Lord,' Hannah added quickly.

'Well, I am glad to hear it. I had thought to have him to dine tonight. We have only mutton at present, I'm afraid, but some fine carrots have come in from the vegetable garden, and potatoes in great number. Is there anything you could do with those ingredients?'

'Quite a number of things, and every one of them palatable,' said Hannah.

'Excellent! Could you cook for us tonight? We have a convict usually do it, a former ship's cook, but he is rather heavy-handed and unused to cooking fresh things. I look forward to seeing what you come up with.

'Walter, would you please be kind enough to help Mrs Mulrooney carry her provisions up to the visiting magistrate's cottage?' Mrs Brewster continued. 'I assure you I will manage the stores well in your absence. I shan't let anything get out of place.'

Walter turned to Hannah and smiled. 'Very important that nothing is out of place,' he said, nodding to himself. He handed Hannah the pot containing the tea, holding the other two in the crooks of his arms.

'It's a responsible job, that of the commissary,' said Hannah as they crossed the little bridge over a small creek which flowed to the ocean, making their way back up the hill.

'Oh yes. I'm assistant commissary to my sister, just until they send a new man from Hobart. And I'm very good at it. Elizabeth says so all the time.'

'It must be true, so,' Hannah said.

He nodded emphatically.

'Mr Gendron,' she said, 'I wonder, could you tell me the name of those creatures?'

There was another pair of them down in the reeds which fringed the beach, the mother munching loudly and the young one nibbling happily away.

'Wombats,' he said. 'Funny, aren't they? They have very rough fur, you know. I wouldn't recommend patting them – I tried it once and it gave me fleas. I was hoping to take one as a pet – I had a little dog, back in Devon, you see. Sweet little fellow, would always run to catch anything I threw. I've thrown a stick to a wombat, and he ignored it. I think they just want to be left alone.'

'Well, leave them alone I shall, then,' Hannah said.

Walter stopped suddenly, turned and looked at her with a strange intensity. 'You mustn't be frightened of them, though,' he said. 'They won't hurt you, not unless you're a blade of grass.

It's important to save your fear for those things that deserve it, otherwise you might not have enough left over when you need it.'

'I think that a very fine suggestion, Mr Gendron. Although I never until recently thought of fear as something that could be rationed.'

'Everything has to be rationed,' said Walter. 'And fear keeps you safe.'

They started up the pathway to the twin cottages in silence, before Walter stopped again. 'Of course, you might want to practise.'

'And what should I be practising, Mr Gendron?'

'Being afraid,' he said. 'Not enough to wear it out, just enough so you can call on it when you need it.'

'Thank you, Mr Gendron, but I don't need any practice,' she said. The image of flames leaping up around a grinning woman with a lighted branch still projected itself onto the inside of her eyelids at night. That fire was still more present to her than the threat of a madman with an axe.

Chapter 4

Monsarrat walked slowly away from the little cottage in which Power had no doubt gone back to scribbling on the mountains of paper on his desk. Monsarrat kept his head down, given the enthusiasm for digging displayed by some of the animals here, so he didn't notice Lieutenant Holloway until the man passed him.

Monsarrat scrambled to catch up, nearly tripping in the process, so that by the time he reached the soldier, he was feeling rattled and put a hand on the man's shoulder rather than calling his name.

Holloway turned instantly, eyes wide and nostrils flaring, offended at the contact. 'Mr Monsarrat! May I ask what the urgency is, that you feel the only appropriate course of action is to grab me?'

'I do apologise, lieutenant, but might I speak to you for just a moment?'

'Very well. A moment.'

'I understand you were the last to see Harefield alive.'

'What are you saying?' said Holloway.

'Nothing. Nothing at all. I simply wanted to get your views.'

'My views? Views are of no use. Evidence is what we need, and that's what you're here to get.'

'And that's what I am in the process of doing. But it would help if people refrained from making assumptions. Simply because Power is who he is, it does not automatically make him a murderer.'

'Does it not?' said Holloway. 'Even if he's not guilty of this crime – and who's to say he's not – he is guilty of others. People admire him, of course. He has the words for it. But words don't feed a person. They did not feed me, when a group of Luddites burned down my father's mill after listening to someone like Power. These men, they bear responsibility for acts committed in their name, but it is a responsibility they are not forced to take.'

'Surely you want the right person to be held responsible for Harefield's death? The one who wielded the axe.'

'Naturally.'

'And you last saw Harefield . . . when, exactly?'

'I sent him to the light. Didn't want to see the cliffs decorated with dead whalers.'

'Just before he died, then. And you saw nothing of concern?'

'Do you not think I would have shared that information, if I had?'

'Of course, of course. If I may ask, though, for an indulgence . . .'

'Yes, you seem the type for indulgences,' said Holloway. 'Parramatta is a town with many diversions, I'm sure. You must find it somewhat sparse here.'

If only you knew, thought Monsarrat. 'I would very much like to see the axe which was used,' he said aloud. 'I understand it is in your custody?'

'Yes. However, I can't see what you would gain by looking at it.'

'Well, I don't suppose I shall know either until I do. By the way, who owns it?'

'Mr Monsarrat, I really can't be expected to know the owner of every implement in the settlement. An individual tool might be issued one day to one man, the next to someone else. You should look to build a path between Harefield's body and Thomas Power, rather than asking to see axes which have no mouths and cannot speak.'

Mrs Mulrooney had done a remarkable job on the little kitchen. She'd found the fireplace colonised by a group of possums, whom she'd gently relocated to a comfortable tuft of grass outside. The fireplace was swept out, the cobwebs banished, and the utensils thoroughly scrubbed and then frowned at until they knew it was in their interests to behave. These activities seemed to cheer Mrs Mulrooney, make the island more of a home to her.

'Will you be comfortable tonight?' Monsarrat asked her.

'Of course,' she said, as if to dismiss the question. 'I have a strong scream if needed, and the magistrate's room has a lock on it.'

Mrs Mulrooney was spotless though Monsarrat noticed a stained shirt and smudged pinafore soaking in a copper in the corner of the room. Between utterances, Hannah Mulrooney murmured her displeasure at a hairline crack in the only mixing bowl she'd been able to find, stirring the butter, flour, sugar together with the handle of a ladle, as no wooden spoon was in evidence.

'Is it within the realms of possibility that I may actually receive a small share of that shortbread?' Monsarrat said.

'Perhaps. It's for the Brewsters and Mr Gendron, though. Big lad that he is, there may not be any left.'

Monsarrat tried not to show his irritation. He was forever missing out on Mrs Mulrooney's shortbread.

'And I won't be able to make any more after this, not today anyway,' Mrs Mulrooney said. 'I'm to make the Brewsters' dinner tonight, and yours as well since you'll be dining with them.'

She spread the shortbread out in a battered but intact pan, and set about boiling water. 'Mrs Brewster was kind enough to come by. Said she thought I would need a tea pot and some cups. Good of her.'

'Yes. Encouraging that she's so friendly. Her husband is a slightly different proposition. I hope, for all our sakes, we can get this business concluded as quickly as possible. Power is charming, as we were promised, and desperate for reading material. I'm lending him my Catullus. In Latin and English translation. Not that he needs the English.'

'And yet you won't let me read it in its English form!'

'Some of the verses are hardly, shall we say, seemly.'

Mrs Mulrooney was a recent addition to the world of readers. She had been taught her letters by Monsarrat a few months previously and had made remarkable progress. He was proud of her, but the whole business did have an unwanted consequence. She attempted to read everything she could get her hands on – from other people's lists to Catullus to correspondence Monsarrat brought home with him. She took any attempt to hide the written word from her as a personal affront.

'Mr Monsarrat, I've seen the arms blown off men by Spanish grapeshot, and you think I'm too squeamish for a dead Roman?'

'Very well, you may read Catullus when I am able to taste some of your shortbread.'

It was then that Monsarrat discovered that Mrs Brewster had also provided Mrs Mulrooney with a cleaning cloth, which in an instant was flicked against his temple.

'Please don't scar me before dinner tonight,' he said. 'There is a matter concerning the Brewsters and Power that I need to investigate, and this is an investigation which I suspect will be unwelcome.'

He told Mrs Mulrooney about the tension between Brewster and Power.

'They both refused to talk about it. Power said it's not relevant,' said Monsarrat. 'But I would rather judge that for myself. Especially as Power has shown me, perhaps unknowingly, that he is not always able to restrain himself. He bared his teeth at me, you see. Not intending to use them, just to show me he had them.'

Mrs Mulrooney smiled. 'We are finally teaching you to think, aren't we?' she said.

'Actually, I was rather good at it previously.'

'But you're better at it now,' she said, with the same certainty with which someone would discuss the direction from which the sun rose. 'Have you an avenue of approach in mind?'

'Not yet. Perhaps dinner will be illuminating. And you? Tell me more about the commandant's wife and brother-in-law.'

'He's an odd one, that lad. Very sweet, I think. And I wouldn't say he was simple-minded; in fact, some of his conversation is intelligent. But he doesn't slot into the world the way most people do. It doesn't seem to agree with him. And Mr Monsarrat, he's frightened.'

'What of?'

'Well, he said that in the past he wasn't frightened when he should have been.'

'Could be anything. Or nothing.'

'Or it could be everything, eejit of a man,' said Mrs Mulrooney. 'And we don't know until we know. So keep half an ear out at dinner for anything anyone says which might nudge you in the right direction.'

I must urge you, my dear, to try not to provoke anyone. It is perhaps futile to beg you to stay silent in the shadows, but I am being selfish. I have seen the ease with which they can lengthen a sentence. I know the superintendent is less depraved than the last one, but even the most upright administrators allow atrocities to occur, and I can't bear to think of it.

I hope you're in good spirits. I well remember how time began to slow when my own freedom drew near, and I hope it is sitting more lightly on your shoulders than it did on mine.

Monsarrat folded the paper, paused before writing the address on it. He knew, in a cooler part of his mind, that to build a little structure of expectation involving a future with Grace was foolish of him. Yes, she could be assigned to him as his wife, as was a colonial practice (and a source of many jokes, domestic and earthy), yet he only maintained his liberty at Ralph Eveleigh's pleasure. But such dreams should be the entitlement of a free man, and he was, however marginally, free. He was tempted to send the letter via Eveleigh, but the man might read it, and Monsarrat would feel he had exposed more of his soul than he should. He had an irrational fear that the message would lose potency if other eyes saw it. So he dipped his pen in the inkpot and wrote: 'Grace O'Leary, Female Factory, Parramatta, New South Wales'.

Whether it would convince Grace, he had no idea. He rather doubted it, and it was unlikely that it would reach Parramatta much before he did. Still, the act of setting it on paper felt almost like a prayer, and he hoped the words would call the reality into being.

❧

Mrs Mulrooney had done her best with limited ingredients, which she served before retiring to the corner of the room, for all the world the waiting servant. She had a way with potatoes, and Monsarrat would be willing to bet that the mash in the tureen in front of him was as smooth as any to be found on the dining table of Government House.

Elizabeth Brewster was wearing a blue silk gown which would have been considered plain in London but must have been by far the finest garment ever worn on this island. Her height, her heart-shaped face, her odd air of command tempered by caution – he squinted and allowed himself to believe, for a moment, that he was looking at a future incarnation of another woman, one who had yet to wear silk.

Elizabeth's eyes were flicking between her husband and her brother, and she would hurry to correct Walter's small infractions before Captain Brewster noticed them – laying a warning hand on his arm when he tried to attack his dinner before grace was said, mopping up splashed gravy before it could be fully absorbed by the tablecloth.

The china had a fussy floral design, gold leaf that had worn away in places, and small chips on the edges of some of the plates which spoke of a journey every bit as rough as Monsarrat and Mrs Mulrooney's. Monsarrat saw how gentle Chester was when he placed his knife or fork onto the plate. He sat on the other side of Walter, occasionally leaning in to listen to an excited account of the latest visitors to the bay, a pod of dolphins.

'I must say,' said Elizabeth, looking to Monsarrat. 'Lovely to have another person at the table. Particularly an educated fellow like yourself. We do tend to get quite inward-looking here. Odd to think of it, but I sometimes wonder whether there is anything left at all overseas. England and France might've started another war, might've blown each other out of existence for all I know. My only war here is against tedium.'

'Together with certain ideological battles you insist on engaging in,' said her husband. 'Which can be just as dangerous as any battlefield skirmish.'

Elizabeth, who – Monsarrat suspected – was a woman of spirit, did not choose to fight the proposition. Yet Monsarrat was glad not to be in a position to intercept the look James Brewster gave his wife as he spoke. She met his eyes with an initial challenge which melted into wariness under his stare.

She recovered herself to turn to Monsarrat and smile. 'I do differ, it is true, from those who believe in a divinely dictated order of society,' she said. 'I have seen nothing which proves to me that one class of person is inherently inferior to another. A misfortune of birth is all the difference between a lord and a labourer, in my opinion.

'Doctor, you see men in all kinds of states. Are they truly that different once all the social trappings are stripped away?'

Chester cleared his throat, glancing at Brewster. Monsarrat felt for him. The commandant might treat the doctor as an equal, but he was all-powerful here.

'Well,' said Chester, after a short pause, 'convicts do tend to die sooner . . . but with poorer nutrition and hard work it's to be expected.'

'That fact is certainly to be regretted,' said Elizabeth, and her glance wavered a second towards her husband. 'But you don't believe they're fundamentally different. That they're flawed from birth?'

'I've seen nothing to suggest . . .'

'Thomas Power is certainly different,' Brewster interrupted, slamming an open hand down on the table so that Monsarrat feared for the china. 'His brand of treason comes with a thin coating of manners and palaver. Just enough to make his self-worship palatable for those of a gullible mind.' This time he avoided looking at his wife, a determination which seemed every bit as aggressive as a naked stare.

Elizabeth straightened her shoulders, flared her nostrils in a way Monsarrat had seen Mrs Mulrooney do when anxious but trying to cover it. 'Well, one has a chance to think here,' she said. 'And my thoughts, I assure you, are my own.'

There was silence, for a moment. I should, Monsarrat thought, fulfil the ancient duty of the dinner guest. To change the subject following an argument between hosts.

'My housekeeper mentioned that the commissary keeps you rather busy,' he said to Walter. 'Hard to think of a more important job, feeding an entire settlement.'

Elizabeth and Brewster looked at each other while Walter reached his fork over to Elizabeth's plate to spear a neglected carrot.

'A responsible job, as you say,' said Brewster. 'And one we had to fill rather quickly. Hence the unusual arrangements.'

'And, I wondered . . . why the haste to find a new commissary?'

'Well, there were, as I said, some administrative irregularities,' said Brewster, his tone making it clear that he felt irregularity deserved a place among the seven deadly sins.

'They think the commissary was stealing,' said Walter, speaking with his mouth full. 'Some supplies went missing, and Mr Harefield said it was the commissary's fault, and suddenly everyone was saying it.'

Brewster glared at Walter. 'Enough!' he hissed. 'Elizabeth, if you can't control him, I swear . . .'

He looked around then, realising that the only eyes which weren't on him were those looking away in embarrassment. Walter's were beginning to fill, the corners of his mouth sagging.

Brewster regained his composure. 'You persuaded me, Elizabeth, to appoint your brother acting commissary. Perhaps you should think how that reflects on me.'

But, Monsarrat complained internally, you let yourself be talked into it.

Walter looked stricken, his mouth agape, and there was a pause before Elizabeth reached out and made reassuring pats on his arm and then decided to try to scoop up the ruins of the conversation.

'I must say, your housekeeper is quite remarkable. She would not be out of place in a grand house,' she said to Monsarrat. 'Wherever did you find her?'

'She was part of the staff of the commandant of a settlement north of Sydney. As was I.'

'You're a military man, then?' asked Brewster.

Beside him, Monsarrat could feel Chester relax, no doubt relieved to be out of the commandant's line of vision for a while.

'No, I was . . . on the civil staff,' he said. 'The man's secretary.'

'You do seem to have a very precise manner, if I may say, Mr Monsarrat,' Brewster said. 'May I ask how it served you in your conversation with Mr Power?'

Elizabeth's smile disappeared and Walter, who had sought comfort in his dinner, slowed in his chewing.

'The fellow is rather skilled at managing a conversation, and leading it in the direction he wants,' said Monsarrat, determined by powerful instinct to omit all reference to Power's manhandling of him. 'Which would be ideal if one were looking for an entertaining chat. Not so much if one is looking for straightforward answers. He claims that he has too many future plans to have killed Harefield.'

Walter looked wide-eyed around the room.

'But do you believe he's guilty?' asked Brewster.

'I do not yet have sufficient information to form an opinion,' Monsarrat said. 'But I would say he does have plans. That he'd hang for a spectacular cause but not for the sake of a mere personal grudge.'

'He would like you to think that,' said Brewster disdainfully. 'Don't be fooled by him, Monsarrat.'

'I shall be vigilant, Captain Brewster,' Monsarrat felt it was wise to assure his host.

'Well, he's not the only convict on this island. Tomorrow I will introduce you to Oliver Trainor, the overseer I've been trying to keep away from Darlington. He knew Harefield well. They occasionally decided to dispense their own justice rather than waiting for mine.'

'Oh? Harefield was violent?'

'Harefield was ... a rough man,' said Brewster. 'Fit for his purpose, you could say, but not one for graces – to be expected, I suppose, for who would he use them on in the normal run of things? Elizabeth didn't care for him.'

'It's not a matter of caring for him or otherwise,' said Elizabeth. 'I just thought he was a brute.'

'I must say,' Chester said, 'I've tended to more than a few wounds caused by him.'

'He didn't like me,' said Walter, suddenly. 'Said I was useless. And ... and other things.'

Elizabeth smiled. 'You are worth ten of him, dearest,' she said, her words suddenly choked. 'He didn't appreciate your intellect.'

'And I didn't appreciate his fists,' Walter said.

'His fists?' Monsarrat said. 'He never assaulted you, did he?'

Walter nodded, but James Brewster shook his head.

'Not quite,' he said. 'He got a little frustrated with Walter once – there were some dolphins off the beach, you see. Walter was gazing at them just as Harefield was trying to unload a sack. He yelled at Walter to get out of the way, otherwise he'd ...'

'Flatten me,' Walter interrupted. 'He said he'd flatten me, and he—'

'Yes, well, there you are then,' said Brewster.

'Harefield,' said Elizabeth, 'was as much of a bigot as those who believe the poor are born deficient and destined to stay that way. Anyone incapable of hoisting a barrel on one shoulder was useless, according to him. He failed to appreciate strength if it didn't reside in the muscles. You know, Mr Monsarrat, Walter can do very complicated sums in his head, and in a fraction of a second. It's a skill which is useful in the administration of a penal colony.'

'I'm sure that's the case,' said Monsarrat. 'May I ask, if you bore Mr Harefield no love, how many others felt the same way?'

'Harefield was difficult to like,' Brewster said. 'He dealt in rumours, true or not, spent words like money. People enjoyed his gossip until they were the subject of it. Some of the overseers and convicts made time for him. It was rumoured he supplied rum to be sold on, to a fellow called Milliner.'

'So Dr Chester told me,' said Monsarrat, smiling at the doctor. 'Did you not demand to inspect Harefield's boat, captain? Or his quarters?'

'It is a small community, Mr Monsarrat. I wouldn't expect you to understand the way things work. Mr Harefield had the ability to take us across the water. I didn't begrudge him and some of the rest of them a drink from time to time. As long as it didn't lead to violence or vandalism, and it didn't. Command means taking these kinds of decisions.'

'A sore head won't help them work any faster on the reservoir,' said Elizabeth, 'but rum might ease some of their less easily eradicated pain.'

'In any case,' Brewster said, 'it is one thing to follow orders on the running of a penal settlement, another to make it continue to function from day to day. Sometimes it requires an approach which is a little, shall we say, imaginative.'

'Tell me, Captain, and forgive me for speaking so plainly, but you'll appreciate the need for efficiency,' Monsarrat said. 'Am I correct in assuming that you have been on friendlier terms with Power in the past?'

Brewster frowned awkwardly, cleared his throat. 'Well . . . he was good company for a time, as I'm sure you can imagine,' he said. 'But he began behaving in a singularly inappropriate manner, an indecent—'

Elizabeth held up a hand. 'Forgive us, Mr Monsarrat,' she said, 'but in places as isolated as this, rumours can be fatal and must not be given life through repetition.'

She turned to her brother, smiled, put a hand on his arm. 'Otherwise they become grotesque monsters from which the innocent need protection. And I will always protect the innocent.'

Brewster pursed his lips, considered his hand and nodded sourly.

⁓ↄ∾ↄ⁓

The fire must have died some time during the darkness. It had been a warm enough summer's day, but the night had brought a chill unknown in these months in Port Macquarie or Parramatta. It was a long while, Hannah thought, since she had withdrawn her feet from the paving stones of the bedroom floor, unwilling to press them to such a cold surface.

She forced herself to wash, even so. It was one area where she would allow herself no compromise. If she behaved like a convict, lost all regard for personal hygiene, she was far more likely to be treated like one.

Despite her sturdy boasts to Monsarrat, Hannah did not like being transplanted. She could not draw strength from the hearth when the hearth kept changing, and she would likely feel ill at ease until the kitchen and everything in it had been organised into submission.

Clearly she hadn't banked the fire up enough, she thought, or else the wood here burned differently. She shivered at she thought of fires misbehaving. At least this one was obviously just lazy. She had coaxed it back to a semblance of life, enough to apply some heat to the bottom of the kettle by the time Mr Monsarrat walked in.

'You'll be expecting tea, I imagine,' she said.

'I expect nothing, but I'm grateful for anything,' he said. 'It was chilly last night, wasn't it?'

'It's nothing compared to what we both felt before we made the long journey to the new land all those years back. We've gone soft, the pair of us,' she said.

Monsarrat smiled. 'I'm sure you're right. I have only very dim memories of the properties of snow. I suppose I might not see it again for some time.'

'Well, Mr Monsarrat, if the past years have taught me anything, it's the dangers of supposing. So tell me, what did you make of your evening?'

'There's obviously the issue of these rumours, whatever they are,' said Monsarrat. 'Interesting that a martinet like Brewster ignored Harefield's sly grog trade. Can't believe no one searched the man's hut.'

'Well, young Jeremiah's in there now,' said Hannah.

'Jeremiah?'

'Jeremiah Jones, the boatman! Pay attention, Mr Monsarrat. Perhaps he might like some tea.'

'Anything for the man who got you across that sea,' said Monsarrat.

'Who might not object to having his lodgings searched.'

'What about the fact that Mrs Brewster does seem rather keen to protect her brother – and more than a little nervous of her husband? As you say, that must be why she works alongside her brother in the stores.'

'Oh, you'd be mistaken to underestimate Walter,' said Hannah.

'Hm. He is, though ... unusual.'

'Yes, he is. That's a supposition I will allow you, though, as I've already told you, Walter is no fool. So don't make the mistake of assuming he has nothing of use to say.'

She realised she sounded like a schoolmistress upbraiding

a refractory student, and Monsarrat bristled slightly. 'Very well then – what am I missing?'

'Do you remember what Mrs Brewster said on the subject of rumours?'

'Yes, that she would do anything to protect her brother from them.'

'Eejit of a man. She said no such thing. She said "the innocent".'

'Well, if anyone's innocent ... and who else would she have been talking about?'

'I don't know. Perhaps no one. But your recollection of the conversation is flawed. Take care to hear what is said in future.'

'Indeed I shall, and we are still left with the fact – one which I'm certain I didn't mishear – that there was some sort of damaging rumour involving Power. On an island this small, everyone surely would know about it, whatever it is.'

'They probably do, Mr Monsarrat. You just have to ask the right person in the right way.'

'And the right way would be?'

'You have to do it side-on,' she said. 'Meander up to them, find a way in through conversation about anything else, or nothing in particular.'

'Well, I'm to see the overseer soon. I will try to take your advice and – how did you put it? Approach him side-on.'

Chapter 5

Oliver Trainor, Monsarrat realised, was not the sort of fellow one approached side-on.

He was a sturdy man who didn't seem to have sides, with a barrel torso resting on top of muscular legs. His head, almost entirely bald, was covered in lesions caused by years of blistering under the unforgiving sun. Monsarrat was fascinated – it seemed clear Trainor had been elevated to the position of overseer because of the very air of threat that had got him transported in the first place. A man who must do enough hard-knuckled disciplining to keep the commandant happy, but not so much as to motivate his charges to kill him; a man caught between criminality and the state. But then, Monsarrat knew, he himself was such a being. A ticket-of-leaver who was an investigator even of his betters – not that the betters here knew it.

To reach Trainor, Monsarrat was directed by Captain Brewster to follow a small path, which had been gouged by the feet that had trod it before him and by the wheels of stone-carrying carts. The path cut through the thick trunks of the venerable gums and the sweet green undergrowth, into which some wombats were attempting to make headway. Occasionally a brown waterfowl would scutter across the path, and once or twice Monsarrat saw a subtler movement at the edge of the track, a cylindrical writhing which he tried to ignore.

Having come from a crowded penal settlement by way of a thriving town, Monsarrat was unused to the absence of the sounds of humans. He indulged himself on the walk, imagining he was alone on the island, that he would always be so, that there was no longer any point in pretending as there was no one to pretend for. He found the thought oddly comforting.

He was also comforted by the sight of the reservoir. The snakes (if that's what they were – and at this latitude he thought it was possible there were creatures yet to be seen by the colonists) would probably try to avoid this place: men swearing, rocks dropping one on another as the reservoir slowly began to encircle the waterhole it was being built to tame, would surely have scared them off.

Monsarrat identified Trainor not only by what he had heard of his size but also by his constant yelling. Monsarrat walked up, introduced himself and held his hand out but Trainor ignored it, glancing down and muttering, 'I don't think your shoes will survive here.'

Monsarrat feared he was right. The leather which he took care to shine each night was covered in mud, and no doubt absorbing much moisture.

'I care little for the state of my shoes at the minute. I'm more interested in finding out what befell your friend.'

'My friend? Harefield? I wouldn't call him friend. I suspect few here would.'

'I was given to understand that you and he were on cordial terms, Trainor.'

It felt odd, still, to address someone else as a subordinate, to rob them of a given name or an honorific, and thereby part of their humanity. But if Monsarrat was to pass himself off as somebody used to power, it was essential.

'We never fought,' said Trainor. 'I helped him when I could, but we did not seek each other's company. Neither of us much felt the need for companionship, except for the female variety, which is not readily available to us here, although I suspect Harefield did his best to rectify that on his trips.'

'You must have envied him those trips. You are a convict yourself, yes?

'As it happens.'

'Your sentence?'

Trainor looked down again.

'Your sentence, man!' said Monsarrat, trying still to play the role of a man in authority.

'Fourteen years, attempted murder,' Trainor said sullenly.

'I see. And what was your trade?'

The overseer hesitated. 'Woodcutter. I was a woodcutter,' he said finally.

'Ah. Now that is interesting. I imagine the implement you used in your crime was an axe, then?'

'It was, as it happens. But I pulled myself up in time and the man lived. With a few broken bones and a limp.'

'So you have some skill in wielding such a weapon.'

'I did not kill Harefield, if that's what you think. No reason to, and plenty of reason not to. In any case, not much skill needed for an axe. Just the right amount of heft, and the right timing. A child could kill with an axe if they swung it at the right angle.'

'Indeed? And you were doing what at the time of the murder?'

'Back in the barracks. Anyone here will tell you that.'

Trainor turned, and the convicts who had been working at as slow a pace as possible to enable them to listen suddenly redoubled their efforts.

'Did Harefield get along with anyone else?'

'Only the Hatter, really.'

'The Hatter?'

'Milliner. His little joke. Harefield brought rum for the Hatter to sell the convicts, took a cut of the profit. There were more rum lately for me, but it all had to go through Mill— Oi! You want to go and quarry one to replace that?'

Trainor was striding towards the source of a loud crack. Two convicts were standing above a split slab of rock which had proved too heavy for them. With the gaze of their overseer diverted, Monsarrat noticed that some of the other men had slowed in their work again. One of them, in fact, had stopped entirely and was staring at Monsarrat with an avidity he found disturbing. He quickly averted his eyes, telling himself he did not want the fellow to come to the notice of the overseer. If he was honest, though, the man was making him uncomfortable. His fierce, unmoderated gaze transmitted an indiscriminate hunger which had nothing to do with conventional behaviour.

Such a person might be dangerous. But they might also be useful.

'I shall let you get back to your work,' said Monsarrat as Trainor stalked back to him. 'It seems your supervision is required. Might I ask, though – I would like to take one of your men back to Darlington with me. Some heavy lifting which needs doing.'

'And plenty in Darlington to do it. I can't spare you anyone.'

'I see,' said Monsarrat, casting around for a pretext and remembering the crates outside the commissary. 'Well, I suppose Mr Gendron will have his afternoon mapped out for him, then. An awful lot of baggage still needs to be moved into the commissary.'

'It's Mr Gendron what needs help?' asked Trainor.

'Yes. But, as you say, plenty in Darlington to give it. I'm sure if I told the commandant that none of your lads could be spared, he'd find someone.'

'If it's Mr Gendron . . . I believe he's owed some help. I can spare a man for him. But he needs to be back here after the dinner break, mind. Take your pick.'

Monsarrat turned to the man who had been staring at him. 'This fellow here looks good enough.'

'Shanahan!' yelled Trainor. 'Go with this gent here, and make sure you're back in time or you'll be the worse for it.'

The man nodded and walked towards Monsarrat, still staring. He looked to be around Monsarrat's age, with shoulders which seemed to run naturally to narrowness, but for the constant lifting he must have to suffer. Narrow-hipped, he moved with a surprising grace – the kind of movement one would suppose required thought.

'Come on then, Shanahan,' Monsarrat said. 'We best make haste if we are to have you back before the dinner bell.'

⁂

There was so little to do here. It was enough to drive a woman out of her wits. And Hannah had slept uneasily and had a confused dream, in which her son Padraig came to her and said he would marry Rebecca Nelson of Parramatta. It left a stain of unhappiness and anxiety over the morning light.

By mid-morning she had swept the grate out three times, and imposed her usual fierce scrubbing on the table, a rickety specimen which had seen little use from the visiting magistrate and was not accustomed to the attention. She had made bread and shaken the crumbs off the bread pan out of the back door.

There was now really nothing at all to do. This was a problem. She noticed her injury more when she was bored and, when her mind was too quiet, she sometimes fancied she could see smoke curling its way up from her ankle, nipping at her skirts.

But pretence – a skill which had saved her life in Ireland and many times since – was always a distraction. Perhaps if she offered help, she might have an excuse to stay long enough to learn something at the commissary.

The cottage door complained a bit, not used to being opened and closed with such frequency, and she had to take care to sit it in its frame as she was leaving. Probably a wasted effort, she thought – anyone with the propensity to steal from the hut would simply get some clothes and an empty teapot.

Those with theft on their records were hard at work now anyway, and five miles of erratic sea raged between them and escape, with the coastal mountains of Van Diemen's Land standing out blackly against the sky, offering little succour.

Leaving the cottage, Hannah noticed two things. The bread-crumbs were gone. And in their place stood a large grey bird with the long neck of a goose and a short green beak. The creature had its head side-on to her, taking her in with an accusing gaze, although what she could be accused of she couldn't guess.

'Hoi!' she said, clapping her hands. Such behaviour would be enough to see off any geese she had met in the past, from those of County Wexford to their cousins in Parramatta. The creature, however, did not move. It opened its green beak and let out a harsh, echoing sound, its own aggressive version of a honk.

'Hoi! Away with you! I won't have your droppings fouling this step. I've already washed it this morning.' She clapped her hands again, twice.

The goose did move now. It didn't scramble away with protesting honks, as she had expected it to; it turned and very slowly walked towards her until it was standing right at her feet. Then it bent and pecked her shoes.

She felt herself oddly disinclined to kick the thing – coming from a background where those more powerful kicked without thought, she felt it was incumbent on her to behave better towards this odd bird than others had behaved towards her. Instead she stamped her feet up and down and yelled again.

'If you don't stop that and leave, I will be serving you to Mr Monsarrat for dinner tonight!'

Her words had the desired effect, to a point. But instead of the satisfying flapping and fleeing she had expected, the goose simply straightened its neck, emitted an offended glare, turned and waddled off.

'The animals here need to be taught some manners, so they do,' she muttered to herself, making her way down the hill towards the commissary, where she assumed she would find Elizabeth Brewster.

She found her rather sooner than expected. There was no guard outside the gate leading into Thomas Power's area of confinement, but Elizabeth Brewster stood there, staring up at the walls, utterly still.

Hannah walked slowly, quietly, telling herself it was because she didn't wish to startle the woman. But Elizabeth was startled soon enough when the gate opened and a private emerged. He stopped when he saw Elizabeth. 'Mrs Brewster ... I'm sure your husband would be pleased to know that the prisoner is secure. I too was checking.'

'Naturally, Ennis,' she said. 'As I would expect. And I was . . .'

Hannah was scant feet away by now. She took the remaining steps which separated them. 'Waiting for me, she was,' she said to Ennis, then turned to Elizabeth. 'I am so sorry for keeping you, Mrs Brewster. I don't move, I fear, as quickly as I once did. And I was bailed up by a goose.'

Elizabeth and the soldier both laughed.

'The geese are more likely to bail someone up than any bushranger I've heard of,' said Ennis, in an accent which would not have been out of place in Hannah's childhood. He winked at her and she smiled. 'I'm keeping an eye on Mr Power,' he went on. 'He didn't have a guard until the recent death. Had the run of the island.'

Ennis looked very young. He had allowed some stubble to darken his chin. It could have been out of laxity, Hannah thought, but his uniform was clean, no old stains or missing buttons. More likely stubble was a new experience for him, one he associated with virility. He would be reluctant to shave off such evidence of manhood.

'Please don't trouble yourself, Mrs Mulrooney,' Elizabeth said. 'However, we should now make haste. To . . .'

'The commissary, Mrs Brewster,' Hannah said. 'You required some assistance there, as I recall.'

'Yes, the commissary. Good day, Ennis. I will ensure my husband is aware of your conscientiousness.'

They walked down towards the bridge over the small creek, startling a wallaby which had been examining the grass at its edges. 'I must thank you, Mrs Mulrooney. I was lost in thought.'

'No trouble at all. I get lost in thought at times myself. Sometimes a woman just needs to be turned and set on the right path.'

'Quite so,' said Elizabeth. 'May I ask, while we're on the subject, where you were bound?'

'Well, I was going where I said I was. I have scrubbed every corner of the visiting magistrate's house, and I'm sure the man will be glad of it when he is next here; however, I don't like to be idle and I thought that perhaps some assistance might be welcome.'

'As indeed it would. Walter will be there, of course. And a highly intelligent man he is too, in the channels in which his mind runs.'

Walter was not in fact in the store, but scouring the vista – they saw his broad back down on the dock. He appeared to be talking to Jones.

Elizabeth fished in her pocket for some keys. 'Mrs Mulrooney, I wonder, would you be kind enough to fetch him? I don't wish

71

to leave the store unattended, particularly with all these crates still outside to be unpacked – they shouldn't have been left here this long.'

Hannah picked her way through tufts of grass and the holes dug by the industrious grey-furred denizens of the island towards the dock, meeting Jones as he was walking up it.

'All well with Mr Gendron?' she asked.

Jones smiled. 'Ah, yes. I get things for him from time to time. Interesting bits of wood. Shells, that kind of thing. He likes them. Nice to be able to bring someone joy.'

Walter seemed not to hear Hannah approach. He was staring out across to the arm of earth and rock which protected the bay, absently fiddling with a striped shell.

'You have a new trifle, I see,' she said gently, more as a means of getting his attention than from any curiosity about the shell.

He didn't seem surprised to see her in the least. 'Do you know,' he said, still staring at the dark shapes playing under the surface of the water, 'something used to live in this?'

He held the shell up to the sun, squinted at it. 'They're like young pups, aren't they?' he said.

'The shellfish?'

'No! No, the seals,' he said, nodding at some splashes a little way out to sea. 'They were closer in this morning and I was hoping they might be this afternoon as well. They'll pop their little heads up and dart around. Sometimes I go for a swim and they will come and say hello to me, then duck down back under the water as though expecting me to chase them. Poor things, they don't know anything outside their own experience, don't know I have not the lungs for it. But I do enjoy them.'

'Well, they sound charming to me, Mr Gendron, and I'm sure I'd enjoy them as much as you, had I the chance to see them. That is if I didn't have an abiding fear of the ocean.'

'Ah, you must not fear the ocean. It can be a little cross, but as long as you learn to spot when it's getting temperamental and get out of the way in time, it's safe enough. I would be happy to bring you in to greet them.'

From anyone else, the impropriety of this suggestion would have made Hannah walk away instantly. But there was an innocence about Walter. He did not know that an offer to take a woman – even one old enough to be his mother – into the ocean for a swim was the height of bad manners. He simply wished to introduce her to his friends.

'That's kind of you, Mr Gendron. However, I must decline. I'm not much of a swimmer, have survived this long without being one and expect I'll survive however long the Lord has apportioned me in a similar state of ignorance as to the mechanics of moving through the water. But I'm afraid I need to draw your attention to less interesting matters – chiefly, the crates to be unpacked outside the commissary store.'

For a moment, Walter looked stricken. 'I was planning to get to them, I was. I just wanted to give the seals a chance to come closer. It seems, though, they have let me down, so I might as well get to it.'

'If I may, Mr Gendron, I would like to make you a proposal.'

Walter giggled, a sound she had rarely heard from a man, one more childish than girlish, and oddly disarming.

'It's been a long time since anyone made me a proposal,' he said.

Another woman might have blushed. But Hannah, accustomed to those who needed organising, recognised someone who simply needed a little nudge, not derision or reprimand.

'Mr Gendron, one must take care not to laugh at other people's comments.'

Walter's face immediately rearranged itself into an expression of concern. 'Of course,' he said. 'I meant no offence.'

'And none has been taken,' said Hannah. 'I would like to think that you may rely on me to speak honestly with you, and you may do likewise in the assurance that I will never take offence when none is intended.'

He frowned for a moment, and then nodded. 'That sounds like a reasonable bargain,' he said.

'Indeed it is. So my *suggestion* – you will note I have not used proposal, as it clearly gave you such amusement – is this. You will accompany me back to the commissary, where your sister is waiting. You will offer to do whatever she asks, and once we get a bit done you may then come back here and resume your vigil for the seals, and I'll finish what needs finishing. How does that sound?'

Walter nodded. 'Wonderful,' he said. 'Although I can't help thinking I'm getting the best end of the bargain.'

'I don't think so,' said Hannah. 'You are saving me from almost certain death, either from boredom, or from geese.'

Chapter 6

Monsarrat found that silence could often be quite an effective cudgel. He decided to employ it now, for a full five minutes as he trudged through the bush with the odd, staring man at his side. After a while, though, the silence began to disconcert even Monsarrat. Without turning or looking at the fellow, he asked, 'What's your name, again?'

'Shanahan.'

'Shanahan . . .?'

'Begging your pardon. Shanahan, sir.'

'Thank you. But I was actually in pursuit of a Christian name.'

'Niall. Niall Shanahan.'

'Niall Shanahan. And tell me, Niall Shanahan, what brings you here?'

'Several boats, sir,' said Shanahan, and chuckled, though Monsarrat did not see the joke.

Monsarrat stopped in his tracks. Shanahan took a few paces ahead before he realised he was now walking alone. He could have kept walking towards the settlement, following his orders and displaying a contempt for Monsarrat at the same time.

But Monsarrat was betting he wouldn't. It was a bet he hoped he didn't lose.

His gamble paid off. Shanahan turned and walked back to Monsarrat. 'A laugh, it's a rare thing here. I could not resist the opportunity. I beg your pardon.'

'My pardon is given,' said Monsarrat, hating himself for the high-handed language and beginning to think Shanahan an honest fellow. 'And if I may ask the question again, and get a serious answer this time, what brought you here?'

'A pig, sir. I stole a pig, from my father's landlord because we had nought to sell for oatmeal. We was hungry with what they call in Ireland "the summer famine".'

'I see. Yet there are many who are hungry who do not steal.'

Monsarrat shocked himself to hear the words coming from his mouth. They were the arguments of the likes of Socrates McAllister, the crooked and moralistic magistrate who ruled from the bench in Parramatta. I must, he thought, not allow myself to be fooled by the fiction Eveleigh has foisted on me.

'That's true, as it goes, sir,' said Shanahan. 'But I can only plead the evidence of my own belly, and those of my sisters and brothers. None of them would have continued much longer without feeding.'

'Very well, the evidence of your belly is accepted, for now,' said Monsarrat. 'Another question, then. Why on God's earth were you staring at me earlier?'

Shanahan stopped, thought for a moment. 'It's rare to see anyone new here, you see,' he said. 'Simple as that.'

'Hmm. So you must know everyone on the island, then.'

'I thought I did, sir,' said Shanahan. 'Didn't think there was anyone that handy with an axe though. I've probably passed him that killed Harefield, spoken to him. So have you. Makes us all a bit uneasy, in case the axeman has set himself against others still living. We're all watchful, I tell you.'

'Him?'

'Not many women here, sir. You may have noticed.'

'Hm. You must be talking about the murder, all of you.'

'Well, most are happy he's gone – a lot of people have run foul of him at one time or another. None of us had an opportunity to do anything about it, though.'

'I see. And let me ask you something else. What do you know of Thomas Power?'

Shanahan inhaled deeply. 'It's not true, what they say, sir.'

'And what do they say?'

'That he was using me. As a messenger. They were a little bit kinder to him than they are at present. And when he saw me, you see, he clapped his hands and insisted. Insisted I become a member of his retinue, as he calls it.'

'Why would Mr Power insist on you, particularly?'

'Because I worked for his father, you see. For a time, before I took up farming. As a groom, in the stables of Scarforth Castle in Kerry. He said it was wonderful to see a face from home, and he would be delighted if I could join him, help him with his reminiscences, that sort of thing.'

'And the commandant agreed to this?'

'Yes, and let it run for some months. I got Power hot water, tea, whatever he wanted. Provided conversation, when he asked for it, reminiscences of Scarforth Castle and the glory of his father. But the commandant wouldn't let it continue after ... well, after.'

'After what, Shanahan?'

'The commandant hasn't told you, sir?'

'Yes, he has, of course. I am simply after your own recollection, and do not wish to pollute it with anyone else's.'

'Well, after the business with Captain Brewster's brother-in-law. It was Harefield who put it about, you know. It wouldn't have been given any credence but for him. He'd give rum to those who could pay, and Power is the richest man on the island. Harefield said he saw the ... incident with his own eyes. I heard he withheld the rum for a while until his customers would say that they saw something too.'

'Can you imagine your patron then committing so savage a killing? Such primitive work with an axe?'

'I can't imagine that, sir. But the damage the bosun could do was of the kind to stir up a big anger. I'm not saying it is Power. But it's startling what a man can do in anger.'

'Why did you lose your position with Power?'

'The commandant said the business must've been going on for a long time, even as far back as Ireland. That I must've been aware of it, even participated in it. I most certainly did nothing of the kind. I like women, so I do, as few of them as I get to see. And so does Mr Power, I can swear. At least, if his pursuit of the maids at Scarforth Castle is anything to go by, he is the same as everyone else. But there are those who can't help it, you see. Perhaps they can't help seeing sin where there is none. So when it happened, well, Harefield decided to put things about. That there was, you know, something indecent going on. More indecent than the usual, that is.'

'And by something indecent, I presume you mean ...'

'Yes. That Power and Walter were having some kind of tryst.'

⁓

'But Mrs Mulrooney said I could go and look at the seals again,' said Walter.

'Now, Mr Gendron, you know I said no such thing. I said that perhaps if we got some good work done now you may go and see what creatures decided to visit you.'

Elizabeth Brewster, to Mrs Mulrooney's surprise, was smiling. 'Mrs Mulrooney is quite right, Walter,' she said. 'There is work to be done, here, you know. You must justify the money His Majesty gives you.'

'Of course I will! I would hate to disappoint His Majesty. But, well, the seals will be disappointed if I'm no longer there,'

Walter said. 'And Mrs Mulrooney...thank you, my kind friend, and you must let me know if I'm ever in a position to repay you.'

'I assure you, Mr Gendron, I shall. For now though, you can repay me by dragging in one of those crates so that we can get started on unpacking it.'

Walter nodded solemnly and almost sprinted to the door.

They worked in silence for a while. Walter opened the crate and stared at it; Hannah and Elizabeth extracted the parcels of meat and sacks of grain.

'It's stupid of them, you know,' said Elizabeth. 'Those in Hobart. If they just gave us the livestock we asked for, we would not need to rely on them for provisions as much.'

'What is it you need?' asked Hannah.

'Well, James asked for two working bullocks to help till the land, and a few sheep. Not much, you would have thought.'

Hannah, who had no idea whether a few bullocks and some sheep represented a reasonable request or not, had to stop herself laughing at the flash of an image – the bullocks sitting in the small boat, bunching their hooves together so that they could fit on the benches, weighing it down so that it was almost vertical.

'The request was denied?' she said.

'Yes. They pointed out that the penal settlement at Macquarie Harbour over on the west coast of Van Diemen's Land relies on manpower only. But the penal settlement at Macquarie Harbour is also a lot closer to shore. They cannot expect a self-sufficient settlement without giving us the means for that sufficiency, but that's what they appear to want.'

'You are not well disposed towards Marley and his like?' said Hannah.

'I didn't say that,' said Elizabeth a little sharply. Then she sighed. '*But*, for a man whose title is comptroller of convicts, he has little control and even less interest. Certainly no appreciation of the challenges of building and running a settlement such as this one.'

Hannah was surprised to hear Elizabeth speaking so plainly. But she reminded herself that perhaps conversation which involved another female voice was welcome.

'This is not your first posting, then?' she asked.

'Oh, Sydney for a while. But nothing like here. If a commissary had been . . . indisposed, another would have taken his place before a morning had passed. Here, though . . . Well, we make do.'

Hannah nodded. This woman would not have acknowledged her had they passed in the street in Parramatta, but class fell away in the face of the need to make do.

'It must have been worrisome to be without an experienced boatman even for that short time before Jones arrived, especially needing all these provisions. Do any of the convicts have any nautical skill?' she asked.

'Some of them. But we would never consider giving them charge of the boat – we would never see it again. As it is, they've proved reasonably adept at escaping. A few months ago, five of them built a bark canoe. They were found over at Orford a few days later. The poor fellow who stumbled on them stumbled away again with a lighter purse. They've taken to the bush now. Haven't been seen since. They may already have starved for all we know, but it doesn't change the fact that they are willing to make the crossing in the flimsiest of vessels. If we gave them a sturdy cutter like ours, they might sail all the way to Sydney.'

'Well,' said Hannah. 'Myself, I don't hold with the sea, even when it's calm. I can't imagine wanting to trust myself to a sheet of bark lashed onto some sticks.'

'Nor I. And really, it is not nearly as bad here as some other penal settlements. The stories that come out of Macquarie Harbour . . . Some of them here are rotten to the core, it's true.

But others, well, they're just misguided. I'd hate to see them taken in by the more hardened lags, caught in an escape attempt and then submitted to the kind of punishment they dish out over there.'

'Yes, your prisoners certainly do seem to be treated well. Mr Power, I'm given to understand, is particularly comfortable.'

'Not as comfortable as he was, nor does he deserve to be,' said Elizabeth. 'But – you are Irish, of course.'

'Of course.'

'He must be something of a hero to you, then.'

'Must he?'

'Well, he has fought for you.'

'Others have fought for me died for me,' Hannah said, more harshly than she intended. 'I have fought for myself.'

Elizabeth frowned for a moment, no doubt unused to being addressed so baldly by a domestic.

'Mmm,' she said after a while, 'we must all fight for ourselves, after our own fashion.'

'If you don't need me, further, Elizabeth, I'd just as soon go back to the seals,' Walter said. He had been watching them as they talked.

'Very well then, Walter,' Elizabeth said, in a tight, clipped voice.

'I might also look in on Thomas. I haven't seen him lately. I know you say he's well treated, but he must be missing his books.'

Elizabeth gave him a sharp look. 'On no account are you to visit Mr Power.'

'Elizabeth, I'm not sure you are entirely in a position to tell me what to do.'

Elizabeth exhaled, picking distractedly at a thin splinter from the crate which had lodged itself in the side of her hand.

'You know yourself it is James's command that Mr Power receive no visits from us.'

'Elizabeth. I'm not a stupid man. They say I'm simple. They say I'm worse than that, too. And it is all a lot more bearable when one has a friend.'

'You do your friend no service by keeping the attention of the settlement on him even more than it would be otherwise,' said Elizabeth.

Walter's brows drew together and then sprang apart, his eyes narrowing as he tried to determine his sister's meaning, and widening when he apprehended an insult.

'I should like to be your friend, Walter,' said Hannah quickly. 'When Mr Monsarrat and Mrs Brewster can spare me, I would very much enjoy it if you could show me some of the places where you walk, tell me about the seals and the dolphins, perhaps introduce me to a few wombats. Maybe even help me understand how to vanquish those dreadful geese. Would that be all right? With your sister's permission, of course.'

The muscles of Elizabeth's face seemed to relax a little. 'I am sure there would be no harm,' she said.

'Excellent,' said Walter. 'It will be lovely to be able to show something to someone. Elizabeth, may I . . . ?'

'Yes, yes, off you go.'

He grinned and walked quickly towards the door, as though afraid he might be called back.

'Thank you, Mrs Mulrooney,' said Elizabeth after he had gone. 'I fear that with too much time on his hands, our Walter goes wandering to places he shouldn't. It will be nice to know that a steady person such as yourself has charge of him.'

'I will get as much out of it as he does,' said Hannah.

'You will certainly get a great number of outlandish stories. I might say, it's important to remember that's what they are – stories. Walter is right, he is not a stupid man. He is, though, an imaginative one, and sometimes lacks the ability to tell the difference between the real and the fabricated. Please bear that in mind.'

They continued unpacking the crates, Elizabeth making inconsequential conversation about how dear the baby wombats were, and the impossibility of getting a tea set sent to the island without at least one item emerging cracked from the sawdust packing.

'We seem to be reaching the bottom of this crate,' she said after a time. 'I'll need to call Walter back to haul in another one.'

She was saved the trouble. A few minutes later, as Hannah was positioning a small container of tea on the shelf, the commissary door opened gently.

Say what you will about Mr Monsarrat, thought Hannah. He knows how to treat a door. Doesn't go slamming them against the wall like some I've known. At the thought her breath stopped briefly in her throat, as she remembered a now dead laughing man who'd had a habit of abusing doors.

Monsarrat was followed into the room by a wiry, sunburnt convict with a grimy face.

'Shanahan!' Elizabeth exclaimed. 'He was sent to the reservoir,' she said to Hannah. 'Explain your presence here, if you please.'

Shanahan looked alarmed, his eyes flicking from Monsarrat to Elizabeth.

'I do beg your pardon, Mrs Brewster,' said Monsarrat. 'I hope I have not unwittingly caused a problem. I went to the reservoir to speak to the overseer and noticed the crates outside the commissary. I asked him for the use of one of his men to move them inside for you. I do hope you don't find me presumptuous.'

'Well . . . As you say, the crates do need moving. I will forgive you, Mr Monsarrat, as your intentions were clearly the best. However, I would beg you not to take such an action again without my husband's express permission.'

Monsarrat bowed. 'Forgive me. But since he's here, shall we put him to work? Mr Trainor is expecting him back at the reservoir by the dinner bell.'

Elizabeth nodded to the convict, who moved outside and started shifting the crates.

'I must say, Mr Monsarrat,' said Elizabeth, 'you have quite a treasure here in Mrs Mulrooney. She has volunteered to assist me in the commissary, and it is assistance of which I very much stand in need, I can tell you.'

'I agree wholeheartedly with your assessment, Mrs Brewster.'

'It's rare, don't you think?' said Elizabeth. 'To find a convict, or a former convict, who seeks out work rather than avoiding it?'

Hannah, standing behind Elizabeth, felt her jaw clench. She knew she should be used to being spoken of as though she wasn't there, or as though she was insensitive to praise or criticism. She should be, but she wasn't, and she deplored a world where one needed to make such accommodations.

She saw Monsarrat glance at her, raise his eyebrows in warning to stay silent.

'I have always found Mrs Mulrooney to be the most conscientious of workers,' he said. 'And as it is only me in the magistrate's cottage, she will be available to provide you with as much assistance as you need.'

'The assistance and the company will both be welcome. As for you, Mr Monsarrat, how do your investigations go?'

'Slowly, at present, madam, I fear.'

'It was one of the convicts, no doubt,' said Elizabeth. 'Harefield had certain . . . well . . . unorthodox commercial relationships with some of them. James turned a blind eye, most of the time. But when a disagreement over money erupts between such people, blood is often shed. You must know that.'

'As soon as I find the evidence to support that certainty, madam, I can assure you I will bring it forward. However, I do need to interview Power again. And of course I take your point about operating without your husband's permission. I don't suppose you know where I can find Captain Brewster?'

'He shouldn't be far, Mr Monsarrat,' Elizabeth said, a little hazily, as if she actually had trouble imagining her husband at work. 'Perhaps in his office – a little further down near the boat shed. I believe the correspondence from Marley and the lieutenant-governor is considerable. He could be up at the hospital site – he calls in on Chester each day. Given we have been denied livestock, we need to make sure that those on whose strong backs we rely are kept healthy for the purpose. And if we are responsible for their moral welfare, surely their physical welfare is ours too. Do you not agree?'

⁓

Monsarrat found James Brewster pacing the perimeter of the hospital site.

'The hospital is one of my priorities,' Brewster said, beside the fringe of convict-made bricks. 'I always intended that if I was given charge of a penal settlement, it would be one of the first buildings constructed. I do not want to bring up children anywhere without the means to see to their health. And of course those who come after me will know who built it.'

'I wasn't aware that you had children,' said Monsarrat.

Brewster frowned. 'We don't, not yet. I had thought, by now . . .' He paused for a moment, straightened. 'Elizabeth has enough to deal with as it is. Walter, you know.'

Hastily and somewhat awkwardly Monsarrat changed course and told Brewster about bringing Shanahan from the reservoir.

'I would have preferred to be consulted, of course,' said the commandant. 'Not that there is a problem with using convict muscle to bring those crates in, but I would have chosen any convict except that one.'

'Oh? Is he deficient in some way?'

'Morally, yes. Was in thrall to Power; supposed to keep an eye on him, but failed to mention that he had once been the man's father's servant. He paid for that little omission with a month on bread and water. And a flogging, of course. He was lucky we need the labour – I restricted the lashing.'

'Ah. Well of course there's a maximum allowable.'

'The new governor will change that rot. Macquarie was too soft. He didn't have to deal with them on a daily basis. Those of us who do are paying the price for his leniency.'

'Indeed. You needn't worry, though – Mr Trainor insisted Shanahan return quickly to the reservoir, and I am under the impression that he metes out a fierce punishment when his orders are disobeyed.'

'That he does. One of the more brutal overseers I've come across, but effective, as the brutal often are. He is judicious in the way he disciplines his men. Those who know that the punishment will be severe are more likely to stay loyal, and loyalty is important in a place like this, held together by the ocean and the mountains.'

'As you say. That ocean and the mountains – I presume they're as effective at constraining Thomas Power as anyone else. So I hope you see no risk in my visiting him again. I have a few more questions.'

'All right. I suppose you may go this evening. He enjoys singing of an evening, and I'm getting sick of the sound of Irish rebel songs like "Boolavogue" floating over that wall. He can't sing if he is talking to you. And if your investigation comes to a satisfactory conclusion, he will not be singing at all.'

Chapter 7

Walter was standing on the beach as Monsarrat passed. Perhaps he was looking across the waters for the ripple of a seal's fin. And indeed a few whaling boats were now to be seen between here and the distant bay. In Monsarrat's experience of whalers, they did not make the effort to throw down anchor without a reasonable hope of return.

Mrs Mulrooney had come back to the cottage and was pacing up and down by the back steps. There was still an unsteadiness to her walk, but she appeared to be applying her preferred strategy of ignoring the pain and refusing to acknowledge any injury. She was glaring at a small group of large grey birds which had gathered nearby, and were glaring back.

'I found one of them in the kitchen, Mr Monsarrat. I mustn't've closed the door properly, and the creature was pecking away at some crumbs under the table. That I missed them is something for which I have reprimanded myself, you may be assured, so there's no need for you to do it.'

'I would not think to reprimand you, my friend,' said Monsarrat. 'I rather think it generally goes the other way, does it not? In any case, I'm aware you're not feeling your best.'

'It is the sea, Mr Monsarrat, and then this strange family we must deal with. And the idea I hear from some that Mr Power has done this savage thing.'

She narrowed her eyes, huffed, and closed the door with such vehemence that he almost expected her to drag a chair over to it to prevent it being battered down by the bills of the geese. She took her broom and tried to drop to her knees – prevented by her ankle from doing so with any fluidity – seeking to chase out any further crumbs which might precipitate another invasion.

'Please,' said Monsarrat, 'leave that.'

She rose, glared at him again. 'Of course, as you command, Mr Monsarrat,' she said, forcing out the words in a resentful spit.

'Now, why this? Why the petulance?' said Monsarrat.

'You call it petulance? You and herself, standing there discussing me like I was a chattel. I deserve better, Mr Monsarrat, truly I do.'

Her jaw was set and her lips tightly pressed together in a manner he rarely saw. He knew that in her it was a sign of strong emotion being contained. He was particularly concerned that she was making no attempt to swat him with her cleaning cloth. His infraction clearly transcended such a trivial punishment.

'If I have offended you, I apologise,' he said, sitting down and gesturing her to the other chair at the table. 'You know, though, that we need to maintain the fiction.'

'The fiction?'

'The pretence that I am your superior, while we both know that in actuality I am anything but.'

She sat back in her chair, hopefully somewhat mollified.

'As to the matter of geese for dinner,' he said, 'they do look plump, and I would be delighted to consume anything which has upset you so; however, I fear the geese will have to remain unmolested for now. I am this evening going over to see Thomas Power.'

'And I am to sit here and hold off the geese?' she said.

'If that's what you really want to do,' said Monsarrat, ducking when he saw her reaching for the cleaning cloth at her waist.

'Of course it's not what I want to do, eejit of a man. I have spent the day unpacking provisions with a woman who views me as a useful implement with the added advantage of conversation. I'll tell you, though, I did notice something interesting.'

'I suspected as much.'

'Herself – Mrs Brewster. Seems quite annoyed at Power.'

'I presume she is, along with her husband.'

'Why, then, was she standing outside his enclosure, staring at the wall?'

'Was she? Possibly to make sure he stays in there? Although one presumes that he has a guard for that.'

'The guard wasn't in evidence,' said Hannah. 'Not at first, anyway. He walked out a short time later, grinning until he saw her. She gave him the fright of his life, I think. And he her. She did not look like the wife of a commandant who had caught one of her husband's subordinates being lax in his duties. She looked like somebody who had been caught out herself.'

'And did you ask about it?'

'Of course I didn't! Not directly. You've heard them go on about Power. They're not going to be answering any direct questions from the likes of me.'

'Possibly not,' agreed Monsarrat.

'One thing I have ascertained is some sort of oddness between Power and Walter,' Hannah went on. 'The lad seems to idolise Power, but Captain Brewster speaks of him as though he were the devil incarnate.'

'Ah, well there, I find myself in the unusual position of being able to tell *you* something. If convict gossip is to be believed, I've deduced that some people think something's going on between Walter and Power.

'Their friendship, you mean?'

'A . . . a *special* friendship, if you take my meaning . . .' He could not meet her eyes as he spoke, choosing to find himself suddenly fascinated with a patch of wall.

'No need to blush, Mr Monsarrat,' Mrs Mulrooney said. 'I've lived among convicts and soldiers for more than twenty years now. I'm well aware of how some men tend to enjoy each other's company. Do you *believe* it?'

'I'm not entirely sure. I have also been assured that Power enjoys the company of ladies . . .'

'There are some who enjoy the company of both, Mr Monsarrat. Don't look so shocked, eejit of a man. You know that.'

'Yes, well . . . Moving on. I was rather hoping you'd come with me tonight.'

'To meet the man himself?'

'Yes. Mr Power may reveal something he doesn't intend to, in a manner which doesn't involve words. And as far as that type of listening goes, no one can equal you.'

~∾~

Private Ennis was again absent from his post.

'If Captain Brewster finds out, I expect the lad will be in a deal of trouble,' said Mrs Mulrooney.

'Probably already is,' said Monsarrat. 'I suppose we should knock.'

Mrs Mulrooney looked at him with something between exasperation and pity. 'What would be the point of appointing a guard if Power is able to open his own gate to visitors?'

'True,' Monsarrat said. 'I don't want to cause the man any trouble but I suppose I'd better go and find Brewster.'

'He seems a good lad, though . . . very well then, we'll knock, for all the good it will do.'

And she marched over to the slab of wood, pounding her little fist against it. To Monsarrat's amazement, there was a rustling inside, and the gate was yanked open. The guard stepped out and closed it firmly behind him. He glanced at Monsarrat, and then smiled at Mrs Mulrooney.

'Hello, missus. Geese leaving you alone?'

'For now, yes, young Ennis. If they come back, though, I may have to borrow your bayonet.'

'You're the only one I would trust with it,' he smiled. 'Looking for Mrs Brewster?'

Monsarrat found himself oddly irritated. The young man was ignoring him entirely. He must be getting used to the deference which came with a supposedly unblemished past.

'Why would she be looking for Mrs Brewster here?' he asked.

Private Ennis glanced at Monsarrat, and then at the ground. 'No reason. Mr Power receives few visitors.'

'Yet you seem to have been visiting.'

'Not visiting, bringing the prisoner his meal.'

'Well, now that you've completed that task, you may perform another service and open the gate for us.'

Ennis, keeping his eyes on Monsarrat, reached backwards and pushed the gate open.

'Unlocked, private?' asked Monsarrat. 'Somewhat careless, isn't it?'

'Where is he going to go, sir?' said Private Ennis, spitting on the ground. 'You need wings to leave here.'

The yard where Power had paced up and down the other day was empty now, although the ruts the man had worn in the ground were easy to see.

A moment later Power came racing out, waving a piece of paper. 'Ennis!' he cried, looking at the private. 'You forgot your letter. After all the work we put into it, you don't want to just leave it lying around here, surely.'

Private Ennis blushed, turned away. 'Not my letter,' he said. 'You must be mistaken.'

91

'Oh. Yes . . . Very well then, I suppose I am. In any case, thank you for the wonderful meal.'

'I didn't cook it,' said Ennis, and slammed the gate behind him. Monsarrat could hear the pointed rattle of the key in the lock.

Power languidly smoothed the letter, held it up to the light, then slowly folded it and placed it in the breast pocket of his jacket. It was a garment Monsarrat could never have afforded, a light, fine blue wool with buttons which he suspected were real gold. Once Power had stowed the letter to his satisfaction, he turned to his guests.

'Mr Monsarrat, what a delight. I was told you might be visiting again. And you have brought a friend. It is too long, I must say, since a female walked through that gate.'

'This female will walk back through it if that kind of talk continues,' said Mrs Mulrooney.

Power raised his eyebrows. 'And a compatriot, my ears tell me.'

'No compatriot of mine speaks in your accent,' Mrs Mulrooney said. 'Being born on the same soil does not make you my brother.'

Monsarrat stared at her, both in shock and in an attempt to convey a warning. Power, though, was nodding enthusiastically. 'Quite right you are, quite right. I'd bet there are many who speak like me who've made it their business to try to deprive you of your liberty. The fact that you are here tells me they succeeded.'

Mrs Mulrooney's glare intensified.

'I shall make you a bargain,' said Power.

'Are you in a position to?' Mrs Mulrooney said. 'After all, one of us is free, one of us is not.'

Power smiled. It seemed genuine enough to Monsarrat – not the smile of a snake about to strike, not the smile he had seen on the faces of corrupt magistrates and clerical zealots and cruel soldiers.

'I'm not sure whether I am in a position to or not, but I intend to anyway,' Power said. 'And the bargain is this – you agree to hear my story and to at least entertain the notion of hating me slightly less.'

'And in return?'

'If you are still intent on despising me afterwards, I will accept it wholeheartedly.'

Mrs Mulrooney was silent for a moment, then nodded.

'I understand – I do – why my voice might make you ill-disposed towards me. Blame it on the English Jesuits who educated me. I can promise you, though, that I am as aware as any Irish-born man that my people have not been emancipated. Most of them are forbidden an education by law and prevented, by law as well, from holding public office – from being a lawyer, from serving above the rank of sergeant in the army which oppresses them. And naturally they are prohibited from being elected to Parliament. They live and die in the cracks and crannies of the Irish nation, and I am willing, under all the flippancy and vanity, to die to give them a better future.'

Mrs Mulrooney glared at him and then looked away. 'You pay with words,' she said. 'Others have paid in blood.'

Power smiled. 'I would never deny such a proposition, madam. I beg for the chance to tell you of my adventures in the cause of Irish freedom.'

Monsarrat had read some of Power's speeches over the years, widely reported as they had been, even in the English press. And he had met such men before. If Power was permitted to dominate the conversation, they would have a long, entertaining and utterly fruitless evening.

'I must say, Mr Power, this is a tale I look forward to hearing myself. And I do feel that we should allow it sufficient time for it to unfold. Sadly, I do not happen to possess time in that quantity at the minute. As well, I'm here on the indulgence of the commandant, who expects me to talk to you about . . . other matters.'

Power inclined his head, smiled again. 'Of course, Mr Monsarrat. The commandant's indulgence is not a thing one wishes to take for granted. Now, there is still the matter of me having only one chair. I used to have more, you know. That was when people were allowed to come and sit with me. Mrs Mulrooney, if I were to bring the chair outside, would you consent to sit in it?'

Mrs Mulrooney still looked stern, with all of the diffidence of somebody being asked for a favour they would rather not give. She looked into Power's sitting room, and frowned. 'Are you sure you can spare it, Mr Power? You may soon be without a desk, as it will surely collapse underneath all those papers.'

Power clapped his hands as though Mrs Mulrooney had just paid him an extravagant compliment. He darted inside, came back with the chair, which he set on the cottage's small stone veranda, near the three steps which led up to it.

'You can be our queen, and we shall be the acolytes at your feet,' said Power, smiling as he put the chair in place and gently eased himself down onto one of the steps. Mrs Mulrooney glanced in Monsarrat's direction, rolled her eyes, seemingly not caring whether Power saw her.

'Before we get started,' said Power, 'May I ask, what prompted you to bring this marvellous woman here, Mr Monsarrat?'

'Mrs Mulrooney is my housekeeper. And a woman of significant wisdom, whose opinions I value.'

'Not that it's any of your concern,' said Mrs Mulrooney. 'I might be the Queen of England and you would not have the right to ask.'

'Ah, your housekeeper,' Power said. 'Yes, I have heard of arrangements such as this one.'

Mrs Mulrooney looked down at him from her seat. 'I'm *sure* you mean arrangements where someone makes tea, sweeps out the grate.'

Power cleared his throat. 'Of course. Forgive me. Do you know, since my movement was restricted – no more long rambles over the hills – it has played havoc with my imagination and on occasion I see things which aren't there. It's the stress of no longer being able to pretend that I am free, even if I could do so only by walking far enough not to be able to see Darlington.'

'It is forgotten,' said Monsarrat, although the expression on Mrs Mulrooney's face indicated that it never would be.

'Kind of you. Now, I'm presuming that you would like to discuss the murder of our unfortunate bosun.'

'Yes. However, the most pressing issue at present is your relationship with Walter.'

Power looked startled but recovered himself quickly. 'Walter Gendron?' he said.

'And is this island so lousy with Walters that you need to clarify his surname?' Mrs Mulrooney said.

Monsarrat decided not to look at her, for fear of another eye roll, but if she was going to make her dislike so apparent, he may need to find an urgent errand for her.

'Yes,' said Monsarrat. 'I am sure you, of all people, know what a crucible for gossip a small penal settlement is.'

'You have prior experience yourself, I take it?'

'It is impossible to spend any time in this colony, Mr Power, without finding oneself in close quarters with all manner of people,' Monsarrat replied, reminding himself to be careful on this subject.

'As you say, the most outrageous stories circulate, and seem to get a coating of plausibility with each retelling, so that by the time they reach the twentieth ear, or the thirtieth, they are dipped in the gold of truth.'

'So I presume you're aware of these particular stories,' said Monsarrat.

'That Walter and I had some sort of *tryst*? Yes, I'm aware of them. It is because of them that I am no longer welcome at the

Brewsters' table. So those particular rumours have cost me the last friendship I had in this place.'

'I see. The Brewsters gave them credence, then?'

'Oh yes. Particularly after Harefield came running up to James Brewster one day. Flapping his short arms and saying he had seen Walter and me embracing.'

'Why would Captain Brewster be inclined to believe Harefield?'

'I'm not sure he did, at first. But then he came to ask me about it. And I don't like to lie – please don't snort, dear lady, it makes me concerned for your health – so I told him what had really happened. I told him it was true.'

Chapter 8

Monsarrat had been telling Mrs Mulrooney the truth when he said he knew this sort of thing happened. He had heard of it in places like Port Macquarie. In a place where a tiny number of the settlement's 1500 inhabitants had been women, it was quietly accepted, went unremarked on. And Monsarrat could understand it. A friend, an ally, was someone who could take on the aspect of a lover, even for men who might normally have desired women; longing made more intense under the pressures of loneliness, boredom, isolation and the overwhelming absence of females.

Blind eyes were frequently turned in penal settlements, and Monsarrat had once heard a soldier remark to another that as long as it kept them quiet, pliable, no one was inclined to interfere.

But a prisoner of Power's stature was a different matter. Not a faceless road-gang lag or a lime burner with his skin beginning to slough off his face. Not a poacher or a pickpocket. This was a revolutionary, one whose death at the end of a rope might incite further uprisings. One who had refused his freedom as it would bind him to a promise not to leave the colony.

Monsarrat was probably the most knowledgeable person on the island when it came to the colony's laws. And one of those laws imposed a penalty of death for sodomy. Such a charge would also strip Power of a large part of his lustre. Should it be brought, Monsarrat believed the authorities would be delighted.

'You ... you aren't telling me, surely, that you and Walter have had some sort of ... *relationship*?'

Power held Monsarrat's gaze for what seemed like minutes. Then he threw his head back and burst out laughing.

'Good God, man, you'd think I had just confessed to murdering the King!'

'Both actions would result in your death, Mr Power.'

Power's laughter subsided. 'This is true enough. However, I must caution you, Mr Monsarrat, to listen to what I am saying. I did not confess to the crime of sodomy. I confessed to receiving an embrace from Walter Gendron. One does not necessarily indicate the other.'

'You are right, I do need to be more cautious in my listening. A dear friend of mine frequently tells me that.'

Monsarrat knew with absolute certainty that had they been alone Mrs Mulrooney would have applied the corner of a cleaning cloth to his temple, with significant force.

'Oh, I always listen, Mr Monsarrat. It is quite remarkable what one can discern from the things which remain unsaid,' Power said.

Monsarrat heard Mrs Mulrooney give a grudging 'hmmf' from the height of her chair.

'All very true, but I'm more interested in what exactly did happen.'

'Well, Walter ... He is quite a singular fellow.'

'Yes. I should say so.'

'People call him simple. He is a long way from it, though. He is highly intelligent, a skilled observer and has an imagination unequalled on this island, perhaps in the colony. He simply lacks the ability to navigate the world. A place like this – actually it's not bad for him, not bad at all. He is insulated from the dangers of a larger settlement and he has the love and protection of his sister. And until recently he had my friendship.'

'Why did you withdraw that friendship?' said Monsarrat.

'I didn't. It was cut in half by these walls, and by the will of the Brewsters. When I had the freedom of the island, Walter would come with me from time to time on walks. We would hunt for fossils up near the cliffs, or we would try to spot the vapour ejected from the head of a whale. Walter would fabricate these marvellous stories about what the seals he saw in the bay were thinking, or where the dolphins were bound as they dipped in and out of the waves. It was the most . . . restful acquaintance. My life, you see, has until this point been anything but restful.'

'And when they restricted your movement, did you maintain the acquaintance?'

'I flatter myself he enjoyed my company as much as I enjoyed his. We would sit where you are sitting now, Mr Monsarrat, and talk of whatever took the lad's fancy. He would ask why magpies knew to grow white feathers on one part of their body and black ones on another. He would ask by what agency the leaves knew to fall from the trees at the same time. He would wonder aloud whether the wombats had any means of non-verbal communication by which they warned of danger or alerted others to the presence of food. Apart from my walks, it was by far the most liberating experience I could have had here. And I must tell you, I miss his company dreadfully.'

Monsarrat was reasonably certain Power could make just about anything sound believable, but this last statement, his wistfulness for Walter's company, seemed genuine.

'And the incident which led to the rumours that are currently circulating the island with all the ease of one of those odd geese?' asked Mrs Mulrooney. She seemed to have slightly warmed towards Power. Possibly it was a result of his kind words about Walter.

99

'Well, he was here with me one morning. I think from memory we were talking about the concept of free will, how to make it reconcile with the whole idea of transportation. Anyway, our late friend Harefield rapped on the gate, was let in. A package had arrived for me from my sister in Ireland. She knows that I go mad without books, and she had been kind enough to send a copy of the novel *Walladmor* by the German Alexis, which I understand is all the rage in London at the moment, along with the argument that he stole it from Walter Scott. Well, dear Walter, he does like that sort of thing, so I gave him the book. Told him to take his time reading it, to return it to me when he was replete. And he was so delighted he jumped up and down a few times on the spot like a little boy and then embraced me. Nearly squeezed the breath out of me, if I'm honest. Harefield was still there. He stood looking at me for a moment, then turned and left.'

'So you say Harefield reported this to Brewster?'

'I knew he would,' said Power. 'And I knew he would put as much of a slant on it as he could. That one, he saw information as power. Quite right he was, too. He liked to hold himself forth as the source of truth on the island. He would say, "I am the one who leaves and returns; I am the one who knows what is happening beyond this island." Naturally, as the most skilled sailor here, he was essential to everyone's survival. So people would go to great lengths to avoid upsetting him. And then there was the matter of the liberal quantities of rum that he brought here. Well, the geese certainly didn't bring it.'

'No,' said Mrs Mulrooney. 'All they bring are droppings and fright.'

Power laughed. 'Bellicose creatures, aren't they? Who can blame them? We did, after all, invade their home. You and I, dear lady, we know how that feels, don't we?'

Mrs Mulrooney pressed her lips together and turned to examine a particular cloud scudding across the sky.

'Was Brewster angry?' asked Monsarrat.

'Livid. He cut off all contact. Is no doubt hoping against hope that you are even now finding evidence against me.' Power patted Monsarrat on the shoulder. 'But you and I, of course, know there is none to find.'

The gesture, and the assumption which went with it, irritated Monsarrat. You, he thought, with your books from your sister and your complaints of the harshness of your incarceration. You who have never had to break a rock, or swing a pick, or scrabble for grain. Who rejected freedom when it was offered, to feed your own legend. You do not tell me what I know and what I don't.

'I know no such thing, Mr Power,' he said. 'I will be calling on you again.'

Power didn't react to the slight, or pretended not to. He slowly unfolded himself from his perch on the veranda. 'Rather uncomfortable, don't you think, for those of us with long legs to be sitting so long? Not that I begrudge the chair, of course.'

He offered his hand to Mrs Mulrooney, who ignored the gesture and rose as though he wasn't there. He aimed a conspiratorial wink at Monsarrat, walked towards the gate, casually rapped on it with the back of his hand.

As Private Ennis opened it, Power leaned towards Mrs Mulrooney and whispered something to her. Her frown remained in place but she nodded and walked through the gate, her chin high and her shoulders square as though her skirt was that of a ball gown with a long train.

'Do make sure you come again soon, Mr Monsarrat,' Power called. 'I have enjoyed our conversation.' He turned to the private. 'Now, Ennis, you do realise that we are only halfway through *Tristan and Isolde*. Shall we get started?'

'What did he whisper to you?' asked Monsarrat as soon as they were out of earshot of the cottage. With only the light from the moon, full as it was, it was difficult to tell whether Mrs Mulrooney's face was still set. Her words, though, when she forced them out, were truncated, strangled by an anger Monsarrat did not fully understand.

'He asked me to visit him,' she said.

'Visit him? You?'

'Don't sound so surprised, eejit of a man. I doubt there was any intention of impropriety in the invitation. He said he wanted to talk about Ireland. And he said he wanted to talk about Elizabeth.'

'Elizabeth? Mrs Brewster? What on earth could he have to say to you about her?'

'And how would I know that? I'd hazard it's about her behaviour at the wall of his enclosure today. Whatever she was feeling, hatred, or not, I can't tell you, but she certainly seemed to be feeling something.'

'Would you like me to accompany you?'

'Perhaps. Perhaps not. If a chaperone is needed, I am sure young Ennis would serve. I will visit him tomorrow. With the commandant's permission, of course – we have to be forthright with him, Mr Monsarrat. If he decides we are sneaking around behind his back, that will be an end to it. Will you arrange it with him?'

'Yes, yes. I must say, I'm fascinated to hear what you find out.'

'Don't get too exercised about it, Mr Monsarrat. Whatever I find out will be half the truth, or even less.'

'How can you be certain of that? You may indeed discover something significant.'

'I may, and if I do it will be no thanks to Mr Power. I do not trust him, nor anything which comes out of his mouth.'

'I could see you'd taken rather a set against him. How did the man earn your enmity in such a short period of time? I thought he'd be a hero of yours.'

She glanced at him, and the anger in her eyes almost made him stumble.

'Do you see a scar on the man?' she said. 'A missing finger? A ruined scalp where the hair will never grow again? It is very easy for him to talk of revolution and his glorious part in it. He does not have to lie down and die in the mud, or bury what he loves, or leave it rotting on a hillside. And I might tell you, Mr Monsarrat, that I have met his kind before. Many times. My childhood was full of them – men who enjoyed rolling words around in their mouth, not caring whether they reflected the truth or not, believing the way they sounded was more important than the message they conveyed. I can't tell you whether Power was responsible for splitting the head of the bosun. But I can tell you that of the words he lets tumble out of his mouth, not many of them will reflect the truth. Deciding which do will be the challenge.'

James Brewster's office was a small, squat, brick building near the commissary. Sparse, even by military standards, a folding camp table covered in papers, a smaller sideboard, similarly swamped, and a tallow candle by the window for use when duties kept him in his office after nightfall.

There was blotting paper and a blotter and an assortment of pens on which the ink had been allowed to dry, which Monsarrat found offensive. How difficult is it, he thought, to wipe the things after you use them? It was certain that after this morning's activities, more ink blotches would need to be cleaned up. Brewster did not have a clerk but was still encumbered with the administrative necessity of putting the settlement's progress down on paper and sending it off to Lieutenant Governor Arthur in Hobart, who may or may not actually read it.

He was busy working on a dispatch when Monsarrat arrived, his pen jumping from ink pot to page and back again, spraying fine black droplets as it went, as he committed to paper his thoughts on the building of the hospital, or the progress of the flax crop.

Monsarrat was consumed by a sudden desire to step in, sit down, tidy the papers, clean the pens and await dictation. He smiled to himself for a moment. What have you become, he thought, that your most passionate urges relate to the ordering of disorder, to the taking of dictation?

The idea of passion, though, plunged him into thoughts of the downy cropped hair of Grace O'Leary; wondering how fast it was growing back; the amber flecks in her eyes; his fear that the convict system might yet assign her to a faraway master. He wanted, for a moment, to bolt down to the dock and ask Jones to sail to Sydney and up the reaches of the Parramatta River, to reassure himself she was still there. It was astounding to him that in these lunatic imaginings he felt most free, and happy.

The sound of the scratching of pen on paper stopped and Brewster was looking at him, one eyebrow raised in a silent question.

'Captain, I am sorry to disturb you. I was wondering if I might have a moment?'

Brewster smiled, gestured to a chair which sat on the other side of his camp table. 'Have you progress to report on the investigation?' he asked. 'As I am writing to Hobart anyway, I would like to include any developments.'

'Sadly no, sir. Unfortunately, in my experience these things are seldom easy to resolve.'

'I understand that. I had hoped, though, that you would have found some intimation of Power's involvement.'

'Nothing firm, no. Though it is on that matter that I wish to speak to you.'

Brewster nodded, folded his hands on the desk in front of him and leaned back, ready to receive whatever supplication might come.

'It seems Mr Power is rather taken with my housekeeper,' Monsarrat said.

Brewster's eyebrows shot up.

'I mean nothing indecent by that, of course,' said Monsarrat.

'Of course not. Power's interests run in a different river,' Brewster said.

Monsarrat saw no benefit in getting into a debate with Brewster on the matter.

'What I mean to say, sir, is that he seems to have taken a liking to her because she is Irish.'

'Yes, he does like reminders of home. Shanahan, of course . . .'

'Quite. In any case, he has expressed an interest in continuing conversation with Mrs Mulrooney. I think it wise to allow that to occur. He may be more at ease while conversing with her. May let something slip, if there is anything to discover.'

'Very well, she may visit him – either you or Private Ennis must attend, though. We shan't have any more secret trysts.'

'No, indeed, such a thing would be most inappropriate. And there is one other request. The axe. Lieutenant Holloway seems reluctant to show it to me, but it's essential I examine it. To conduct a murder investigation without seeing the murder weapon would be quite irregular.'

'I suppose so. Although what an axe can tell you . . .'

'Perhaps nothing, but the enquiry should be made.'

Brewster gave a noncommittal grunt.

'And at the same time, I should like to visit the light where the crime occurred,' said Monsarrat.

Brewster exhaled sharply. 'Very well. I don't think it's the best use of your time, but I suppose it must be done. I'll give you a note to take to Holloway in the guardhouse. He'll make sure you have what you need.'

Chapter 9

Holloway seemed less than delighted by his commandant's instruction to provide all assistance to the interloper.

'As I've told you, I have already examined the weapon,
Mr Monsarrat. There is nothing to find.'

'Yes, your commandant agrees with you, and I'm sure you're
both right. Nevertheless, I was not sent over these great leagues
of ocean to fail to examine an implement which is within
arm's reach.'

Holloway grunted. 'What makes you think it's in arm's
reach?'

'I was speaking metaphorically, Lieutenant Holloway.'

'As it happens, you're not far from the truth,' Holloway said.

The guardhouse was a small, windowless building, brick, like
all the rest, though in this case the convicts had been forced
to construct a prison for the worst of their kind. The floor was
dirt, already compacted and trampled flat by a great many feet,
leaving Monsarrat with the impression that in its short existence the guardhouse had already been called on to fulfil its
function. No one was in residence at present so the benches
jutted out from the walls, empty for now, although Monsarrat

had the uncomfortable impression that Holloway would like to see him occupying one of them.

The whole structure was no larger than Mr Eveleigh's office at Government House in Parramatta.

Why do we do this? Monsarrat thought. Why do we lay claim to all this vastness, and use it for buildings of such strangulated proportions, quickly filled with the wails of those contained in them.

Holloway went to a small table. On the earth beneath it was a bundle wrapped in grimy canvas. He reached for it, put it on the table and unwrapped it as though he was in the process of displaying a precious golden candlestick or a jewelled sceptre.

I must not antagonise this man, Monsarrat thought, not for the first time since arriving. The rash, headlong aspect of his nature was growing weary of the continued pretence, the ongoing need to guard against speaking, thinking or acting like a former convict. It wished, like a child, to grab a hold of the entire situation, throw it in the air and see where the pieces fell.

'I must say, I question the wisdom of keeping a weapon such as this in close proximity to a cell where the most refractory among you are sometimes detained,' he said, wishing with every word that he could swallow it back.

He was unsurprised by the reaction from Holloway, whose face reddened. 'I would have thought it was obvious to use the most secure building in the settlement.'

Monsarrat nodded slightly, barely restraining himself from pointing out that the situation was subject to change by the very nature of the purpose of the settlement.

He went over to the unwrapped bundle, looked at the implement lying on the bed of canvas. He drew out the blue leather case which now accompanied him everywhere and extracted the ornate magnifying glass – Eveleigh's parting gift, although at the time Monsarrat had not realised that it came with an identity which was false and difficult to maintain: the uncomfortable pretence that he had always been free.

The axe was hardly tiny and really he didn't need the magnifying glass. But he was making a point to Holloway. I am vigilant. I miss nothing. He did not, however, need magnification to see that the axe was considerably shorter than average, with a narrower head. When he picked it up, he noticed that the head wobbled slightly in its notch. He put it down again, flourished the magnifying glass in a way which even he found a little overdone, and held it a few inches above the blade. The blade, as it turned out, was quite an odd thing.

Each of the axes Monsarrat had seen on the island had been unpocked by rust. They were used too frequently for that, and considered so essential by their owners that they were frequently wiped, even waxed or coated with fat to prevent any corrosion. This blade had not been the beneficiary of similar treatment. It was decorated with small blooms of rust, some of which had been there long enough to begin to pit the metal.

But its sharp edge was different. It had a sheen to it that not even the best cared for axes usually possessed. Through his magnifying glass, Monsarrat could see the lines on the metal made by the movement of a whetstone.

The edge of this blade had been sharpened. Very recently.

Monsarrat ran his finger down it, and was unsurprised to see a small line of red emerging. 'Lieutenant Holloway – your opinion on a certain matter, if you please.'

The man straightened his spine, held back his shoulders. He clearly did not like or trust Monsarrat, but seemed happy to be solicited as an expert.

'Is there any reason that you can think of as to why someone would allow every part of an axe to fall into such a state of corruption but the cutting edge?'

'People do, on occasion, let their implements rust, Mr Monsarrat. Perhaps the owner of this one suddenly noticed and took steps to correct it.'

'Doesn't seem much point though. Fixing the cutting edge when the blade is being eaten away.'

Holloway shrugged.

'And come to that – have you made any progress on finding out who owns this axe?'

'Axes are axes, Mr Monsarrat,' Holloway said. 'As I've told you, very few of them are owned by one individual. They use whatever they can grab to cut wood. That's all there is to it. It's likely this axe did not have one owner, was simply used from time to time by whoever had need of it.'

'So it could not belong to Power?'

'Do you really think, Mr Monsarrat, that we would leave him in possession of an axe? Some of the other convicts are allowed to use them. Him? No.'

'I would have thought not, but neither would I have thought to find such a weapon in a place of confinement for the worst convicts on the island.'

'Power could have found it easily enough,' said Holloway. 'There are some who I've threatened with a reduction in rations for leaving their axes propped up against their wood-piles rather than taking them inside. Not convicts, either. One or two privates less careful than they should be. When he had greater freedom, Power could easily have noted those who were careless. The man could talk his way out of hell, and I doubt he would have had any problem talking his way out of his enclosure – not with Shanahan as his only guard. It would have been simple for him to find this.'

'But he has not been provided with such an item.'

'Certainly not. It is not needed, in his case. The only people who don't cut their own wood here are Power and the Brewsters.'

❧

The patch of earth on which the visiting magistrate's cottage stood had, like the Brewsters' house, an excellent view of the bay.

And the bay was becoming rather crowded, Hannah thought. Three whalers were waiting in the distance, hoping for a chance to pierce the flank of a beast larger than a carriage. They may well get that chance, too. From her vantage point, she could see what the whalers probably couldn't – further out, beyond the sheltering arms of the bay and the northern tip of the island, small puffs of water vapour rose every few minutes from the surface.

Closer in, too, the bay was busy. Arched dolphins were threading themselves into and out of the water, in a way which would have delighted Walter Gendron. Hannah envied them their ease, their smiling beaks suggesting they were equally happy in both water and air, while she was barely a mistress of one and terrified of the other.

Standing on this smear of earth as the sea licked the cliffs and was carried on the breeze into her lungs, she thought, I am as far from home as it is possible to be. The realisation nearly felled her. This is not you, she admonished herself. This place has no power over a woman who has survived . . . She recoiled at where the thought was leading her, as the sea spray seemed to transform into smoke and the geese's cries into the laughs of a madwoman.

A distraction was needed, and the activity on the small dock below her provided it. Jones was standing in his cutter, arms reaching up to accept a tied bundle of turned chair legs, and bales of flax. She presumed he would be returning with other crates, ones containing the necessities that the settlement was unable to provide. The refusal of the request for bullocks and sheep meant the only red meat came in casks and entombed in salt. As for other forms of meat – the geese, she thought, must surely be utterly stupid creatures. She had made herself very plain – continued incursions on the small cottage would be rewarded with a wrung neck, and possibly a nice stuffing of breadcrumbs and walnuts, if such things could be found here.

She would have thought that her tone of voice, her mimicry of their flapping as she chased after them, had made her intentions quite plain. I must have gone soft in Parramatta, she thought. There was a stab of unease, a lick of distaste at the prospect of grabbing a goose by the neck and twisting. It was something she would have cheerfully done in Wexford, and even more cheerfully so during her early years in the colony, had a goose presented itself, had they not all been reserved for the tables of the rich.

Then again, she was becoming accustomed to the idea. Even more so this morning, when she had opened the back door of the cottage to find a step splattered with white excrement. She had looked around for the perpetrator, seeing none until one of the creatures had clearly felt the urge to confess to its abuse of the cottage's back step. It had been on the roof of the commandant's house, and now stood, stretched its wings and flew down to her, its neck lolling as its wings worked so that its head was in front of its belly. It landed a few feet from Hannah, turned its head side-on to fix her with one of its cruel eyes, and honked.

Hannah inhaled. It had been a while, anyway, since she had tasted goose. And the sooner it was over, the better for both of them. She walked slowly towards it, not wanting to send it into another gangling flight. She felt slightly guilty at the fact that it seemed to anticipate no danger, just stood there looking, perhaps hoping she had some shortbread crumbs in her pocket. As she reached out for it though, it was startled by another voice and flew off with its head dipping in front of it.

'Mrs Mulrooney, I am sorry to interrupt.'

She turned to see young Private Ennis. Who was guarding Power now, wondered Hannah?

'It's no trouble,' she said. She had no argument with him, only his prisoner. 'That goose is very grateful to you, in any case.'

'Yes, not bad eating, when we get them,' said Ennis. 'You'd think the wombats would be a feast. All bone and fat and gristle though. Kangaroo isn't bad when we can catch them, which isn't often. Fast buggers, they are, and we've no hounds to chase them down. You have to be careful not to cook them too long, else it's like eating a shoe. But I'm afraid you'll have to forget the geese for now. I've been sent here by the commandant. He has asked me to fetch you to Mr Power.'

'Ah. The man wishes to reminisce about a country he thinks we shared.'

'Did you not? I understood you were Irish? You certainly sound it.'

'We shared the same island. But not the same country, not really. His country is decorated with estates and fine houses and streams that always yield fish and plump livestock which can be slaughtered at will for the table. My country was one of anger and blood and courage and loss.'

Ennis opened his mouth and then closed it, clearly unsure of what to say.

Hannah sighed. 'I'm sorry, *a buachaill*. It's the air here, you see. I find it's deranging me,' she said.

'Yes . . . I've seen it have that effect on others as well. But why did you call me a . . .'

'*A buachaill*. Forgive the familiarity, private. It's just that you put me in mind of a dear friend who is gone. It means "my boy".'

'Oh. Well, I can certainly tell you I've been called worse, even last night in the barracks. Now, as that goose has gone back up to roost on the commandant's roof – would now be a convenient time for you to come with me?'

Monsarrat was beginning to wonder about Holloway.

He had assumed the man's obstructive stance came from his wounded pride, from being thwarted at his chance to be a hero in bringing a killer to justice. But the obstacles Holloway was putting in his path seemed to Monsarrat to speak of more than bruised self-regard.

'I would strongly counsel you against going up there,' Holloway said, when Monsarrat told him of his intention to visit the light.

'On what possible basis? It was the scene of the murder! The very event I'm here to investigate!'

'Ah, you see, but the track . . . it is very difficult.'

'Not too difficult for Harefield to ascend every night. And I imagine you'll want to get Jones up there soon enough, with all the whalers in the bay. One assumes the lights should not remain unlit.'

'Well, the commandant has yet to decide who'll change the lights now. Until he does, no one should visit the place.'

'I intend to do so anyway, Lieutenant Holloway. And I have Captain Brewster's agreement to it. You are, of course, most welcome to accompany me, should you have any . . . concerns about what evidence the place may hold.'

Holloway stepped back, as if struck. 'My only concern, Mr Monsarrat, is for your safety.'

'I am more than equal to it, lieutenant. I have been in challenging situations in the past.'

'Have you indeed?' said Holloway. 'Well, let's hope you don't meet with any mishaps. The snakes can be particularly aggressive, and they do not find cheaper shoe leather much of an impediment.'

⚜

Monsarrat was not interested in finding out whether Holloway was correct in his assessment about the snakes' attitude to poor-quality leather. In fading light, he kept to the narrow dirt path, glancing from side to side constantly as he went, searching periodically for the striped flank of a tiger snake on the edge of the path. A man on his work gang had run foul of one of them and his symptoms had progressed quickly from headache to nausea to death. Once or twice Monsarrat pulled up with a start at the sight of something long and thin across the path, which revealed itself on closer inspection to be a stick or a tree root. What did the Irish convicts make of this island so different from their home country, where St Patrick was said to have eradicated the snakes? And behind Power's brave front, were the snakes of this place a further weight on his soul and occasional visitants to his hut and his nightmares?

Monsarrat was surprised that neither Holloway nor Brewster had shown more urgency to reinstate the light, given the number of whalers he saw when he reached his destination. And there was the skeletal structure which supported the light, a tower of wooden struts about one and a half times the height of a man, nailed and lashed together, at the top of which sat a large, rotund oil lamp.

The light may be prosaic, but the cliff on which it rested was extraordinary. Layers of ancient sand had been compacted through the weight of the grains into a striped pattern which seemed too artfully rendered to be natural. The remarkable sight had lain under dirt and vegetation until the persistent sea had eventually eaten away a chunk of the cliff, revealing the beauty underneath.

Monsarrat wondered whether Harefield had enjoyed the sight, or whether he had simply begrudged the walk and the prospect of making his way back to the settlement as night fell and the snakes were emboldened.

Apart from the threat of serpents, though, Monsarrat saw little evidence of the dangers Holloway had warned him about. There did not seem to be any unsteady sections of cliff, holes or impediments. A small slope on the way up to the headland, yes, but nothing that would trouble a man who had at one time been used to traversing the scree at Port Macquarie.

Monsarrat looked up at the tower and its neglected light. He had assumed, seeing the structure from a distance, that Harefield would have simply climbed it. Now he realised he was wrong. A ladder lay nearby. It was broken, snapped in two. Monsarrat wondered whether Holloway was aware of it, or was even now cursing himself for not removing it.

Harefield now occupied a plot of land a little further down from the hospital, from which, had he stood on the land which was now his grave, he could have seen the light spring up. But Monsarrat had not arrived soon enough to examine the body, which would have putrefied in the summer heat had it not been taken care of.

Surgeon Chester had spoken of the lacerations associated with a fall, a fall which Monsarrat had assumed had taken Harefield from the top of the cliff to the bottom. But what if his descent had started earlier? If he had come within inches of igniting the flame in the large glass jar, only to have the ladder pulled away? That, Monsarrat thought, would not have taken nearly the same strength as dragging the man to the cliff's edge if he was still alive and struggling. All it would have taken was a stealthy approach and enough wit and speed to step out of the way as the ladder brought Harefield to earth with it.

And there was someone on this island with an excess of wit, and plenty of time to practise stealth while pacing around his small yard.

Chapter 10

Hannah was uneasy about why Thomas Power would want a private meeting with her. She could, she supposed, understand the impulse to talk to someone who had walked under the same sky, when they were both at this remove from their childhood home, and Power had recently lost access to the company of not only the Brewsters but also Walter. Or perhaps he is just using me as a mirror, she thought. Someone to tell him of his bravery, his courage. Someone to reflect his glory back at him. 'If that's his intention,' she muttered to herself as she and Private Ennis approached Power's cottage, 'he's more of an eejit than I thought.'

'I'm sorry, did you say something?' asked Ennis.

'Nothing at all. Just a rambling woman. I assume you're going to unlock that?' she said, nodding at the green gate in the white wall.

He did, and gestured her in. 'I'll be in here with you the whole time,' he said as she passed him.

'Ah. I shouldn't worry. If you have other duties, you should get about them. Power is no threat.'

'Not to your person, but possibly to your reputation,' he said.

'And that, here, can be just as dangerous. You wouldn't be the first to discover that.'

Power was sitting at a small table in his parlour, scratching at a piece of paper with a wood-shafted pen. Stacks of used paper were piled up on the desk and around it, Power's thoughts spilling over, seemingly in no particular order, onto the floor, inching their way towards the hearth. Some had reached their destination. Hannah noticed scraps of burned paper in the grate.

Power looked up when Ennis cleared his throat. 'How wonderful!' Power said, springing to his feet. 'Mrs Mulrooney, I am delighted that you decided to come.'

'I had little better to do,' said Hannah.

'Now, we can sit and talk, if you'd like. But I rather fancy a walk around the yard. Not that it will challenge us much – we will probably do twenty laps in the next half-hour. Do you have any objection?'

'None that I can think of at present. If one occurs to me, I'll let you know.'

Power chuckled again, and gestured to the small patch of earth.

Hannah was used to Monsarrat's slow, deliberate tread, hands clasped behind the back, as he leaned slightly forward, thinking about anything except where he was putting his feet. Power, despite his constraints, seemed intent on eating up as much ground as he possibly could, and on letting the earth know he was there by planting his feet solidly with every step. She had the odd sense that they were engaged in some sort of foot race.

'I suppose,' said Power, 'that you are curious as to why I wanted to see you.'

'I presumed the quality of my conversation was sufficient enticement,' she said.

He chuckled. 'I can't resist unvarnished honesty, even if someone is being honest about their loathing of me.'

'Should you tire of it, I'm sure you can find more than enough disciples, even here.'

'Possibly. Could I trust them, though, to show me a true reflection of the world beyond these walls? No, there are few people who walk in here with exposed intentions. You are one. Walter was another.'

'Walter? What possible intentions could he have had? You're not referring to ...'

'What? No. No. Walter wanted to talk to someone who would give him credit for some wit. He asks questions. I rarely had answers for him, but we lost hours in speculation.'

'He ... do you think he is in any danger?' asked Hannah.

Power stopped pacing, looked at her sharply. 'Why?'

'Something he said.'

'Well, there are those who don't ... appreciate him,' Power said, resuming his pacing. 'Those who measure a man by his ability to lift a log or steer a boat don't see the point of Walter. Harefield could be scathing, the chief scorner. Though Walter has Elizabeth to protect him.'

'Elizabeth ... Mrs Brewster?'

'Quite,' said Power quickly. 'But now to you. I invited you here for your recollections.'

'My recollections of what?'

'Well, that depends. Perhaps if I explain ... How much, Mrs Mulrooney, do you know about the crime for which I was transported?'

'Some sort of revolutionary you think yourself, I believe.'

'Well, the unsuccessful sort, as here I am. And to be honest I was not a big preacher of revolution when I was in Parliament.'

'What did you preach?'

'I wanted the yoke of British rule lifted from Ireland. And that in itself was enough, in the eyes of many, to condemn me. But, you see, I felt that a nation born in blood would never

118

properly heal. So I set about agitating for an Irish National Guard, a council, that sort of thing.'

'I have had little news of Ireland for some time,' said Hannah. 'I've no one left there.' And I wish I knew how to find the one I have here, she thought.

'I presume I'd have heard if your efforts had been successful,' she said.

'You're right, they weren't. They were opposed by two different groups. The British government, of course. And the more physical Liberty Association – a group I formed myself, to promote a peaceful, ordered liberation. But there will always be those who want barricades and blood. The government wanted me to shut up and wait for my father to die so that I could inherit the estate and the baronetcy that went with it. Suppose they thought that'd settle me down. And some of the Liberty boys wanted nothing less than an armed revolution.'

'Well, I hope they had better luck than the last group of revolutionaries,' said Hannah.

'They didn't. Oh, they tried. There was an armed insurrection under the name of the Liberty Association, but without my approval; without any organisation, either, any strategy. It failed. And I was arrested and charged with high treason.'

'And convicted, I assume, given the fact that you are here rather than on your father's estate. Why not just take your ease there? Why get involved at all?'

Power sighed. 'A question that has been put to me before. I am a rare beast in Ireland, a Catholic landlord, and my grandparents were ordinary folk. You see, I cannot use difference of religion as the basis for looking at my tenants as a lesser breed. For if they are lesser, then so am I. Do you realise that at the moment they are precluded by law from education, from serving in juries, from being officers of the court or the army, and from attending universities? They have not been emancipated. And they are not someone else's people. They are my people. A British parliament keeps them slaves. Only an Irish parliament will liberate them.'

'And time will liberate you,' said Hannah. 'And you'll have the means to return. Unlike so many others.'

'True. While my liberty has been taken, though, I have been left with a lot of time to think. And what my thoughts chiefly turn on is this – is there, perhaps, a better means of achieving Irish independence? I will, when my sentence expires, return, of course. And I fully intend to take up where I left off. But how to do it? How to give it the best chance of success, because if it fails I doubt very much that they will bother transporting me again. I have already paid a high price for my efforts.'

Hannah could hear the rush of her own blood. Her throat constricted and her teeth jammed themselves together. And here it was – the anger which could only be called forth by what she viewed as an insult to certain of her dead.

'You have paid a price, but it is not a high one,' she said, looking straight ahead as she feared she would hit him if she saw any hint of self-satisfaction on his face. 'Your castle sits waiting for you, when you're able to return and reclaim it. Those you love did not die in the mud, were not tortured, or piked through on their doorsteps. So you may think yourself a hero of the revolution, even though it was a revolution you did not order. But heroism is easy for those who don't pay the full price.'

Power stopped walking, frowned, turned to her.

'Ah. I see. I did suspect . . . it's why I wanted to talk to you. I have experience of only one revolution, you see. I have spoken, at every possible opportunity, with anyone I can find who has had experience of another. And you – you said that you'd been ticketed for twenty years. Assuming your sentence was seven . . . Well, it puts you in Ireland at the time of the 1798 uprising. So nearly a successful revolution. The closest to revolution Ireland has been. And you saw it too, yes? You were there?'

Hannah turned away. The image of tufts of red-gold hair rising from a ruined scalp was one which she had not admitted into her conscious mind for many years; in fact not until very recently, when she had told Monsarrat the story of her past. Now, suddenly, it was one which would not leave her.

'Yes,' she whispered. 'Yes, I was there. And I cannot speak to you of strategy or armaments. But I can tell you that for every fine speech made, every aristocratic revolutionary who fancied himself a leader, a hundred men, a thousand, died. Because those who make the orders are rarely those who make the sacrifices.'

Hannah didn't tell Power all of her story. She did not feel he deserved it. It had taken her some time to give even the most rudimentary details to Monsarrat. The memory of her fiancé, Colm, painful as it was, was still intense, and she feared that sharing too much of it would diminish him, make him insubstantial.

She didn't tell Power of walking home after the battle that changed everything. Passing burned or burning cottages, knowing hers would be among them, hoping her father had got out in time. He had, but he had not been allowed to go far. She had found him piked through on a doorstep which now lacked a door. She had buried him and spent the night on his grave.

She didn't tell Power of watching in Enniscorthy's market square, of not recognising Colm among the prisoners. There had only been a few tufts of red-gold hair left on his scalp. The rest had been destroyed when the British had poured pitch over his head and lit it. She realised it was him just before he was lined up and shot.

And she didn't tell Power about giving birth in the cramped confines of an Irish cell to a boy who would grow to inhabit the wild vastness of Australia.

But she did want to leave Power in no doubt as to the nature of her sacrifice, and how she felt it compared to his. 'My man gave his life, you know,' she said. 'Tortured and shot.

And my da – defending his farm, and piked through, for all that. So please do not tell me, Mr Power, of the wonders of revolution. Of the glorious sacrifices. Your glorious sacrifice has been to sit here for a couple of years, hoping the world doesn't forget you, doing everything you can to make sure it doesn't while seeming not to care, after which you'll be back to your castle in the south. I can never go back. I cannot afford the passage, but even if I could, the Ireland I left no longer exists.'

Power had left off his pacing entirely. He was standing stock-still, looking at the ground. When he looked up, Hannah was rattled to see the intensity in his eyes. Some might have taken it as an indication that their story had moved him. Hannah, though, was enraged further. How dare you? she thought. How dare you claim my grief? How dare you steal my sorrow?

He seemed not to notice the angry set to her face, walked up and took both her hands in his. 'My dear woman. I cannot begin to thank you for the sacrifice you have made for our country. I assure you, I will make sure it is repaid.'

'I do not require repayment,' she said.

'Well, you certainly deserve it,' he said. 'Thank you, truly, for telling me.'

'I'd like to ask you to put it out of your mind as soon as possible. I ask you not to mention it to anyone. It is my private history, not one to be used as gossip or the foundation for a speech.'

He nodded, seemingly chastened. 'I am going to take the trouble to defend myself only because I respect you, Mrs Mulrooney, as a veteran of the struggle. I could have stood for the House of Commons of London for County Kerry. I needed only to share the interests of those few powerful men in the county who have a vote. I could have then gone to London and traded my vote with the English Whigs to get a place in the Cabinet, become a great man and utterly forget my peasants except in so far as they might owe me rent.

I did not do that. I proposed that we should have an Irish government and parliament, and the reward for that . . . well, you see it.'

Hannah felt unexpectedly chastened. 'I respect your motives, sir,' she muttered. 'But that doesn't mean they can't get ordinary people like me killed.'

She thought, best to end this now, and rushed to say something more before he could speak. She saw his mouth open. And now,' she managed to say, 'I best be getting back up the hill. Mr Monsarrat will want feeding.'

'Of course. I did, though, have another reason for asking you here,' said Power.

'Quickly, then,' she said.

'It feels inappropriate, now, to be bringing it up after what you've told me.'

'All right, so, I'll be leaving.' She had no interest in standing there while he wrestled with a conscience that she suspected was not as sensitive as he pretended.

'Wait! Wait, please. Ask I will, and I'll deal with the consequences later. And as I am holding your story to myself, I'd ask you to do the same. Tell me of Mrs Brewster. Is she well? I wondered, have you seen any evidence to suggest that she thinks of a poor prisoner like me?'

∾◦∾

'Why on earth would he ask that?' said Monsarrat. 'And just as importantly, what on earth did you say?'

The light on the island was beginning to grow soft, to diffuse itself, to retreat over the corrugated horizon. They had decided to see it on its way, watching the bay and the whalers further out as the dusk blurred them.

It was Monsarrat's suggestion – there was an agitation to the way Mrs Mulrooney was moving around the small kitchen where he found her on his return from the light near the painted cliffs. She was always moving but there was usually a smoothness and grace to it, the ease of a woman who was settling into accustomed rhythms, even in an unfamiliar kitchen. Tonight, though, the movements were jerky. Less efficient, too, he noticed, as she returned to the kettle for the fourth time, picking it off the hob to hang it on the hook over the fire before replacing it. He had carried the bench outside so they could watch the bay and make sure the day was truly over, that it didn't sneak back.

At his question she had smiled and made no move to flick him with her cleaning cloth, and now her stiffness seemed to be slowly receding with the sun.

'I suppose there are a number of possible reasons,' said Mrs Mulrooney.

'Surely, only one,' said Monsarrat.

'Perhaps. Or perhaps he wishes to know whether even when Private Ennis is absent, he is being watched.'

'Either way – what did you say? Did you tell him you had seen her staring at his wall?'

'Certainly not. I simply observed that she was a woman with many calls on her time. He does not need to know everything that transpires outside his wall.'

'I suppose not. Although he does seem to know a fair bit. No doubt Ennis is feeding him information in exchange for letters home. I used to do something similar for people at the Caledonia Inn – take their sentiments and force them into finely tuned words, transcribed for dispatch. People are remarkably desperate to make a good account of themselves when they are represented in front of their families by a piece of paper.'

'Yes, well – Ennis seems to like him, but I don't think he trusts him. He was cautious when he brought me there.'

'No one seems to trust him. Marley, everyone here, seem desperate for Power to be convicted of this murder. Yet he'd have had to leave his compound for long enough to get to the light, and procure an axe. Hard to see how those things could be done, even without a guard.'

'One thing I'll tell you,' said Mrs Mulrooney. 'I seem to have shamed him into being a little neater. His papers, they were mostly stacked and there were fewer of them. Presumably he tied some of them up, put them away. Anyway, they were certainly less in evidence than our first visit.'

'Yes. Well, you inspire the worst of us to better things, Mrs Mulrooney.'

She glared sideways at him, and he held up his hands. 'I assure you, I am not mocking. You must stop seeing derision when there is none.'

She exhaled slowly, sinking into herself as the breath left her. 'I've been in a bad temper this whole time,' she said. 'I regret it, Mr Monsarrat. No, truly I do. The sea journeys, with a horrendous stretch in a carriage to separate them, have put me in an interminable snit. And my ankle still pains me. I shall try to improve, I promise.'

'You're entitled to far more than testiness,' said Monsarrat, wondering how many people could cope with worry over a silent son and memories of an encroaching fire. 'As long as I have access to your intelligence, your skills of observation, I don't need your good humour, though I will welcome its return.'

She smiled briefly, and Monsarrat had the disturbing impression it was all she had energy for. She let the weight of her back rest against the wall and they looked for a while in silence as the sea absorbed the last of the day's light.

For all that Mrs Mulrooney had promised goose for dinner, they were still there half an hour later, and the sky was now a deep shade of blue, preparing to tip over into blackness.

Suddenly Mrs Mulrooney leaned forward and pointed down into the darkness of the bay. It was a cloudless night and the moon was not quite full, but it was full enough to allow them to see the sails of a whaler approaching the bay, perhaps now a hundred feet out.

'I've been looking at them for the past two days,' said Mrs Mulrooney. 'I've yet to see them this close in, either the whales or the whalers.'

'The water here would be too shallow for whales, surely? And the whalers never put in here for provisions. So yes . . . It does seem a little close.'

The whaling ship had stopped moving. In the silent twilight they had not heard the sound of an anchor chain rolling through the hawse. But Monsarrat could see an undulating darkness against the water. He held up his hand to warn Mrs Mulrooney to silence, but she was watching just as intently as he was.

In the absence of the squabbling of sea birds, geese, or the yelling of the overseers on the hospital site, the rises surrounding the cove acted like a natural amphitheatre, carrying sound up to the watchers on the cliff. The sound they carried on the air now was the slap of oars on water.

Monsarrat unfolded himself quickly from the bench, hitting his head on the overhanging eve of the house and not even bothering to rub it as he sprinted across to the commandant's residence. Mrs Mulrooney followed as quickly as her skirts and ankle would allow.

⁓

'What do you mean, landing?'

'Exactly what I said, Captain Brewster,' said Monsarrat, struggling to hide his frustration. All the man had to do was walk outside and look down towards the bay to see what he meant. Belatedly, the same thought seemed to be occurring to Brewster. He turned to Elizabeth, who was coming in from the back of the cottage with some split logs for the fire.

'Stay where you are. We don't know who they are or what they intend,' he said. 'Mrs Mulrooney, stay here with my wife.'

Mrs Mulrooney did not make the slightest effort to conceal her frustration. The most interesting thing that had happened since they arrived, and she was trapped in a cottage.

Brewster started purposefully striding towards the door, before returning to the living room and picking up a musket which had been standing in the corner.

'Ennis should be outside Power's door,' said Brewster. 'We'll have him raise the alarm, get the whole garrison down to welcome these knaves.'

Ennis, however, was not at his post. When Captain Brewster and Monsarrat were still some distance from Power's enclosure, they saw the gate open. Out of it had exploded a tall man, coatless and running faster than Monsarrat would have thought possible for somebody who had only a small patch of dirt to exercise in.

Because it was obvious, by both his bearing and his haste, that the man bolting down towards the shore was Thomas Power.

Chapter 11

Elizabeth Brewster got to her feet as soon as her husband had left the room and began pacing up and down between the fireplace and her chair with every bit as much latent frustration as Power displayed pacing his yard.

'Don't agitate yourself,' Hannah said gently. 'Whoever they are, I'm sure your husband and Mr Monsarrat will stop them causing any trouble.'

'I am not concerned about the men who are landing,' snapped Elizabeth. Then she shook her head. 'Forgive me, Mrs Mulrooney. It's the tension, you see. Waiting, wondering whether ... Whether ... they will achieve their objective. Whatever that might be.'

'Of course. But come away from the window, now. Your husband is unlikely to be the only one with a musket down there. I don't know how far those pieces of shot can fly, but I would rather not find out.'

'All right,' Elizabeth said, and came back to her chair, only to leave it again a minute later and resume pacing.

'This hasn't happened before, then? Strange visitors with unknown desires rowing ashore in the dead of night?'

Elizabeth uttered a rather flat, mirthless sound. 'No. No, the only boat we see is the *Swift*, the brig which brought Power to us. And of course our own cutter.'

'Why don't we take our minds off it,' said Hannah. 'I shall make you tea, shall I?'

Elizabeth strode over to Hannah, gripped both of her forearms. Hannah was surprised by the woman's strength. 'How can I think of tea when he is in danger?' Elizabeth yelped.

It was not the first time Hannah had heard the high, strained tones of a woman whose wits were becoming jangled. This one was not trying to kill her, at least. Hannah took the same approach as she had with Rebecca Nelson. Calm. Practical. She hoped it would soothe Elizabeth, and herself.

'I am sure your husband is in no danger at all. Don't forget, he has a garrison here. No doubt he's alerted them and they're bearing down on our visitors right now.'

The reassurance did not seem to calm Elizabeth. Tears were beginning to skirt her high cheekbones. 'He ... Yes, of course, you're right. Walter is still in the stores, but I'm sure he'll have the sense to stay there.' She seemed to make a conscious effort now to compose herself. 'And tea would be lovely, if you'd be so kind.'

Hannah, who'd had to use every ounce of her self-control to avoid jumping out of the chair and running down to the ocean's edge after Monsarrat, was happy to at least have a task to perform. She went to the kitchen and left Elizabeth to her pacing.

As she boiled the water and warmed the pot and measured the leaves, she told herself that naturally the 'he' Elizabeth was fretting about was her husband.

❧❦❧

Monsarrat opened his mouth to cry out, to call Power back before the man did something foolish and irreparable. Brewster, though, clapped his hand on Monsarrat's upper arm, gestured him to silence. 'I want to see where he is going, what this is about,' he whispered.

The air had given up its heat with the setting sun, but retained a moist heaviness which seemed to make Brewster's words far louder than they should have been. They followed as quickly as they could while maintaining a degree of stealth. Power flew across the little bridge over the stream and was now nearly at the beach, showing no signs of slowing.

'I'll raise the garrison myself,' whispered Brewster. 'You go after him. I'll fire my musket into the air when I want you to break cover, try to detain him. Hopefully the distraction will help.'

Monsarrat found himself oddly reluctant to chase after Power, to prevent him from escaping – because it seemed increasingly likely that what was occurring was an escape attempt. He understood all too well the impulse to find the world one lived in wanting, and to decide to take steps to change it; steps which would inevitably upset those in authority.

He did not consider such things a crime. Not necessarily. Not when one was redressing an imbalance, and trying to do so peacefully. But he knew that he had absolutely no choice in the matter. He must apprehend Power as part of his duties as a government representative.

So he sprinted down the hill, sacrificing stealth to speed. He was the taller of the two and had had more opportunities for exercise, so he gained quickly on Power.

He was very nearly not quick enough. By the time he made the beach, Power was already splashing into the sea, sending up great showers of salt water with each frenzied step. And the tender for the whaling boat was drawing closer. Within seconds it might be close enough for Power to climb aboard, and to slip away from this island off an island and into an unknown future.

Brewster, though, was as good as his word. As Monsarrat found himself splashing into the waves – gasping as the chill water gripped his legs, cursing not having time to remove his shoes, which would now be permanently ruined – he heard the startling crack of a musket.

The men in the boat slowed in their rowing, and Power stopped and looked around. He might not have been able to see the soldiers who were coming out of their barracks, some sleep-addled, others a little the worse for rum, one man holding playing cards. But he could certainly see Monsarrat. For an instant he tilted his head and fixed Monsarrat with a glance, as though he was considering a point someone had just made to him during a friendly debate in a gentlemen's club. *I thought we understood each other*.

But both Power and his unknown friends soon recovered themselves, and the boat started moving more quickly towards the shore as a determined Power waded out. Power was not afraid, thought Monsarrat with grudging admiration.

Then another sound. A deep keening, gathering into a wail of such desolation it stilled the men who had been galloping towards the beach.

Monsarrat turned. The smudge that was Walter's white shirt could be seen against the black outline of the commissary door. His voice bounced off the waves and seemed for a moment to paralyse those who heard it, as though he were some sort of disingenuous siren.

'Thomas! Thomaaas! You said you wouldn't go! You cannot leave! Do not leave me, Thomas. Please, my friend!'

The spell of his despair could not hold back the regiment for long. Behind him, Monsarrat heard the sound of running feet, of shouts. Soldiers were thundering down towards the sand.

Power, of course, heard the commotion too. He stopped again, stood, planted his feet against the waves which were lapping around his waist, and held his hands up to his mouth.

'Turn!' he yelled. 'Turn, or be captured. Thank you, my friends. But you can see we are discovered. I shall not be coming with you tonight. I would not have you join me in captivity.'

The men in the boat were close enough for Monsarrat to see the outlines of their faces. They were also close enough to hear Power.

'We'll not leave,' one yelled back. 'We came here for you and we'll leave with you!'

'No,' yelled Power. 'You must turn. They will not treat you well. Turn, I beg you!'

Monsarrat continued to wade towards him, widening his stance, stopping whenever a wave came up against him, and then starting again, wondering whether he would need to dive below the waves and swim through the black water.

He was not the only one who was getting his feet wet in pursuit of the famous prisoner. He could hear splashes as others plunged in. He would be upon Power in a matter of moments and they would be seconds behind.

The men in the boat saw them too, as those on the ship must have – the sails were being unfurled, bright patches springing out of the darkness.

'Your captain has more sense than you, my friends,' Power was yelling now. 'Turn back!'

And a thicket of oars rose in the air on one side of the boat, plunging into the water again and again until it was side-on to the shore, and then facing away from it, and then being rowed with almost unnatural haste towards its larger counterpart.

Power turned towards Monsarrat, held his hands in the air, and said, 'I commend myself to your care, Mr Monsarrat. You may have the capture. I do hope, my friend, that it sits well with you.'

Chapter 12

'They were friends. That is all they were, and that is all I will say.'

If it was possible to lounge on the rudimentary benches jutting from the wall of the guardhouse while wearing wet clothes which were beginning to stiffen with salt, Thomas Power was managing it, as if it were beneath his notice to shiver. He had far more room behind the bars than Brewster, Monsarrat – who was freezing in his own wet clothes – and Holloway did on their side. He was not bothering to turn his head to answer Brewster's questions, instead seemed caught in a contemplation of the ceiling timbers.

'And how did you communicate with these friends? By dolphin?' Brewster said. 'You surely don't expect me to believe that a whaler was coincidentally in the area, that a rowing boat coincidentally came ashore as you ran down to meet it.'

'Oh no, certainly not. But I'm afraid the rest will have to remain a private matter between myself and them. I have been, my friend, tortured in the past and have managed to keep information safely between my ears. I do not intend to change that habit.'

'I am not your friend!' said Brewster. 'Nor am I a torturer. You may find, though, that there are those who will interrogate you in future who will not hesitate to stoop to such practices. I urge you, confess all to me now and it will go easier for you once you leave this island.'

Power stared up at the ceiling. Monsarrat was impressed by his composure at being recaptured. 'I shall take my chances with whatever barbarian has decided to put on a red coat. And I regret it, Brewster. Not the attempt, but the position it has put you in. However, you will hear no more from me on it.'

'Answer me this then. What in God's name have you done with Ennis?'

Private Ennis had clearly not been at his post. Neither had he been among those to splash into the bay.

'Oh, he is quite safe. Probably not conscious yet though. You will find him on my cot. You mustn't think he had anything to do with this – a friendly lad, certainly, but a loyal one to the Crown and his masters. I have been taking a mild sleeping draught these past weeks, you see. At first I thought to use it for my own purposes – there's little to do now except write and sleep, but the latter always seems to elude me. I've worn away more topsoil in my yard at three in the morning than at any other time. Chester is a rather wakeful man himself, and takes pity on those similarly afflicted.

'But then I conceived another use for it – I offer Ennis some of my tea, from time to time. You really must feed those boys better, Brewster. He was always happy to accept it, and earlier tonight it contained a little more than tea. He will perhaps be somewhat groggy on waking, but no more so than some of those who ran into the water after me.'

Brewster turned to Lieutenant Holloway, who had been hovering by the door, unwilling to miss the spectacle of this most hated man being interrogated.

'Check on Private Ennis, Holloway, please.'

'He deserves to be harmed, sir, if I may say. Taking an inducement from a prisoner is what it is. If it hadn't been for our vigilance, he would have a lot more to answer to.'

Holloway glared at Monsarrat as though angry at him for apprehending the man, and stalked off.

Monsarrat felt a pang of pity for Ennis. To be woken, head pounding, from a slumber to the sight of Holloway's scowling face was something no young lad deserved.

After the lieutenant had gone Brewster seemed to deflate a little more. He sat in the chair near the rickety wooden table, the one on which the axe had rested, and slumped his shoulders forward.

'Thomas ... What are we going to do with you? You may well hang.'

'And would you be there, James? Watching with a face of granite as I drop? Would you be the one to nod to the hangman?' Power sighed, rubbed his eyes. 'I'm sorry that our friendship was unable to survive what were – no, hear me out, I know I've said it before but I will say it again – baseless accusations from Harefield. But don't trouble yourself with regard to my life. They won't hang me. They don't want to make a martyr. They fear that if word of me at the end of a rope gets back to Ireland, the country will rise again.'

'There's a difference between a martyr and a murderer! How like you to assume that the possibility of being made the former hides you from the consequences of being the latter! And why do you think your name still has the force it once did – across all those leagues of ocean?'

Power frowned. Perhaps, thought Monsarrat, he doubts he is still a favourite of progressive people all over the earth. And loss of that repute must be Power's greatest fear.

'It doesn't matter what would happen in the eventuality of my execution. It's enough that they think it might provoke a revolt. They are still stinging from the outrage after they hanged, drew and quartered Robert Emmet twenty years ago,' said Power.

'Thomas, for all your vanity, I never thought you a coward,' said Brewster. 'Yet you try to escape just as a murder of which you're suspected is being investigated. What am I to make of that? Confess, and I will do my best to have any death sentence commuted.'

'I happily confess to the crimes I own,' said Power. 'This is not one of them.'

Brewster walked up to the bars and pressed his face to them, so that his nose was inches from Power's. 'Then I will make it my business to secure your conviction and send you to hell, and not one Irish farmer will put down his loy and pick up a pike after you shit yourself on the gallows.'

He spat, and the gobbet landed on Power's salt-stained shirt. Brewster hissed, 'Your attempt at escape means I will now get hectoring letters from Hobart Town. Come Monsarrat!'

Power's eyes had a febrile gleam. The excitement from the escape attempt had not yet been replaced by any despondency.

'To be honest with you, commandant,' said Monsarrat, 'I am not feeling particularly restful after tonight's events. Would you have any objection if I stayed for a short while?'

He leaned towards Brewster, and spoke quietly into his ear. 'The man is a braggard, so I will see if I can make him brag.'

Brewster thought for a moment, then nodded. 'Very well then. And you will report to me on the content of your conversation.'

'Of course.'

'I bid you goodnight. Mr Monsarrat, I hope that when you eventually come to it, you sleep well. Power, I hope you never sleep again.'

Through all the shouts, all the musket shots, Elizabeth Brewster had remained with her face glued to the window. There was no more musket fire, the yelling from the shore had died down and she had returned to her chair, a cup of cold tea on the side table beside her. She took a few sips and then left it.

Hannah tried not to mind. The woman was agitated. There were those for whom tea was a calming elixir, but Elizabeth was clearly not among them. Now she was staring into the fire, and had been doing so for so long, was so utterly still, that Hannah occasionally looked at her chest to make sure it was still rising and falling. The exhaustion of their hours-long vigil sat lightly on her, a woman whose features wore the pallor of a marble statue.

Elizabeth reanimated at the sound of the door opening. She stood quickly, smoothed her gown as though expecting a reprimand, laid a hand on the mantle, perhaps for support in the face of whatever news her husband brought. Perhaps tiredness had frayed the caution with which she usually addressed her husband, but Hannah was surprised by her strident tone.

'I have been sitting here suffering through musket shots and shouting, not knowing whether to expect a group of men at the door, demanding God knows what. Tell me, right away, what happened?'

Brewster scowled for a moment. But as his wife had found her voice, he seemed to have lost his to the events of the night. He went to his seat near the fire. Hannah moved to a corner of the room and stood there, the position of the servant, never seen but always listening.

'Power tried to escape,' Brewster said. 'A well-planned attempt, too. He has had help.'

Elizabeth was nodding, clearly willing him to get to the crux of the matter. 'But what,' she said, '*happened*? Did he succeed?'

'No, he did not. He was recaptured when he was within twenty feet of the boat which was rowing ashore towards him.

By Mr Monsarrat, actually. Speaking of which . . .' He turned, looked towards Hannah. 'You may go now.'

Hannah's mind was racing as she nodded, bobbed demurely to Captain Brewster and turned to leave. Mr Monsarrat must close off this endless cycle of rumour and insinuation surrounding the possible culpability of Thomas Power in the killing of the bosun, as well as lay to rest any speculation around Power and young Walter, a lad who had won his way into her good graces. And Hannah saw before her, in the exhausted face of the commandant and the pinched, strained set of his wife's mouth, a possible means to achieve that. Proof may not exist, but if it did she knew where she was most likely to find it.

She stopped halfway out the door.

'Sir, may I ask . . .'

'Oh what, for God's sake, what?' he yelled. 'I have had my fill of questions from women! Neither of you have the right to ask me anything.'

Hannah stepped back a pace. 'Of course, sir. I simply wished to offer my services towards a particular endeavour . . .'

'Christ and his saints. Very well, what?'

'I would imagine, sir, that Mr Power will not be returning to his lodgings. That there will be a need to make them ready for new occupants. In exchange for the hospitality you have shown us, I would be delighted to take on this task.'

Brewster exhaled heavily through his nostrils, a provoked bull. He shook his head, and she thought for a moment he would order her out.

'You might as well,' he eventually said. 'Hardly the most urgent task, but I suppose it'll have to be done.' He slashed his hand through the air in a gesture of dismissal.

Hannah bobbed again. She hated it, the hypocritical servility, the willing self-abasement. But she accepted it as a necessary part of her protective colouration.

'Oh, and Mrs Mulrooney – any papers, any books, personal effects of any kind that you find are to be brought straight to me. Is that clear?'

'Of course, sir,' Hannah said, turning to leave before the man changed his mind. And she would keep her promise; she would send anything she found to him. Because Brewster had not said anything about forbidding her to peruse them first.

Power seemed to force himself to some animation when he was alone with Monsarrat. He swung his legs off the bench, sat up and turned his cornflower gaze on Monsarrat.

'Don't suppose you have a water skin,' he said.

'Oddly enough, Mr Power, I did not have time to provision myself before running down to the beach to recapture you.'

There was a small rumble in Power's throat, a sound which might have developed into a grim chuckle. 'And I must say, Mr Monsarrat, you pursued dutifully, but rather . . . What's the word . . . ? Hesitantly.'

'My ruined shoes give the lie to that,' Monsarrat said. 'And I was the one who raised the alarm.'

'Yes, before you knew what alarm you were raising. Oh, you waded in. Didn't have any choice, of course. Did what was asked of you,' said Power. 'But when it came time to lay hands on me – well. There was a second's hesitation. And I do believe I understand why.'

'You understand little about me, Mr Power.'

'That may be, but it's still more than you would credit. I know what you are, Mr Monsarrat.'

Monsarrat could not resist the offer of a character assessment from Power, even though it might not be flattering. 'What I . . . What I am? And what might I be, in your estimation?'

'Mr Monsarrat, I have spent a significant proportion of my life agitating for liberty, and another significant proportion of it deprived of my own. I know the marks, the signs, of one who has been similarly deprived. The eyes which find the ground too readily. The deferential way of speaking, even as a representative of the governor addressing the commandant of a small penal settlement. The caution. And, I flatter myself, the only lightly veiled sympathy for a fellow exile.'

He looked at Monsarrat, clearly expecting some sort of confirmation. He will get nothing from me, thought Monsarrat.

'No, I wouldn't respond either,' said Power, after a moment. 'You have done well, I think, to rise to such a position. Only one thing concerns me, Mr Monsarrat. I set much store by honesty. I did not lie even about my intention to try to escape. Why, then, would you conceal something so fundamental?'

Monsarrat's intention not to allow Power the satisfaction of a confession from him, when he was the one supposed to be seeking the confession, melted in front of the slight. The man could question his background all he wanted, but when he questioned his integrity something needed to be done.

'As it happens, the decision was made for me,' said Monsarrat. 'It was obviously felt by the man who sent me that providing knowledge of my past would impede my ability to do my job. A job, I might remind you, which involves investigating Harefield's murder. A murder which now looks even more likely to be laid at your door, as whoever dispatched the man killed the only person on the island capable of giving chase, had you been able to get to that whaler of yours.'

'And yet I didn't escape before they got a new bosun, did I? Did not even try. Would you not think I would have done it the night after the man's death, perhaps?'

'Perhaps you were not able to arrange it in time. Can't have been easy.'

'No. And in killing Harefield, I remind you, I would also have removed my only method of communication.'

'On the subject of communication . . . How did you manage it?'

'I'm afraid I can't enlighten you on that score, Mr Monsarrat. But Harefield was not part of it.'

'Those letters you wrote for Ennis, the ones to his mother . . .'

'Nice lad, he is,' said Power. 'Misses her too, and no doubt the feeling's returned from across the seas. He has images of her sobbing by the fire for him. So he writes only of cheerful things, which requires no small amount of imagination in a place such as this.'

'In those pages for Mrs Ennis, were any other letters concealed? Ones never intended to get to England?' asked Monsarrat.

Power smiled, but said nothing. The man's self-assurance, his urbanity even in a guardhouse on an island as remote from civilisation as the moon, was irritating, coming from that rarest of convicts – someone with the means and connections to secure a passage home after his sentence expired. Power would eventually have everything he had lost in the pursuit of liberty restored to him, as long as he was not convicted of Harefield's murder.

'There is one question you have not asked me,' said Power. 'An obvious one. I'm surprised we haven't discussed it by now.'

'You refer to the axe?' said Monsarrat. 'To how you might have procured it, and how you might have left your enclosure long enough to use it.'

'Precisely so,' said Power. 'Hard as this may be to believe, Mr Brewster is not in the habit of leaving me with weapons.'

'Yet you managed to leave your enclosure to run down to the ocean, by drugging the young man you said you liked so much.'

'Yes, I suppose I should regret that. No permanent harm will come to him though, and far better he be unconscious and therefore incapable of being implicated. In any case, that's a trick which would only work once. Ennis might lack the imagination to frame the letters to his mother in a way which will allay her fears. But he is smart enough to realise that if he finds himself losing consciousness around me on a regular basis, there is probably more than exhaustion at work.'

'You do realise that there are more than a few who will say your escape attempt puts your guilt beyond doubt. And they'll point to your treatment of Ennis as evidence of your depravity.'

'And I can offer them no proof to the contrary, not the kind that would satisfy them, anyway,' said Power. 'I can simply lie here, examining the ceiling, wishing it was the deck of a whaler that was taking me to America.'

'Quite a journey,' said Monsarrat. 'Why America?'

'Friends there,' said Power. 'Together with a certain anti-authoritarian streak which would make me welcome.'

'You know, of course, that having attempted and failed, you are unlikely to get a second opportunity,' said Monsarrat.

'Oh yes, well aware. My only escape now lies within my mind. On that, Mr Monsarrat, I wonder if I might ask you a favour. I have a treatise on public administration to finish. Would you be kind enough to drop in some pens and paper when you're next passing? Because without those I really will be imprisoned.'

Chapter 13

It was only a few hours from dawn by the time Monsarrat made his way back up the hill. He expected to find the cottage cold, the fire out. It was still burning, however, and had been set to the task of heating the kettle while Mrs Mulrooney moved quickly from shelf to table to stove, scrubbing imaginary blemishes. Within minutes she had a cup of tea in front of him.

'We have a real mystery on our hands now,' she said.

'Oh, that's a relief, because the one about who killed the bosun was getting rather boring,' said Monsarrat, picking up his teacup to avoid a swat – she would never risk spilling the sacred liquid.

'Should we think more,' she said, 'about the friendship between Power and the Brewsters?'

He sighed. 'We know Power was accused of some sort of romantic activity with the lad. You know how protective Mrs Brewster is of her brother, and her husband's advancement would be threatened if such word got out.'

'Yes, yes, we know all that. What we don't know, Mr Monsarrat, and I feel we very much need to, is the nature of the relationship between Elizabeth and Mr Power.'

'You can't be suggesting . . .'

'I'm not sure what I'm suggesting. All I know is that there's something worth suggesting, something that at least bears a second look. Her staring at his wall. Her reaction when she heard about the failure of his escape – she was upset, Mr Monsarrat, and Brewster thought it was out of relief at his return, but it may not have been. Power asked me about her too, of course.'

Monsarrat set down the cup, slightly too loudly against saucer so that the noise drew one of Mrs Mulrooney's worst glares.

'My dear lady, this is even more circumstantial than the case that would have Power implicated in the murder of the bosun. It is a distraction.'

'And how many distractions have we come across that turn out to be central after all?'

Monsarrat inclined his head, an acknowledgement that she may have a point. 'How, though, does that help *us*?' he said. 'How does that advance things, so that we can deal with the matter and return to Parramatta? I know you're not eager for another sea journey, my friend, but I think we are both in rather a hurry to get back.'

Mrs Mulrooney frowned. 'I do wonder how young Helen is coping. Whether the hearth fire's behaving itself – and I know fire bears watching, now more than ever. If there have been any letters from Padraig. And I'm fully aware, Mr Monsarrat, that a certain Female Factory convict will be free soon.'

~~~

Why, Hannah wondered, had the man left his papers out?

Thomas Power certainly must not believe that an ordered desk made an ordered mind – and there was some doubt in hers as to whether his mind *was* ordered anyway. But he had known he was about to leave the island, or try to. He had known the ship was coming. Yet here on his small desk, moving slightly

144

in the morning breeze, were pages in various states of completion. Some neatly written in a hand of which Monsarrat would have approved, some scrawled and crossed out, and some little more than receptacles for ink blotches. The pen rested in an ink pot in which the pigment was beginning to dry and crack. She had never seen Monsarrat treat a pen with such disrespect. His were not made to spend the night marinating in ink, were always cleaned and put away.

Perhaps Power hadn't known precisely when to expect his salvation. Perhaps there had been a signal. But he couldn't have seen it here in his enclosure, and there had been no cannon shot or bell.

At any rate, as the pages had been left here Hannah saw no reason not to peruse them. Ennis hadn't come into the cottage with her, had instead opted to stand, very visibly, outside the gate through which he had failed to prevent Power escaping.

'I'm embarrassed, to be honest with you,' he'd said to Hannah after he had collected her from the visiting magistrate's cottage that morning. 'To let any prisoner escape . . . But Thomas Power!'

'You've got no cause for embarrassment,' Hannah said. 'The man drugged you. Betrayed your trust.'

Ennis had frowned. 'There is that . . . He knows a lot about me, you know, that man. Every thought I have sent to my mother has gone through his hands. But the fact remains – I should not have accepted tea from him. I'll get a dressing-down from the commandant. Or a nasty punishment, if he gets Lieutenant Holloway to take care of me. In the meantime, I'd best not let you leave with anything tucked away in your pockets.'

'I promise that the only papers leaving here will be doing so with you, not me. And while I'd warn you against accepting anything from Power, if you'll take a cup of tea from me after we are finished here I'd be delighted.'

He had smiled and waved her in.

After staring at the untidy man's desk for a few moments, Hannah turned her attention to his grate, and immediately felt despair. Was no one here capable of keeping a fireplace clean and swept? And really, what else had the man to do with his time? But she knew why Power had not taken pains over the cleanliness of his cottage. He had grown from infancy with staff paid to do everything for him. And while he may preach liberty and equality, those sentiments clearly did not extend to cleaning up after himself.

She set the pan and brush she had brought down near the fireplace, defeated for a moment by its squalor. The desk, then, first. It might yield something to cheer her.

The first page she picked up appeared to be a letter to an unknown confidant. No salutation, no address, no polite inquiries into the recipient's health. Instead the page was full of Power's own despair.

'I confess, the deprivation of movement has affected me most grievously,' he wrote. 'It has coincided with a malaise of spirit of which I cannot rid myself. My captivity is now evident from morning to night, amplified by my small rooms and the walls within which I am permitted to move. I no longer have the luxury of walking until I can see nothing of the works of men, and imagining myself free, perhaps even alone on this island. The restrictions on my reading materials and writing paper are also weighing heavily.'

Self-indulgent tripe, Hannah thought. But not the letter of a man who expected to escape.

She sifted through the other papers. There was one titled *A Treatise on the Colour of Magpie Feathers*, which Power seemed to have largely made up. Below the title, he had written, 'for Mr W. Gendron, natural scientist'.

She set aside those she could make sense of. Hannah had only recently come to reading, with Mr Monsarrat as her teacher. She had, he claimed, made remarkable progress, and he seemed as proud as if the achievement was his own. She didn't begrudge him – she was willing to admit in a small and quiet corner of her mind that she could at times be difficult to teach.

Still, the first documents she had read had been transcribed in Monsarrat's neat hand. Some of Power's writing was a different proposition altogether, wandering drunkenly across the page and ending in a splash of ink. Many of the pages seem to be musings on the trip here and his treatise on public administration. Hannah could hardly imagine a drier subject, but she supposed his recent confinement had left him with little option. Certainly, when she looked around the small room, there was a distinct absence of the books she would expect from someone of Power's education and inclinations.

She stacked all the papers, put them to one side of the desk. She would have to impose a severe scrubbing on it. The man clearly did not use a blotter, and ink had seeped through countless pages, pooling on the wood and then soaking into it in roseate blotches. His careless use did not, however, account for the smell from the corner of the room, where a stack of tin dishes stood, the remnants of past meals. It was apparent they had not been collected in some days, and chicken bones picked clean of flesh told her that his rations were significantly better than those of most convicts. He did not appear to appreciate vegetables or soup, though, some of which had crusted over and were beginning to putrefy and grow lovely lozenges of mould.

She snorted. It was one thing to think cleaning beneath yourself. It was another to have so little regard that you allowed food to fester in front of you.

The grate was the next task – there was no getting away from it now and she was dreading it: it cradled what must be several weeks' worth of ash and the charred stubs of logs and twigs, and she knew from experience that the stone of the hearth would be irreparably stained from being smothered so long. She also knew she would likely walk back out of the gate wearing some of the ash.

She went to the gate, rapped on it, and Ennis's face appeared around it.

'You don't look like a fellow who would desert his post,' she said.

'Neither am I, missus.'

'Nevertheless, I'm afraid I'm going to have to ask you to do exactly that for a short while. Have you seen the way the man lives! Does he always keep ancient food in the corner of the room? Perhaps he enjoys the colours it creates as it rots.'

Ennis chuckled. 'Difficult not to notice, with the smell,' he said. 'I would amuse myself sometimes by thinking that my mother would have his hide if he behaved like that under her roof. I would have told her about it, let her know I was better raised than a nobleman, but, well, I couldn't ask himself to write that!'

'A sensible woman, your ma sounds,' said Hannah. 'But even though our friend is no longer here, we still need to clean up after him. And I don't think anything less than a good soaking will work on those plates. Would you go and fetch a bucket of water and some soap from Mrs Brewster at the stores?'

Ennis looked hesitant.

'I promise, *a buachaill*, that you will not be chastised for it. The commandant himself has asked me to carry out this task, and I'm sure he would wish you to assist me.'

He sighed, shook his head. 'All right. In the interests of the greater good of the Empire, through making a corner of it a little less putrid.'

'Good man yourself,' she said, smiling.

She was tempted to secrete some of the less legible documents inside her waistband during Ennis's absence. It would feel like a betrayal, though, of a lad who had already been betrayed.

She had resigned herself to giving her pinafore a thorough soaking later, when it would be covered in smuts from the fireplace, and now knelt before the hearth with the pan and brush she had brought, startling a little at the creak of inexpertly laid floorboards beneath her knees. She inhaled what was likely to be her last breath of untainted air, and made a start.

As she had expected, billows of ash rose every time she disturbed the stratified remains of past fires. Her pan was full quickly, and she suddenly realised she had given no thought to what to do with its contents. She had noticed some holes dug by unknown night-time creatures underneath the foundations of the cottage and resolved to empty her pan there, where they would go unnoticed and rain would wash them away.

She tipped the contents out carefully, trickling them down so they didn't fly back up in her face. As she did so, she noticed that the grey mass of ash was not uniform.

During her frantic sweeping inside, her eyes half closed against the grit, she had failed to notice a few flecks of cream-coloured parchment. She set the pan down and picked them out. There were two. One was no larger than the pad of her thumb, and had part of a letter inscribed on it. Possibly a 'W', although what she could see of it did not match the jagged rush of Power's hand. It was more similar to Mr Monsarrat's writing, precise and flourished. The other fragment was larger and contained a part of a single word, 'nal', perhaps written by the same hand that had written the 'W' on the first fragment. It had the same evenness, with the loops on the 'L' giving it a little flamboyance.

Someone who scatters papers like falling leaves, preserves his scrawl, but burns a page with copperplate handwriting, she thought. I may just have found a wrinkle.

She went back in to load her pan, and this time watched carefully as she was doing it, feeling the grit clog up her eyes and forcing herself to keep them open. She was rewarded after a time with a third snippet of paper which the fire had declined to consume. It bore the end of one word, and the beginning of another: 'nal wi'.

Ennis would be back soon. As she moved towards the gate, listening for his footsteps, her eye snagged on a patch of grimed white. She picked it up, turned it over. A piece of cloth, embroidered with delicate blue flowers and green sprigs. Part of a dress maybe, or a handkerchief, and quite fine – or would have been before it had spent some time soaking up the dirt of Power's yard. And it did not seem to have fallen there by accident. It was not torn, as though caught on a nail. It had been very deliberately cut into a narrow strip.

While taking full documents would have been a betrayal of Ennis and insubordination in light of the commandant's order, no one had said anything about scraps of charred paper or fragments of cloth. Still, Ennis must not see them. She cast around in her mind for a secure way of conveying them, then gingerly untied the string which was holding the collar of her shirt closed and secreted the snippets of paper into the neck of her shift.

She had just tied her shirt again when she heard Ennis opening the gate. He was carrying a pail of water and a misshapen lump of soap. When he saw her he laughed. 'We should use all of this on you instead of the plates,' he said.

She adopted a look of mock sternness. 'And there will be no more of that from you, young Ennis, not if you want some tea later.'

'Well, it's clear you're not to be trusted unsupervised, Mrs Mulrooney,' he said. 'And having a liking for tea – and I do understand your shortbread is quite fine as well – I'd better keep you under close supervision. Here, bring those plates out. I'll make a start on them while you hunt down that dragon that's breathed all over you in my absence.'

Chapter 14

Monsarrat held out very little hope of getting further information from Power. He knew Brewster intended to try, Holloway too. They would not have any more success than he had, but he was still hoping to be present. Perhaps a misdirected word, an odd look might put him on the right path. Because for now he was no closer to discovering the identity of Harefield's murderer than he had been when he'd first set foot on the island. No closer to ascertaining who had sharpened a rusty axe, who had brought down the ladder, whether that ladder had had a man on it at the time. And hardly much closer to knowing why exactly Harefield had been put to death.

Holloway and Brewster both clearly thought they knew the why of it, but that was little comfort to Monsarrat. The dispatch of an experienced mariner could only be a boon to any attempt to escape by sea, despite the fact that another had been engaged in the interim. And they clearly felt they had no need of a man from the rarefied reaches of the governor's staff to make that conclusion official.

Holloway was standing behind Brewster when Monsarrat arrived at the commandant's office. Brewster was clutching a sheet of blank paper and holding a stick of graphite.

'Good morning, commandant,' Monsarrat said. 'I presume you are on your way to the guardhouse?'

'Mr Monsarrat,' said Holloway, 'you would do well to remember that the commandant's movements are no concern of yours.'

'Of course, Lieutenant Holloway. I merely wish to ascertain whether I could be of any assistance.'

'Stop fighting over me like a pair of alleyway tarts,' said Brewster. 'Yes, Monsarrat, I am going to see Power again. Hoping for enough information from him to put into a report, one that doesn't make me look like an ass.'

'Sir, I have some experience in the taking of depositions and the like,' said Monsarrat. 'So that you can concentrate on your questioning, I would be more than happy to transcribe for you. It might make the whole process more seamless.'

'We have no need of your assistance, Mr Monsarrat,' said Holloway. 'I will do the transcribing, and I assure you it will be perfectly adequate.'

Monsarrat smiled, bowed slightly. 'I have no doubt of it,' he said. 'In that case, Captain Brewster, I might prevail on you for permission to conduct some other enquiries. I would like to interview Mr Jones.'

'Jones!' said Holloway. 'The man wasn't even here when the murder occurred, you realise. You must really be casting around for busywork to want to talk to him.'

'On the contrary, I feel it's important to understand the type of people one encounters as the Maria Island bosun. It may lead us down interesting paths, ones we haven't yet considered. Unless, of course, you prefer me to accompany you.'

'No. Go and talk to Jones. 'But I want an update. And I expect it to show progress, Mr Monsarrat.'

'Of course, sir.'

'Otherwise,' said Holloway, 'the commandant might be moved to write to Mr Marley about the ineffectiveness of the Sydney transplant.'

'I see no reason to go that far, Holloway,' said Brewster. 'Yet, anyway. For now, Mr Monsarrat, I wish you good morning, and I assure you that I will fully brief you on anything that arises from our discussions which might have a bearing on your investigation. As for Jones, he left yesterday, to collect mail from the Hobart coach. I imagine he'll be back sometime this morning, but I couldn't say exactly when. The sea and those on it seem to operate to their own timetable.'

They worked in silence for a while, Ennis attacking the crusted plates with a cloth which was getting progressively dirtier, dipping it into increasingly murky water, while Hannah made repeated trips with pans full of ash out from the fireplace, and then swept those which dribbled out onto the floor.

'I wonder,' she said, when they were nearly finished, 'may I go to check on Mrs Brewster? Just to make sure she has no need of anything. Sometimes, a woman might confide something to another woman in matters about which her husband is ignorant.'

'Of course,' said Ennis. 'I've already left my post once this morning, to do so again would be tempting providence a little too much, I feel.'

'Good lad, then. I'll just drop these dishes in at the store on my way – remarkable job you've done, I thought at one point that we might have to take a chisel to them. First, though, I'd best clean myself up. I suspect the geese will be waiting for me, and I've always considered a white apron the most effective form of armour.'

He smiled, opened the gate for her and gave her a mock salute as she passed.

⌒⌒

Monsarrat found Mrs Mulrooney dunking her shirt in and out of a tub of grey water. She was dressed in an identical outfit, but the shirt she was wearing was starched and clean. Seeing the treatment its counterpart was receiving, the shirt no doubt hoped to avoid attracting the merest speck of dust.

He could not resist smiling. 'Mrs Mulrooney, I didn't take you for the type of woman to let your clothes get into such a state.'

She glared at him. 'Nor am I, as you well know. But I've never seen such a mountain of ash in any grate as that which I found in Mr Power's. I am lucky to have escaped without carrying half of it home in my lungs.'

'And was it worth it?'

'Well, I did find something. Whether it has any meaning, who's to say?'

She nodded towards the table, where she had laid out a few scraps of paper, little more than specks, none of them big enough to contain more than a word. And none of them did contain a full word.

'"Nal" and "wi"' said Monsarrat. 'I'll have to give this one some thought. I don't have my dictionary here, curse it. But I will make it my business to write down every word I can think of that contains those letters.'

'And there is this,' said Mrs Mulrooney, tapping the fragment with the letter W on it. 'A nice hand, I think. Whose, though?'

'Not the commandant's, that's certain,' said Monsarrat. 'I've seen his hand. Yes, this one is quite well executed, and if Brewster's reports are anything to go by, this would be beyond his capability.'

Then she held up the small scrap of cloth, ingrained with dirt, which dulled the bright blue of the cornflowers covering it.

'Could be anything, I suppose,' said Monsarrat.

'But rather feminine for a man like Power, don't you think?' said Mrs Mulrooney.

'Perhaps a souvenir from his wife or . . . or another lady,' said Monsarrat. 'Shall I return it to him?'

'I wouldn't be doing that, Mr Monsarrat. If it was precious to him, he certainly wouldn't have allowed it to become half-buried in the earth. Whether he deliberately placed it where I found it, or whether it was discarded and trampled, I don't know. But it may yet mean something, and if it does we would be silly to let it go.'

Monsarrat sat down at the table, picked up the fragments one by one, examined them again. 'You're remarkable, truly, to have discovered this much among the ashes and the dirt,' he said. 'And I know you want to find something. So do I. Nonetheless, it could be that these are simply leavings which carry no meaning.'

'Why did he burn them, then?' said Mrs Mulrooney. 'You should have seen the state of the man's desk – truly, Mr Monsarrat, you would never countenance it. He has papers there with so many scratchings-out that they cannot be of any further use to him, yet he has not thrown them away, or burned them, or done anything but leave them where they sit. If he has taken the trouble to walk over to the grate with these and placed them there, I would wager that they have some sort of bearing.'

'But what?'

'Mr Monsarrat, I know that you set great store by my powers of observation. But I cannot get any meaning out of these. Yet life sometimes turns on the smallest things, and these scraps may tell us more than the entire mess of documents which Power left so casually on his desk.'

Walter was sitting at the commissary's small desk when Hannah entered, having glared briefly at the sky to ensure it knew not to rain on her drying clothes. His elbows were on the table and his head was in his hands as he squinted at the ledger. His eyes, though, were fixed in one place, while the pen beside him showed no signs of having been used today.

'What's troubling you, young Mr Gendron?' said Hannah, sitting in the chair opposite him. 'I think you have read the same line in that ledger several times already.'

Walter looked up, and she saw his eyes were red and swollen.

'Power was my friend,' he said.

'And I wager he still is,' said Hannah, 'although you might find visiting him a little more difficult now.'

'He wasn't really my friend, though,' said Walter, without seeming to notice the tear which was now rolling down his face. 'If he was, he wouldn't have tried to leave.'

Hannah reached out, took one of the hands which had been propping up his chin.

'Now I want you to stop that nonsense right away, Mr Gendron. What Thomas Power did last night had nothing to do with his regard for you, of that I am certain. He was escaping captivity. He was not escaping your friendship.'

'He was treated well here though,' said Walter. 'I would measure his rations out myself – he got as much as the officers. And he got officers' rations of fuel as well.'

'Ah, men like Power, they don't like to be constrained, do they. They have too many big plans to be forced into little boxes, no matter how well they're fed. And he still believes that he has a role to play in liberating Ireland. That's why he ran, my boy, and you should not take it to heart.'

'He would not have been so constrained if it wasn't for me,' said Walter. 'When I hugged him Harefield saw. He was a nasty man and I know it was because of him that after that James had

Power restricted, stopped him going for walks. Do you think that is why he tried to run? Did he miss the walks?'

'Possibly, and a lot more besides. But he didn't run in the end. He is still here.'

'He might as well not be. James says I can't visit him, and Elizabeth doesn't want to either,' he said.

'Well, it probably wouldn't be appropriate anyhow for the commandant's wife to go and sit with a felon who had just attempted escape. But why do you think she doesn't want to? Is it because, as I understood, she is unwell today?'

'She's crying too,' Walter said. 'She's been crying all morning, so badly that she could not even get out of bed.'

'Perhaps she was sad, like you, that he had tried to leave.'

'No, no, that's not it. I did ask her. I went by there to check why she wasn't at the commissary and I told her that she could cheer up because Power was still here. And you know what she did?'

'I'm sure I couldn't begin to guess.'

'She threw a cushion at me! I mean, what is the point of throwing a cushion? If you are to throw something, surely it should be something heavy.'

'Why on earth did she do that?'

'She called me a fool,' Walter said, and his eyes began to shine again. 'She called me a fool, and she said that she wasn't crying because Power had tried to leave. She was crying because he hadn't succeeded.'

❧

Monsarrat was at a loss for something to do as he waited for Jones – an unaccustomed state for him, and one which he did not like at all. He knew he had to look occupied. If Holloway glanced out of the guardhouse and saw him wandering aimlessly up and down the dock waiting for Jones to return, he would no doubt say, 'Look, here is a man who was sent to do a job we could have done, and he is idle.'

Monsarrat was fairly certain he could talk his way out of that, but he'd rather not have to. Instead, he walked slowly up to the site where the hospital was trying to rise, and the tent next to it which served its purpose for now. Chester was there, of course. Having no orderly, he was called on to use his medical training not only for more complex procedures, but for bandaging, salving and the like.

Right now, he was engaged in bandaging the ankle of Milliner, the convict Monsarrat had met on the day he arrived: the Hatter, through whom contraband reportedly flowed.

Chester looked up, and nodded. 'When I was at the Royal London Hospital, Mr Monsarrat, it never occurred to me that I might one day be asked to treat wombat injuries.'

'Oh? I didn't realise they were aggressive.'

'They are not. But apparently the holes they dig are.'

'They've been digging them where they know we walk, sir,' Milliner said, a contrived breathlessness in his voice. 'Just where a man would put his foot, but covered by bracken, so you don't see it until it's too late. You would think, if you didn't know better, that they were trying to get us to leave.'

'Yes, well,' said Chester. 'Fortunately we do know better, don't we? There, that should help with any pain, although I have to say I can't see any swelling, and I remember well, Milliner, treating you last month for a goose bite.'

Milliner shook his head. 'But they are vicious, those geese. They attack without any threat. They are on you before you know they're there.'

'How is it, then, that you are the only one to have succumbed?'

'They go for the strong ones first, see,' said Milliner.

'And strong you must be,' said Monsarrat, 'for that suppurating wound on your foot to heal so fast. It looks as though it is back to building the hospital for you.'

'Oh, I've been taken off the hospital,' Milliner said. 'The commandant felt my talents suited me for more refined work.'

'Or perhaps he moved you because you weren't doing any work of any kind,' said Chester. Milliner ignored him and kept talking to Monsarrat. 'Turning chair legs, now, sir. We make very fine ones, so I'm told. So they want me back, I imagine.'

'I imagine they do,' said Chester, 'and I will take you.'

'Doctor,' said Monsarrat, seeing a chance right in front of him for some investigating, 'the matter I came to see you on wasn't urgent. I'd be more than willing to escort Milliner.'

'Now that, Mr Monsarrat, would be most welcome. Some-times, you see, people get bitten by something more threatening than a goose. It's the season for snakes, and I have been trying to make up and set aside sufficient stores of ointments which are known to be effective on snake bites. I do need get back to it, so thank you for your kind offer, I accept wholeheartedly.'

'I'm not the only one who's been away from his duties, Mr Monsarrat,' Milliner said as they walked back to the workshop. 'Young Ennis had a nap, I've heard.'

'Have you indeed. Well, I don't believe Private Ennis's nap was, shall we say, voluntary.'

'Oh, I know it wasn't. Laudanum, rumour has it. God knows how Power got a hold of it.'

'I couldn't possibly say. So it didn't run through your hands, then?'

'Mine? Mr Monsarrat, I assure you, I'm not a trafficker.'

Monsarrat raised an eyebrow. 'I have not come here, Milliner, to investigate smuggling and trading in the convict barracks. Nor do I intend to make it my business – *unless* I am obstructed in some way.'

'I am not obstructing you, Mr Monsarrat. What would I deal in? Where would I get it? Have you noticed the ocean surrounding us?'

159

Said to the wrong person, words like that from a convict could see the man spending the night, or longer, with Power in the guardhouse. They could even result in some flesh being removed from his back. Milliner, thought Monsarrat, was good at quick assessments. Good at deciding who would be trusted and who couldn't, at gauging how far he could go. And something about Monsarrat had clearly led him to conclude, as had Power, that Monsarrat was not a true figure of authority.

'I know, Milliner,' he said. 'I know you deal in rum, tobacco. What I don't know is what else you can get. In the absence of any other information, I may have to conclude the worst and report my findings to Commandant Brewster. And to Holloway, of course.'

Milliner shrugged. 'I confess to rum,' he said. 'Tobacco, sometimes. But laudanum? Not much call for it, and no way of laying my hands on it even if I did get an order. No way of laying my hands on anything for anyone, at the moment.'

'Why not?'

'I will simply say that Jones is a reputable bosun, but that others who have held his position have not been above taking their own share. An importer's fee, you might say.'

'Might you indeed. And someone so motivated would surely be able to lay their hands on laudanum.'

'Perhaps, had they been asked to. But they weren't. The only laudanum on the island resides in the commissary, watched over by the commandant's missus and her less than watchful brother.'

'You have little affection for Walter, then.'

'Actually, I am interested in commodities, and he's a kind lad, and a puzzle – will give with no hope of receiving. Gave me some tea, once, when I was coughing up catarrh. I don't understand it, but I welcome it. Come to that, Mr Monsarrat, do you think you could ask the commandant to assign me to the stores? I'm not made for hard labour.'

'Woodworking is hard labour?'

'To men like you and me. Those of us with something of a brain. Businessmen.'

'I am not a businessman.'

'Yes, you are, for have we not just made a business agreement? You have given me information, in exchange for your pledge not to notice any . . . unconventional activity.'

Monsarrat sighed. He did not want to be part of any pact with the Hatter. 'I could renege,' he said.

'Ah, but you won't. You understand the . . . the niceties of it. I can tell.' And he winked, smiled and covered the rest of the distance to the woodworking shop at a skip which should not have been possible for someone who had recently fallen victim to a deliberately placed wombat hole.

❧

Hannah knocked gently on the door of the Brewster cottage. She had noticed that Elizabeth tended to snap if she was in a delicate condition. She didn't want to give her any excuse.

There was no response. She risked a transit to the side of the house, where she could peer into the small window which showed her a partial slice of the parlour. Elizabeth was in her chair, a cup of tea next to her, her head slumped forward so that her chin rested on her chest.

She sees me, Hannah thought, as a convict servant. Convict servants don't rap on windows. Not if they want to remain unseen, able to stand in the corner and hear things. But she would not be hearing anything from Mrs Brewster in her current state.

She tapped her callused knuckles against the pane of glass which protected the cottage's living room from the enthusiastic blasts of wind rushing up the hill from the beach. She looked for a starting, a slight lift of the head, any indication that Mrs Brewster had heard her. But the woman remained still, and slumped and, Hannah thought, terrifyingly pale.

Hannah felt the malevolent tickle, the tightening in her chest which accompanied the realisation that something may be very wrong. She did not know whether she had time to run down to the commandant's office, raise the alarm, or whether time had already elapsed. She raced around to the front of the cottage, trying the door with such force that she fell forward into the hallway when it opened without complaint.

Why, she thought, would Elizabeth Brewster leave her door unlocked in a settlement full of convicts, with an unknown murderer among the few people here?

It was a question Hannah would have to tuck away in the corner of her mind for later though. For now, she let the force of her stumble through the door propel her into living room, knelt beside Elizabeth, gently tapped her cold cheeks. If the woman had been conscious, she would surely have lashed out at such insults, but there was no indication that she was receptive to any amount of tapping.

The teacup, half full, sat on top of a small silver tray. Hannah yanked it off the saucer. Mr Monsarrat had told her how the Parramatta police superintendent had checked whether she herself was breathing after the murderous Rebecca Nelson nearly took her life. She held the silver up to Elizabeth's mouth and checked it. There was a thin film of mist. She grabbed the woman's shoulders and shook, but Elizabeth's head lolled backwards and forwards in an alarming manner.

Hannah ran to the door, looked towards the barracks. She ran down the hill, nearly colliding with Ennis as he emerged.

'Ennis!' she screeched, scouring her throat as she did so. 'Ennis, run! Get Dr Chester, ask him to hurry. It's Mrs Brewster!'

Ennis looked up to where the sound was coming from, shielded his eyes with his hand so he could see her.

'Why? What's happened?'

'Just go, and tell Chester to run as he never has before.'

As he bolted off, she murmured: 'That graveyard is getting crowded. We don't want another plot dug there.'

Chapter 15

Turning away from the woodworking shop, Monsarrat could see a small slice of canvas framed against the crumbling headland that enclosed the bay. By the time he got down to the dock, Jones and his boat were close enough for Monsarrat to see that another man had joined him for the return journey. A man dressed in black with a white bib, like a cleric. Or a magistrate.

Monsarrat was waiting at the end of the dock when Jones drew alongside. His passenger stood unsteadily, moved his way over to the small wooden ladder which extended down from the dock, and began to climb. Monsarrat put his hand out to haul the man up the last few steps.

'Magistrate Ellison. An unexpected pleasure. You mentioned you wouldn't be here for another month.'

'Nor did I expect to be, Mr . . . Monsarrat, yes? But Jones here has given me to understand that a rather interesting event has taken place. I thought some legal expertise might not go amiss.'

'Very generous of you. I fear the commandant has lodged us in your cottage. I'm sure we can make arrangements to stay elsewhere.

'Not a bit of it, sir. You are more than welcome to share my cottage, although it rather lacks in the comforts one might expect in the more populous parts of the colony. For now, though, why don't you tell me what you know of the escape attempt?'

Monsarrat did, and in the process realised how little of it was clear. 'How Power knew the vessel was coming, what signal there was, who gave it, how he communicated – nothing has been found to shed any light on any of these aspects, and Mr Power himself is utterly silent on the matter,' said Monsarrat.

'Ah, but you are the one who raised the alarm, and the first to lay hands on him, how wonderful! I'm sure there will ultimately be an appropriate reward for you, sir.'

'I require no reward, magistrate, but thank you. The whole business has rather overshadowed my purpose for being here, and I would as soon quickly resolve the matter of Harefield's killer and return to Parramatta.'

To where, he hoped, his letter was winging its way to Grace O'Leary, whose face once more floated to the forefront of his mind as Parramatta was mentioned.

'Well, I will do everything possible to ensure that happens with all haste,' Ellison said. 'May I ask, though, where is Power now?'

'He is being held in the guardhouse. Being interviewed by the commandant and Lieutenant Holloway at present, I understand.'

'Best get me there, then. The sooner Power claps eyes on me and realises the gravity of the situation, the better, wouldn't you agree?'

Monsarrat was not overjoyed at the idea of returning to the guardhouse, only to be rebuffed again by the noxious Holloway. With a magistrate in tow, however – and one who had travelled wearing his magisterial garb – Monsarrat felt a little more confident of gaining entry.

Outside the guardhouse Ellison lifted his hand to the door and pounded on it three times. Holloway appeared, his mouth already in a snarl. Monsarrat expected the expression to change when Holloway saw Ellison. And the scowl did slip. But it was evident that Holloway was very unhappy to be interrupted.

The magistrate nodded briefly at him, and stood on tiptoe so that he could see over Holloway's shoulder.

'Captain Brewster, you have had a busy few days, I understand. May I come in?'

Brewster looked up from the pages he'd been scribbling on, grimaced distractedly and stepped outside to greet them.

'We'll all have to breathe in. Henry, we weren't expecting you for another few weeks, were we? I'm afraid I've rather given away your house.'

'Yes, so I've heard, but don't trouble yourself over it. You're right, it was another three weeks before I was due to return. But the news of the activities of our friend here has positively flown across the water, and I thought you might have need of somebody with some judicial authority.'

'No trial needed,' said Holloway. 'He attempted escape. That is the beginning and the end of it.'

'Ah, yes, so he did. And of course he will be punished for it. There remains the matter of the bosun's death. While those two vortices are swirling around in proximity to one another, there is potential for things to get muddled. Legally speaking. I am here to prevent that.'

'And grateful we are,' said Brewster. 'I tell you, if you can get something out of him, I'll give you my own cottage. He is resolutely silent on the matter of whom he planned this escape with.'

'Need there have been accomplices?'

Holloway snorted. 'You are not, surely, suggesting that a whaler happened to make its way to Darlington Bay, where no whaler has come in so close, and then decided to lower

165

a rowboat over the side and make for the shore at the precise moment Mr Power was running down to the beach?'

'Yes, well, I take your point. Still, these things are often not as one initially believes. May I?'

Holloway stood aside and Ellison edged himself into the door. He went over to the guardhouse bars and looked steadily at Power, who turned his head on the bench and returned the gaze, smiling.

'I will do what I can, gentlemen,' Ellison said. 'Because if there's one thing that I can assure you of, it's that Mr Power knows exactly what he should say.'

Power and Ellison continued to stare at each other in silence for a few moments. If they had still been talking, Monsarrat might have missed the sound of running feet on the gravel outside the building.

It was impossible, though, to miss Ennis as he tried to push the door flat against the wall, sandwiching Holloway behind it.

'Oh for God's sake!' said Holloway. 'Is there no end to the interruptions? Private, you are confined to barracks for the next twenty-four hours.'

Ennis nodded briefly. 'As you wish, sir, but perhaps we can discuss my punishment later. It's your wife, captain. You need to come at once. She has been taken gravely ill.'

◈

By the time Brewster had sprinted up the hill to his cottage, his wife was lying on her side next to a pool of vomit. Her eyelids were fluttering and she emitted the occasional cough, ejecting more dribbles down her chin. She showed no inclination to move away from the substance she had just coughed up. It was, Hannah thought, the most beautiful ugliness she had ever seen – a woman of such loveliness, with the pallor of the grave, covered in her own muck and alive because of it.

When Dr Chester had arrived, Hannah was holding Elizabeth's hand, shaking her, dragging her eyelids open and doing anything else she could think of which might elicit a response.

Chester had dragged Elizabeth onto the ground and placed her on her side. He shoved his fingers down her throat, jabbing in and out. For a moment, it seemed hopeless, even disrespectful. The defilement of a corpse. But then she convulsed once, twice, opened her mouth and let fourth a watery stream. Chester was unable to withdraw his hand in time but he didn't seem to mind. He inserted his fingers again and allowed another foul-smelling torrent to wash over them.

Hannah was ineffectually dabbing Elizabeth's forehead with a damp cloth when her husband entered.

'For the love of God, man, what is happening?'

The doctor was kneeling by Elizabeth's side, with one of his trouser legs soaking up some of her emissions. He had her wrist in the fingers of one hand, his pocket watch in the other.

'Still thready,' he said. 'Too much so. But I do detect a slight stabilisation. She may, and I stress may, be recovering. Not quickly enough for my liking, mind, but there is hope, commandant.'

'Hope ... But what could have done this? What possible disease? Are we facing a plague?'

'No plague, commandant,' said Chester. 'Some sort of poison, I suspect.'

Brewster moved around his wife until he was standing at her head. He did not stoop to stroke her forehead or pat her shoulder. Of course there wasn't much room, with Hannah mopping the woman's brow and Dr Chester still tending to her.

'But who would have poisoned her?' Brewster asked.

The doctor cleared his throat. 'Well, clearly that is something to be ascertained in due course. But you must prepare yourself, Captain Brewster, for the possibility that there was no third party involved.'

'No third party? You don't mean . . .'

Hannah had had quite enough of this useless prattle over a woman's body. 'Can I suggest, gentlemen,' she said, barely controlling the quaver in her voice, 'that we leave the hows and whys until after the lady has been attended to. Doctor, can she be moved?'

'Yes. However, she will need someone with her. We do not want to have brought her this far back into life only to have her choke should she vomit again.'

Hannah looked at Captain Brewster. Waited for him to say he would not leave his wife's side, would not even blink until she had recovered her strength.

Instead he glanced at Hannah. 'Mrs Mulrooney, would you be kind enough? Perhaps another woman . . . Well, she will need to be cleaned, I expect.'

'Very important that she be in a state of cleanliness at this juncture,' Hannah said, immediately chastising herself for the sarcasm. But truly, the man was the living end. He was quickly beginning to rival Thomas Power as the island's most maddening denizen. He might, if he kept at it, even surpass the geese.

'Of course, sir,' she said, slathering her words with as much civility as she could bear. 'I would be delighted to do whatever is needed for Mrs Brewster as she recovers.'

Brewster merely nodded. Chester stood, seeming not to notice the vomit which was now dribbling down the leg of his trousers. 'Good woman,' he said. 'I will look in on you in a short while. Keep the cool cloth on her forehead. Make sure she's still responsive, that her breathing is steady. And fetch a basin from the kitchen. It's likely we haven't seen the last of . . .' He looked down at his trousers.

'There's a canvas cloth drop sheet in the boot room, Mrs Mulrooney,' Brewster said. 'Fetch it, if you please. That way the coverlet will be protected.'

He turned away immediately, and it was probably just as well. Hannah didn't know whether he would have noticed the unrestrained contempt in her gaze.

Chester and Brewster carried Elizabeth into the bedroom, laid her on top of the canvas Hannah had grudgingly placed there. Elizabeth was beginning to moan now.

'I hope she's not in any pain,' said Hannah.

'No, no, that's a good sign,' said Chester. 'It means she's beginning to recover.'

'Commandant, where are her nightclothes kept?' she asked.

'There in that dresser,' said Brewster, waving his hand in the general direction of the corner of the room. 'If she seems quiet, could you clean whatever that is on the floor of the parlour.'

'Sir, she really should not be left even for a moment,' said Chester.

'Oh, I'm sure a few minutes won't hurt. You're efficient, aren't you, Mrs Mulrooney? Now, Chester,' Brewster said, steering him towards the door, 'I would like to talk to you in private.'

Chapter 16

As soon as Ennis had brought the news, those in the guard-house had jostled to be the first one out and on their way up the hill. Monsarrat assumed it was worry motivating Brewster's headlong rush, but they had taken only a few steps when Brewster turned. 'Whatever is happening, a stampede will not help it. Kindly stay where you are, gentlemen. I will be back as soon as I can.' And with that he sprinted, perhaps less quickly than Monsarrat would have, up the hill.

Monsarrat was left standing there with Ellison and Lieutenant Holloway in a puddle of frustrated expectations. Eventually Holloway said, 'I best get back to the prisoner.'

Ellison reached out his hand to touch Holloway's forearm, a gesture which Holloway tolerated without any answering move.

'Lieutenant, I applaud you for your conscientiousness. However, there are certain legal conventions to be observed here. Perhaps it would be best, with your approval, of course, if I spent some time with him myself.'

Monsarrat could see the conflict playing out in Holloway's face – the desire to assert his reflected authority at war with the soldier's love for regulation, for the observation of statute.

The hidebound soldier won.

'As you wish, magistrate,' he said. 'I will join you in half an hour, with your approval. I have, as it happens, another matter to attend to in the interim.'

'Of course, lieutenant. I look forward to seeing you.'

Monsarrat did not quite know what to do with himself. He could see Jones struggling to hoist some crates from the stern of his little cutter up to the dock, his task made more formidable by the lack of cooperation from the tides, which were now at their lowest ebb.

'Almost done, but uncommon of a gent like yourself to offer, thank you,' said Jones, after Monsarrat had gone down and offered him help.

'You're lucky Power didn't take this boat,' said Monsarrat.

'How could he do that from the guardhouse?'

'During his escape, I mean.'

'Oh. Well, he couldn't have, Mr Monsarrat. It wasn't here. Neither was I. Regular mail trip, you see. I often stay over.'

'Regular. So he knew there was a good chance you wouldn't be here?'

'I suppose so. Hardly a secret.'

'Hmm. Much mail this week, by the way? I am hoping to receive a letter from Sydney.'

'No. There often isn't a lot. Mr Ellison occasionally gives me a letter for the commandant. He tells me he usually writes to Mrs Brewster, too, after a visit. She always tries to make sure he's comfortable, well fed. He likes to thank her.'

'And who collects the mail here? Do you bring it around yourself?'

'No, I just bring it to Mrs Brewster. I think Walter takes anything which needs taking to the commandant, the surgeon and the barracks.'

He looked behind Monsarrat's shoulder, raised his eyebrows as Holloway came thumping down the dock as though he was about to prevent another escape.

'Anything?' he asked Jones.

'Mr Holloway, I only took that letter for you four days ago. I would not be expecting an answer for another few days yet.'

Holloway glared at Jones, then turned to Monsarrat.

'And you have nothing to occupy you in the investigation of the death of Jones's predecessor?'

'I remind you, Mr Holloway, that I am not part of your staff and not yours to command, as I'm not a soldier.'

Holloway ostentatiously drew his eyes from Monsarrat's toes all the way up to his face. 'No, you're not, are you? You're not of the stuff for it. The question is, what stuff are you made of, Mr Monsarrat? That is something I would very much like to know the answer to.'

As Holloway stalked off to the barracks, Monsarrat found himself pitying whichever subordinate he encountered in such a temper.

Monsarrat spotted Dr Chester, who was walking quickly down the hill, stumbling on the rutted ground as he went. By the time he caught up with Chester, the doctor had his hand on the commissary door.

'Is all well, doctor?'

Chester turned sharply, opened his mouth, closed it. Looked at the door and back to Monsarrat, and stepped towards him.

'To be honest,' he said, almost whispering, 'everything's a long way from well. Mrs Brewster has . . . well, she's suffering. Thank God she has your Mrs Mulrooney with her.'

'And Mrs Mulrooney – she is well?'

Monsarrat knew what nursing the young Honora Shelborne in Port Macquarie had cost his friend. He did not know whether she could pay such a price a second time, after all that had happened since.

Chester nodded. 'And coping admirably. You may have to do without her for a while, though.'

'Of course, if it will be of assistance to Mrs Brewster and the commandant.'

At the mention of the commandant Chester snorted derisively. 'Forgive me, Mr Monsarrat. The whole thing seems to have stripped away my circumspection.'

'I thought you and the commandant were on good terms?'

'It is a very small island, Mr Monsarrat, and one which contains few people whom James Brewster considers even vaguely appropriate to socialise with. I happen to be one of them.'

'You don't care for him?'

Chester jammed his lips together for a moment, then shook his head. 'When I came here, Mr Monsarrat, I had thoughts of improving the health of this island. Nutrition, sanitation, that sort of thing. I laid a plan in front of Brewster. Do you know what he said? These prisoners weren't worth it. I was to stitch them up when needed and ... how did he say it ... save my more libertarian impulses for my return to Sydney. I dine with him on occasion because I can't avoid it. And for Walter. I always leave as soon as is polite.'

'For Walter? You have concerns?'

'The boy is an innocent, frequently he finds himself catching the edge of the commandant's tongue. Perhaps worse – who knows.'

❧

Elizabeth was breathing evenly now. She was clean, in a nightdress, and Hannah had removed the insulting canvas from the bed so that Elizabeth could lie where she belonged.

There was a rocking chair next to the bed, which Hannah sat in, listening to the occasional complaint from the geese outside, the shouting of men on the hospital site. Watching the light change as the day wore on. And checking for any sound from the woman nearby. She was thinking a lot of her last vigil by the bedside of a commandant's wife, one that had also resulted from poison. That poison had been administered by a beautiful young man with an ugly wound which could only be salved by the death of Honora – who had done him no wrong. But Elizabeth Brewster had tipped the poison down her throat willingly if Dr Chester's hunch was to be believed. And while Hannah had no quarrel with Chester, whether or not it was to be believed was a matter on which she had yet to settle her mind.

The occasional baleful honk of the geese was replaced by a crescendo of them, all honking at someone approaching the house, someone with the temerity to do so without bearing shortbread.

The door to the outer room opened, and then the door to the bedroom. Chester, wearing a different set of trousers, craned his head around the door frame. 'Feels odd, don't you know, letting myself into the commandant's bedroom like this.'

'I am sure Mrs Brewster wouldn't mind,' said Hannah. 'You are here for her, after all.'

Chester approached the bed, ran his eyes over the woman in it. 'I perceive some colour. I will be sure to report that to Walter – he's distressed, as you can imagine. You are to be commended, Mrs Mulrooney. She looks clean and comfortable, and that dreadful canvas is gone. Has she woken? Said anything?'

'Nothing anyone could understand,' said Hannah. 'A few mumblings, that's all.'

'Mumbling is better than nothing,' said Chester, picking up her wrist. 'Her pulse is stronger. She seems to be out of immediate danger.'

'I'm sure the commandant will be delighted to hear it,' said Hannah.

'Yes . . . I wonder, Mrs Mulrooney, would you bring him the word? He is back in his office now. Some urgent dispatches needed writing, apparently. I don't believe constant watching is required now, and the commandant might have another task for you while his wife is incapacitated – assuming Mr Monsarrat can spare you, of course.'

'Oh, I'm sure Mr Monsarrat will do what's needed for the greater good,' said Hannah.

'Yes. He does seem the type. In fact, have him call on me later, if you please. There is a matter I would like to discuss with him.'

Hannah stood, bobbed and left Mrs Brewster in the care of the doctor. Perhaps, she thought as she walked down to the bay, she was being uncharitable towards Captain Brewster. Perhaps he was every bit as shaken as he should be but had adopted the practice of some men, who saw emotion as weakness, burying it in clipped orders and blank faces. Perhaps now he was pouring his agitation out into reports.

He emitted a flat 'come' when she knocked.

'Commandant, the doctor bids me inform you that your wife is recovering. She is still not awake, but it seems she is no longer in imminent danger of death.'

Brewster raised one eyebrow. 'Thank you,' he said and went back to his document.

She had hoped he would jump from his desk, race up the hill, take his wife's hand and kiss it. But she had known, really, that he wouldn't.

'Sir . . . The doctor suggested I ask you whether there is any service I may perform as your wife recovers.'

Brewster leaned back in his chair, massaged the bridge of his nose with his thumb and forefinger, and exhaled slowly. 'I have had Walter in here twice today. Asking about where the sugar is kept, whether there is enough salt pork. Will probably inquire about the location of his own backside next. I understand you assisted in the commissary before. Can you keep an eye on him again tomorrow? And clean yourself up a bit. Your apron looks disgraceful.'

Hannah nodded, murmured a platitude about her hopes for his wife's recovery, and backed out. As she was closing the door, she saw he had already gone back to his document. She was about to turn towards the commissary when she noticed a familiar dark figure on the dock, leaning slightly forward as he walked, hands clasped behind his back. She went down to meet him. He looked up, smiled distractedly when he saw her. 'How fares Mrs Brewster?'

'She will live, by the looks. I have to say, Mr Monsarrat, sitting beside a woman in a bed, dealing with the scorn of an officer who hates convicts . . . It's all feeling a little like Port Macquarie.'

'As would any isolated penal settlement, I imagine,' he said. 'A large group of people who wear a criminal stain, and a smaller group of people who are tasked with making sure that they don't escape, kill each other, or rebel, and you will get a similar result, wherever you go. But this is not altogether like Port Macquarie, Mrs Mulrooney. This place is in the grip of a man who seems incapable of feeling. And this time he's in charge.'

'Yes. The commandant is proving an odd one, that's for certain.'

'As a matter of fact, I was speaking of Thomas Power.'

Hannah sighed. 'Oh, he's not such a bad man in himself,' she said. She could see Monsarrat adjusting himself to her new tolerance of Power. 'I would not take up a pike for him and go to the barricades,' she assured him.

They walked back up past the commandant's cottage, along the small track which had taken Monsarrat to the light, towards those extraordinary striated cliffs. Hannah told him about the scene at the Brewster's house, the detachment of the commandant, but soon felt herself running out of the strength needed to entice any more words out of her mouth.

'You are quiet, my friend,' said Monsarrat.

Hannah looked sideways at him. 'You forget. The weight of it. The way it chokes you, to be in a small place like this, in this case knowing that the only law is administered by a man who seems almost criminally uninterested in his wife. Tell me, do you feel the commandant has given you everything you need? Has he opened all doors for you as you pursue this murderer?'

Now Monsarrat was quiet for a while. Eventually he spoke. 'To a point. He has not put any overt impediments in my way, but I suppose you could say that he has been less than accommodating in some regards.'

'And why, tell me, do you think that is?'

'I had thought that he was used to running things at his own pace here, that he saw the insertion of a man from Sydney into this settlement as no reason to change his way of doing things.'

'Perhaps, Mr Monsarrat, you need to think again. Because an odd idea is beginning to take hold of me, one that refuses to go away, even when I call it nonsense. I am wondering whether our killer is currently sitting in his office, scratching away at reports on the flax crop.'

Chapter 17

If the suggestion had come from anyone else, Monsarrat would have dismissed it immediately. Brewster was revealing himself to be a lacklustre administrator, someone whose preferred response to a terrible event seemed to be a desire to pass the issue onto a visitor like Monsarrat, and then complain of lack of immediate progress. He was not, Monsarrat would have thought, the type to take matters into his own hands in such an emphatic way as committing murder himself.

But the notion was coming from Mrs Mulrooney. A woman who, Monsarrat had to admit, was probably more intelligent than him.

'Very well then,' he said. Neither of them felt like sitting and both found comfort in movement. The falling night meant they couldn't go far, but they were pacing back and forth along the first stages of the path which led to the light. 'I suppose you had better tell me why you think the commandant himself might be responsible.'

'Well,' she said, with the excited air of somebody about to indulge in their favourite pastime, 'first of all, I'd better tell you who else I suspect of wrongdoing.'

'It is an island full of convicts. Fertile ground, I would have thought.'

'Do not make a jest of this, Mr Monsarrat, clever as you think yourself. A woman's life nearly ended because of it.'

The smile left Monsarrat's face, and he nodded solemnly. 'I am sorry. It has been a confusing few days, and sometimes making light is the only way to convince myself of my ability to survive it. Go on. Who are the malefactors in your view?'

'Using big words will not make me think you any more intelligent, either,' said Mrs Mulrooney. 'What would that mind of yours say to the suggestion that Elizabeth Brewster and Thomas Power were . . . closer than one might expect?'

'By closer, you mean . . .'

'As close as it is possible to be.'

'*Lovers*? Why?'

'I told you, I have seen her standing by the wall surrounding his cottage, staring at it. When I visited him the day before he tried to escape, remember he asked me about her. And she was very agitated the night of the escape.'

'Well, her husband was conceivably in danger. None of us knew whether those in the boat had a musket.'

'Yes, I assumed the same, at first. But her upset could also have been because of Power's recapture. Walter says she was crying because Power hadn't succeeded.'

'But if Elizabeth was in love with Power, wouldn't she want him to stay?'

'Perhaps not. Perhaps she knew where he was bound, was planning to join him.'

'And if they *were* involved,' said Monsarrat, 'I wonder if she . . .'

'Was responsible for signalling that the ship was near? I would say so. She was just coming in when we went to the cottage to warn the commandant. Neither of us heard a bell or a shot, or saw a light. But Power must've had some means of knowing when to make his dash down to the beach. And she could easily have had a hand in making sure messages went back and forth, although how . . . Well, I haven't worked it out yet. But I am increasingly certain that she was complicit in his escape.'

'I will grant you, it does sound plausible,' said Monsarrat. 'Jones tells me she often takes the mail and delivers it. But how does this convince you that her husband is our killer?'

Mrs Mulrooney stopped for a moment to allow a large wombat and its child to trundle across the path, the baby with its nose to its mother's rear. They were close to a clearing where some felled trees littered an open, grassed area with a view of the ocean. She made to sit down on one of the logs, patted the vacant section next to her. Monsarrat would have preferred not to sit, actually. When one's legs were so inconveniently long, sitting on a log was rather uncomfortable, with the choice between bringing your knees up to your chin or stretching out ridiculously. But he knew better than to disobey when Mrs Mulrooney beckoned.

'Now, this is where I get a little uncertain,' she said. 'This is where I make assumptions, which I detest. But assumptions are all we have right now, so here are mine. Brewster, somehow, discovered the liaison. It was he who was responsible for poisoning his wife.'

'But even the doctor suggested there was no one else involved, and the lady herself can't tell us.'

'Not at the moment. But she may yet.'

'And why would Brewster have killed Harefield?'

'Perhaps he suspected Harefield of carrying messages for Power. Perhaps Harefield had also discovered the liaison and was threatening to expose it. Let's not forget that the man had already been spreading speculation about another romance. If another scandal he spread were to become common knowledge, what would that mean for Brewster's advancement?'

'I see your point.'

'And ask yourself, Mr Monsarrat, who knew where Harefield was likely to be? Who could avail himself of any axe in the settlement? Who is the only person who would not be questioned over his whereabouts if he was not where he was expected to be for an hour or two?'

'The path you are leading us down, my friend, is the most tangled on this island.'

Mrs Mulrooney smiled. She walked over to the edge of the clearing closest to the cliff. Monsarrat followed, dragged as always by the force of her personality.

'It will make Brewster look good, I should think, to have prevented Power from sailing off,' she said. 'Let's assume for a moment that he found out about Power's escape. That he knew when it was to be, the manner in which it was to take place. Which would look better in his report? Increasing security to prevent it? Or bravely charging down the hill, musket in hand, leading his men as they splashed into the water after the miscreant?'

'Actually, I was the first in the water.'

'Well, I would be amazed if your involvement made it into the official report.'

'Why then did he not come immediately when we pounded on his door?'

'That I don't know. Perhaps he knew he had time, thought it couldn't hurt to pretend to be ignorant of the situation.'

Monsarrat was silent for a moment. 'It's an interesting story,' he said, finally. 'One which has possibilities.'

'And they will remain just that unless we are able to find something else, something stronger. Because at the moment we've built a very pretty framework, and we've managed to drape the facts over it so that they fit quite nicely. But the whole thing might collapse with the first puff of wind.'

Magistrate Ellison's arrival had caused all sorts of upheaval. It had of course upset Holloway. His was no longer the second-most authoritative voice on the island, and he had potential competition when it came to influencing the commandant. Monsarrat did not know yet if the magistrate had been able to extract anything from Power. He thought not, and Holloway would be crouched in wait for a misstep. But the disruption extended to more prosaic matters as well. Chiefly, where Ellison was to sleep.

Brewster had come up with a solution. When Monsarrat and Mrs Mulrooney returned, Brewster and Ellison were standing on the patch of grass between the two cottages overlooking the bay. The soil here was heavy with moisture, swelling and opening fissures between patches of grass, objecting to these structures which stood where the wombats had once grazed. The two men were looking out to sea and Brewster was gesturing wildly, drawing his arm in a slash down from the cottages, past Power's old enclosure to the bay, no doubt describing the escape attempt and its frustration at his gallant hands.

I must stop thinking like this, thought Monsarrat. I must not assume that he is motivated by sloth and glory. An odd combination, to be sure, but not an unknown one. There were those whose aversion to work was only matched by their hunger for glory. These warring impulses could create an odd tension. Who knew what someone in their grip might do?

For now, it seemed Brewster was actually doing something. 'Ah, Monsarrat. We have a few matters of logistics to discuss. Night will be upon us soon, and we now have an additional guest.'

'Naturally, I will cede the cottage to the magistrate himself,' said Monsarrat. 'Perhaps a bunk could be found for me in the soldiers' barracks. Mrs Mulrooney, though . . .'

'Everything is arranged. I will spend the night in the barracks,' said Brewster. 'Mrs Mulrooney can stay in our cottage with Elizabeth. As for the magistrate, he will indeed stay in his cottage, with you.'

⚜

Mrs Mulrooney had managed to procure some salt beef from the commisary, and had given Jones a coin in exchange for a plump bream. Brewster was dining with his officers in the mess, probably reliving the glory of Power's aborted bolt for the horizon, so Monsarrat and Ellison ate a meal prepared by Mrs Mulrooney before she went to the cottage next door to take up her vigil.

'Not married, are you, Mr Monsarrat?' said Ellison, after they had been eating in silence for a few minutes. 'I can tell, you know. You are perfectly comfortable with yourself, not used to being an appendage.'

'As it happens, no, I'm not. That may change, though.'

Was he right? It was the first time he had heard the words come out of his own mouth. It was time, he supposed, to either marry or make an equally strong commitment to confirmed bachelorhood. Had he not met Hannah Mulrooney and Grace O'Leary, had he not in them found an affirmation that mankind was not perpetually venal and grasping, he might have opted for the latter. Now, though, he felt he would not mind a companion, even if it did mean he had two women instead of one telling him what to do.

'Power is married, you said?' he asked.

'Oh yes. Seven children. Before Marley cracked down, Power wrote his wife long, rambling letters, you know. Criticised everything about this place, said he was treated deplorably, told her the convicts here were of the worst possible description. Can you imagine if he was at Macquarie Harbour?

'You know a lot about him,' said Monsarrat.

'I make it my business to know a lot about everyone.'

'And no female companionship during his long exile,' said Monsarrat. 'Must be difficult.'

'Ah, well, he manages . . .'

'Manages? On an island so full of men?'

'What I meant,' said Ellison quickly, 'is that he manages to survive without.'

'Candidate for the sainthood, I'd say.'

Ellison smiled. 'I've heard Mr Power called many things, Mr Monsarrat, but that's the first time I've ever heard him called a saint.'

Ellison took a surprisingly healthy pull on his glass of port, drawn from a bottle which was now nearly empty.

'As for marriage, I would not be in such a hurry if I were you,' he said. 'My wife – God rest her soul – was a wonderful woman. But, and I feel a little disloyal saying this, life has become less complicated since her departure. One can get very used to pleasing only oneself. And, if you forgive me, at your age you've had a lot of time to get used to it.'

After another draught of port, he leaned across and patted Monsarrat's knee companionably.

'Your housekeeper seems a sensible woman. Nice face, too. Is she married? Silly question, of course – she would hardly be called Mrs Mulrooney if she wasn't.'

'She is currently unattached. Although a very busy woman,' said Monsarrat.

'Of course, of course. Not frivolous, though, by the looks. The frivolous, they don't do well here.'

Mrs Mulrooney shuffled in just then to clear away the plates.

'I've some shortbread, if that's of interest to you,' she said. 'Together with tea, of course. Magistrate, if you don't mind my saying, adding a little tea to that port you've been drinking might not be the worst of ideas.'

Ellison threw his head back and laughed. 'You are quite right, my dear. Tea and shortbread would be delightful, thank you.'

184

Mrs Mulrooney looked over his head to Monsarrat and raised her eyebrows, and Monsarrat responded with an almost imperceptible shrug.

She deposited the shortbread in front of them a few minutes later, and carried in a tray with the tea things.

'I'll have to leave you gentlemen to pour for yourselves, I'm sorry,' she said. 'Dr Chester is with Mrs Brewster and is expecting me just as soon as I can get there.'

'Very good of you,' said Ellison. 'You must go, of course. Do not fret, Monsarrat and I will be able to take care of ourselves, and we promise not to burn the place down.'

Mrs Mulrooney cast a sideways glance in Monsarrat's direction, a look which told him she wasn't reassured.

After she had scurried into the darkness of the commandant's house, Ellison turned and clapped Monsarrat on the shoulder. 'Well, dear boy,' he said, with an avuncular familiarity made possible by the better part of a bottle of port. 'I hope you'll excuse me, but I do need to attend to some paperwork this evening. Perhaps, if you've no use for the kitchen table . . .'

He leaned towards Monsarrat, the fumes on his breath hazing the air between them. 'Should you ever want a hiding place whilst you're here, there's a loose floorboard near the hearth,' he said. 'You will find secreted there another bottle of fine port. I would offer you a glass, dear chap, but you've already told me that you don't indulge. Might I prevail on you to help me retrieve it? I believe it might be a long night.'

Chapter 18

Brewster and Chester were on their way out of the cottage when Hannah got around to the front. 'If there is any change in Mrs Brewster's condition,' the doctor said, 'please send for me at once.'

'Of course, doctor. And shall I send to the barracks for you as well, Captain Brewster?'

Brewster let out a short bark of a laugh. 'I have no medical training, I would be worse than useless. I am sure you and Dr Chester between you can manage.'

Hannah bobbed, all of her conscious mind bent towards preventing the contempt she felt making itself apparent in her face. 'Very good, gentlemen. Have a pleasant evening.'

She turned and walked away without waiting to be dismissed.

Hannah had hardly thought about the wealth which awaited her in Sydney since she'd landed on Maria Island. Here it seemed irrelevant. No amount of money would make the geese leave her alone, or bring Elizabeth any more quickly back to health, or soothe Walter's troubled mind.

But she thought of it now. All of those men I've heard you send to work on that house you believe no one knows about, she thought. All the lumber, and all the labour. I could probably pay for it many times over.

She made straight for the bedroom where Elizabeth lay, still in the nightgown she had worn the day before. The woman's pallor made her fine features look as though they were carved from blue-veined marble. Her eyes were open.

'Mrs Brewster, your husband sent me to take care of you. I hope you don't mind if I come in,' Hannah said.

Elizabeth contorted her mouth in what might have been attempted smile. 'I am grateful to have you here, Mrs Mulrooney. You are far more capable of attending to me than my husband.'

'I shall certainly do my best, madam. Now, to start, shall we get you into a clean nightdress? You have been wearing this one for far too long.'

Elizabeth inched herself backwards, so that she was sitting up, and Hannah put some pillows behind her head. 'Just over there,' Elizabeth said, waving her hand towards the side of the room. 'In the . . . oh. I suppose it would have been too much to expect . . .'

The wardrobe was in a dark corner of the room and of dark wood itself. The doors were open and clothing was spilling off the shelves onto the floor, clearly a result of James Brewster's swift packing for his barracks sojourn.

'He always does this,' said Elizabeth. 'Never occurs to him to put back what he's taken.'

Her eyes, Hannah noticed, were beginning to shine, and her jaw was set from the effort of preventing tears emerging.

'Don't distress yourself, now,' Hannah said. 'This is easily fixed. I'll get you a nightdress, we'll get you washed and later I'll set the wardrobe to rights.'

The next half-hour was taken up with delicate negotiations over how Elizabeth was to bathe. While she said she yearned to be clean, she was not inclined to reveal herself to anyone, even another woman.

'Dr Chester says you're not to be by yourself,' Hannah said.

'Yet I've been by myself for most of the afternoon and seem to have survived the experience.'

'All right, so,' she said. 'I will make you a bargain.'

'Will you now?' Elizabeth said. She smiled, not unkindly. The gesture showed Hannah she needed to expand the terms she was about to offer.

'Forgive me, Mrs Brewster, but your teeth – they could use some attention. I'll give you the privacy you want to attend to them, wash and dress. But I will be on the other side of the door and if I hear anything – the thump, say, of you falling to the floor – I'll be coming straight in. Without knocking.'

So Hannah stood against the blank-faced wood and listened, encouraged by sounds of gentle movement and the occasional drip of water.

'You can come back in,' Elizabeth called.

Her hair was wet but brushed, and she must have scrubbed her cheeks because they were a healthier shade of pink. She lay on top of the bed in her clean nightdress.

'And now – tea,' said Hannah. 'It has healing properties, you know.'

She started to smile at Elizabeth, but faltered when she remembered the woman had very nearly died from drinking a substance out of a teacup. Once more, in Elizabeth Brewster she could not help seeing the shade of Honora Shelborne, and she started to cry.

Hannah Mulrooney was not a crier, and prided herself on not being so. But the memory of the deaths of two young people always squeezed the air out of her lungs. Honora was one of those people. Even in Parramatta her ghost could be called forth by the sight of a passionfruit vine or a woman on horseback. Here, as Hannah stood by the bedside of this other beautiful wife of a commandant, there were three women in the room.

It would never have occurred to Elizabeth to find out anything about the life of a woman she viewed as a loaned servant. That was the difference between her and Honora. If the situations were reversed, Honora would have made it her business to know about Elizabeth.

The small degree of callousness which sat between them, though, was not enough to inure Elizabeth entirely to another woman's tears, particularly as they were springing from someone she viewed as practical above all else. Elizabeth pushed her hands down onto the mattress and hoisted herself further back so that she was sitting straighter than she had in more than a day.

'Whatever is the matter?' she said. 'The wardrobe, surely, isn't that much of a mess.'

Hannah smiled weakly, acknowledging the attempt at a joke. 'It's nothing, forgive me,' she said. 'I was remembering something . . . someone, but it is passing.'

'It can rush in on you, can't it? Grief,' said Elizabeth. 'Especially here. The isolation magnifies it. There are too few other souls to absorb it, so it is able to turn its full attention on you.'

Hannah risked the familiarity of patting Elizabeth's knee. Elizabeth took her hand and squeezed.

'I find,' said Hannah, 'that speaking of grief can help. Can't make it go away, of course. But giving a small piece of it to someone else can make the difference between . . . well . . .'

Elizabeth took her hand away, smiled to show it was not a rebuke. 'There is truth in what you say,' she said. 'But some grief is all of a piece. You can't break chunks off and give them away. There is still solace to be had, though. You mentioned tea?'

Hannah patted the bed briskly, stood. 'Indeed I did, and it will be with you shortly,' she said.

She found a bud vase in the kitchen and snipped a small gardenia off from those growing outside the cottage. On the

189

tray, with its teacup and pot covered in matching blue cornflowers, it looked rather pretty, she thought.

So did Elizabeth when she brought it in. 'This is lovely!' she said. 'The wonder of having someone else make the tea . . . You have no idea.'

Hannah went and knelt by the wardrobe door, folding clothes and putting them back where she hoped they went. Trousers and chemises and pillow slips. And, in one corner, handkerchiefs. She knew women who saw no point in folding handkerchiefs. She herself saw the unwillingness to fold a handkerchief as the beginning of the end of civilisation. So she picked them up and transformed them into neat little squares. The last one she picked up had a strip or two torn from it. And a design that Hannah had seen before. It was covered in blue cornflowers.

She had just made tea in a service covered in the same flowers, obviously a favourite of Elizabeth Brewster's. But that was not the first time she had seen the design. The first time was on the snippet of cloth she had found in Thomas Power's yard.

~⟞⟞⟶⟵~

After Monsarrat had said good night to the magistrate, who had already made a reasonable dent in the bottle of port from under the floorboards, he went into the small servant's room, where his nightshirt had been laid on the cot by Mrs Mulrooney before she left. He didn't change into it though. He lay down, fully clothed, and waited. He had no idea how long he would have to wait – some men could hold their liquor far better than others – but wait he would. It was not gentlemanly, he told himself, to riffle through another man's possessions, even if that man's bloodstream was so awash with port there was almost no chance of discovery.

There was something concerning about the magistrate. He appeared to harbour sympathies for Power, and certainly seemed to know a lot about him. Odd, too, that a magistrate whose jurisdiction covered not only Maria Island but also townships like Orford and Triabunna would race to the dock to make the journey over on such short notice.

There was probably nothing in it. But the situation seemed what Mrs Mulrooney might call wrinkly. And he would rather see those wrinkles smoothed out, one way or the other.

He nearly fell asleep himself, his waistcoat buttoned and his cravat tied. His eyelids kept drooping, and it took increasing strength of will to haul them open again. He did not have to struggle for consciousness, however, when he heard unsteady footsteps making their way towards the bedroom. Half an hour, he thought, and then I will chance it.

And it seemed he had chosen well, because when he opened the door of his room some time later, the snores could be heard throughout the house. Of course, the man may well have taken his papers to bed with him. But this was his house, and there was a chance he might feel comfortable enough, and be drunk enough, to leave things out.

Monsarrat had judged the situation correctly. Ellison had gone rolling off to his room, leaving his pen, ink and papers where they lay. The snores were still reaching Monsarrat, so he felt safe enough to pick up a page and read it. It was mundane, a letter from Ellison to his valet. He hoped to conclude his business here speedily, he wrote, and he would be home as quickly as he could. The next page was equally mundane, the paperwork of a functionary in a remote outpost. Crimes committed, sentences imposed. Samuel Johnson, for example, had been given one hundred lashes for stealing food from his master's larder. Harriet Wells, one week in the Cascades Female Factory for drunkenness. Crimes which could have been committed in Parramatta, or in Port Macquarie, and sentences which were neither extreme nor lenient.

But Monsarrat noticed that Ellison used a slightly different hand for the more official documents. The letter to his servant was written in a serviceable hand, clear and legible but lacking in any of the style which Monsarrat liked to think his own handwriting possessed. The official documents were a different matter. They were characterised by flourishes, curlicues and a number of other embellishments.

Monsarrat reached into his pocket, withdrew the scrap of paper containing the letter W which Mrs Mulrooney had found in Thomas Power's fireplace and held it against the same letter on a report to the lieutenant governor. One sentence started: 'Whereas Henry Dunkin, convict, has appeared before me on charges of . . .'

The letters were, as close as they could possibly be, identical.

Chapter 19

Hannah Mulrooney liked to be up by dawn. She enjoyed the feeling of getting a significant chunk of the day's business done before anyone else was about. Monsarrat considered himself an early riser, but she saw him as an amateur, a trier.

As the sun was rising she looked in on Elizabeth Brewster, who was sleeping peacefully now, the room as neat as it had ever been, her clothes safely contained behind the wooden doors of the wardrobe, together with a small scrap of torn blue-and-white fabric.

Elizabeth's colour had returned to the point where Hannah thought she could justify a trip outdoors, watching the day seep in from a bench outside the magistrate's hut, the same one from which she and Monsarrat had seen the whaler coming in. There was, Hannah thought, a held breath while the sun was in the process of getting itself fully aloft. A slight pause between the birds who yelled themselves hoarse at the first of the light, and the men and women who greeted it slightly later. It was at this time of day she could think best.

And she had a lot to think about.

She was already reasonably certain that Power and Elizabeth had been lovers. But if the strip of cloth was a token, why had it been discarded? And why would she not have given him a more meaningful object? Perhaps she felt it would be discovered, but it would be an easy thing to give him something like a ribbon from her hair. If it had been found by James Brewster, Power could easily have claimed it belonged to his own wife, that he'd carried it all this way across the seas.

The facts did not quite sit well together, did not mesh in the way they should. As she worried at them, she heard a noise, which she always resented at this time of morning. A footstep. Another soul laying claim to a part of the day that she considered hers alone.

Monsarrat was up even earlier than usual. He looked the worse for it. He had not shaved – unusual for him – and a dusting of whiskers was darkening the lower part of his face. His cravat was loose, and one waistcoat button was undone.

'You need to take yourself in hand, so you do, Mr Monsarrat,' she said. 'This kind of laxity in the way you present yourself – what would Eveleigh think?'

'He would be appalled, I have no doubt,' said Monsarrat. 'As I might be when I get sufficient rest to allow myself to care. I do, however, have a reasonable excuse. It was a late night.'

'You never got into that drink with him, did you? You know you've not the head for it, Mr Monsarrat, nor the stomach neither. Asking for it, drinking that sort of stuff.'

Monsarrat straightened his shoulders, seemed slightly put out. 'I didn't, as it happens. And I think he was quite relieved about it, too. Do you know he had another bottle secreted under a floorboard near the hearth? We must've walked over it several dozen times. And by midnight last night there was nothing left of that either.'

'He didn't drink two bottles of port in one sitting!'

'Oh, he did. And part of the reason I look the way I do this morning is that that much port can produce some quite remarkable snoring. But I made sure I put the time to good use. Ellison was kind enough to leave his papers on the kitchen table.'

'Was he indeed? Considerate of him. Save you the trouble of riffling through papers that were put somewhere private. You can tell yourself that you saw whatever you saw by accident. A little easier on the conscience.'

'That it is,' said Monsarrat. 'I still felt terrible going through them. Until I noticed something you might find interesting. Those fragments you found in Power's grate – the letter W. It's identical to the way Ellison writes it.'

Hannah pursed her lips. 'Now that is of interest. Is it a common way of writing it, though? Is there a usual way of doing such things among clerks?'

'There are a great many little rules, and I shan't bore you with them all. But the way one forms letters should be neat, certainly; each should have a decorative element to it. Beyond that, there is a broad range of individual differences. And I have never seen anyone write a letter – even a simple W – in the same way as the next man.'

'We know where the cloth came from too now,' Hannah said. 'I found the handkerchief it was torn from in Elizabeth Brewster's wardrobe. How it got to Power's yard, though . . .'

'Will hopefully reveal itself. In the meantime, I've been searching my memory for an example of a situation where a magistrate would write to a prisoner. Unsuccessfully. Whatever Ellison's reasons were for communicating with Power, it seems they were likely to be . . . unofficial.'

'Yes . . . like his unofficial hoard under the floorboards . . .' She turned towards the bay, which was beginning to sparkle now as the sun rose higher. 'I wonder . . . Mr Monsarrat, while I'm trying to extract information from the commandant's wife and pretend to enjoy the company of that sot Ellison, do you think you might like to do some work as well?'

'I might. What did you have in mind?'

'For an intelligent man, you can be idiotic, did you know that?' she said. 'The floorboards!'

'The floorboards?'

'The floorboards near the grate in Power's old cottage. We might find something useful has been under our feet all along.'

～～

Monsarrat could still hear the low growl of Ellison's snoring when he padded to his trunk to collect a small, well-thumbed book. He did not know whether Brewster had risen in the barracks, but it was early yet and if he was to endure the anxiety which went with pretending to be something he wasn't, he might as well use it to his advantage.

So when the young private who was stationed outside the guardhouse – and judging by his unfocused look had been so all night – was told to open the door in the governor's name, he had no hesitation in doing so.

Mrs Mulrooney was a fierce advocate of approaching things side-on. But an oblique strategy, Monsarrat feared, would not work with Power. The man was skilled at building verbal snares himself, would not fall for whatever clumsy device Monsarrat could construct.

So being direct seemed the way. It might yield nothing – very probably wouldn't – but it was the best he had. That, and a tactic which the uncharitable might describe as bribery.

'I imagine this is becoming quite tedious,' said Monsarrat. 'I did put in a word with the commandant, the paper and so forth. I do hope he obliged you.'

Power sat up and winced – no doubt due to being forced to lie on a rough board all night.

'Not yet,' said Power. 'Still, I am used to tedium now. I was in the process of constructing the next entry of my journal in my head – where I hope it will remain until I can transfer it to paper. Thank you for inquiring, by the way.'

'Not at all. I imagine you'll thank me rather more profusely when you see what I have for you,' said Monsarrat.

He fished the small book out of his pocket, turned it side-on and passed it through the bars. Power was on his feet in an instant. If he was still stiff, he was ignoring it in his eagerness to see what was in Monsarrat's hand.

'Catullus! My dear fellow, you did mention his volume has a place of honour in your library, and it makes the gift all the more welcome. Catullus can always cheer a fellow up. I do thank you quite profusely.'

'The only thanks I require, Mr Power, is that you not make the commandant or Mr Holloway aware that you possess this volume.'

'You need not trouble yourself on that score, Mr Monsarrat.' Power thumbed through the pages. 'And in Latin. Neither Brewster nor Holloway would know what they were looking at.'

'I must confess, neither do I,' said Monsarrat. 'Oh, not the book. Latin poses no problem for me – as a boy I translated these poems into English, you know. At least, those that were appropriate for a child's eyes.'

'Around a quarter of them, then,' said Power, smiling.

'Quite. So the Latin doesn't confuse me, but something else does, and it's a point on which you may be able to assist me.'

'I shall do whatever I can. As long as it doesn't turn on the issue of my escape and anyone else who may or may not have been involved.'

'As to that – I honestly don't know. What I do know is that you've been corresponding with Ellison. And it strikes me, as someone who is reasonably familiar with the workings of a penal settlement, as odd. I have never encountered a case where a magistrate would correspond with a felon.'

Power raised his eyebrows, walked slowly back to his bench and sat down, tucking Catullus into the breast pocket of his jacket and patting it. 'This volume will be safe with me, Mr Monsarrat. As will any information regarding who I do or don't correspond with. And as you say, it would be highly irregular for Ellison to be writing to me, or I to him. What on earth makes you think such a thing has occurred?'

'A scrap of paper found in your fireplace, actually,' said Monsarrat. 'Bearing the letter W, written in an identical script to Ellison's.'

'You are basing this supposition on a single letter?' Power chuckled.

'That and a few others. Fragments of them, anyway. I'm not sure what the complete words were, but you really must be more careful to ensure that when you burn something, it burns fully. Together with the W, you left another scrap of paper. The words "nal" and "wi". I have spent a lot of time, Mr Power, over the past day casting about the words which end in "nal", and there is one I keep coming back to. Signal. And the other one – will? With? Whatever the rest said, those letters are identical to ones in a recent report by our friend Mr Ellison.'

'You do seem to be casting about, Mr Monsarrat. Those papers were innocent. From my brother, actually. Writing from Ireland to tell me how marginal the crops were this year, with the winter frost coming early. I burned them simply because my desk was getting crowded.'

'You burn the letter from Ireland, but not the list and scratchings-out and first drafts of your journal that my housekeeper found on your desk?'

'Reminders from home can be painful, as I'm sure you're aware. Do not forget, Mr Monsarrat, that I know I am not the only one in this room to wear the sentence of the court. When I put that to you during our last interview, you did not deny it.'

Monsarrat couldn't resist smiling at the facility, the ease and speed with which Power responded.

'What I'm not entirely clear on, Mr Power, is how you got correspondence into Ellison's hands, and vice versa. Of course I recall you helping young Ennis with a letter to his mother. Perhaps those bundles contained additional information, the kind you could no longer write on your own behalf?'

'Well, you certainly seem to be enjoying your fantasy, so I'm not going to impede you in the spinning of it,' said Power.

'Very well then. Let me add another element to this story. A lady. One who somehow managed to get messages to you, even after you were placed under guard. One who could no longer risk being seen in open conversation with you, nor had the access even if she wanted it.'

Power clapped his hands. 'Very good! All good stories need a lady, don't you think?'

Monsarrat reached into his pocket again, pulled out the strip of fabric embroidered with little blue flowers, fiddled ostentatiously with it. 'Perhaps this lady somehow managed to tie bundled messages up in strips of cloth and throw them over your wall.'

Power laughed. 'Really, Mr Monsarrat. You struck me as an educated man. How can someone who's been translating Catullus since boyhood not have a rudimentary grip of physical laws? I suggest you try such a feat yourself. I think you'll find that no one, particularly here where the wind is present more often than absent, would be able to lob a small scrap of paper tied in a tiny strip of cloth all the way over a high wall.'

'Is that what she did, then?'

'No one did anything.'

Monsarrat stood. 'Very well, Mr Power. I'm delighted to have entertained you, and now I will leave you to your dead Roman. I thought you might like to know, though – I'm planning a visit to your former lodging today. I thought the floorboards near that fireplace might bear closer inspection.'

He stood and walked to the door. He tried to do so without looking back, but was unable to resist a brief glance over his shoulder. And he saw the expression on Power's face had slid, rearranging itself from its customary amused superiority into something close to fear.

Ellison was well and truly up and about by the time Monsarrat got back to the cottage. All the papers had been cleared away from the kitchen table, which was just as well, as Mrs Mulrooney promptly reclaimed the room, so that within half an hour Ellison was sitting in the small parlour, a cup of tea at his elbow.

'This woman is a marvel,' Ellison said as Mrs Mulrooney came in with a fresh pot. 'And young Walter tells me that the stores are in better shape than they have been in some years.'

He turned to Hannah. 'Mr Mulrooney is a fortunate man indeed,' he said.

'Mr Mulrooney is . . . no longer,' Mrs Mulrooney said.

'Oh, I am sorry,' said Ellison, looking anything but. 'I wonder, my dear – most irregular, I know – but would you join me in a port this evening?'

'Kind of you, but I never touch it,' she said. 'In any case I am due at the stores.'

She was not, as far as Monsarrat knew.

'Never mind,' Ellison said, in a reassuring tone which gave the distinct impression that he saw Mrs Mulrooney's dislike for alcohol as no impediment. 'A cup of tea, then. And I have plenty to occupy myself while you set the commissary stores to rights.'

Mrs Mulrooney opened her mouth to utter what Monsarrat was sure was a refusal.

'I would be delighted to have tea with you,' she said quickly, looking anything but delighted, and Monsarrat had the sense she was forcing the words out before she could change her mind.

'How wonderful! If you'll excuse me for now, I'm going back down to Brewster's office. I have some interesting conclusions from my conversations with Thomas Power to bring to light. I may also need to acquaint him with some other facts.'

When he had gone, Mrs Mulrooney tramped up to Monsarrat. 'Do you know, I was about to make you shortbread? You'll have none now. How dare you let me promise to have tea with such a rogue.'

Monsarrat was already feeling guilty. He knew she had volunteered to further the investigation. Mrs Mulrooney's sentence had long expired, she had escaped the paper jail of tickets of leave and conditional pardons. She had nothing to lose should they fail to find the perpetrator of Harefield's murder, but, for Monsarrat's sake, had just agreed to tea with a man she no doubt found odious.

'Ellison is right, you are a marvel. No, don't hit me, I mean it. I've had less luck than you will hopefully have. I was unable to make any headway with Power. He did look a little alarmed at the prospect of me visiting his old cottage, but he scoffed at the idea of Elizabeth Brewster throwing messages over the wall to him tied in strips of cloth. He even suggested I try it, that I wouldn't be able to get such a light object over a high wall.'

'Try we should, nonetheless,' said Mrs Mulrooney. 'But what makes you feel I'll have better luck?'

'I suspect, Mrs Mulrooney, that our magistrate may be something of a braggart after a little port. If you were to convince him to brag about helping Power . . .'

'I shall see what I can do, so. Perhaps he has yet another bottle secreted under those floorboards.'

Chapter 20

There was a surprising amount to do, running a store. In a place where the majority of people had been found guilty of criminal activity, particularly theft, everything had to be re-weighed and re-measured regularly if you wanted to avoid opening a sack only to find there was half as much as there should be. Hannah realised Elizabeth probably had a system which made sure none of the precious food slipped out the door, but if she had, it appeared she hadn't shared it with her brother.

Hannah had first gone to find Captain Brewster in the barracks, where she had received a curt nod in response to her suggestion that she look in on the stores for the duration of his wife's incapacity. Walter was there, of course. He may have only a nodding acquaintance with the administrative necessities of running a store, but he would never desert his post.

He was, though, doing nothing. At least, nothing towards getting the barrels and crates unpacked and in some sort of order. He was at his customary position behind the desk, flipping the broad ledger pages filled with crammed writing, looking for all the world as though he was searching for a particular entry.

'Good morning, Mr Gendron,' said Hannah.

Walter looked up. He wore half-moon spectacles, which Hannah suspected were an attempt to make him seem more authoritative, because he pushed them up on his forehead whenever he examined the ledger. He was frowning as she came in, and when he saw her he stood quickly, knocking over an ink pot in the process. The ink had been allowed to dry, so only a few black flecks spilled onto the desk.

'Elizabeth . . . She's not . . .'

'Now sit yourself down, Mr Gendron. You mustn't go assuming the worst. It's the opposite, actually. She is recovering well – she is obviously a woman of strong constitution.'

'Yes. She would be cross at me for saying this, but she can chop wood as fast as any man.'

'I've no doubt of it, as I'm sure circumstances have called on her to do that many times in the past. While her body is recovering, though, her spirit seems to be flagging a little. There's still a sadness to her.'

Walter sat down again, tapped the top of his half-moon glasses so that they fell from his forehead to his nose. 'That's because of Thomas.'

'Why should she be sad about him? His escape was prevented, and her husband will no doubt receive some sort of commendation for it.'

Walter frowned. 'He deserves no commendation.'

'Why ever not?'

'Thomas should be on his way to America now,' Walter said. 'I could have visited him there, seen him happy. I am angry with James about that. I'm not very pleased with your Mr Monsarrat, either.'

'You mustn't be cross at him, Mr Gendron. He did what he thought was right.'

'But that's all Thomas did too! Sometimes you do things for the best reasons. If they turn out to have the worst results, should you be punished?'

'Well, I would say no . . . But it's not really up to me.'

'Nor to me. But he should have been let go. He should never have been here. All he did was try to free people who had committed no crime.'

'I may – *may* – share your opinion on that, Mr Gendron, but it is a dangerous one. Who told you that? Was it Mr Power?'

'No, it was Elizabeth. She said he has done no wrong, that he is being punished for wanting to give some freedom to people who don't have any. They have more patience with that sort of thing in America, she said. And after he had gone . . .'

Walter gave a little start then, seemed to be hearing his words for the first time, as though they'd been spoken by someone else. He pushed the spectacles back on top of his head and returned his attention to the ledger.

'After he had gone, Mr Gendron? What were you going to do then?'

'Be happy, I suppose,' said Walter. His eyes were flicking around the room, not settling on anything – he seemed on the verge of becoming distraught.

'Well, do you know what makes me happy?' Hannah said. 'Tidying up. And there appears to be a good amount of it to do here, if I may say so, Mr Gendron. Why don't you and I get some of these crates open, get everything measured out? We nearly lost one of the inhabitants of this island; to lose some of the provisions as well would be the height of carelessness.'

Walter hauled the crates and barrels that Hannah pointed to, fetched the containers she asked for, got the scales and clocked them onto the desk so that they rattled alarmingly, sending a rat which Hannah pretended not to notice scurrying to the door.

'You're very . . . very calming to be around, Mr Gendron, if I may say,' said Hannah. 'Your sister must be looking forward to getting back here with you.'

'I think she'd rather be with Thomas,' said Walter.

'James?'

'No, Thomas,' he said simply, looking at her intently, crinkling his brow with concern. 'Are you tired, Mrs Mulrooney? You don't usually mishear things.'

'I am that, now you mention it,' said Hannah. 'In between looking after Mr Monsarrat, Mr Ellison, and your sister – delighted to be of service, of course – but yes, I suppose I am a little fatigued. I have one more task ahead, though, before I rest tonight. We are running low on logs for the fire, and Magistrate Ellison does like to stay up late.'

'I can ask James to send a convict with some wood?'

'Not a bit of it. Aren't they all busy building this settlement? No, like your sister, I'm able to handle an axe when the situation demands it. The only problem is, I currently don't have one. I don't suppose there's one here I could avail myself of?'

'I'm sorry, Mrs Mulrooney. There was one – not much of a one, either. It is not here now. Elizabeth may have thrown it out. The head was all wobbly anyway.'

❧

Power was right – it was impossible to launch a small piece of paper and an insubstantial scrap of cloth over a high wall. Nor was Monsarrat about to test his challenge, and risk questions should anyone see him throwing snippets of paper and cloth into the air. But if there was one commodity Maria Island had in abundance, it was forest and rocks and stones. A piece of paper crumpled around a good-sized stone, and tied with the strip of cloth, sailed easily enough over the wall.

He must think I am dim, thought Monsarrat. Yet when Monsarrat had mentioned the floorboards near the hearth, Power had looked as worried as Monsarrat had ever seen him. Of course, Monsarrat was supposed to be investigating the murder of the bosun, not how Thomas Power had received a signal that the means of his escape was near. Monsarrat could not help feeling, though, that the two were connected.

There was no guard on duty now that there was no one to guard. The gate was not even locked.

Once he was through it, Monsarrat stooped to pick up the wrapped-up stone he had flung over the wall. It would be hard to explain if it was discovered.

The cottage was empty and clean now. Some of the flagstones surrounding the fireplace still bore the shadows of months of ash, and if Mrs Mulrooney couldn't eradicate them they would be there until doomsday. He knelt and one of the boards creaked underneath his knee. He rapped on each of them in turn until one rewarded him with a hollow sound.

They were not, as it turned out, nailed down. Monsarrat was able to lift them for the price of a few splinters under his fingernails. The smell of damp was overwhelming – the cottage had been constructed by men who were not trained for the job and the floorboards were scant inches from the ground, so it was easy to see the small bundle of oilcloth resting on the bare earth.

Given the damp, it seemed quite extraordinary that the papers had not rotted. Perhaps they hadn't been there long. Some of the older ones were beginning to display roses of mould, but these hadn't obliterated the script. The letters were in a delicate hand. A feminine one, fancied Monsarrat. They were unsigned and undated. Some were a little florid – they spoke of finding joy where none was expected, and the even greater joy in developing what the writer referred to as a 'deep regard' for a man who had risked so much for the sake of his people. The pages at the top of the pile bristled with febrile excitement, speaking of America and the contentment that might be found in a place where the writer's earlier marriage would be easy to deny and the recipient's revolutionary activities celebrated. The letters further into the collection were more mournful, distressed at the truncation of the writer and recipient's contact.

And interleaved with these letters was one in a different hand. It described an inappropriate relationship, and the price that needed to be paid for silence.

There was little doubt in Monsarrat's mind from whom these had come.

⁓

'Doesn't surprise me, you know. I told you she had a grip you'd expect to find on a labourer.'

'I still find it hard to imagine,' said Monsarrat. 'Her sharpening the axe, stalking Harefield all the way up to that place, pulling him down from the ladder. And making a substantial dent on his shoulder before throwing him off the cliff.'

'Mr Monsarrat, you are being – what's the word you like to use? – obtuse. You find it hard to imagine because she is a woman. Need I remind you of Rebecca Nelson?'

She was right, Monsarrat thought. He would not have thought Rebecca Nelson capable of driving an awl into the eye of the man who had tormented her, and engineering a plan to have Mrs Mulrooney die in her place.

'I think we can safely assume – yes, I know you don't like it but we can – that the relationship Harefield was threatening to expose was between Elizabeth Brewster and Thomas Power.'

'And there's something that I need to tell you,' Mrs Mulrooney said. 'The axe that killed Harefield. It came from the stores.'

'Did it indeed?'

'Yes. And the person who liberated it from its place in the corner was not James Brewster, but Elizabeth.'

'You think we may have been looking in the right house, but at the wrong person?' Monsarrat asked.

'Well, she chops her own wood – she could have taken it for that. Then, if our other theory is to be tested, it would have been a simple matter for the commandant to get hold of it.'

'It is difficult, as I said, to see Elizabeth trudging her way to the light through the darkness, carrying an axe. Even to get some respite from her husband. But I agree that we must consider it.'

'Yes. Although something is troubling me. She was upset, certainly. But murderous? We are missing something, Mr Monsarrat.'

'Perhaps there is nothing to miss.'

'We need to find out if she did drink the poison on purpose.'

'You are the one best placed to do that. Perhaps you should simply ask her. And Ellison had a hand in all this too, I am certain. Jones says he often left mail with Ellison to put on the Hobart coach. It would be a small matter for Power to conceal messages in other correspondence.'

'And I should just ask him? Whether he was conspiring with Thomas Power in the man's escape? I'm sure my charms are such that he will confess immediately.'

'Yes, I see your point. But my friend, if there is anyone who can see the wrinkles in whatever he says, it is you.'

Chapter 21

'I must say, this is wonderful stuff,' said Ellison, dabbing some crumbs from the side of his mouth. 'I always thought my late wife made the best shortbread in the colony, but you may well have surpassed her – I should whisper that, in case her shade can hear me and decides to pay a reproachful visit.'

He chuckled. Oh yes, Hannah thought. The passing of your wife, poor woman, must be a source of endless amusement.

'Would you care for some more tea?' she said, wondering if he would notice that her smile was stiff and fixed.

'Yes, I should think so,' he said. 'More of that special tea, if you'd be kind enough. Don't think I didn't taste the rum in it, dear lady.'

'He lifted the newly filled teacup, pouring the contents down his throat in one gulp. Hannah winced at the rattle as he replaced it on the saucer. This is how tea sets get chipped, she thought. And they're not to blame, not when they are handled by someone like this.

'Were you always free, my dear?'

I am not your dear, thought Hannah.

'No, as a matter of fact,' she said.

'Bread, was it? Cabbage, perhaps? To feed your beloved mother?' Bread and cabbage thieves with hungry mothers must have come before him on a reasonably regular basis in the course of his work.

'My mother stopped requiring food on the day I was born,' she said, unable to keep her anger at his casual treatment of suffering out of her tone. 'And it was butter. To sell so I could feed my son.'

'Ah yes, it's always something like that.'

He looked at her then, perhaps noticed the thunder on her face. 'You must not think me hardened,' he said, suddenly quiet. 'I hear the same story over and over, and yes, some are fabricating mothers or children, but most aren't, and I have seen their suffering.'

Perhaps the rum was doing its work. If so, she would allow it to continue to do so. It would be a small price to pay if there was to be a useful, drunken revelation at the end of it.

'I got my ticket twenty years ago,' she said. 'My time is long since served.'

'Good God, twenty years! And am I correct in presuming you were transported for seven?'

'You are.'

'So that would mean you left Ireland . . . late last century?'

'Early in this one, by the time the courts ran their course.'

'So you were in Ireland for the revolution?'

'Yes. A time I would prefer not to discuss.'

'Of course. And when you were trying to feed your son, where was Mr Mulrooney?'

'In his grave. Put there by the British.'

It was technically true. The only real Mr Mulrooney – her father, Padraig – was a victim of the British, every bit as much as the man who, had he lived, would have become Hannah's husband. She apologised to both of their ghosts for using their memory in such a deception.

'What extraordinary experiences you must've had! How exciting, to be party to such history.'

'It was horrifying. It nearly killed my soul as well as my body. It was not exciting,' she said. She remembered to attach the smile back onto her face. It was bad enough being questioned by Power on the subject, but to hear a magistrate talk with such apparent fervour of an event which the government viewed as treason was even more disconcerting. Nonetheless, she did not want to discourage him from taking further steps down the indiscreet path he was on.

'You seem to know a lot about it,' she said. 'Most don't speak of it, on either side.'

'Oh yes, you might say I've made a study of it. How a disorganised force of gentlemen, priests and farmhands nearly overthrew the might of the British government. Extraordinary, and revelatory.'

'Why study such things? So you can prevent them from occurring again?'

'It won't happen here, not on any grand scale,' he said. 'Place is too big, the majority of the population are in chains of one kind or another. No, my interest is this: liberty is like water – it finds a way through. Do we build the wall against it until it punches a hole and breaks through, destroying everything in its path? Or do we allow it just enough space to move at a trickle?'

'Thomas Power might well agree with you,' said Hannah.

'Oh, I'm not like Power. Never been found guilty of treason, for a start. Can't help but admire the man, though. There is a felon with imagination.'

And imagination, thought Hannah, is easy to come by on a full stomach.

'You must think it a dreadful shame that he is confined where his imagination can benefit the wombats and the geese but very few others.'

'A shame? He did break the law, of course. But I don't imagine for a moment that this is where he will die. I am sure that at some point he will be back out in the world, letting his imagination gallop on.'

'Were you disappointed that he was unable to escape?'

'I would say disappointed is a strong word, Mrs Mulrooney.'

'He must have had help. From the mainland. Unless you can train one of these geese to carry messages to a whaler.'

Ellison chuckled, held out his cup for some more of that noxious brew that she was forcing herself to serve him. 'I am imagining he must've. But it is imagination again, you see.'

'All the imagination in the world can't get a letter across the ocean,' Hannah said.

'No, it can't. Do you know who is good at it though? That fellow Jones. He's a ticket-of-leave man, I'd wager. A few of you ticketed convicts around. Do you carry your papers with you in case someone checks?'

'I don't. But we were asked to leave Parramatta quickly. Mine are in my trunk at home, but I assure you they exist.'

If ever a man deserved flicking with the cleaning cloth . . .

'And tell me, my dear – do you know anyone else in possession of such documents?'

'Here? As you say, perhaps Jones is one. Beyond that . . . No, I can't think of anyone.'

Ellison looked at her thoughtfully for a moment. 'Yes, Jones. Far better than the last bosun. Actually tries to avoid the worst of the waves. I swear, sometimes Harefield took delight in terrifying me as much as possible on the crossing. Brewster has chosen well this time.'

Hannah recognised an attempt to change the subject when she heard it. 'Seems a nice enough fellow, that Jones,' she said. 'What little I've seen of him – which is usually when he's on his way into or out of the boat.'

'Yes, he makes a run nearly every day. We were lucky to get Harefield to do it once a week.'

'We?'

'The commandant, of course,' Ellison said.

'Of course. Well, I would prefer never to have to cross an ocean again. I can't imagine doing it daily.'

'Ah, you have to be born to it. It certainly helps if there is a charming woman on the other side of the crossing . . .' As he spoke, Ellison stood unsteadily. And suddenly he was on her, moving far more quickly than she would have believed possible, clamping his arms around her waist. She turned her head just in time to avoid his lips landing on hers, instead receiving a wet, open-mouthed kiss on the cheek, which made her feel ill.

Barely thinking about it, she followed some advice her father had once given her should she be the recipient of unwanted male admiration: she brought her knee up as hard as she could between the magistrate's legs.

He yelped loudly and in an instant was bent over gasping with his hands on his knees.

'What a terrible man you are, forcing yourself on a woman like that! And a magistrate! Imagine if word got around! Remember, my employer has the ear of the governor's secretary.'

He looked up at Hannah through eyes which were watering, opened his mouth and closed it again, putting her in mind of a fish. She took his arm, helped him back to his chair, waited while he recovered himself.

'Now, kindly explain yourself,' she said.

'I am terribly sorry,' he said, still short of breath. 'I was under the impression you would welcome it.'

'You were under the wrong impression, then.'

'In that case, I must beg your forgiveness.'

Hannah stayed silent.

Ellison straightened and took a gulp of tea. 'And now, my charming friend, if you will excuse me, I feel it is time to retire.'

He pushed back his chair, letting it scrape along the floor rather than lifting it, stood and bowed. Hannah hoped for a moment he would lose his balance and topple over. He didn't; he straightened again, smiled at her and weaved his way out of the kitchen. Just before he reached the door, he turned to Hannah and said, 'I do ask you to pardon my rudeness. And might I ask you a great favour? That the events of this afternoon remain between the two of us?'

⸱⸰⸲

The following morning, Monsarrat lowered himself on to the bench next to Mrs Mulrooney.

'He knows,' she said, keeping her eyes on the bay. 'Knows, or at least suspects.'

'I'm afraid you will have to give me a little more information, my friend. Who knows what?'

'Ellison has suspicions. About you. I'm certain of it – about your coming here as a convict.'

She turned to look at him then, saw that his lower jaw was slightly thrust out, a habit of his when he was trying to disguise some sort of internal upheaval.

'And do you think he intends to use that information?'

'If he does, he risks me talking about his attack on me.'

'His attack?' Monsarrat was on his feet, was about to stride toward the building. Mrs Mulrooney grabbed his arm and dragged him back down to the bench. 'Don't trouble yourself with it. He tried to kiss me' – Monsarrat grimaced and opened his mouth to speak, but she held up a hand to hush him – 'which was indeed disgusting, but at least does mean we now have information he would prefer wasn't aired. And unlike his collusion in Power's escape, we can prove it.'

Monsarrat sat again, slowly. 'Yes. We have only the flimsiest of evidence that he actually wrote to Power.'

'I wouldn't be sure, Mr Monsarrat. Mr Ellison appears to lack a head for rum – very possibly he is used to drinking port. After a few measures of the stronger stuff, he did express a fair amount of admiration for Thomas Power. And more than a little sympathy with his views.'

'Well, if you set those letter fragments beside such statements, it does make a more compelling case, doesn't it?'

'Let's make the case, then, shall we?' said Mrs Mulrooney. 'Before Ellison can waddle up from the dock with a letter confirming his suspicions about you.'

'They are suspicions, by the way, that I think our friend Power, that lover of equality between men, might have put in his head. But I will give him one last opportunity to explain himself. The letters I found under his floorboards. I will put them to him, see what he says.'

'And what if he sheds a light on nothing at all?' said Hannah. 'What will you do then?'

'We are now in possession of a lot of information, all of it highly suggestive. I've been trying to make the facts behave themselves, make them light up a path to a inevitable an conclusion. I have failed in that, so to be honest I don't know what I'll do.'

'I do,' said Hannah.

'Of course you do.'

'You will go to Captain Brewster. Remember, the person who reaches the commandant's ear first is the most likely to be believed.'

'I'm sure you're right. And he will probably remind me – if he doesn't arrest me – that I was brought here to solve a murder, not to reveal co-conspirators in a failed escape attempt. And what do I say to that?'

Hannah frowned. She should, really, tell him to turn everything over to Brewster. Including the letters from his wife.

But she did not wish to cause anyone pain. Brewster's pride would be wounded, which meant Elizabeth's suffering was likely to be far longer, and her unhappiness would compound Walter's.

'You say,' she said, 'that you are close to proving the identity of the killer and you do not wish to compromise the investigation by giving any further details. He will squawk, of course, but if you hold that line there is little he can do.'

'Sounds reasonable. Except from that point on he will ask me every few hours whether I'm yet able to tell him who the killer is.'

'It's my hope, Mr Monsarrat, that you will be.'

Chapter 22

'That is my personal correspondence, Mr Monsarrat. You should not have read it, and I most certainly will not be commenting on it.'

Power turned away from the bars towards the corner of the cell. He was a man of exquisitely tuned gestures, so his movement could not be accidental.

'It ceased to become personal correspondence when you tried to escape, Mr Power,' said Monsarrat. In that moment, he despised himself every bit as much as Power did. He sounded like the functionary he had pretended to be since that first interview with Marley in Hobart. But this interview seemed likely to be the last chance he would have to extract any information from Thomas Power.

'How long,' asked Monsarrat, 'have you and Mrs Brewster been ... friends?'

'I don't believe I named a lady,' Power said, still looking at the wall. 'Nor has she fixed her signature to those letters.'

'She doesn't need to.'

Power turned around, went to his bench and sat. 'Why are you here, Mr Monsarrat? Do you wish to add further credence to your distasteful fantasies about me and the commandant's wife?'

The accusation of prurience stung. 'I harbour no such fantasies, Mr Power. As a matter of fact, I have come to do you a kindness.'

Power snorted. 'It would need to be quite a kindness to make up for my continued presence here on this island.'

'Well, as it happens, I wanted to give you news of Elizabeth Brewster's condition.'

Power leaned forward, his hands on his knees. 'This is, Mr Monsarrat, a kindness indeed, and I will accept it as such.'

'Mrs Brewster recovers well. She is sitting, taking food and water and the occasional turn about the gardens in the company of my housekeeper. She is expected to be back at the commissary within a few days.'

Power lowered his head for a moment. When he looked up, he was blinking. 'And Walter?' he asked. 'Is he . . . is he safe?'

'He was distressed by his sister's incapacity. And, surprisingly, by your failure to escape – nearly as much as he would have been had you succeeded. But why would he not be safe?'

'Mr Monsarrat, there are on this island those who believe that anyone without a strong back and a strong mind has no business consuming air and rations.'

'I see. And you fear some of those might take it upon themselves to stop Walter consuming either?'

'I would like to think not but I commonly find that there is a large gap between what I would like to think and reality. You will have noted the presence of rum in large quantities on this island, despite the fact that it is forbidden to the convicts.'

'Yes. The Hatter's doing, I understand, with not a little help from Harefield before he was put to death?'

'Those men would have put even the great smuggler Black Humphrey and his brethren to shame. They were not, though, responsible for what happens when the rum hits the stomachs of some of the worst convicts. And when some of them drink, they think on how much they enjoy eating – and how little they get to do so.'

'And they blame *Walter* for that?'

'Well, he's a convenient scapegoat. And then he started running the stores, nominally at least. And they do not see him doing the consistent labour which they believe is the only currency that should buy food.'

'There are always convicts who believe they have a greater right to resources than anyone else,' said Monsarrat. Oh Lord, thought Monsarrat, I'm speaking like a Sydney Tory!

'Ah, yes, but rarely do they have such an easy target. Walter does not have the protective red coat, nor the quick fists which might earn respect from some of them. And he is a trusting soul. It would occur to him too late that when a group of men is circling him, they are doing so for less than friendly reasons.'

'Has he been attacked? Surely they wouldn't dare – not someone so closely connected to the commandant's household?'

'Would they not? James does enjoy observing the proprieties when there is pomp involved. But when it comes to making some things plain – such as the fact that his brother-in-law is under his protection – he verges on negligent. And, as I said, they were drunk.'

'Do you know who they were?'

'Yes. They were unwise enough to mount an ambush just outside my gate. That they were also in sight of the commandant's house tells you all you need to know about the level of protection Walter could expect from that source. And these were in the days when I had the run of the island. I was coming back from a walk and saw a knot of arms and legs rolling around, getting wombat ordure smeared all over them. At first I thought it was a convict brawl. They happen, as you know, with alarming regularity. But then I heard the sobbing from underneath the bodies. I yelled at them to get off him. They obeyed. Walter was at the bottom of the pile.'

'Was he badly injured?'

'No. Some bruises, a few cuts, nothing severe. But he was terribly frightened. It turned out he had been threatened with injury if he did not accede to their demands – one of them would arrive at the commissary at dawn every morning to collect some extra rations.'

'Would they have been able to get out of the convict barracks to do that?' asked Monsarrat.

'One of them didn't need to sneak out of the convict barracks,' said Power. 'Because one of them wasn't a convict. One of them was Harefield.'

'Harefield? For God's sake, why didn't Walter report him to the commandant? Why didn't you?'

'Well. You have read my correspondence, Mr Monsarrat. You know the answer. It is contained in the only letter not written by a lady.'

'The inappropriate relationship. Harefield was blackmailing you and Mrs Brewster.'

'I did not name a woman, you will note.'

'You didn't need to, Mr Power. Whether or not his accusations are true, though . . . Why would Brewster take Harefield's word over his own wife's?'

'Harefield made it his business to demonstrate his mastery over the back and forth of information on this island,' said Power. 'He was good at it, too. Believe me, Mr Monsarrat, I know better than most how important it is to keep a story going in the public mind, and the skill required to do so. I have done it, even from here. In my case, the public is in England and Ireland. In Harefield's, it was here. He needed to show me that he could make any story he chose take root and grow.'

'His rumours about you and Walter,' said Monsarrat. 'They were a demonstration as well as a threat?'

220

'Indeed. As you know, the embrace actually happened – Walter's way of thanking me for *Walladmoor*. And really Harefield's rumour-mongering was horribly clever. He isolated me from the Brewsters, and made it more likely that I would be executed.'

'Executed? On a charge of sodomy? I know it's a capital offence, but if everyone who was the subject of some sort of rumour of wrongdoing was convicted, the gaols and the grave-yards would be more crowded than ever.'

'I don't think his intention was to have me tried and convicted of sodomy. Not in a court, at least. Mr Monsarrat, do you know why they haven't killed me yet? And let me assure you, they would dearly love to.'

'Presumably because they do not wish to make you a martyr.'

'Precisely. But they only run that risk if my supporters across the seas continue to view me as a hero. It is one of the reasons I continue to write to the papers, to send tracts back for publication. If whispers skim over the waters and find their way into the ears of the more loquacious society matrons, or into the pages of the newspaper, I will be a distant degenerate, easily dismissed and forgotten. And just as easily dispatched, without the risk of revolutionaries rallying around my corpse.'

'Was Harefield that sophisticated?'

'Possibly not, but he had an instinctive ability to twist information to suit his ends, and he wanted me to know that he was able to use it, and to devastating effect. So I'm afraid the assault on Walter went unreported and unpunished. For the most part.'

'The most part?'

'Well . . . there was Milliner.'

'Oh yes, the Hatter. Rum middleman and skiver.'

'Like Harefield, he recognises when a weapon has been put into his hand, and does not hesitate to use it. He likes Walter – innocence in the body of a man is a rare thing here. So he retaliated by letting it be known that no more rum would be available – because Harefield was refusing to supply it. Suddenly those who had been Harefield's accomplices in the assault on Walter looked at him a little differently.'

Monsarrat recalled Shanahan's words about Harefield withholding rum. 'And I presume Milliner extracted a price for making rum available again.'

'Yes. He made Harefield swear to leave Walter alone. He gave advantageous rates to those who were willing to keep an eye on the lad, and he refused to sell to those who had been party to the attack on him.'

'So who were they?'

'Men like Trainor. Harefield attracted a coterie of lesser intellects to whom he seemed the most knowing man of all. Most of them are working on the reservoir, where their strength can be put to good use and their amorality is less likely to infect Darlington. But I would not recommend that you try to speak to any of them on the matter. Tickets of leave have been offered to those with information which leads to the identity of the murderer and no one has come forward. And they have a particular brand of justice: if they are not afraid of beating the brother-in-law of the commandant, God knows what they would do to a stranger from Sydney. As you will have noted, people here run the risk of falling off cliffs.'

Chapter 23

Elizabeth was still lying in her bed, subdued and propped up on a sea of pillows. Hannah could think of nothing worse than lying in bed all day, the smell of heated dust drifting around, watching the sunlight through grimed glass. Elizabeth, however, seemed desperate to stay where she was, inside her cocoon where events on the island could move along without her, leaving her untouched.

'I don't wish to rush my recovery,' she said. 'Yes, I am doing well. But if one takes these things too fast, one can relapse. At least, that's what Dr Chester says.'

Hannah was sure she had been there nearly every time Dr Chester had examined Mrs Brewster and she couldn't recall him saying anything of the sort. But arguing was a waste of energy which could be better used elsewhere.

'As you wish, of course,' she said. 'It's just that . . . Well, the garrison like to see you about. I think they have more faith in their command when they see what a fine woman he married.'

One he doesn't deserve, she thought.

'And Walter,' Hannah said, 'misses you terribly. I'm doing my best, helping at the stores. But he wants you back there.'

Elizabeth groaned, then, sank back into her hillock of pillows. 'Would you be so kind as to go and see him again today?' she asked. 'I trust you to keep an eye on him.'

'Mrs Brewster, I would like to speak plainly.'

'Of course,' said Elizabeth. 'I doubt I could stop you even if I wanted to.'

'Well, I am sorry to ask you, but I feel I must. What is it that you fear? What is such a horrendous prospect that you confine yourself here? What is keeping you now to your bed?'

Elizabeth frowned, and then sat straight up, squaring her shoulders and lifting her chin. 'I fear nothing, Mrs Mulrooney. Kindly do not speak to me in such a personal fashion again.'

Hannah was annoyed at herself for pushing things too far.

'As you wish,' she said, curtseyed, and left the room.

She had no intention, of course, of leaving it alone. She would simply have to take her own advice and find a way to approach things side-on.

◦◦◦

Monsarrat hurried along, this time careless of avoiding tree roots or trying to distinguish branches from snakes on his way to the reservoir. His shirt was sticking to his body underneath his wool coat. Why do we do this to ourselves, he thought. Dress for an English winter in a colonial summer. He flung it into the bushes at the side of the path as he ran. He thought of Trainor, the trunk-necked overseer. A rare ally of Harefield. The man had mentioned his access to rum had recently improved. If that was true, presumably he was also among those who had been denied rum in the wake of the attack. So one possible reason for his new rum supply was that he had made it clear he knew something, and needed his silence bought by liquor.

Trainor wasn't even watching the men on his work crew when Monsarrat stumbled into the clearing, his shirt soaked through with sweat, and a nasty scratch from an overhanging branch on his cheek. The overseer was casually barking orders over his shoulder, not checking whether they were being carried out or not, seemingly more intent on picking his teeth than getting the reservoir built. He looked up briefly at Monsarrat, seemingly almost without registering him, then to the sky, and jammed his dirty fingernail back into his mouth.

Monsarrat walked up. 'Mr Trainor. A word, if you please.'

'You look as though you've been in a fight, Mr Monsarrat.'

'I imagine you would know a reasonable amount about fighting yourself. Tell me, did you enjoy beating a man who is unequipped to defend himself?'

'Don't know what you're talking about, sir.'

'Deny it as much as you like. I understand your mate Harefield was holding some information over Mrs Brewster. You, on the other hand, have nothing to hold over me. So unless you would like me to acquaint the comptroller of convicts in Hobart with your situation, you would be best advised to cooperate with me.'

'That depends on what you mean by cooperation,' said Trainor after a pause.

Even now, the man was far too cocky, especially for a convict. Perhaps being isolated out at the reservoir, where he was the undisputed authority, had given him a false sense of the scope of that authority. He needed some perspective.

'Were any of you offered tickets of leave in exchange for information which might have led to the apprehension of Harefield's killer?'

'No. Wouldn't have accepted them if we were, either – tickets have been offered before, you know, and oddly enough have never come into being. Don't suppose you're offering one?'

'Oh, I'm offering something quite different. A chance to get to know Thomas Power in the guardhouse.'

'You? You've not the authority!'

'I have all the authority in the world, Trainor, as a representative of the governor.' Monsarrat hoped that whatever correspondence might be bouncing across in Jones's cutter would not undermine the truth of that statement. 'Would you like to test me? See if I am telling the truth? Or would you rather just tell me why the Hatter suddenly decided to restore your rum supply?'

'Who says he did?'

'You said yourself – there had been more rum lately. Milliner had been holding it back from you, thanks to your role in beating Walter. He obviously had a change of heart. He is a businessman, is the Hatter – at least he seems to be. It does not strike me as the type of thing you would do out of sheer loving kindness.'

'You don't know him, and you don't know me.'

'I know convicts,' said Monsarrat. 'And I know a transaction when I see one.'

Trainor pursed his lips. Monsarrat could see the man's tongue probing his cheeks.

'People say things all the time here,' he said, eventually. He exhaled slowly, seemed to almost enjoy the process of letting the air leak out of his lungs. Then he clapped the palms of his hands decisively on the top of his thighs. 'It is possible that someone like the Hatter might have . . . let's say, relaxed certain of his rules. It's the kind of thing he would do if somebody saw something he would rather they had not seen.'

'And what might somebody have seen to earn such consideration?' Monsarrat asked.

'Harefield on his way to the light.'

'Not an unusual sight, I would have thought.'

'No, but it was the last time anyone saw him.'

Monsarrat paused. If the answer to his next question was yes, he was closer than he had thought to identifying the murderer.

'You saw him on the day he died?'

'Yes. But I saw the commandant's wife, too, following him. She was holding an axe.'

Even though Elizabeth Brewster's guilt was a possibility Monsarrat had discussed with Mrs Mulrooney, he still found it jarring to hear this so plainly, from the mouth of a man who exhaled more brutishness in each breath than Monsarrat would have thought Mrs Brewster capable of in a lifetime. And yet in bodily strength she was not of such delicacy that she could not wield an axe, and her love of Walter was so intense that one could possibly imagine her wielding it with emotional and physical force. Monsarrat found it a credible but appalling image.

'Did he know she was there?' asked Monsarrat.

'Didn't look like it. He was a fair way ahead, and she seemed to be taking pains to move quietly. She must've been bending all her will to that, because she didn't notice she was being followed herself.'

'Who on earth would have been following her?'

'Who do you think? Who follows her around like a dog all day long? Walter was not about to let his sister go plunging into the bushes at dusk by herself, was he?'

❧

As she trudged down to the stores, in wooded ground beneath the mountains named – in a place where there was not even a parson – Bishop and Clerk, Hannah was aware of being followed by several pairs of broad webbed feet, their owners honking in irritation, no doubt asking her why it had been so long since she had made shortbread. She turned, and some of them walked around her until they were on the other side. 'All right, you have me surrounded,' she said. 'Now what are you going to do?'

One of them looked up staring, its irritated red button eyes at her. The creature opened its beak and gave a harsh honk.

'You may very well say that,' Hannah said. 'But I've been too busy to make shortbread, let alone for the likes of you to nibble up. You'll just have to wait like everybody else, and that's an end to it.' And she marched straight at the geese blocking her path, who wisely waddled out of her way.

'I thought I heard them,' said Walter, as Hannah opened the door to the commissary. 'The geese. They're outside?'

'No, Mr Gendron, please don't trouble yourself on their account, eejit birds that they are. I shooed them off.'

'They might come back, though,' Walter said. He went to the door, opened it a crack, looked out and closed it quickly.

'Stupid big feathery lumps, even if they were to pay you a visit, it would surely be no concern.'

'You don't know what they're like,' said Walter. 'Not really. They can surround a person. You know what happens when people get surrounded, don't you?'

Hannah nodded but was not sure how to answer. It was a frightening but perhaps, in the end, harmless experience to be surrounded by those angry, inquisitive beaks.

'My father used to tell me that everything in nature operates on the same principle. No matter what kind of bird you're looking at, they fly because of the way their wings move in the air. No matter what kind of tree, they will need sunlight to survive. And I have found another principle. Whenever things surround you, they mean to do you harm.'

'What things surrounded you?' Hannah asked.

Walter inhaled, held his breath for a moment, and opened his mouth. Before he could speak, however, the door of the commissary was thrust open.

Hannah was reasonably certain Jones had not intended to push it with such force but had been assisted by a gust of strong wind blowing up from the bay. When she looked out over his shoulder, she could see lines of white froth punctuating the great expanse between Darlington Bay and the main island.

'A rough crossing for you, was it?' she said.

'One of the rougher ones, missus,' said Jones. He was scratching his skin through the bristles of his dark beard, which was flecked in parts with dried salt. 'Had to stay at the inn last night – there was no chance of attempting it then, not with the light failing. And the wind – she couldn't decide yesterday which direction to go in. It would have been waves from all sides. At least now they're mostly from the north. Easier to manage when you know what to expect.'

'I don't know how you do it, young Jones, I truly don't,' said Hannah. 'As you know, I've a mortal terror of the sea, even when it's pretending to be good, flat as a table.'

Jones chuckled. 'Not a pretence it indulges in much, not here anyway,' he said. 'But there will be some who will be cross at me for not taking the risk. Some here are wanting their mail. Ellison was there. Holloway too. Pardon, missus, if Mr Ellison is a friend of yours, but neither of them made any attempt to help with the other cargo. I handed them their letters and off they trotted. I tried to call Holloway back – there was a letter for the commandant as well, and I thought he might do me a favour and deliver it – but he was already opening his own and reading it; didn't seem to hear me above the wind. Lucky it didn't snatch his out of his hands and commit it to the ocean. On the subject of letters . . . I was hoping to find Mrs Brewster recovered and at her post, but I see she is not.'

'Sadly, no. She is recovering well, but she must preserve her strength.'

Jones nodded. 'Well, if you see her, wish her a fast recovery from me. I shall deliver these letters myself, then.' He was unable to stop his shoulders slumping at the prospect.

'I am . . . assisting Mr Gendron, at Mrs Brewster's request,' said Hannah. 'With the approval of the commandant. If making sure letters reach their destination was one of her tasks, I am sure that Mr Gendron and I can accomplish it.' She patted

Jones on the shoulder. 'And you, Mr Jones – after all the letters have found their recipients, I shall bring you some tea. If you don't mind my saying, you look done-in.'

He nodded. 'I am, at that. No bed for me last night, so I was in the stables. If you wouldn't mind . . .'

Walter had been listening to the two of them talk, and had straightened, flicking his spectacles back down onto his nose. 'Oh yes,' he said. 'I know precisely where they need to go, every last one of them.'

Jones smiled. 'Good lad, Walter. Will I take you fishing later?'

Walter beamed. 'Anything I catch, you can have for your supper,' he said.

'I will most certainly take you fishing then! We'll just wait for the sea to settle down a bit first though, shall we?'

After Jones left, holding the door firmly as he closed it so that the wind didn't slam it, Hannah spread out the letters. 'Now tell me, Mr Gendron, where should I take these?'

'A few for surgeon Chester,' said Walter, tapping the envelopes. 'These names here – Jackson, O'Reilly – they're convicts, I believe. Not official correspondence, I wouldn't think – no envelope, just folded with the names written on the front. Mothers, sweethearts. They have to go to the convict barracks. There should be an overseer there. And these are for James.'

'Indeed, Mr Gendron, and I shall make sure they get to him.'

'I can deliver them if you like. James might be pleased with me if I did.'

'Ah, no, Mr Gendron. You are needed here, so you are. Such a tempting target, this place must be, with all the food within its walls. We need someone with broad shoulders like yourself to guard it.'

Walter nodded, stood straighter. 'You may rely on me, Mrs Mulrooney, I assure you,' he said. 'I always do the right thing.'

Hannah set out with the parcel of letters. She did not turn towards the outbuilding where James Brewster had his office, or to the convict barracks to find Trainor. She went up the hill, ignoring the occasional complaint from her ankle, towards the two little cottages in which the island's power was concentrated in the persons of the commandant and the magistrate.

She had thought to walk into the visiting magistrate's cottage for all the world as though she expected no one to be there, to see if Ellison was poring over a letter. She might sit opposite him, enquire whether he would like a cup of tea. Shortly after she had acquired the skill of reading, she had taught herself to do so upside down. If he were perusing a letter and laid the pages on the table, she might be fortunate enough to get a glimpse of its contents.

Instead, on her way up she paused outside the wall of Thomas Power's former home. She wondered whether it were possible that the letter addressed to James Brewster had something to do with Power. Equally, it could be a manifest of the next ship to bring a batch of convicts to the island. But if Power's fate rested on the contents of this letter, she would very much like to know. Of course, it was the height of bad manners to read someone else's mail. In this circumstance, very possibly against the law as well. But those social conventions, those laws, had never worked in her favour and she felt surprisingly little guilt in setting them aside.

There was no wax seal, thankfully. Hannah knew Monsarrat had some ability forging them, although it was an art he had not practised for some time as far as she knew. But there would be no time to create a replacement for this one.

She moved around to the uphill side of the building before she opened Brewster's letter, and ran her eyes down to the bottom before starting at the top. The signature, slanted and spiky but legible – unlike some she had seen – was Robert Marley's. And the letter itself informed James Brewster – and Hannah

Mulrooney – of the approach of a brig which was to convey Thomas Power to the penal settlement at Macquarie Harbour.

Hannah folded the letter, shuffled it in between some of the others so that if she was seen on her rounds it would not be obvious. She thought for a moment of taking it directly to James Brewster, handing it over, making no further mention of it. But there was a woman lying in a bed, scared even to press her feet to the floor for fear of what the world outside the walls might hold. This letter very probably contained confirmation of Elizabeth Brewster's worst fears. Hannah wondered whether it would be a cruelty or a kindness to tell her.

Whatever she decided, she could not be seen to have knowledge of the contents of the letter before the commandant did. She walked slowly back down the hill, telling herself she was trying to avoid wombat holes, giving herself as much time as she could to make a decision.

There was no answer at first when she knocked softly on the door of the commandant's office. Perhaps he was used to larger fists pounding on the wood. She tried again with more force, earning herself a small splinter in one of her knuckles and a response from inside. 'Very well! Come, if you must.'

The captain was writing as she entered and likely did not realise who his visitor was. When he looked up he frowned for a moment, as though trying to decide whether she really was who she appeared to be. 'Mrs Mulrooney. I was expecting . . .'

She waited for a moment, until it became apparent he was not going to finish his sentence.

'I'm helping in the commissary, sir. At your command, of course, if you recall.'

He nodded.

'I understand that one of your wife's tasks was to deliver the mail, so I've taken that on as well. There's a letter for you.' She extracted it from the middle of the pile, held it out to him. He snatched it, frowned at it.

'I have also looked in on your wife this morning,' she said.

He looked up again. 'You don't expect me to read this in front of you, do you?' he said.

'Of course not, sir,' she said, making the bobbing movement she had come to hate and backing out of the room.

She felt compelled to redress the imbalance caused by Brewster's indifference and go and check on Elizabeth again. She should, she thought, be grateful to the commandant. He had helped her come to a decision. Because apart from Chester and Walter, as far as she knew, only one man on this island had shown any concern for Elizabeth's recovery. And he was sitting not in the commandant's office, but in the cell of the guardhouse.

Chapter 24

Monsarrat had never wanted to speak to Mrs Mulrooney more. On the walk back from the reservoir, he turned Trainor's revelations over in his mind. Chester had said that the wound to Harefield's shoulder was deep enough to have been made by someone with significant strength. It was one of the factors which had made Monsarrat hesitate to believe that Elizabeth Brewster was capable of the crime.

But if Elizabeth had just gone to confront Harefield – even, perhaps, to ask what the price for silence was – that made more sense. And if she was followed there without her knowledge by a man to whom she was as much a mother as a sister, a man who saw his former attacker now turning his aggression on a woman most precious to him, would he not defend her?

It all needed more investigation, of course. But the details fitted together, a solution that made Monsarrat uncomfortable, and failed to give him any feeling of success. He had no wish to see Walter hanging for the murder, or to hear that Elizabeth had tried again to drink a fatally strong cup of tea and this time it had succeeded in taking her life.

Once more he cursed Eveleigh for sending him to this isolated post and making his position doubly difficult by failing to reveal his background. And now he faced a terrible choice: reveal what he knew and see an innocent choking at the end of a rope, or stay silent, say he was unable to discover the culprit, that he was returning to Parramatta, and risk finding not only that his ticket of leave had been revoked for his failure but also that Elizabeth might be accused of the murder. If she was, he suspected she would willingly go to the gallows in Walter's place, and her death would be equally obscene.

Monsarrat did not know whether he could survive another penal stretch, and while convicts could marry other convicts, there was certainly a chance that an alliance between him and Grace O'Leary would be prevented if he threw away the credit that would be due to him were he to solve Harefield's murder.

Nonetheless, he would lose what was left of his soul if he revealed what he knew. Some would see it as justice. But justice was not its own entity. Its meaning was determined by those who were authorised to interpret it – and they always did so to serve their own ends.

Monsarrat decided then to serve a justice which would not end with him watching the confused look on a good lad's face as an execution hood was dragged down over his eyes. He felt sure Mrs Mulrooney would agree with him. But he wanted to hear her anoint his decision with her hard-won approval, to hear her tell him that he was an eejit of a man but that he was, for once, right.

At least there was one thing he need no longer worry about – if he was stripped of his freedom, he would know that she was taken care of. She was a woman of independent means now. She need not rely on his employment or anything else.

There was, he realised, one hand he could play. One revelation which might partially redeem him and see justice done. Brewster would no doubt think Ellison should be punished for aiding Power's attempted escape. Monsarrat felt he should be punished for his lurch at Mrs Mulrooney. Whatever the crime, the result would be the same.

He hoped Mrs Mulrooney had not returned to the cottage that morning after her shabby treatment at the hands of Ellison.

In fact, she was on the path between the two. As he rounded the corner where the trees stopped, he could see her striding purposefully up the path and letting herself into the commandant's cottage. He was at a loss then. He chided himself for it – even as a false lawyer he had once in Exeter held courtrooms enthralled, or at least not utterly bored, and as the convict clerk to the commandant at Port Macquarie he had proved himself an indispensable part of the administration. Why, then, did he feel he needed the blessing of an Irishwoman who could not read this time last year, before taking action?

He knew the answer, was ashamed of himself for even asking the question. Mrs Mulrooney was a far better person than him.

'Mr Monsarrat! You look as though you were the one who spent the morning trying to avoid the worst waves on the way from the mainland.'

Jones was walking up towards the military barracks, where he had a cot along with the soldiers. He was ruddy from sun and wind, but the shadows under his eyes told of his broken night's sleep.

'Jones, hello. Yes, I suppose I must look frightful. I ran to the reservoir, and walked fairly swiftly back.'

'In that case, I'm surprised you don't look worse. But if you're after some restorative tea from your housekeeper, you might have to wait. She has been delivering the mail. The type who is never happier than when she has a task, by the looks of it.'

'Yes, you've described her exactly.'

'And please don't take offence, Mr Monsarrat,' Jones said. 'I am very happy that the only mirror on the island is attached to Mrs Brewster's dressing table. I myself probably look a little rough too.'

'A difficult crossing?'

'Aye, and a difficult job unloading at the end of it, with the boat bucking, and two able-bodied men standing on the dock choosing not to assist me.'

'Who?'

'Holloway, naturally. He believes his commission should exempt him from anything as menial as unloading boats. And Ellison was too engrossed in his letter. Nearly walked off the dock at one point.'

'I see. Well, Jones, I shan't keep you. One thing, though – do you know where Ellison is to be found?'

'In his cottage, I believe. He headed up there almost immediately and I haven't seen him come down since.'

It took some time after Jones had gone for Monsarrat to work up the will to move. His legs were complaining about their abuse. But even if they hadn't been, he wasn't sure where to tell them to take him. Up the hill to confront Ellison or down it to expose him.

If the letter contained confirmation of Monsarrat's convict past, as soon as its contents were shown to Captain Brewster, anything Monsarrat said would carry no weight. So it seemed best for Monsarrat to put his case to Brewster and hope that he had enough time to make it compelling before Ellison walked in waving a piece of paper which would ensure Brewster stopped listening to anything Monsarrat said.

❧

Hannah had managed to convince Elizabeth out of her bed and into a chair while she straightened the covers and shook the pillows. The back which had sat so straight at dinner when they first arrived was now bent and slumped, as though Elizabeth lacked the will to keep it straight, and the once luminous skin was now dull and unnaturally pale. Hannah thought that perhaps she might take the news slightly better if she felt more comfortable.

When Elizabeth was back in the bed, the two sides of one pillow rising up to cover her ears, Hannah paused. Once words escaped, they could not be put back into a cell. Elizabeth's eyes were beginning to close, though. If there was to be a revelation, the time was now.

'I have word, Mrs Brewster,' Hannah said. 'Word concerning Mr Power.'

Elizabeth woke from her drowse immediately, struggling to sit up against the soft mass of goose down. 'He's not ... They haven't done anything rash? He is well?'

'Quite well, as far as I know, for one who is imprisoned,' said Hannah. 'But he will not be there for much longer.'

'They are releasing him? Letting him stay? I knew they would realise eventually that this is as good a place as any for him, escape attempt or not.'

Hannah went over to the bed. 'May I sit?' she said. Elizabeth nodded, and Hannah lowered herself onto the bed and took Elizabeth's hand. 'They are not releasing him, Mrs Brewster. They are sending him to Macquarie Harbour.'

She watched as Elizabeth's skin, paler than it used to be but with the pink of returning health, faded to the pallor of the worst of her incapacity.

'Macquarie Harbour,' she whispered. 'One hears stories ... A brutal place, I understand. Far more brutal than here.'

'I know little of Macquarie Harbour,' said Hannah. 'But I do know that the administrators of Van Diemen's Land consider it in their interest to treat Mr Power well, or at least less horrendously than the other convicts.'

'I've heard of a cell they have there,' Elizabeth said. 'The roof is too low for a man to stand up and the walls are too close to lie down. Food is delivered through a hole with shutters at both ends, so whoever is in there never sees another person or a beam of light. They leave people there for months. Those locked in there are barely human when they come out.'

'They would not put him in such a place, Mrs Brewster,' said Hannah. 'I am sure of it.' In fact, she was sure of no such thing, and it was a fate she would not wish even on the vainglorious Power.

'But if they did,' whispered Elizabeth. 'If they did – it would destroy him. Far more quickly than it would most others. He wouldn't be able to read, wouldn't be able to write. Thomas Power would cease to exist.'

Tears were making their way down Elizabeth's face now. She did not wipe them away, perhaps did not even notice them.

I have already lost one of you, Hannah thought. One commandant's wife who was buffeted by circumstances, easily blamed when she was blameless, easily picked off. You may not be as innocent as she, but I will not see another young woman buried.

'You have a regard for him,' she said. 'It is clear to me, and it will be clear to others if they hear you speak as you do now. I urge you not to.'

'I have . . . no more regard for him than I do for any other soul,' Elizabeth said, contradicted by the tears now marking the coverlet.

'Now let us have truth between us,' said Hannah. 'I bear you no malice, and I would not see you arrested, hanged. But I am not the only one to whom your feelings are apparent. There is a letter, I understand. And it sets a price for the concealment of an inappropriate relationship.'

Elizabeth looked terrified, and Hannah could see her chest beginning to rise and fall at an alarming rate.

'It . . . There is no such letter. It does not exist,' she said.

'I'm afraid, Mrs Brewster, that it does. You showed it to Power, perhaps to ask his advice. Find out what you should do. I am sure you thought he would burn it. He did not. It is currently in the possession of Mr Monsarrat, who has yet to show it to anyone else.'

'I thought . . . I thought he was safe,' she said. 'That we had made sure of it.'

This statement jagged on the inside of Hannah's ear. It was, she thought, as close to an admission as she had heard.

'Mrs Brewster, you must have a care what you say and who you say it to. Such things, they can be misinterpreted. Not everyone here is a person of goodwill, and some would be only too happy to draw a line between such words and the body of the bosun in the churchyard.'

'They would be mistaken,' said Elizabeth, pulling her shoulders back.

'And don't I know that,' said Hannah. Some of Monsarrat and her own arguments in favour of Elizabeth as the murderer made sense. Yet Hannah found it hard to accept the possibility when the office outbuilding contained a man who had the motive, strength and freedom of movement to commit the crime. 'But you must not give anyone else any excuse to even ask the question, in case they decide the convenient answer is that you yourself are guilty.'

Chapter 25

Lieutenant Holloway was sitting opposite Captain Brewster when Monsarrat walked into the small office. The lieutenant was looking happier than Monsarrat had ever seen him, but Brewster was scowling at the fellow in a way that made Monsarrat fear for his safety, let alone his commission.

'You're dismissed,' said Brewster to Holloway, who stood, saluted Brewster and walked past Monsarrat without acknowledgement, changing course to bump into him on his way out the door.

'Well, Mr Monsarrat, you may consider yourself fortunate. Your standing here is now higher than it has been since your arrival.'

'Oh? I wasn't aware that my standing was anything less than high.'

'You must have known that to Holloway you are less than welcome. He felt the investigation of Harefield's murder should fall to him. He had fantasies, the little climber, of writing long reports once he had brought the case to a successful conclusion, of writing pamphlets, or stories for the newspaper. Then you arrived and he was brought back down to earth – just an ordinary lieutenant. And now he'll be lucky not to be an ordinary private.'

'What has he done?'

'Written to Richard Marley. About you. Told Marley that you are doing nothing, that you seem to have no urgency to resolve this matter, or the wit to do so. Suggested that you be recalled and he given the task.'

'Ah. And what is Marley's view?'

'That he should concentrate on his duties and leave the thinking to others.'

'I see. And what is your view, commandant?'

'I agree with Marley. You have been sent here for a specific purpose. But yes, I would have preferred it if you had made more progress.'

'I too wish I were closer to the truth, but I've yet to find evidence that goes beyond circumstantial,' Monsarrat said. And at this he had to stop himself from leaping up and bolting for the door. Because he'd remembered the coat he had flung aside when he ran towards the reservoir. The coat which had in its breast pocket Elizabeth Brewster's letters to Thomas Power, and Harefield's blackmail note.

But to leave now would be to give up the only advantage he may ever have. He must hope the coat would remain unmolested, by wombats or convicts, for a while longer.

'If it is a help, I am in a position to enlighten you on certain aspects of how Power's escape was planned.'

Brewster leaned slowly forward. He looked sceptical, but Monsarrat definitely had his interest.

'You're aware,' Monsarrat said, 'that Power was in the habit of helping certain soldiers of yours with their correspondence?'

'Yes. He loves any opportunity to show off.'

'Well, it would have been easy for him to slide another note in among the pages of endearment, before Mrs Brewster came around to collect the mail.'

'Mr Monsarrat, I would caution you against any implication that my wife was involved.'

If only I were able to make you such a promise, thought Monsarrat. 'I assure you, your wife is not a subject of the current discussion,' he said.

'Very well. I'm willing to entertain the notion that Power exploited the naivety of certain younger soldiers – I presume you mean Ennis – to get messages across the water. But who received them when they got there?'

'I am told that Magistrate Ellison was in the habit of collecting mail from Jones. I believe he informed Jones that he wished to read all letters of a personal nature from convicts or impressionable young soldiers to guard against the eventuality of a conspiracy.'

'Quite right. Solid fellow, Ellison, if a little too fond of the bottle. But if Power was sneaking messages off the island under the skin of a personal letter, why didn't Ellison spot them?'

Monsarrat inhaled, held his breath for a moment. 'It is my belief, commandant, that he did spot them. That he was their intended recipient; that it was he who organised the escape.'

Monsarrat braced himself for whatever reaction was to come. Anger, disbelief, dismissiveness. What he didn't expect was laughter. Brewster leaned back in his chair, looked up at the ceiling and roared.

'Ellison! A secret revolutionary! I must thank you, Mr Monsarrat. There has been precious little to laugh about recently.'

'I assure you, commandant, that I am not joking.'

'You must be! The man is barely sober, except on the bench, where he hands out punishments which are moderate in their severity. He totters between the bench and his house in Orford and the docks, and does the minimum required so that he can return to his bottle quickly. He is not a man given to initiative, to the type of misplaced courage it would take to assist Power.'

'Perhaps he has allowed you to believe that of him, Captain Brewster. I am acquainted with his liking for port, have witnessed it. It may interest you to know though that he has confessed to sympathies which are somewhat anti-authoritarian. And fragments of paper bearing what looks like his handwriting were found in Power's grate after his escape attempt failed.'

'Fragments? What are you talking about?'

'I shall fetch them, with your approval,' Monsarrat said. 'I have compared them to some of Ellison's official documents and I can assure you that the similarity is striking.'

'Hardly seems like much to go on,' said Brewster. 'But I suppose I had best have a look. Please bring them to me. And have a wash while you're about it. God knows what you've been doing, but no one under my command would be permitted to present such a bedraggled aspect.'

The jacket, thankfully, was still where Monsarrat had flung it, somewhat concealed by the bushes in which it had landed, and unmolested as its pockets contained nothing to tempt geese or wombats.

He had no intention now of going back to the magistrate's cottage to wash. Ellison might be there, and he would as soon not see the man he had just, unsuccessfully, accused of treason.

He might, under different circumstances, have felt guilt accusing Ellison. After all, the man was acting in accordance with his own beliefs, trying to bring balance to an unbalanced world. Similarly motivated actions had sent Monsarrat across the seas, or so he liked to tell himself. He never liked to confront the vanity which had also prompted his crime.

But Ellison's lunge at Mrs Mulrooney had driven the fellow feeling out of Monsarrat's mind. Such villainy deserved punishment, one way or another.

'Oh dear, what would Miss Stark say, to see you in such a state?'

Mrs Mulrooney's substantial personality was not matched by her birdlike frame. Her habit of taking short, quick steps, barely troubling the ground with her weight, allowed her to move more silently than most.

'You mustn't sneak up on a man,' he said.

'A man must not allow himself to be snuck up on.'

Mrs Mulrooney must be missing Parramatta to invoke Sophia Stark, a woman she loathed.

'Miss Stark? I imagine she'd feel she had a lucky escape,' Monsarrat said, looking down at his sweat-stained shirt. 'Grace O'Leary, however, would commend me for casting my jacket aside in the service of the truth – after laughing at me, of course.'

'A better match for you altogether, that one, if I may say so,' said Mrs Mulrooney.

'You may, and I would like to meet the man brave enough to try to stop you. And on the subject of men – how are you faring after beating off Ellison's attentions?'

'He is far less persistent than the geese – that I will grant him. I have not seen him today. But Jones has. Gave him a letter, one that might contain certain facts in regard to you, Mr Monsarrat.'

'Yes, that is a concern. I have just been to Brewster to discuss it. Tried to convince him of Ellison's complicity in plotting Power's escape. He was sceptical, shall we say. This is why I am fetching my jacket, you see. I wanted to show him the fragments you found in Power's fireplace.'

'And how did the jacket come to be treated in such an appalling fashion in the first place?'

'I needed to get to the reservoir. Quickly. There was someone there who I believed might have interesting information in relation to Harefield's murder.'

'I hope it was worth it,' said Mrs Mulrooney.

'It most certainly was. I was told that Elizabeth Brewster followed Harefield the night he was killed. And she was followed herself. By Walter.'

'No,' Mrs Mulrooney whispered. She narrowed her eyes at him, looking worried and defiant at once. It was an expression he had seen before. She wore it when she believed an innocent was being threatened. 'No, you will not bring this information to the commandant.'

'I have no intention of doing so, as a matter of fact,' he said. 'Even if Walter is guilty, he is innocent, and we are not the only ones on the island to think so, I am sure.'

'I need your strongest assurance, Mr Monsarrat,' Mrs Mulrooney said. 'Walter Gendron's name will not be mentioned in connection with Harefield's death.'

'You have my word,' said Monsarrat. 'However, I very much fear a conversation is taking place which will make my word worthless to anyone on this island except you.'

'Well, we had best get down there,' Mrs Mulrooney said. 'Regardless of what's being said about you in that room, you need to be there to hear it.'

❧

This time Monsarrat opened the door without knocking. He knew Brewster would be offended at the imposition, but he felt that was the least of his concerns, and he badly wanted to get a sense of the ambience of the room before the men in there had had a chance to rearrange their expressions.

Brewster was sitting at his desk holding a letter in both hands, his eyes flicking over the page, jumping from bottom to top and back again. His jaw was clenched in a way that looked painful.

Ellison, on the other hand, was lounging – if such a thing were possible in the small chair he had appropriated – legs casually crossed, leaning back, looking around the room to entertain himself while Brewster absorbed the contents of the letter.

When he heard the door opening, Ellison turned and smiled broadly. 'Mr Monsarrat! What a pleasure to see you. I must say, I am very much looking forward to hearing your defence.'

'I have done nothing which requires defending, as it happens, Mr Ellison. A statement not everyone here can make.'

Brewster glared at him with fury. 'Have you not, indeed?' he yelled. 'Because this document tells me you are intimately familiar with the need to defend your behaviour! I have in front of me a report from the lieutenant governor's office. The records of a convict who goes by the name of Hugh Llewelyn Monsarrat.'

'The colonial secretary has his share of magistrates, Mr Monsarrat,' said Ellison. 'It's quite a brotherhood. They were only too happy to help me when I read a troubling letter to a convict in Parramatta. One which spoke of the writer's first-hand knowledge of deprivation of liberty.'

Monsarrat thought there was still a small chance that the contents of the document were not as damaging as he feared. Best to extract as much information as he could before going on the defensive.

'I would have thought perusal of the personal correspondence of others beneath you,' said Monsarrat.

Ellison shrugged.

'It does, commandant,' Monsarat said, 'give credence to certain theories: who is in a position to view all letters leaving the island.'

'That is *not* what is worrying me now,' said Brewster.

'May I enquire,' Monsarrat said, 'into the precise nature of your concern?'

'The precise nature! My God, you're like Power. You use words to create confusion rather than to give information.

247

And I am sick of the both of you. The precise nature of my concern, Monsarrat, are your former convictions. Two of them! Good Lord, you sat at my table, ate my food and never thought to mention your criminal past. Had I known of it, I assure you I would have had Jones turn his cutter around as soon as it tied up on the dock the day you arrived.'

Brewster had dispensed with the 'Mr'. A troubling sign.

'Captain Brewster, I am who I have always claimed to be. A member of the governor's staff. My superior is intimately acquainted with my background, and sent me nonetheless. In fact, perhaps because of it. I won my freedom through delivering justice to the murderer of a young woman, a woman not unlike your wife, and the wife of a commandant, for that matter. Not only that, but it must be said that I have more than a passing acquaintance with legal matters.'

'Yes,' said Ellison slowly, 'but from the wrong side of the bench, my friend, would you not say?'

'Regardless of what side of the bench,' said Monsarrat, 'my past status has no bearing on my ability to function in the present.'

'No bearing!' said Brewster. 'You concealed the fact that you are a felon!'

'I am now at liberty. I was granted a ticket of leave by the commandant at Port Macquarie, and it was unconditional.'

This, of course, was not precisely true. Monsarrat's ticket of leave relied on his continued utility, and continuing ability to deal with those cases which could not be resolved through the usual channels. It struck him hard once more that his decision to keep any suggestion of Walter's complicity private would very likely put this freedom at risk. Yet he still felt no urge to trade one for the other.

'Why did you not reveal this as soon as you realised that we viewed you as somebody who had always been free?' demanded Brewster.

'It is hardly unusual, in Parramatta at least, for a senior administrator to be a former convict. Barely one in ten people there arrive free. And for his own reasons my superior decided to omit the information when he was corresponding with Richard Marley about my secondment here,' Monsarrat said. 'I am not clear on exactly what those reasons were; however, I felt it best to respect his wishes.'

'While showing a complete lack of respect for me and everyone else on this island – everyone else who has managed to come here without the encumbrance of chains. Ellison and I managed it easily enough, and many others besides,' said Brewster. He Brewster turned to Ellison. 'I'm indebted to you for bringing this to my attention. And as for you, Monsarrat – your fabrications regarding Ellison's involvement in Mr Power's escape are clearly just that.'

Ellison looked at Monsarrat, and grinned broadly.

'Sir,' said Monsarrat. 'My past does not change the fact that I have evidence of Mr Ellison's complicity in Thomas Power's attempted escape.'

'Scraps of paper! Not even words! Not worth my time, not a second of it.'

'Actually,' said Ellison, 'we had better examine them, commandant. I would not like you to wonder.'

Brewster sighed, massaged the bridge of his nose with his index finger and thumb. 'If you insist. Monsarrat, you said you were going to fetch them. I presume they are there?' He nodded to the coat which Monsarrat was still holding over his arm. Ellison reached out quickly and snatched the coat away, fishing in its pockets.

'Mr Ellison, that is my personal property,' said Monsarrat. 'Most inappropriate to rummage through it. I must insist that you hand it back immediately!'

'Insist all you want, Monsarrat,' said Ellison. 'I am seizing it in my capacity as a magistrate. Who knows, maybe you stole it?'

He continued feeling his way through the pockets, drawing out the charred pieces of paper. They looked to Monsarrat even more insubstantial than they had when Mrs Mulrooney had first shown them to him. They could be taken away by a breath of wind, committed to the bay and the sea is beyond.

Ellison looked at each piece of paper in turn, raised his eyebrows sceptically, and handed them to Brewster. Brewster balanced his spectacles on his nose, held the scraps of paper pinched between his fingers, and turned them over a few times. 'It's difficult – impossible – to see how any firm conclusion can be drawn from these,' he said. 'I have had correspondence from Ellison myself – his hand is even, regular, with little to distinguish it.'

'You'll find, if you examine the records,' said Monsarrat, 'that he employs a different hand in the composition of official documents for the lieutenant general. One which is identical to that which is before you.'

'No, Mr Monsarrat, I will not have it. You have been caught in a fabrication. Your character, which I assumed to be of the best, I now know to be of the worst. It is disgraceful that you seek to impugn a magistrate of long-standing with such insultingly flimsy evidence.'

While Brewster was examining the scraps of paper, Ellison was going back through Monsarrat's coat pockets to draw out the more substantial wad of letters. He unfolded them slowly, as though he were sitting at his desk with a glass of port at his elbow, and began to read. As he did, he made small noises of surprise.

Brewster had finished berating Monsarrat by now, and was looking at the magistrate.

'Well, my dear James, it seems that our friend in the guardhouse managed to attract the attention of a lady,' Ellison said. He continued shuffling the papers. 'Ah,' he said. 'Then someone found out. Look.'

He handed the blackmail note over to Brewster, who read it, squinting. 'Do you know, this looks an awful lot like Harefield's writing,' he said. His mouth began to stretch in a teeth-baring smile. 'You know what this means, Henry, don't you? Harefield was blackmailing Power! After which he is found rolling back and forth in the waves with great big indentations hacked into his shoulders. This seals it. It must have been Power!'

He stood up, still smiling, reading the letter again. But when he looked up, at Monsarrat, the smile had gone.

'This was in your possession. And you have been concealing it.'

Ellison was shaking his head in theatrical disapproval.

'Not concealing it,' said Monsarrat. 'Holding it while I sought more complete information.'

'You're one of them, of course, I must remind myself,' said Brewster. 'Probably holding it back out of fellow feeling. No, no, that would be too honourable a course, if a misguided one. How much was Power paying you to keep this back?'

And here it comes, thought Monsarrat. The shadow which unfurled inside him, always called by anger, pushing out reason. The rush of blood, the knowledge that he was about to say something that could prove fatal to his hopes of resolving the situation in a way which did not end up with Walter at the end of a rope. The affront, though. The spittle, which he could feel on his nose from the commandant's outburst. The assumption that he was dishonest. It was not to be borne.

Monsarrat took a step forward, so that he and Brewster were face to face. 'I would like to remind you, commandant, that I am no longer a convict. Before my fall I was a gentleman. And I retain more of a gentleman's sense of honour than some would credit! Nor am I here under false pretences. I am clerk to the governor's private secretary in Parramatta, and on Maria Island at the request of the administration of Van Diemen's Land. And I insist that you treat me with the dignity that fact

251

calls for. If you impugn my integrity, I can assure you there will be consequences.'

'Integrity! My God, you proved yourself to have none – twice! I will impugn it all I like.'

'That is your choice, sir, and it is my choice to deal with the insult in an appropriate manner. That can wait, though. I can assure you that Power is paying me nothing. He is angry at me for alerting you to his escape – and may I remind you that were it not for my intervention he would likely be on his way to America now – on his way to denounce this place to the United States Congress. You, commandant, would need to write a very long, involved and difficult report on how you managed to let this settlement's most notorious prisoner disappear. If you would like me to acquaint a certain Richard Marley with the fact that you were taking your ease in your cottage while a whaler slid into the bay, I would be more than happy to. Otherwise, I suggest that you moderate your tone.'

Brewster took a few steps backwards and sat down. 'As you say, Monsarrat,' he said, struggling to maintain any semblance of composure, 'this can all wait. Why do you believe this letter may not have been meant for Thomas Power?'

'It might have been given to him – by someone seeking counsel on how to respond to it. It was found interleaved with some other documents which came from an external source. And I would prefer to be addressed as Mr Monsarrat, thank you, commandant.'

Ellison, all the while, had been sitting in his chair, leaning back, enjoying the spectacle and grinning. 'Those other documents you speak of, Mr Monsarrat,' he said. 'Would they happen to be these? They do appear to bear all of the signs of hero worship turned more amorous. There is a feminine hand – not that that necessarily means they were written by a female, of course: one has heard the rumours about Power's proclivities. Perhaps they were written by Private Ennis? Or perhaps that

Shanahan, the convict who used to work for Power's father, the one who has been dispatched to the reservoir? In any case, it is difficult to think of anyone on this island who would be in a position to give Harefield what he wanted. Anyone except Thomas Power, prior to his incarceration. Well, apart from the commandant's family, of course.'

Brewster glanced at Ellison, frowning slightly. 'Give me those letters, if you please,' he said.

'Commandant, no!' Monsarrat cried.

Both men looked at him, Ellison with an expression suspiciously close to enjoyment.

'I would strongly advise you,' said Monsarrat, 'to let me complete my investigation before you look at them. An incomplete picture can be worse than no picture at all.'

'I happen to dislike complete darkness,' said Brewster, holding his hand out for the letters.

Ellison raised his eyebrows, shrugged and handed the papers over, grinning all the while. He had stopped lounging, was sitting forward in his chair unable to disguise his avidity.

Brewster started reading, frowned, shuffled the papers, read again, frowned again, and looked up. 'Mr Monsarrat, is this some sort of joke?'

'I assure you, it is not. Were I to wish to joke with you, I would take pains to ensure you found it funny.'

'And these were found in Power's cottage?'

'Yes, after his escape attempt, after he was put in the guardhouse.'

'So there is a chance they have been placed there by someone else?'

For the first time Brewster wasn't glaring at Monsarrat but looking at him with shock. Monsarrat almost felt for the man.

'I'm sorry, commandant, no. There is very little chance of that. The letters were found underneath the floorboards close to the hearth, a repository which only Power was aware of until I discovered it.'

'Why, James, do you suggest that the documents were put there by someone else?' asked Ellison.

'Because, Henry, as I believe Monsarrat is well aware, they are written in the hand of my wife.'

Chapter 26

By late afternoon, Elizabeth Brewster was sleeping. Just as well, thought Hannah. She would need her strength. Hannah knew Mr Monsarrat would be as good as his word, would protect Walter. But now there were others involved. It was difficult to say where things would end up.

She had just returned from the kitchen with a pot of fragrant tea for Elizabeth on her waking when she heard the door pushed inward with a force which spoke of great anger.

James Brewster appeared in the doorway. 'Get out!' he shouted at her.

The yell woke Elizabeth, who struggled to a sitting position against the mounds of soft pillows. 'There is no need to shout,' she said, seeming to forget any fear in her sudden return to consciousness. 'You should know that. Mrs Mulrooney has been tending to me, and does not deserve such rude treatment.'

'And I? What treatment do I deserve? To be betrayed in the settlement I rule, with the worst of men, someone who could have been taking his ease in a castle in Ireland but chose instead to mount a treasonous rebellion?'

'It was not *his* rebellion,' Elizabeth said.

James Brewster strode into the room towards the bed and Hannah took the opportunity to skirt him, unnoticed, and stand by the door. Elizabeth glanced over at her, a silent plea to stay.

'And you would know, wouldn't you, whose revolution it was? Did he tell you when you visited him in his cottage? Did you and he laugh about how you were fooling me? When you were planning his escape?'

He walked over to the bed, grabbed her elbow and dragged her out so she landed heavily on one knee before getting to her feet. He clamped his hands on each shoulder and shook her so violently that her head snapped backwards and forwards, in a way which made Hannah fear for her neck.

'Tell me! Tell me what you planned, when you planned it!'

He let go for a moment, and Elizabeth backed away. 'There is nothing to tell,' she whispered.

'I have seen the letters, stupid woman! There is a lot to tell, and you will tell it.' He reached out his arm and struck her with the back of his hand so hard that she fell to the floor. There was blood down the front of her white nightdress. She tried to raise herself by one hand, but her eyes were unfocused, blinking, and darting around the room without seeming to fix anywhere.

Hannah raced back into the room, around Brewster, taking Elizabeth's elbow and helping her waver to her feet.

'Commandant, there is no call for that,' Hannah barked, and immediately regretted it. This was a man who was not in control of himself, and who had no love for convicts when he was. My God, she thought. I can't command him as he deserves to be commanded – a sweet tone could be the only defence I have. Her voice, though, when she spoke, did retain some of its raw authority. 'No reason to strike your wife at the best of times, let alone when she is ill,' she said. 'Why don't you go into the parlour? I will bring you tea and set Mrs Brewster to rights.'

The captain looked at Hannah for a moment, and she realised what she had done. Jumped into a situation not even the strongest tea could fix. Put herself in the path of a man in the grip of an unrestrained violence. She searched his face for any indication of what was to come. She found nothing, a stare which reflected no humanity, and no recognition that the women in front of him were as human as him.

Then James Brewster pulled back his arm again, and hit Hannah across the face. 'Convict manners! It's not your place to intervene between husband and wife!'

Hannah had planted her legs when she had spoken to him, because that was what she did when she was confronting somebody. It was as well she had, because it stopped her falling as heavily as Elizabeth had, perhaps saved her from hitting her head, so that at least one of women in the room retained her wits.

She still found herself sprawled on the ground. She slowly got to her feet, dragging herself up by the coverlet, scattering drops of blood onto the bed.

'You must send for the doctor, sir,' she said, feeling a slick wetness emerge with the words. 'Your wife – surely you can see, you have injured her grievously. Whatever you intend, I am certain it is not murder.'

'Murder . . . Now, what an interesting idea,' said Brewster.

'You will not be killing her, commandant. Not without killing me as well.'

'I had no intention of killing my wife. I am beginning to wonder, though – now that you mention it – whether she might be entirely blameless in the matter of the death of the bosun.'

He smiled, a vicious contortion of his mouth. He took another step towards her and she forced down a choking fear that arose with the knowledge that he could come at her again unchallenged.

'Now, I will ask you once more, and I recommend that you do not defy me,' he said. 'Get. Out.'

Hannah turned and walked as steadily as she could from the room – the man might be able to split her lip, but she would not allow him to make her run.

But she did run, as soon as she was clear of the cottages, down the hill and past the commissary to a tent pitched by the construction site.

James Brewster had nearly pawed the door off its hinges when he left his office, sprinting up the hill towards his cottage. Monsarrat made to go after him but was held back by hand on his shoulder.

'Mr Monsarrat – I did not know those letters were from Mrs Brewster. I would never have handed them over. I will do all I can for her now. But I must now speak plainly,' said Ellison.

'Plain speech would be wonderful, but it will have to wait. I have fears for Mrs Brewster's safety.'

'He won't kill her,' said Ellison. 'Bad for the reputation. He would never be tried for it, of course – these things happen, the number of ladies who have come before me saying they have fallen downstairs ... And if they themselves say that – probably under duress, but who's to know – I am powerless to do anything about it.'

'Your fine feelings did not prevent you assaulting my housekeeper, and I fear they won't stop your friend assaulting her either.'

'I am appalled at myself for that, admittedly,' Ellison claimed. 'But Brewster is not my friend. He is an inconvenient part of the landscape, who needs to be worked around, like a rock, although far more susceptible to flattery, fraternal nudges, reminders that he and I are the authorities here – that sort of thing. But there is a matter of urgency at hand. I don't think

Mrs Brewster's life is in danger, but her face may not look as pretty as it did – and you are right, we must protect the innocent. Must we not, Mr Monsarrat?'

'There might be nothing left to protect shortly,' said Monsarrat, and he turned and sprinted up the hill.

There was, he saw, lunging and limping towards him, a creature from a nightmare. A bloodied face, a bloodied shirt, and wild, desperate eyes.

He ran to her, took her elbow. 'Did Brewster do this?' he asked in a voice he was barely able to control.

'Never mind about that now,' muttered Mrs Mulrooney. 'You can give me sympathy later, but for now we need to fetch Dr Chester.'

Ellison was lumbering up the hill behind them. Monsarrat turned, caught him in a glare which must've singed some of the whiskers he had allowed to grow.

'This is a man who will restrain himself, is it? A man who can be trusted not to kill someone. Make yourself a force for good, Mr Ellison – go and fetch Dr Chester.'

'I suggest that you do that, Mr Monsarrat,' said Ellison. He looked at Mrs Mulrooney, frowning. 'Are you hurt?' he said.

'I can't imagine what would make you think that, Mr Ellison.'

'Get Chester, and hurry,' Ellison said to Monsarrat. 'I have a far better chance than you of convincing Brewster that there is nothing to be served by this wickedness.'

<hr>

When Chester saw Mrs Mulrooney – who had followed Monsarrat despite him calling over his shoulder for her to go and rest in the commissary – he took her to a cot, sat her down and started palpating her cheek to feel for evidence of a broken jaw.

'I'm not badly hurt, doctor,' said Mrs Mulrooney. 'Mrs Brewster is, though. She was struck, fell, hit her head. Dazed, doesn't seem entirely certain where she is, although I'm fairly sure that she knows she does not want to be there.'

Chester wasted no time on questions. He told Mrs Mulrooney to rest and ran to the door, with Monsarrat following.

When they got to the cottage Brewster was standing outside, his arms folded.

'I've been told your wife is injured, commandant,' said Chester. 'I would like to examine her.'

'You do not have my permission,' Brewster said. 'She tripped, hit her head. She is resting now. I am certain she will recover shortly.'

Chester was silent for a moment. Perhaps taking time to formulate a careful response to a man who needed careful handling.

'I do hope that's the case, sir; however, surely I should look at her, to make certain.'

'That will not be necessary.'

'Mrs Mulrooney is similarly injured, although not as severely,' said Chester, unable to keep a growing anger out of his voice. 'Was it a simultaneous slip by both ladies? May I at least send her to care for your wife?'

'No, you may send no one. I am standing here until arrangements can be made for a more permanent guard.'

'Your wife does not need a guard, commandant,' said Monsarrat. 'She needs a doctor.'

'Oh, but there was never anyone so worthy of being guarded, Mr Monsarrat,' said Brewster. 'You see, I have achieved what you have been unable to, despite all the advantages of your position on the governor's staff. My wife, gentlemen, is under house arrest. For the murder of Bartholomew Harefield.'

※

On her cot in the empty hospital tent, Hannah felt around the inside of her cheek with her tongue, wincing at the sting as it found a gash. She would usually never spit, but she was not fond of the taste of blood, and she was alone. She stood and spattered a red, watery mouthful onto the earth outside the tent.

She was surprised at herself, actually. Surprised she was still here, had not followed Monsarrat up the hill. She was, she realised with a shock, afraid.

Stop being an eejit of a woman, she said to herself. March on out there, down the hill and up the other one, as you always do. Show them some sense, make them behave. But she was not now dealing with unruly geese; she had come face to face with a vindictive and, she suspected, unhinged man who was the ultimate authority on this island.

Still, it was no excuse for cowardice, she thought. Colm would have been appalled. And at the thought of him, and his death at the hands of someone like Captain Brewster, she stood and after cleaning up her face as best she could, she set off.

She was beaten to the cottage by Lieutenant Holloway, whom she saw scurrying from the direction of the barracks. By the time she was close enough to hear, Brewster was already barking orders at him.

'No one in, no one out. My wife will have the cottage to herself.'

Holloway nodded, ran back towards the barracks, no doubt to fetch a more permanent guard for the commandant's wife.

Hannah stood, assessing the scene. Ellison and Monsarrat emerged. Despite his earlier ardour, Ellison seemed not to notice her.

'Commandant, you should at least let the doctor look her over,' he said. 'I'm sure all is well – but news of these things travels, doesn't it? You and I know how quickly rumours fly across the seas, faster than any boat. If word of this reached Hobart – your imprisonment of your wife and your refusal to allow her a doctor – it would seem as though you had lost control here. And I assure you that such an impression will not get you another commission.'

Brewster frowned. 'You will note, gentlemen, that I did not tell Holloway precisely why my wife was to be guarded. Nor do I intend to.'

'Very wise, very wise indeed,' said Ellison. 'If I might suggest, perhaps you should allude to a threat to her safety – a convict who has taken a liking to her, who you feel will break in and molest her? Allow that to be put about and no one would question the presence of the guard at your door. Particularly if you allow her medical treatment. And a companion. Mrs Mulrooney can sleep in her room and attend her. After all, if this is merely a matter of protecting her virtue, what possible reason could there be for denying her these things?'

Brewster nodded slowly. 'Very well then. Things will come out eventually, of course, but until then . . . Yes. There is no point in Marley being alerted to all of this, unless it is us alerting him, and then with a very carefully constructed tale. Dr Chester, you may go in and attend to my wife. Mulrooney – you too.'

Hannah bowed – more important than ever to observe the niceties now. She froze, though, when he grabbed her by the elbow as she passed him, and saw Monsarrat's look of alarm.

'Once you go in, you will not be permitted out again. Can't have any more messages carried.' Brewster turned to Ellison. 'Clearly it was my wife, rather than you, Henry, responsible for helping Power plan his escape. I must apologise for entertaining the notion of your guilt.'

Ellison had the grace to look slightly uncomfortable, but nodded his thanks.

Monsarrat walked Hannah to the door. 'Does it hurt very much?' he asked. In that moment he held himself in the highest contempt. He should be making Brewster bleed in the dirt, and he badly wanted to.

'I probably won't be eating anything hard for a time, but otherwise it's not too bad. Certainly nowhere near as bad as Elizabeth Brewster's injury.'

'I will walk by the window a couple of times a day. If you need me, rap on it. I hope they send a guard who is reasonable. Private Ennis would do nicely, but you can never tell,' he said.

'Don't worry, Mr Monsarrat. I am being confined in a comfortable cottage – seems to me that I am getting off more lightly than I have in the past.'

He smiled, squeezed her elbow. 'You are braver than any soul I've ever met,' he said.

'Ah, it's not bravery, Mr Monsarrat. If I let her flounder, if she suffocates under the weight of a husband's fists . . . Well, I fear the shade of another young woman would not approve.'

Chapter 27

Chester was squinting in the dying light, looking at the wound on Elizabeth's temple when Hannah walked in. Elizabeth had her eyes open but they were glazed, staring at the wall as if it bore a painting only she could see.

'I think she'll be all right, thankfully,' said Chester, without turning around. 'Here, Mrs Mulrooney – you might find this useful at some point. Come and look.'

She moved over to the bed. Chester drew one of Elizabeth's eyelids closed, and then opened it gently again with his thumb. She did not seem to notice the manipulation.

'Look, here, see? Notice how her pupil is getting smaller? That is good. When that fails to happen, it is a matter of great concern,' he said.

'What needs doing for her?' asked Hannah.

'Nothing that you have not been doing already. Well, almost. I must stress how important it is that you keep talking to her. Trying to draw her out. Don't let her slip into such a deep sleep that we might have trouble rousing her, or even be unable to. Beyond that, simply do as you have been doing. Tea and so on. If you have the wherewithal here to make broth, that might be useful as well. I shall see if Walter can send something up from the stores that you can use.'

'Walter . . . he doesn't know. Dr Chester, I fear if he understood the reality of the situation, he might do something . . . something foolish. Something which cannot be compensated for. It is probably better to let him believe the fiction that Brewster has made up – that she was under threat from a crazed convict but is perfectly safe now that she's being guarded.'

Chester nodded. 'You're probably right about Walter, poor lad. Devoted to his sister. And with Power incarcerated, Mrs Brewster injured and you, dear lady, cooped up here, I do worry for the lad, Mrs Mulrooney. It is a dangerous enough world for those equipped to deal with it. Without protection, I fear Walter will flounder.'

～

Brewster had worn the beginnings of a groove into the dirt beside his front step by the time Lieutenant Holloway returned with Private Ennis.

'There is a need to protect my wife from molestation, private. I will not go into details, nor will you enquire. But you will guard this door through the night and allow no one in – or out – without my express approval.'

Ennis nodded, and then remembered himself and saluted, before taking up his position at the door.

Chester emerged shortly afterwards, opened his mouth to speak. No words were allowed to escape, though, before Brewster said, 'Dr Chester, Ellison. My office, if you please.'

Chester and Ellison glanced at Monsarrat and followed the commandant and Holloway down the hill.

Brewster turned, when he realised that those in his train included Monsarrat. 'Your presence is not required, Mr Monsarrat.'

'Yet I will be accompanying you, commandant, required or not,' Monsarrat said, reverting to a bluntness he did not often get to use. 'I would prefer not to write a report on how information was withheld from me, and how a suspicion of murder was covered up to save your reputation. But I will do so if you leave me no other choice.'

Brewster looked at Monsarrat for a moment. It was not the glare he was expecting. It was a cold, assessing look. Monsarrat had the uncomfortable impression he was being measured in some way.

'Very well then, damn you,' said Brewster.

There was barely room to shut the door in the small outbuilding with the five of them in there. But it was clear the door must be shut in the commandant's view. They had a deception to discuss – or so Monsarrat thought.

'Chester,' Brewster said, settling himself behind the desk. 'What is your opinion of my wife's strength?'

Chester was caught off guard by the question, failed to hide his surprise in time.

'Would you not like me to discuss your wife's current condition?' he asked.

'I would like you to answer my question.'

'As you know, your wife is in frail health at the moment,' said Chester. 'Exacerbated, if I may say, by the hit to the head she took during her . . . stumble.'

'Her assisted stumble,' said Monsarrat.

Chester shot him a warning look. 'She is confused, disoriented, but it is my hope that the condition's not permanent,' he said. 'She needs rest.'

'I did not ask you to tell me of her needs, doctor. Is she, do you think, a strong woman when in health?'

'Possibly stronger than many, given her involvement in the life of the settlement,' said Chester.

'But is she as strong as a man?'

'I would say not,' said Chester. He was frowning now, probably trying to look ahead for further protruding branches on the path Brewster was leading him down.

'And you told me, doctor, when you examined Harefield's body, that the wound to his shoulder would have required a significant amount of force.'

'I . . . Yes, I did,' said Chester.

'Strong lad, that Walter,' Brewster said.

'Commandant,' said Monsarrat, 'I have only been here a short time, and have not managed to discover as much as I would like. One thing I have learned, though, is that Walter is among the gentlest souls I have known.'

'You see it too, then,' said Brewster. 'You must, if you are trying to dissuade me from forming an opinion which I haven't yet articulated.'

There was an intake of breath from Ellison. 'Commandant,' he said, 'this is madness. You know Walter isn't capable of violence.'

'I know no such thing. What I do know is the regard in which he holds his sister. It would be most convenient if I were correct. A murderess for a wife – the stain of that would never leave me. This would be my last command. But a strong young man known to not be in full possession of his wits – such a circumstance, while regrettable, would be unlikely to pose much of an impediment to my advancement.'

'Your advancement at the cost of Walter's life,' said Monsarrat.

'Do you know, Mr Monsarrat, how long I have had to drag that fool around with me? How many tasks I have had to find for him in each settlement so that he might feel useful, so that he might continue to enjoy the wages that come with an official position like commissary without having to do any of the work associated with it? I assure you, I would be more than happy to give that burden up. My wife would be devastated, but she can wail all the way to her own trial.'

'You mustn't do this,' said Ellison. 'It is a mistake which cannot be unmade.'

'You have not the authority, magistrate, to tell me what to do and what not to do. I thought to bring this matter before you, in the fullness of time, but it is apparent you would not give it your objective consideration. You may return to the mainland at your earliest convenience. I will tell Jones to have the boat ready within the hour. In the meantime, we have some questions to ask my brother-in-law.'

<hr />

Elizabeth's eyes were beginning to focus, her gaze snagging on one object after another as she seemed to be trying to ascertain how she had come to be back in bed.

When she tried to sit up, though, she let out a low complaint which brought Hannah to her side.

'You have hurt your head, Mrs Brewster. Do not try to sit up, not yet,' she said.

Elizabeth either didn't hear, or ignored her. She braced herself against her hands, pushed herself upright and was immediately sick over the coverlet.

Hannah expected her to flag, and ran to the kitchen to get a bowl of water and some rags to clean up the pungent mess. When she got back, Elizabeth was standing. She was not doing so without effort, holding onto the brass bedstead. But she seemed alert enough, and in no danger of immediately tumbling.

'Sit here, at the dressing table,' said Hannah. 'I'll change your bed for you. Then you can lie back down.'

'I have no intention of lying back down, Mrs Mulrooney,' said Elizabeth. 'I need to go and find my brother. Would you fetch me some clothes?'

'If that's your wish, but you will not be able to go in search of Mr Gendron.'

'Why ever not? You will assist me, won't you? I must confess, I would welcome an arm to lean on.'

'And you would have it. But you and I, we are not permitted to leave. You are under guard.'

'Under *guard*? How ridiculous! On whose authority?'

'On your husband's. Do you remember, he . . .'

'He struck me, yes,' she said calmly. 'Has done so before, at times of stress. Not for a while, now. He realised that such behaviour demonstrated a lack of control which would not impress his superiors.'

It was odd to hear her speaking of it as a simple transaction, thought Hannah. But she knew that such things happened, and frequently. There were very few courses of action open to women thus abused. Her regard for Elizabeth Brewster swelled in that moment. To bend every waking thought to preventing such treatment, as a means of protecting not only herself but her brother's position here, must have been extraordinarily exhausting.

'Mrs Brewster, did you confess to the murder of Bartholomew Harefield?'

'I did. And will do so again, before any magistrate my husband likes.'

Hannah could not help stepping backwards.

'You need not worry, Mrs Mulrooney,' said Elizabeth. 'I am no danger to you.'

'And don't I know that,' said Hannah. 'As does Mr Brewster. While he is using your confession as an excuse to hold you here, I fear he knows that Walter is the one responsible.'

Elizabeth blanched, then grabbed hold of the bed head to stop herself falling. 'Do you know what he intends to do?' she whispered.

'I do not. But I very much fear he intends to take things forward. Could he be right in believing Walter guilty of such a crime?' asked Hannah.

'Yes,' Elizabeth said, quietly. 'God help me, it was for my protection.'

'Because Harefield was threatening to expose you?'

'Partly. He saw Walter embrace Power, of course. But I sent Walter off very quickly. Feared that the gesture might be misinterpreted – as it was. I didn't know Harefield was watching. So I added my own embrace before following Walter back down to the commissary. Some days later I found a note wedged in the pages of the commissary ledger. Unsigned, but I knew who it was from. There was no chance of my acceding to his request – it might have led to my own incarceration. But I thought if I could talk to him, offer to intercede with my husband for better pay, more rations, something along those lines, perhaps it might have been enough.'

'You followed him to the light, then?'

'Yes, as little as I wanted to.'

'This is a rough man who assaulted your brother. Were you not frightened he might do the same to you? There would have been no help to hand, not in the middle of that bush.'

'Oh, I was terrified,' Elizabeth said. 'But if Harefield made good on his threats it would kill me anyway. This was my only path to survival. I was not unarmed though. I had the axe. It was next to useless – and Harefield knew it too – he had borrowed it once and returned it, saying the spoon from my kitchen would have been of more use. And had he seen it in my hands, seen me trying to wield it against him, he would have laughed. So I sharpened it. There's a whetstone behind the commissary, you know. It was put to good use. I even rubbed some oil into the blade so that Harefield would be in no doubt that the implement I carried was capable of significant damage. But I did *not* intend to use it.'

'I am assuming Harefield did not accept your terms,' said Hannah.

'He would not even speak to me. Just climbed the ladder as though I wasn't there. I grabbed hold of it, shook it. Simply to get his attention. But I must have used more force than I believed I was capable of, because he came crashing down. That's when he lunged at me, sent me sprawling to the ground, knocked the axe out of my hand, pinned me by the shoulders. And he had the most horrible grin on his face. The man's breath, good Lord, I could smell the teeth as they rotted out of his head. I closed my eyes, and then I felt his weight suddenly come down on me. I was certain he was going to . . .'

Elizabeth paused, looked down. Hannah patted her hand. 'You must not worry about speaking of such things in front of me,' she said. 'It is a tale of the kind I've heard before, and very much fear I will again in future.'

Elizabeth was breathing quickly now, and Hannah gave her a cup of water and stroked her hair.

'I should have screamed but my throat was dry. There was no point anyway – no one would have heard me. I waited, waited for him to do what he was going to do. He didn't move. I opened my eyes and Walter was standing there, an axe in his hand, and Harefield was bleeding.'

'All over you,' said Hannah.

'He's a dear thing, Walter,' said Elizabeth. 'You can see it, I know. I have protected him since we were children – my father had so longed for a son, and when he got Walter – well, he couldn't see his charm, couldn't see past what he viewed as his deficiencies. And my mother – so hidebound, she was. She never defended him when my father raised his fists. It was my job to do that. I would stand between them, and my father stopped short of striking me. Usually. I suppose Walter thought it was his turn to protect me.'

'And he did protect you.'

'Yes. He stood there for a moment, looking at Harefield and the axe in his hands, and then he turned to me and started to cry. Wailed. I haven't heard him make that sound since our father locked him in a stable overnight to punish him for his inability to ride a horse. And then he knelt, tried to take Harefield by the shoulder, shook him and said, "Wake up, wake up". No one could have survived those blows, though. And Harefield's shoulder was flopping backwards as Walter was shaking him. Then he said how sorry he was – that he hadn't meant it, but he knew Harefield was going to hurt me.'

'Poor Walter. And he must've been splattered with blood.'

'Yes, he was. So was I. We were fortunate night was drawing in. We bundled his bloodied shirt up and took it back for burning. Then we dragged Harefield over to the edge.

'I warned Walter he must never, ever tell anyone. And he's not given rise to any suspicion as far as I know, until now. I can't let him hang, Mrs Mulrooney.'

'No, indeed. I can assure you I'll do anything I can to help prevent it,' said Hannah.

'We are under guard, you say?' said Elizabeth.

'We are,' said Hannah, 'Private Ennis, who guarded Mr Power.'

'Ennis. I wonder if he'd . . . Come sit with me, Mrs Mulrooney. We will avoid the side of the bed that I've managed to soil. I very much hope you will agree to grant me a favour.'

⧼⧽

'As you insist on invoking your status as the governor's man, Mr Monsarrat, you may come with me while I interview Prisoner Gendron. I wouldn't want you writing a report of obstruction.'

Prisoner Gendron. In those two words, Captain Brewster reduced his brother-in-law to another inconvenience which needed managing on an island full of inconveniences.

As Ellison made to follow Brewster to the commissary Brewster turned again, glaring at the magistrate. 'Jones will be departing shortly and you will be with him,' said Brewster. 'There is very little point, magistrate, in you attending this interview.'

'Do you not think you should have someone with legal training there? Simply for administrative proprietary?' said Ellison. His tone was calm, almost casual, but his eyes were flicking from the commissary to the dock and back again.

'I don't think that will be necessary,' Brewster said, walking away.

Monsarrat looked at Ellison, grimaced and turned to follow Brewster, but the magistrate called him back.

'Mr Monsarrat, she will be taken care of, arrangements will be made. Please let her know, if you're able to.'

At the commissary Brewster yanked open the door, gestured Monsarrat inside, closed it. Walter was at his usual place behind the desk, staring at the ledger. He stood when Brewster entered. 'James! What a surprise to see you here. I was just going over our provisions. We have enough salt pork to last until next week, but the rice is running low. Do you think Jones could get some? I saw him getting the boat ready.'

'Walter, sit down,' said Brewster.

'Let me just show you – over here – look, we have everything organised on the shelves now,' Walter said, walking to the back of the room.

'I said, sit down!' Brewster yelled. In the confined quarters, his voice echoed off the timbers and the newly organised pots and barrels and crates, making Monsarrat start. He could not imagine how much more frightening it would be for Walter.

Walter did as he was told, moving his half-moon spectacles from his forehead to his nose, possibly to conceal the shining in his eyes.

273

Brewster leaned on the table, pushing his torso forward until his head was directly over Walter.

'Why did you kill Bartholomew Harefield?' he said.

Walter gasped. He opened his mouth, closed it again and shook his head. 'Elizabeth said—'

'Elizabeth can say what she likes. I will never again listen to her. Did you do it because he had found out about her friendship with Power?'

'But you knew she was friends with him! You were too! So was I, and I still am!' He inhaled sharply, and then shut his mouth in a firm line.

'You did, didn't you?' hissed Brewster. 'It must've been most inconvenient when Harefield found out about the liaison between those two.'

Walter had clearly decided that any reaction was going to be used by Brewster to build a case. He sat back like a petulant child, mouth shut, staring.

'I wouldn't have believed it of you, Walter. You are a very stupid man, yes, but I had always taken you for an honest one. Now I know that you have been part of this deception all along, it is not something I can forgive. And the taking of Harefield's life is not something which can be forgiven by the courts, either. You are coming with me.'

'I can't, James! You know I can't. I need to stay here, to run the commissary.'

'Walter, you have never run the commissary. You have never done any such thing. It will be a relief to get someone qualified in here, someone who does not need your sister's supervision, which is just as well, as she won't be there to give it. You know, I assume, what an accomplice is.'

But Walter had decided on silence again, his lips pressed so firmly together that Monsarrat could hardly see them.

'That is what your sister is. Your accomplice. When you hang for Harefield's murder, she will hang with you. I shall not attend though. I have no love left for her, and I will be too busy preparing for my next posting. Stand up and come with me. It's only fair that I give you some time to say goodbye.'

Chapter 28

'Please, *a buachaill*. I am not the one under arrest. I do hate to ask you to disregard the commandant's orders but it's crucial that I get out. I will be back within ten minutes.'

Private Ennis was shifting uneasily from one foot to the other. It was clear he did not understand why the house-keeper had been confined with Mrs Brewster. After all, why should she be protected from a convict who was stalking the commandant's wife? Orders, though, were orders, no matter how inexplicable.

'You heard him, missus. Were it up to me, you'd have the freedom of the island, but Captain Brewster said nobody out.'

'But . . . but Mrs Brewster has been ill, you see. She has no clean nightclothes, no clean sheets. I must go down to the commissary to see if such things are available there. You surely wouldn't begrudge a little comfort to an ill woman.'

The private was clearly at odds with himself, poor fellow, and she felt bad for putting him through it. His discomfort, though, was minimal compared to what she would suffer if Walter was executed.

Eventually Ennis exhaled through his nose like a young bull. 'Ten minutes, Mrs Mulrooney. In thanks for the shortbread and the tea, and your company. After that, I will have no choice but to report your absence.'

Mrs Mulrooney grabbed the young man's shoulders, stood on her tiptoes and kissed him on the cheek. 'That's from your mother, you dear lad. Ten minutes. I will have returned before then, and the door will close behind me as though I was never gone.' She lifted her skirt and began hobbling down the hill towards the dock, where a rotund figure in a black suit with a white bib paced.

She did not know which of the saints made sure she didn't trip in her heedless rush, and resolved to light a candle for all of them when she was next in a position to do so. In the meantime, she sent into the air a quick prayer of thanks to St Jude, the patron saint of hopeless causes, in the hope that hers would not remain so.

She glanced about the dock to make sure Brewster was not prowling, and then scurried to the spot where Ellison was standing, looking across the water. She touched him on the shoulder, and he jumped and turned.

'Mrs Mulrooney! I would have thought you'd be delighted to see me leave the island without any further talk between us.'

'And so I would have been, I'll be honest with you. But I'm here on behalf of Mrs Brewster.'

'How is she?'

'Fretting about her brother, but otherwise extraordinarily strong, given the circumstances.'

'She's fretting with good reason, I'm afraid,' said Ellison. 'The commandant is interviewing him as we speak. With your Mr Monsarrat.'

'He will advocate for Walter. Will do his best, anyway,' said Hannah. 'But I doubt he can prevent Walter's trial, his execution. Especially now that certain people have seen to it that Mr Monsarrat's previous crimes have come to light.'

Ellison frowned. 'I regret it. I regret nothing more, though, than showing Mrs Brewster's letters to her husband. I did not recognise her hand – the messages always came from Power himself.'

'You have made a number of mistakes, haven't you?'

'Yes. And damned if I know how to clean them up.'

'I have been cleaning up messes for decades,' said Hannah. 'And I have a suggestion for you. From Mrs Brewster, actually.'

He nodded as she told him the plan, slowly, and then more emphatically.

'There is always a chance Brewster will refuse to accept my authority,' he said. 'That he'll throw me off the island – indeed as he is in the process of doing. But I do believe this is the best chance we have. And if it doesn't work . . . well, I'll consider it my duty to contrive a means of escape for them. A pity that there is no one to carry letters, or to signal the approach of a ship.'

'Ah yes, the signal,' said Hannah. 'What was it, by the way? Tell me quickly! How did Mr Power know to run down to the sea?'

Ellison allowed himself a smile. 'She became quite good at it, actually,' he said. 'She showed it off to me, once. She told me that she would go for long walks to practise until she felt her voice blended into the sounds of the island's other creatures.'

'But what sound was she making?'

'That peculiar rasping honk of the geese. I couldn't tell hers apart from one of the real ones in the end. Three of them, a five-second silence, and then another three. Anyone listening would have heard nothing but a creature making its annoyance felt.'

'They have a use for something then,' said Hannah, thinking of Grace O'Leary imitating an owl to warn her friends of a patrol. 'Perhaps I won't wring one of their necks, even if I get another opportunity.'

Ellison began to smile, but stopped when he spotted the commissary door opening. 'Get behind me,' he whispered, 'Then move around behind those crates, when you can do so without being seen. I'll do my best to get Brewster back inside, and you can follow the gully up the hill back to the cottage. Stay low. Because the necks of the geese are not the ones at risk now.'

❧❧❧

Walter was openly sobbing.

'I would hold you in the utmost contempt,' James Brewster said, 'but I do not believe you're worth the exertion.'

He walked to the door, pulled it open, stepped outside. 'Are you coming?' he yelled back, without turning.

Walter got to his feet but didn't move. Brewster looked as though he was going to open his mouth and launch another insult but he was interrupted by a call from the dock.

'Commandant!' Ellison's voice was distant, but getting closer. 'Commandant – please listen to me. I do believe I am in a position to save you from an embarrassing legal blunder.'

'I doubt it, magistrate,' Brewster called back. 'I've told you to wait for Jones . . .'

But by now Ellison had gained the front steps of the commissary, had taken the commandant's elbow and was attempting to steer him back inside. Brewster roughly shook his elbow out of Ellison's grasp, but did walk back through the door.

'I suggest we shut this,' said Ellison. 'I am sure you would wish this conversation to remain confidential.'

'There seems to be very little that is confidential here anymore,' said Brewster.

'All the more reason to make sure we are faultless in how we manage things now.'

'Faultless? Oh, I certainly am. I am about to take a murderous simpleton up to join his sister under house arrest.'

'Yes, well, that's just it,' said Ellison. 'House arrest, with only a handful of people who know the real reason. Do you know, James, there are those who would say you are refusing to follow due process just to save yourself embarrassment.'

'If you're accusing me—'

'I'm doing no such thing, dear boy. I am simply telling you that sort of concealment could land you in a spot of legal bother. But if you were to allow the law to take its course – to bring the culprits to justice, regardless of who they are – there are some, many actually, who would say that that is a mark of a fellow of great integrity. I for one would certainly ensure that those whose opinions matter saw it in that light.'

Brewster paused. 'What are you suggesting?'

'The brig which will convey Power to Macquarie Harbour is due, am I correct?'

'Yes, thank God.'

'What if it were to take not one prisoner, but three? I would accompany Mrs Brewster and Mr Gendron – sorry, the prisoners – and on arrival in Triabunna I would escort them to Hobart, where they would be imprisoned and tried. While we are waiting, I would be more than willing to draft a report for Richard Marley and the lieutenant general. Emphasising your impartiality, your honesty. You may read it, if you like – change it, even. We can send it on ahead with Jones, so that it reaches their eyes before the prisoners arrive in Hobart.'

'If word of this gets out, they'll never stop laughing . . .' said Brewster.

'If you do not do as I suggest, and word of it gets out, you will be arrested. I assure you I will bend my efforts to that end, every bit as much as I will to the preservation of your reputation should you decide on the wise course of following my advice. And please don't forget, my dear James, that I have seen the convicts you send across to work on your Orford house.

I have noted their names, the dates when you sent them. Your conviction would be a simple matter.'

Brewster began to pace. His head was down and he bumped into one of the shelves. An earthenware pot fell off, shattering and spilling out tea leaves. He looked at it for a moment and resumed pacing.

'You will write this report today, then. I will read it, change it should it need to be changed, and Jones, as soon as possible, will take it across the water.'

'Of course, James,' said Ellison. 'The very course of action I was suggesting.'

Brewster sighed. 'You had best start on that document, magistrate, if we are to have any hope of getting it to Hobart in good time.'

'Naturally. I will begin at once. I must say though, such a missive would benefit greatly from a beautiful hand, and the speed at which we need to accomplish this precludes my own – I write appallingly when I'm rushing.'

Ellison turned to Monsarrat, smiled. 'Mr Monsarrat, do you happen to know anyone with any experience as a clerk?'

⁓⦵⁓

Monsarrat and Ellison walked in silence up the hill, Monsarrat having to pause every now and then to allow Ellison to catch up.

'I must say, I am better fitted to a life of the mind than of the body,' Ellison said. 'No, don't wait. Walter won't have any kind of life if we don't hurry up.'

He sat down heavily at the table when they entered the magistrate's cottage, looking around and then frowning as though he had expected Mrs Mulrooney to come in with a cup of tea.

Monsarrat laid out the papers, fetched his own pen and ink, and sat down. Into the night Ellison spoke eloquently and easily, describing the crime, the means of its perpetration, and how James Brewster had been the man to ultimately discover the culprit. He also noted that Brewster had single-handedly prevented the escape of Thomas Power.

'Making me a little bit nauseated, actually,' he said to Monsarrat after a while. 'I'm sorry for the fabrications.'

'Just sorry for them? You are hauling a lad who might as well be innocent to Hobart for almost certain execution. I know murderers must be punished, but Walter . . . ? It would be like hanging a child, as happened in the old, bad days.'

Ellison sighed. 'Do you know, Mr Monsarrat, sometimes I think your housekeeper has more wits than you.'

'Oh, I know she does.'

'This was her idea,' said Ellison.

'To send them both to Hobart for trial?'

Ellison frowned at him. It was a look he knew well on the face of Mrs Mulrooney. Had Ellison had a cleaning cloth in his hand, Monsarrat would have ducked.

'They will never get to Hobart, Mr Monsarrat, of that I assure you. They will spend the night – under my guard, as I told Brewster – at the inn at Triabunna. I will wake up in the morning with a painful but thankfully temporary wound on the back of my head, and they will be gone. They will have slid over the water early in the morning in a small boat, which will take them to a whaler bound for America.'

'*Well*. That . . . does rather put a different complexion on things,' said Monsarrat. He felt embarrassed for failing to look beneath the skin of the plan, and for failing to recognise Mrs Mulrooney's marks all over it.

'While we're on the subject of apology, Mr Monsarrat. I do wish I hadn't acquainted the commandant with your background.'

'So do I. Presumably you wanted to destroy my credibility in case I accused you of working with Power.'

'Yes, and that did work rather well, didn't it?' Ellison said, smiling.

'If you were expecting congratulations,' said Monsarrat, 'don't expect any from me.'

'Nor would I, dear boy. I do intend to atone, should a suitable opportunity arise. In the meantime, you and I have something a little more urgent to do. Shall we resume? I am not sure we have yet applied enough hyperbole to the remarkable fortitude of the commandant in bringing a killer to justice.'

Chapter 29

'Do you truly think there's a chance that we might escape?' asked Elizabeth. She had slept badly and woken in the early hours, waking Hannah in turn. Now, with the sun well and truly up, she was slumped in a chair.

'Well, I believe it's the best chance you have,' said Hannah. 'I suppose it all comes down to how much you trust Mr Ellison.'

'Oh, he has been marvellous,' said Elizabeth. 'I don't believe he would do anything to harm us.'

'I must say, you and I have had different experiences of him,' said Hannah. 'Why do you hold him in such high esteem?'

'Being the wife of James Brewster is tiring. Being the sister of Walter is tiring, Mrs Mulrooney. Please don't misunderstand, I adore my brother. But he does need a certain amount of protecting. Nonetheless, looking after him is not nearly as exhausting as being married to a man whose regard for you depends on how he thinks others will see you. On whether you are pretty enough, pliable enough, to make a superior think, Well, he must not be such a bad fellow with a wife like that. The one area in which James has never taxed me is conversation. I don't think he entertains the notion that

284

I might have an opinion on any matter beyond the walls of this cottage. And if he has, he certainly would not care to hear it.'

'Yes, I can see how you would find that stifling. Suffocating, in fact.'

'You know, Mrs Mulrooney, when you are in the middle of the heat of summer, you don't understand just how uncomfortable you are until the cool change arrives. On his first visit here, James paraded around like some sort of actor. Barking commands, demonstrating his authority. Whenever anyone is on the island from outside, he behaves as though he is the general of a large army, rather than somebody whose main task is to stop convicts from killing each other and hopefully to encourage them to get some work done. So when Mr Ellison first called on us, he said that he could see James was frightfully busy – and James always nods when somebody tells him how busy he is – and wondered whether I might show him the more scenic parts of the settlement. I took him up towards the painted cliffs, and as we walked he asked me what I had read recently.'

'Seems an inoffensive question,' said Hannah.

'Oh, it is. It's just one I am not accustomed to being asked. I am not sure James realises I can read. Anyway, I told Ellison I had recently been reading William Hazlitt's *The Spirit of the Age* and he clapped his hands and laughed as though I'd said the wittiest thing in the world. He said it was one of his favourites. He offered to bring me books that he had finished with. He said he was sure a place like this smothers an intelligent soul. And one day, in a package of books he brought me, I found a volume by Thomas Paine. *Rights of Man*, it was called. A dangerous book to have, full of revolutionary ideas. Some would say even possessing a copy amounted to treason.'

'Why would he take such a risk?'

'He hedged it. When I held it up he said he had no idea how that scurrilous piece of work got in there, that he had confiscated it from an educated convict. But he made no move to take it back, and so I read it. In secret, of course – God knows what James would have done if he had found it. And the ideas – the depiction of the world where people are not treated like cattle. Perhaps it might even be a world where striking someone is forbidden, even if you are married to them. So I made no move to give it back to Ellison straight away, and when I returned it to him I said that it was as well he had confiscated it because such a book might give a person notions. And we wouldn't want that.'

'He was recruiting you,' said Hannah.

'Yes, he was, although of course I had no idea of it at the time. He had been a friend of one of Power's co-conspirators, one of those who gave up his parole, who promised not to escape in exchange for a ticket of leave which would keep him here until his sentence expired. The fellow had pushed Mr Ellison out of the way when a cart horse broke free and went cantering through Triabunna. And the man had felt bad about his own freedom when his great friend Thomas Power languished across the water on a matter of principle. So Ellison agreed to help him and therefore Power.'

Hannah started, aghast when she heard the door open. Private Ennis was still at his post. When she had returned, he had pretended not to see her as she moved as silently as possible past him and into the cottage.

Elizabeth was staring at the bedroom door. Possibly wondering who would come through it. Possibly fearing she knew.

'Mrs Brewster,' a voice called out down the hallway. 'Mrs Brewster, would you kindly come into the parlour?'

Elizabeth slowly exhaled. It was not the voice of her husband. Nearly as bad – Lieutenant Holloway was the one calling. But at least he was unlikely to strike anyone.

Hannah helped Elizabeth put on a robe, knot her hair up, and drape herself in the shawl.

Holloway wasn't alone. A blurred shape came hurtling towards the women as soon as they stepped into the other room. Walter, seemingly heedless of his great, broad-shouldered mass, ran at Elizabeth and Hannah. 'I'm sorry!' he wailed. 'I'm sorry, I'm sorry, I'm sorry. You said not to tell. But James made me!'

Holloway scowled at Walter. 'I should have put you in irons,' he said.

He turned to Elizabeth.

'Your brother has confessed to the murder,' said Holloway. 'He will be held here under guard until a transport is ready. You will go in the same boat which will convey Power on the first section of his journey to Macquarie Harbour, after it disgorges another gaggle of convicts on to this island. Until then, please be aware that you are now considered prisoners and will be treated as such, if any attempt to leave is made.'

He looked at all of them in turn, including Hannah, clearly seeing no reason not to include her in the category.

'Now, come and sit down, Walter,' said Elizabeth, looking exhausted now Holloway had left. 'Here, have my seat. You like my seat, don't you? And I daresay our rations will continue unchanged, at least as long as there is still food in the kitchen. Perhaps Mrs Mulrooney should make you a cup of tea?'

He nodded vigorously, began to wail again.

Hannah rushed off, sending up a quick prayer to St Lawrence, the patron saint of cooking, giving thanks for her continuing access to a kitchen. When she got back, Walter had his head in his hands, his shoulders heaving.

'James doesn't like me,' he was saying. 'He's angry with me all the time.'

'It's all right, Walter,' Elizabeth said, stroking his mop of unkempt dark hair.

'Why is he angry with me for Harefield when I did it for you?'

'He is angry with both of us, no doubt,' said Elizabeth. 'But you're not to worry, Walter. Things will work out, and there are plans being put in place right now to make sure they do.'

'Can we still go to America with Thomas?'

Elizabeth looked up sharply, raised her eyes at Hannah. An acknowledgement that there were questions to be asked, and that Elizabeth hoped they would not be asked now. A plea to leave them until later. Hannah nodded.

'Possibly America,' said Elizabeth. 'But not with Thomas, I'm afraid, Walter.'

'But I don't want to go if he's not coming. We can't leave him behind!'

'I'm afraid that's precisely what we will have to do, eventually,' said Elizabeth. 'He will not be here on the island for long, in any case. Did you not hear what Holloway said? You and I are going to take a trip with Magistrate Ellison, in the same boat as Mr Power.'

When Walter beamed, Elizabeth shook her head. 'It will not be a pleasure trip, I'm afraid. I expect Mr Power will be travelling below decks. As might we.'

'Should we tell Thomas what we're doing? So he's not confused?'

'No, Walter, I'm sorry, but we can't leave here until it is time to get on the boat.'

'Then I shall not be able to say goodbye to the seals, either?'

'They will understand,' said Hannah. 'They are used to us coming and going, and there may be others along the way.'

'I should have thought to try and train them,' said Walter. 'Perhaps they could have been coaxed into carrying messages.'

'Ah, but we've Mrs Mulrooney for that,' said Elizabeth, smiling at the housekeeper.

'And I'm given to understand that there is a certain odd goose on the island who is also quite good at giving a signal,' said Hannah. 'I would dearly like to hear its call, before it flies north.'

Elizabeth laughed quietly. 'Perhaps you may yet get the opportunity,' she said. 'Geese, after all, are very obliging when someone is willing to listen to them.'

⁓

James Brewster put down the document, and nodded. 'It is adequate,' he said.

It was, in fact, almost complete fabrication. It cast Brewster as a highly intelligent, perceptive and courageous officer who would not allow even marital affection to interfere with the carriage of justice.

'I imagine you will want to write your own letter to go with this,' said Ellison.

'I don't think so,' said Brewster. 'You seem to have captured the situation perfectly well.'

'Ah, but surely you want to acknowledge Mr Monsarrat's role? The perspicacity of his investigation, and his part in preventing the escape of Mr Power.'

'I understood, magistrate, that the entire purpose of this document was to acquaint the lieutenant governor with my role in bringing the guilty to justice, and mine only.'

'Yes, of course, and you are absolutely right, James. However, the mark of a true hero is his humility. Please don't forget that I deal with these people in Hobart all the time, and I have a reasonable sense of what is likely to impress them. If you were to say that here is a report which describes, in perhaps too glowing terms, your part in all this, but that mention must be made of the services performed by Mr Monsarrat – well, I think it would create a very favourable impression.'

'All right. If you think it is what they want to hear.'

'It is, it is. Mr Monsarrat and I would be delighted to draft something up for your signature, wouldn't we?'

'I will be of service in any capacity needed,' said Monsarrat.

'Will you, indeed,' said Brewster. 'You've been of very little service to me.'

'Except in preventing what would possibly have been the most embarrassing escape in the history of the colony,' said Ellison mildly. 'But of course, I can always acquaint those in Hobart with the facts myself.'

'No, write the damn thing and bring it to me. But be quick about it – Jones is leaving within the hour.

Ellison stood, bowed, and said, 'As you wish, naturally.'

'I must thank you,' said Monsarrat, as they made their way back up the hill to work on the second document. 'Anything which convinces my superior in Sydney that I am worth freedom due to my usefulness – well, it is a great service you do me.'

'Not at all, Mr Monsarrat. And it must be said that after certain packages are sent across the seas, it might be in order for me to take some time away from Van Diemen's Land. I would like to think I would find a welcome in Parramatta.'

'You most certainly will, from me. I cannot speak for Mrs Mulrooney . . .'

'I have done my best to make peace with her,' said Ellison. 'She is a sound woman, and a fair one. I do not believe I will ever be foremost in her thoughts, but I do think, hope, I've done enough to avoid her throwing the slops bucket at me should I ever appear at your door.'

'Well, as to whether any of us have done enough to avoid that . . .'

Ellison chuckled. 'And I wonder, Mr Monsarrat, whether I might ask you another favour.'

'Of course.'

'Sadly it is impossible for me to see Thomas Power again. Your little accusation saw to that. I would, however, very much like to get a message to him. Might I request that you tell him something?'

'It depends what it is. But if it falls short of treason, I've no objection.'

'If you would be kind enough to tell him that the flax crop here is not expected to do well anymore, but that we hope there might be a prospect of a better harvest at Macquarie Harbour.'

'Very well. If you wish me to discuss flax.'

'Oh, flax is so important, Mr Monsarrat. Without it, there would be no sails. If we were not able to cultivate a strong enough crop, it's highly likely that all of us would be trapped in a penal limbo forever.'

Chapter 30

Monsarrat had not seen Mrs Mulrooney for two days. This was the longest he had been without her company almost since he had met her and he lamented her absence.

The report, with its accompanying letter dripping with false humility, had skipped over the waves with Jones. Since then Brewster had been ignoring Monsarrat's existence as much as possible, and Monsarrat and Ellison had settled into an odd, fraternal existence in the magistrate's cottage.

This morning Monsarrat tried to apply the basic principles of tea-making Mrs Mulrooney had taught him, producing a pot to which Ellison did not seem to have any objection. For Monsarrat, though, used to Mrs Mulrooney's brews, it was watery and unsatisfying.

Mrs Mulrooney must, he thought, be finding it very stifling in that cottage with only Walter and Mrs Brewster for company. Brewster had given an order that no provisions were to be delivered to them, but Ellison had talked him around. 'How would it look, dear fellow? You are maintaining the fiction that she is under guard to prevent molestation from a convict, so if she is suddenly deprived of rations ... well, people will talk.'

Monsarrat still made use of the bench he had dragged against the cottage wall. Ellison had given up the pretence of doing any work in the evenings and joined him, sipping from an earthenware cup which contained a dark red liquid.

Both Ellison and Monsarrat were now ghosts on the island. Monsarrat was alarmed by how easily the lack of activity convinced him to accept a cup or two of port from the magistrate's seemingly unending supply. They did not, however, have over-long conversations. Both of them knew that Monsarrat was well aware of Ellison's part in the attempted escape, but should Monsarrat ever feel inclined to bring his role in the whole business to any official attention, he could not point to a single statement in which Ellison had admitted guilt. And any attempt to lay blame at Ellison's door would also be frustrated by Thomas Power, who had still admitted to nothing.

Monsarrat had visited Power, as Ellison had asked him to. He had anticipated some resistance from James Brewster, but as Monsarrat was no longer in a position to influence his advancement one way or another, Brewster appeared not to care and waved a casual permission when Monsarrat visited his office to ask.

It seemed almost impossible that Power was unaware of the jolting developments of the past few days. That not a whisper had managed to trickle in through the guardhouse door. But Brewster had given orders that Power's guard – at the moment an older private who obeyed the commandant without question – should station himself outside the guardhouse rather than inside, to prevent him being influenced by the man.

Power nodded, thanked Monsarrat when he delivered Ellison's message about the flax. When Monsarrat told Power of Walter's crime, though, the fellow rested his head in his hands for a moment, forcing the heels of his palms into his eyes. It was a tactic Monsarrat knew well. When male tears were seen as an almost fatal weakness, most knew how to prevent their emergence.

'That brave, stupid boy,' said Power. 'He's too good for this place, Mr Monsarrat. He is a pilgrim here, comes from somewhere in which there is no need to protect one you love with an axe. I fear for him – there will always be those who do not understand his gentleness, or take it as a weakness.'

'He will continue to have the protection of his sister,' said Monsarrat. 'I do not know exactly where they are bound, or what she intends to do for money . . .'

'Oh, that's taken care of. She will know where to go, the same place I was going. No, I shan't tell you where. But arrangements have been made for funds to be available. The only difference is she will be passing herself off as a widow, rather than a woman married to a baronet.'

'You don't intend to attempt another escape on the journey then?'

'Mr Monsarrat, please. I know you're an intelligent man, so do me the same credit by not asking such questions, ones which are destined to remain unanswered. Anyway, an attempt by me to escape would draw attention to Elizabeth and Walter, make their own liberation less likely. It's too dangerous. They won't hang me, but they would have no such scruples about putting Walter at the end of a rope.'

'That's . . . admirable.'

'Yes, well, I am occasionally capable of selfless action, despite what Mrs Mulrooney might think. Please give her my regards, by the way. Whether she wants them or not.'

'What will you do, then? If escape is no longer your goal?'

'Read. Write, if I'm allowed to. Wait for the end of my sentence, at which point I will buy a passage on a ship bound for England and then Ireland. Everyone will profess their delight at my return, although many of them no doubt will have found life rather restful in my absence, will dread the upheaval. My children will not recognise me and my wife will pretend that my absence was a minor inconvenience.'

'And rebellion? Any more ambitions in that regard?'

'I will act as the situation demands. I always have. Those of the Catholic faith in Ireland risk imprisonment for practising their religion, a situation I cannot allow to continue, and will not when I eventually return. May I ask you a question, Mr Monsarrat?'

'Why not.'

'Knowing what you know, would you still alert the commandant to a whaler in the bay?'

'You're asking me nothing less than whether I would be a party to treason.'

'I'm asking nothing of the sort, Mr Monsarrat. We are simply speaking hypothetically.'

'Well, hypothetically . . . With the life of an innocent at stake . . . Oh, don't preen, I'm not talking about you . . . I might find my eyesight was somewhat impaired in the gathering dusk.'

Power smiled. 'I thought as much,' he said. 'You will always be a convict, Mr Monsarrat. Now please don't take offence,' as Monsarrat began to stand, to make for the door. 'Those on whom justice has descended most heavily are the best placed to recognise what is truly just and what isn't. Believe me, my friend, I intend it as a compliment. And I do hope that if you are ever in a position again to allow justice to be served through what we might call unconventional means, you will look to the convict for counsel, rather than to the functionary who is trying to bury him.'

⁓

Monsarrat did not tell Ellison of his conversation with Power. He told him that his message had been delivered and Ellison did not press for any further details.

After a few shared cups, Monsarrat was beginning to recognise the signs that Ellison had consumed more port than was wise. His eyes, which in sobriety darted about his surroundings, assessing each object for its threat or utility, became unfocused and roamed languidly from tree to cottage to goose. His shoulders would begin to slump and he would start taking Monsarrat on rambles through his past, a subject on which he never conversed while sober.

'Do you know, Monsarrat, when I was a boy my father forced me to whip a tenant? He was bailiff to the local lord, you see, always thought I would continue in that line of work after him. This poor fellow, an old man who should have been taking his ease, had lost his son to a fever and was forced back into the fields. Wasn't as good at it as he used to be, and was barely able to stand straight, so of course his returns would not cover his rent. Yet my father took none of that into consideration. He saw a tenant who was unable to pay and who deserved a whipping.'

This was the kind of story Monsarrat knew Mrs Mulrooney would be familiar with.

'Presumably that's why you pursued a career in law?' he said. 'So you could intervene in such disputes?'

He felt a small nick of jealousy as he asked the question. If he'd had the opportunity to legitimately pursue such a career, he would not have been transported for forging legal credentials. He pushed aside the thought that, legal or not, his desire to practise law had little to do with helping the oppressed.

'Initially, yes,' Ellison said. 'But I found I was constrained. The law has provisions for many contingencies, but compassion is not among them. Whenever I ruled in disputes between tenants and landlords, and when my ruling did not favour the landlord, a more senior magistrate would soon be visiting me, informing me of the necessity to uphold the social order. That's the thing about the rich, you see. The law is supposed to be blind, but if you can afford to invite it over to dine and get it blind-drunk instead, you can get any outcome you want.'

'Did you adjust your rulings?'

'A little, at first. Sometimes it was easy because on occasion the landlord was actually in the right. Not often, though, and I came to hate myself, went back to my old ways of interpreting the law, as though justice was the only principle that mattered.'

'Must've made it difficult, then, to maintain a career.'

'Oh, impossible. That's why I am here. They found a place for me that was as far away from England as could possibly be conceived. I was reluctant to go, but of course I had no choice, not really. And it did turn out rather well. There is nobody here to prevent me from getting up to mischief. My nearest superior is in Hobart, and intervening with the magistracy down here would involve a lot of work, letters to the colonial secretary and so on. I have not made too much trouble – as far as they know – so they have let me be for the most part.'

He sighed and leaned against the bench, so that Monsarrat felt its back peel away slightly from his own. In the next instant, though, Ellison was sitting upright and then standing steadily, as alert as somebody who had not just put away the better part of a bottle of port.

'Down there,' he said, pointing to the bay.

Monsarrat looked. The ship which he had taken to be a whaler had not changed course and headed out to sea. It was continuing to bear down on Darlington Bay.

'This is not a ship you need to alert the commandant to, Mr Monsarrat,' Ellison said, as he swung his travelling bag. 'He will be aware of it. That, if I am correct, is the brig which will take Power to Macquarie Harbour, and Elizabeth and Walter to true justice.'

Chapter 31

Monsarrat stood on the beach with Ellison, watching as the new convicts were rowed ashore, veterans of sea voyages now, even the ones who had been born many days' ride from the first whiff of salt air. Most kept their heads down – a survival tactic with which Monsarrat was well acquainted. Invisibility, here, was safety, and something within many of them would be whispering that if they could not see their tormentors, they themselves would remain unseen.

Others, though – the more recently arrived, perhaps, or convicts like himself who had managed to avoid the work gangs – looked around at the looming Bishop and Clerk saddle-back mountain which rose behind the settlement, and at the slice of sand which extended from one side of the dock. A few cast their glances in the direction of the small congregation of headstones on the other side of the dock. Wondering perhaps whether that was their ultimate destination.

The convicts were lined up on the shore to be harangued by Holloway. Ellison leaned over towards Monsarrat. 'Now the processional starts,' he whispered.

Brewster was not going to miss the opportunity of seeing

Thomas Power being loaded onto the brig. He emerged from his office building, and walked straight-backed to the guardhouse.

The soldier opened the door, went inside and returned a minute later with Power, who was shackled.

'Why on earth are they ironing him?' asked Monsarrat. 'What do they think he will do, fly away?'

'Oh, Brewster has no fears about the security of the prisoner,' said Ellison. 'This is for show. The man who chained the unchainable. Had he the wherewithal, I wouldn't doubt he would have commissioned an artist to sketch the event.'

With Power constrained, Brewster put his hand on the man's back and shoved roughly, so that he stumbled over the chain between his legs. Power righted himself quickly enough though, straightened his shoulders and marched down to the dock at such a pace that Brewster had to hurry to keep up with him. As he passed Monsarrat and Ellison, he said out of the corner of his mouth, 'Good day to you, gentlemen. I don't anticipate seeing either of you again, but I will be happy to be proven wrong.'

And for the second time, Monsarrat watched Power wade into the water to a waiting tender.

Brewster drew alongside them, watching as one of the sailors helped Power to stand alongside the boat. 'Look at that – His Majesty's Navy is unable to resist treating the fellow with respect. Beyond me, truly.'

'Yes, James,' said Ellison. 'I know it is.'

'Hmm. Well, if you will both excuse me, I have some urgent tasks to attend to.' And he turned and stalked up the beach.

'He is not farewelling his wife?' asked Monsarrat. 'Not even watching her as she boards?'

'Oh no. Treating Power as he did was a means of reminding anyone who cared to watch of his gallant capture of the man. He wishes to claim actions which belong to you – and which if I'm not mistaken you would prefer to disown. His wife, though – very few are aware of the circumstances surrounding her and Walter's departure. But enough are. Enough to make him want to distance himself from her in the most emphatic way possible. I imagine he's also arranged things so that Thomas Power, who's presumably being locked below decks as we speak, and his wife do not board the ship at the same time. I very much doubt they will have any opportunity to confer on the short journey.'

As soon as the commandant had disappeared, Power's irons were taken off so he could board the tender that would take him to the brig without risk of drowning.

Perhaps Private Ennis had been instructed to watch from the cottage to make sure those inside did not emerge until the commandant was safely back in his office, his door closed, because a minute or so later Monsarrat could see Elizabeth and Walter make their way down the hill, Elizabeth leaning on her brother's arm, and the very welcome sight of Mrs Mulrooney behind them.

While the commandant was not represented as the little party moved closer to the bay, others were. Dr Chester strode down from the hospital. Some of the kinder convict overseers could be seen lining the path to the bay, reaching out to pat Walter's shoulder as he went, and bow their heads to Elizabeth Brewster. Walter smiled and waved at them, and Elizabeth nodded solemnly. Jones, who was temporarily redundant due to the presence of a much larger ship in what he considered to be his waters, was making his way from the boathouse.

And from the hospital site Milliner watched, completely still. The man would have months, years, to stare at the void of water as he tried to get out of work, tried to avoid being abandoned to Trainor's tender mercy at the reservoir site, where he would stand beside Shanahan as another mule for whipping.

Monsarrat wondered if the Hatter would be watching when he and Mrs Mulrooney slid away from the island. He suddenly felt an odd and unjust remorse. He would be leaving men like Milliner to an obscure fate, to an existence in which the colonial seasons, upside down, blew July gales and brought withering heat in December, while they themselves stood still. But for his investigation the year before into the death of an innocent woman in Port Macquarie, Monsarrat knew that he would have been the one looking at an ocean as the days lengthened and shortened and lengthened again without the slightest regard for him.

Chester got down to the bay before the little party. 'I do hope,' he said to Ellison, 'that the lady will not have further need of the type of assistance I provided to her recently.'

'I believe, Dr Chester, that her removal from this place – and from the influence of its commandant – will guard against that eventuality,' said Ellison.

Chester nodded. 'We shall be diminished without her, though, and especially without Walter. Every settlement needs a young man who can see eternity in a raindrop.'

Jones, too, had drawn level with them. 'It will be you, tomorrow, Mr Monsarrat. The commandant has given orders for me to take you first thing in the morning.'

'I am not subject to the commandant's orders regarding my movements,' said Monsarrat, jealous as only a marginally free man could be about standing up for his own discretionary rights.'

'Well,' Jones conceded, 'I must say, I don't like the look of those clouds. See how they're being smeared across the sky by the wind? They do not bode well. So you may have the opportunity to enjoy the commandant's company for longer than you had imagined.'

'I would rather avail myself of the opportunity to enjoy yours,' said Monsarrat.

Jones chuckled. 'In that case, if you have a fondness for card games, I happen to have a deck. Carry it with me everywhere – far better way to pass the time during a storm than being tossed about on a boat.'

'And you're familiar, Mr Monsarrat, with the location of my little cache,' said Ellison. 'I believe there is half a bottle left. If you and Jones do find yourselves playing cards while the wind howls about, please do avail yourselves of it.'

The little party from the cottage was upon them now. Elizabeth was casting anxious glances in the direction of her husband's office, perhaps fearful he would burst out and drag her back. Her steps quickened when she saw the ship that would take her out of the orbit of her husband's fists.

When Walter saw Jones, he broke into a galloping run.

'Mr Jones, you will take care of things here, won't you? Especially the seals, but the dolphins as well. They need watching, you know,' said Walter.

'Aye, lad, I give you my word. Although no one can keep them in line quite like you can.'

Walter nodded solemnly and then enfolded Jones in a broad-shouldered hug. When he stepped away, Monsarrat could see the tears on his cheeks, and pretended not to notice that Jones had started blinking rapidly.

'I wish you the best, Mr Gendron. Look after that sister of yours,' said Chester. And to Elizabeth, who had just reached them, he handed a packet. 'A remedy for anxiety,' he said. 'Use it sparingly, and it is my wish that you don't have to use it at all.'

'I do believe the need for it will diminish with distance,' said Elizabeth. 'Thank you.'

The tender which had just rowed Power out to the brig was returning now, and a nimble young seaman jumped out to help drag it aground on the sand so that Elizabeth could board without ruining her skirts.

'Good of him,' said Ellison. 'I know the consideration is the lady, but I'm glad of it nonetheless. I am not constructed to hop easily in and out of boats.'

Elizabeth started towards the boat, and then turned and walked towards Mrs Mulrooney, who had been hanging back from the group. She took both of the housekeeper's hands, kissed her on both cheeks. Elizabeth was, Monsarrat thought, already recovering some of her colour, which seemed to increase as the time to board drew near. For the first time in days, he believed that if he squinted, he could convince himself she was Grace.

Walter clearly felt his sister's farewell was too restrained, and lifted Mrs Mulrooney off her feet in a hug which must've driven the breath out of her lungs. Then he and Elizabeth turned and held each other's hands as they walked towards the tender.

Ellison positioned himself at the back of the boat so that its nose rode slightly out of the water, making the work of the seamen who were rowing more difficult. While Elizabeth and Walter climbed the rope ladder onto the brig with ease, Ellison had to be half-pushed and half-pulled onto the deck.

Monsarrat looked sideways at Mrs Mulrooney, noticed that her face was wet. 'I believe,' he said, 'that they will find peace where they are going.'

'I hope so, Mr Monsarrat,' Mrs Mulrooney said. 'Mrs Brewster – she isn't Honora Shelborne, but then nobody is. But she is not the worst of them. And young Walter – there is a purity to him, and this colony makes it its business to snuff purity out. It is to be hoped that the place where they are going is kinder.'

'Well, it is no longer a colony,' said Monsarrat. 'Perhaps in claiming their independence, the Americans have found room for a little more tolerance than can be found here . . . Oh, look.'

He pointed to the brig, where Ellison was waving. Monsarrat believed it was impossible to tell where the magistrate was aiming his eyes, but was certain that the wave was meant for only one person standing on the beach.

'I know he treated you shamefully,' said Monsarrat. 'And it is inexcusable, but you must confess, he does have *some* redeeming qualities.'

'I must do no such thing,' said Mrs Mulrooney. 'Although ... Walter would likely have hanged without his intervention, so I will refrain from praying for him to be afflicted by gout. Probably too late for my prayers, anyway.'

And she glared at the waving figure as the anchor of the ship rose, a look which Monsarrat thought Ellison must surely have felt. Perhaps he did, because the frantic movement of his arms slowed and then stopped.

Mrs Mulrooney began to smile, then to laugh. 'Listen, Mr Monsarrat!'

The thickening clouds did nothing to impede the sound which travelled towards them. The sound of a goose, honking three times, stopping and honking again, and seemingly doing so from the middle of the bay, where no goose had any business being.

⸎

Jones was right about the weather. That afternoon the sky became increasingly crowded with smudges of grey, which joined with each other, relaxing suddenly and releasing their moisture all at once. It was the kind of rain which the colony of Van Diemen's Land specialised in. Instant, impenetrable, reducing the visibility from hundreds of feet to a few inches within the space of a minute.

Monsarrat extracted Ellison's remaining bottle from the cache underneath the floorboards, and struggled through the nearly vertical rain to the boathouse. Jones turned out to be a skilled card player. It was fortunate they were not playing the kind of game which involved wages, or the small amount of money Monsarrat had brought with him to the island would have been completely depleted.

'Do you know,' said Jones, having to raise his voice over the sound of the rain against the boathouse shutters, 'the commandant wanted me to take you back across the water today. Today!'

'The sea could be completely flat for all we know,' said Monsarrat. 'You'd have to walk right to the end of the dock to see it.'

'I did,' said Jones, 'and nearly got washed off. They're standing up like an army, those waves. We would not make it a hundred feet. The wind is no respecter of persons and their good leather shoes. On the way back I saw my handcart rolling down the wharf. Looked like it was drunk, rolling from side to side until the wind pushed it into the sea. God knows where it is now – it might reach Hobart before you.'

'Well, I'm grateful to you for declining the commandant.'

'I have no more desire to drown than you do, Mr Monsarrat. He threatened to relieve me of my duties and I invited him to do just that. It must have occurred to him that any bosun is better than none at all, so he stalked off after yelling at me to get you gone at first light tomorrow.'

'I'd best not drink too much port, then,' said Monsarrat. 'I'm not often taken ill at sea, but I imagine a bellyful of this stuff would contribute.'

'It does, I can tell you that from experience,' said Jones. 'But we'll see, will we? I'll not be taking you and that dear woman across the ocean until it has decided to behave itself.'

Monsarrat smiled. Mrs Mulrooney's shortbread was clearly a far better diplomatic tool than the commandant's manner.

When he eventually walked back up the hill, the rain had eased slightly. At least he could keep his eyes open, did not have to keep blinking against droplets hurled into his face by the wind.

In the magistrate's kitchen, Mrs Mulrooney was scrubbing the table for the fifth time. 'I'm looking forward to going to work on a table in Parramatta,' she said, looking to see what mail there might be. 'Padraig, I've been trying to write a letter to him. I want to ask him to come back, Mr Monsarrat,' she said. 'Do you think the sale of that jewellery would have occurred by now?'

The jewellery which would give her affluence. 'In all likelihood,' said Monsarrat, smiling at her. 'We will find out when we reach Sydney, in any case.'

'And when will that be?'

'Soon, I hope. I am anxious to get back as well.'

Mrs Mulrooney smiled. 'If there's one thing I can assure you of, Mr Monsarrat, it's that Grace O'Leary will be waiting for you in Parramatta. After all,' she said, smiling more broadly, 'she doesn't have any choice.'

'If I had a cleaning cloth . . .'

'Ah, but you don't. You wouldn't know what to do with it. Don't think I haven't noticed the remains of your attempts at tea, Mr Monsarrat. Those poor little leaves, abusing them so when they were just trying to give you some flavour. I've put the kettle on for some more, but I let it boil away. I can't seem to settle to anything. Worrying, you know, about Elizabeth and Walter. That this storm might have put paid to their plans to get away.'

'Well, they would have made it across to the bay before the storm hit. And don't forget that Ellison is currently the only one in Triabunna – in fact, the whole of Van Diemen's Land apart from this island – who knows why they are there. His report to Marley is unlikely to have reached Hobart. I think they'll get away safely enough. I imagine they are watching for the first break in the weather. As is Jones, by the way. We may well find ourselves taking the first leg of the journey back to Parramatta tomorrow.'

Mrs Mulrooney crossed herself. 'I hope Jones isn't going to make us hop into a boat in this weather, or anything like it. Then again, I would rather make it over in wild seas than stay anywhere near that man.'

Brewster had moved back into his cottage and had brought a convict who had previously served as a footman in to cook and make tea and tidy the place.

'I saw him,' said Mrs Mulrooney. 'Just before the rains hit. He was pacing around the side of the house, looking at the water. God knows what he was thinking. Nor do I care, to be honest. I hope, Mr Monsarrat, that there will be a consequence to all this for him.'

'Apart from the consequence he is already enduring, I doubt it. It was the price of Walter and Elizabeth's freedom to cast him as the hero. He will tell the story of his heroism to himself over and over again until he has convinced himself it is the truth. Above all, he will keep seeking advancement, and probably get it. He'll be fine. That kind always is.'

'And what about our kind, Mr Monsarrat?'

'We will do as we always do. I will do my best not to run foul of the administration again, to retain my freedom. I will visit Grace. And I will continue to try to be worthy of your friendship. As for you, though – you're very probably a rich woman now. What will you do?'

'I tell you, Mr Monsarrat, the sooner I get my son back to my side, the happier I will be. And now I'm in a position to set him up in a public house – wouldn't it be wonderful if that public house could be in Parramatta? So when we get back I'm going to bend everything towards that. When you leave me alone long enough with your incessant demands for tea, and your wailing about how you never get any shortbread.'

Chapter 32

Monsarrat wouldn't have believed he'd see Hannah Mulrooney smiling on a boat, yet today she seemed unable to stop. The storms of Van Diemen's Land were now several hundred leagues to the south, and the Parramatta sun was shining on the river as the boat was pushed along towards home by the incoming tide.

In anyone else, Monsarrat would have believed that the smile was prompted by the fact that a significant sum of money had just been deposited with the Bank of New South Wales. But this woman was more likely to be smiling at the prospect of home after nearly a month's absence, her own kitchen with utensils which knew how to behave, and a promise of people to fuss over.

He would not have thought her capable of showing any more delight, until she noticed who was at the dock. A slight woman in a clean but plain muslin dress which, Monsarrat knew, was nevertheless the finest gown she had ever owned, stood waiting. Her hand had been claimed by a little girl, who was scanning the river while clinging to a small cloth doll, as though expecting it to be stolen. Mrs Mulrooney gasped and her eyes began to shine.

Helen started talking before Mrs Mulrooney had set foot on the plank which a seaman had placed on the gunwale, leading down to the dock. 'I've been doing as you asked, missus, and the cottage is still standing and in good order. I've been scrubbing the table every day, just like you said, and staring at the pots and pans, although what good that does, I don't know. It has been done, though, I promise.'

For someone with a fear of the water, Mrs Mulrooney stepped remarkably quickly down the flimsy plank which was all that stood between her and the Parramatta River. 'How did you know we would be back today?' she asked Helen.

'We didn't, missus. Eliza insisted we come down here every day, looking for you. Have done for the past week.'

Mrs Mulrooney straightened, as Monsarrat walked down the plank himself and saw to their luggage.

'Oh, there's no need to walk, missus. James – Mr Henson, that is – has gone to fetch a cart. He's been looking in on us, from time to time. Well, every day.'

When they were settled in the cart, Mrs Mulrooney said, 'Helen, you have been setting the mail aside, of course.'

'I would have, missus, but none has come.'

'Are you certain about that? It wasn't left to the side of the door?'

'No, I've looked, like I promised.'

Mrs Mulrooney frowned. 'Nearly a month since I first wrote to him,' she said. 'I would have thought . . . Never mind. I believe, Helen, that Mr Monsarrat may have some questions for you.'

Helen looked expectantly at Monsarrat. He cleared his throat – he did indeed have a question, though one he would have preferred not to ask in an open cart with the genial Henson in earshot.

'I don't suppose, Helen,' he said, 'that you have visited the Factory in our absence?'

Helen frowned. 'Only once, sir, and then just for a short time. I know nothing of any of the doings there, or any of the women.'

Monsarrat nodded. He doubted that Helen was telling the truth. First-class prisoners were allowed visitors on Sundays, and if Helen had gone and sat with some of her former penitentiary mates, she would know more than a little about the goings-on behind the arched gates with their fancy clock. But convicts, when they did not want to give away information, could be stubborn. And Helen, who had been through horrors, did not deserve an interrogation.

The cottage, when the group drew up to it, had clearly been cared for with an attention even Mrs Mulrooney couldn't fault. Monsarrat felt great relief to be home, which was sorely tempered by a niggling but persistent alarm that had started to ring when Helen had demurred at providing any information about the inmates of the Female Factory.

❧

It was odd, the next morning, to be walking up the hill with the colonnaded stone building at the top, skirting around the back past the Government House stables towards the office outbuilding where Ralph Eveleigh had had to do without a clerk for a few weeks.

Eveleigh barely looked up when Monsarrat rapped on his door. He finished the document he had been working on, looked up and gestured Monsarrat to a seat. 'I have had correspondence from the comptroller of convicts, Richard Marley, in Van Diemen's Land. It seems you were instrumental in the prevention of an escape which would have caused the lieutenant governor some blushes.'

'I was indeed in the right place to stop the infamous Thomas Power in his attempt,' said Monsarrat.

'Yes, well, given that, Mr Marley is not quibbling about the fact that it was the commandant, not you, who identified the killer of the bosun.'

'I am glad to hear it.'

'You should be,' said Eveleigh. 'Your continued freedom relies on your utility.'

'And my utility, it would seem, relies on the concealment of my background, sir.'

'Ah' said Eveleigh. 'Yes. Well, they are a little more conservative down there. I doubted you would have found any cooperation, had it been known.'

'Perhaps if you had informed me of your decision in that regard, sir, I might have been less surprised.'

'Yes, well, I'm sorry about that, but I knew you would never agree to it. And I trusted you to have enough intellectual agility, shall we say, to manage the situation when you found out.'

'Intellectual agility is one thing, sir, but if you'll forgive me, I do not like being put in a position where I have to dissemble in order to achieve what you sent me there for.'

Eveleigh sighed. 'Monsarrat,' he said, 'I expected you would feel this way, and to be honest, I would probably feel the same in your situation. But our nicer emotions must sometimes be forced to submit to practicalities.'

'Well, the practicalities of the situation were that when a certain magistrate discovered the truth, I was very nearly drummed off the island.'

'Yes, magistrate . . . Ellison, is it?' He riffled through a stack of papers on his desk. 'I had another letter yesterday from Marley. He begs to inform me that since the culprits were delivered from Maria Island, they seem to have disappeared. Odd, no? He wonders if we know anything about it.'

'Yes, it is odd,' said Monsarrat. 'Ellison always struck me as very upright. Unimaginative, a lover of rules. A typical magistrate.'

'Well, if he were typical of our Parramatta magistrates, I really would be concerned. Marley has had enough help from us, in any case. They can deal with that one by themselves. I assure you, I will not be sending you back there, nor anywhere for some time.'

'I am glad to hear it, sir. I was hoping, in that regard, to ask you a favour, and what I have to ask is not onerous.'

'Yes . . .'

'Sir, I wish for permission to visit Grace O'Leary this Sunday. She is still a third-class convict, and not allowed Sunday visitors. But perhaps if you were to intercede with the superintendent . . .'

Eveleigh shifted in his chair, looked at the ceiling for a moment. 'Mr Monsarrat, it will probably alarm you to hear that certain magistrates here have discovered your regard for the Irishwoman. And there is one in particular who wants to cause you trouble. Reverend Bulmer has taken it upon himself to prevent any further relationship developing between you and the O'Leary woman.'

'How on earth? She will be free next month!'

'Yes, but she is not free yet. And you know yourself, Mr Monsarrat, that once a convict is assigned away from Parramatta, he or she does not necessarily come back when they earn their freedom.'

'But what has this to do with Grace? I don't . . . You can't mean . . . ?'

'I'm afraid I do. Reverend Bulmer had Grace assigned to a property in the west. I don't know where, nor does anyone but him. Mr Monsarrat, she is gone.'

Monsarrat almost gasped aloud at the desolation he felt in that moment.

'In that case, sir, I need your permission to search for her.'

'I don't think a day or two's journey will bring you closer to her. And a day or two at a time is all you will be able to afford.'

'Sir, may I then request a leave of absence?'

'I must deny it, Monsarrat. I am sorry. Last week, a man was shot in Sydney.'

'And cannot the constabulary deal with that?'

'No. This one is earmarked for you. The slain man was the editor of the *Sydney Chronicle*. It seems he ran afoul of some of those who also have made it their business to torment you. There are conflicts within conflicts within conflicts – requires a delicate touch. So I'm afraid, Mr Monsarrat, that this must take up the bulk of your time. And we must resolve it before the governor arrives.'

'Why? Surely this will not be the only unsolved murder he confronts.'

'Ah, but this one is dangerous. Perhaps fatal for the unwary. I do, Mr Monsarrat, wish you the best of luck.'

Authors' Note

We have taken more liberties with history in *The Power Game* than we have in previous Monsarrat books.

Maria Island is a lesser known sister to the famously brutal Tasmanian penal stations at Macquarie Harbour (established in 1822) and Port Arthur (1830). It was envisaged as a gentler place, a settlement for colonial offenders whose crimes were not sufficiently serious to warrant the institutionalised torture purveyed at more infamous penal stations. In fact, administrators during the late 1820s believed convicts were committing minor crimes to get sent to Maria.

Once they got there, though, some of them tried to leave, and the escapes by canoe described in this book were a frequent headache for the administration.

It is believed Aboriginals from Oyster Bay journeyed frequently to the island.

Triabunna, from where the Maria Island ferry departs now, appears in this book but was not founded until 1830. Today's visitors to Maria Island can see buildings from throughout the island's penal history, which began with the foundation of Darlington in 1825. A few of the buildings (such as the commissariat store where our fictional Elizabeth and Walter laboured, which now houses the visitor centre) would have been there in 1826 when Monsarrat and Mrs Mulrooney arrive. However, most of Darlington dates from later in its first period as a penal station, which ran to 1832, or from its second incarnation from 1842.

While they may be anachronisms, most of the buildings in *The Power Game* did actually exist at one stage or another. The commandant and visiting magistrate's houses stood where they stand in Monsarrat's world, for example, and the reservoir Monsarrat visits is around an hour's stroll through the bush from Darlington.

There are a few notable exceptions. We are not aware of a light as described in this book (although whalers frequently visited the waters around Maria Island). The man on whom the character of Thomas Power is based (more on him in a moment) had a cottage which was next to the convict penitentiary, and not walled in – we've restricted him for narrative reasons.

There are also some living anachronisms in this book. Because of its remote location and undeveloped bushland, a number of threatened species were introduced to Maria Island in the 1970s. These include the Cape Barren geese (which are every bit as strident as portrayed in the novel), kangaroos, wallabies, wombats and Tasmanian devils. Many of these animals can be seen in great abundance by visitors to the island today, but would not have been there at the foundation of the penal settlement.

William Smith O'Brien

The greatest living anachronism in this book is William Smith O'Brien, the inspiration for the character of Thomas Power (although Power is a more flamboyant character than O'Brien, who was said to be reserved).

O'Brien, like Power, was an Irish nationalist and son of a baronet. A leader of the Young Ireland movement, he was arrested for high treason in 1848 and sentenced to be hung, drawn and quartered – a sentence which, fortunately for him, was commuted to transportation.

In an attempt to neutralise the Young Irelanders as a political force, O'Brien and others transported with him were offered freedom within the colony in exchange for their 'parole' – a promise not to escape. It was a promise O'Brien was unwilling to make so he was sent to Maria Island, arriving there in November 1849.

Nine months later, O'Brien was captured while attempting to escape on a whaler sent by sympathetic supporters in America. He spent the rest of his sentence at Port Arthur, eventually getting his parole and serving as a tutor before being granted a free pardon and returning to Ireland in 1856.

From these remnants of historic tapestry we hope we have managed to produce a narrative engrossing enough to justify the liberties we have taken.

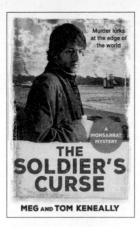

In the Port Macquarie penal settlement for second offenders, at the edge of the known world, gentleman convict Hugh
Monsarrat hungers for freedom. Originally transported for
forging documents passing himself off as a lawyer, he is now
the trusted clerk of the settlement's commandant.

His position has certain advantages, such as being able
to spend time in the Government House kitchen, being
supplied with outstanding cups of tea by housekeeper Hannah
Mulrooney, who, despite being illiterate, is his most intelligent
companion.

Not long after the commandant heads off in search of
a rumoured river, his beautiful wife, Honora, falls ill with
a sickness the doctor is unable to identify. When Honora dies,
it becomes clear she has been slowly poisoned.

Monsarrat and Mrs Mulrooney suspect the commandant's
second-in-command, Captain Diamond, a cruel man who
shares history with Honora. Then Diamond has Mrs Mulrooney
arrested for the murder. Knowing his friend will hang if she is
tried, Monsarrat knows he must find the real killer.

There's much more at stake than just murder...

A MONSARRAT MYSTERY

THE UNMOURNED

MEG AND TOM KENEALLY

'A series that promises to add a new dimension to the Australian crime scene . . . Things can only get more interesting' *Sydney Morning Herald*

For Robert Church, superintendent of the Parramatta Female Factory, the most enjoyable part of his job is access to young convict women. Inmate Grace O'Leary has made it her mission to protect the women from his nocturnal visits and when Church is murdered with an awl thrust through his right eye, she becomes the chief suspect.

Recently arrived from Port Macquarie, ticket-of-leave gentleman convict Hugh Monsarrat now lives in Parramatta with his ever-loyal housekeeper Mrs Mulrooney. Monsarrat, as an unofficial advisor on criminal and legal matters to the governor's secretary, is charged with uncovering the truth of Church's murder. Mrs Mulrooney accompanies him to the Female Factory, where he is taking depositions from prisoners, including Grace, and there the housekeeper strikes up friendships with certain women, which prove most intriguing.

Monsarrat and Mrs Mulrooney both believe that Grace is innocent, but in this they are alone, so to exonerate her they must find the murderer. Many hated Church and are relieved by his death, but who would go as far as killing him?